Praise for
Chelsea Quinn Yarbro

"Yarbro's vampires are benign, rational, civilized beings more worthy of the term 'humanity' than many of the mortals they encounter...a backward-looking version of *The Handmaid's Tale,* set in a dystopia that once was all too real."
— *Locus*

"Yarbro's romantic, colorful cycle of historical horror novels (*Hotel Transylvania, Blood Games*) focuses this time on Olivia, the noble Roman lady who becomes a lover of the vampire Count Sant' Germain in the time of Nero. Hundreds of years later, in the sixth century, Olivia is forced to flee Rome as war flares. In the more repressive and vigilantly Christian city of Constantinople she is suspect as a foreigner and an unmarried woman of wealth. When her patron, General Belisarus, falls out of favor with the Emperor Justinian, she has no protection from the zealous Court Censor ... The book has a real, cumulative power as a portrait of an intelligent, cosmopolitan woman caught in a paranoid web of politics and religious persecution."
— *Publishers Weekly*

Also by Chelsea Quinn Yarbro
published by Tor Books

HOTEL TRANSYLVANIA
THE PALACE

Chelsea Quinn Yarbro

A Flame In Byzantium

TOR

A TOM DOHERTY ASSOCIATES BOOK

A FLAME IN BYZANTIUM

Copyright © 1987 by Chelsea Quinn Yarbro

A TOR Book
Published by Tom Doherty Associates, Inc.
49 West 24 Street
New York, NY 10010

Cover art by Sanjulian

ISBN: 0-812-52804-2   Can. ISBN: 0-812-52805-0

Library of Congress Catalog Card Number: 87-50471

First edition: October 1987
First mass market printing: October 1988

Printed in the United States of America

0 9 8 7 6 5 4 3 2 1

for
RICHARD CHRISTIAN MATHESON
for forty-two excellent reasons
and one to grow on

Author's Note

Byzantine civilization was considered the center of the Western world during that period of time sometimes called the Dark Ages: roughly from the fifth to the twelvth centuries. During that period, Constantinople and the Byzantine Empire stood as the most prosperous and enduring state in Christendom, a bulwark against barbarism and (from the later seventh century onward) Islam alike. As such, it was regarded—especially by the Byzantines themselves—as the most perfect example of everything that had been lost to Europe since the collapse of the Roman Empire.

Although the Byzantines spoke Greek and were strictly and repressively monotheistic Christians, they considered themselves to be the political and cultural descendants of Imperial Rome and were very proud of this heritage, no matter how inaccurate their claim to it was. The Byzantines saw themselves as an improvement over Rome, without the license and tolerance of the polytheistic Romans; the Byzantines were proud of the restricted social order they had achieved. This in turn led to repressive cultural patterns that presaged later religious and social persecutions, which continued in Christian countries for centuries after the Byzantine Empire itself fell to the advancing Islamic Turks.

Constantinople was made rich in large part by trade, for its location at the mouth of the Black Sea gave it access to the Mediterranean trade as well as most of the caravan routes of Asia. For this reason, if no other, it was a sought-after prize for many of the various invaders of Europe. The continued resistance to such invasions contributed to the general attitude of isolationism that marked much of the political tenor of the Byzantines in their treatment of any and all foreigners. In such an environment, paranoia was not so much a neurosis as a means of survival.

It is important to be aware that at the time of this novel, most of the historians were political officers, employed by the Court Censor and strictly mandated to present a very specific view of persons and events. As a result, many of the contemporary records are questionable at best, being slanted by the requirements of Emperor, clique, religious leader, or prevailing power shifts. Accurate data are not easily found or identified. Often unpopular opinion suffered the usual fate of unpopular opinion in an absolute monarchy/theocracy: it ceased to exist.

Because of the Byzantine attitude toward records, there is much information that is not available, or disputed: the date of the birth of Justinian; the age and profession of Theodora before she became Empress; the year of birth and parentage of Belisarius, and the year and nature of his death; the year and nature of the death of Antonina. The questions are endless and at this distance, unanswerable. For the purposes of this book I have drawn in part from the *Secret Histories* of Procopius, although much of his information is highly biased; on merchants' records of the period; on the military reports that still remain, both Byzantine and those of their opponents; on some of those few letters and journals that have survived the centuries and the censors. For Belisarius' campaign in Italy I have used some of the records kept by Italian religious communities regarding the conduct of the army and the problems of supply which were a constant concern.

As with my other historical horror novels, this book is based on actual events and employs actual historical figures as characters; but they, as well as the fictional characters, are used fictionally, as are the settings and events, and should not be construed as representing or intended to represent actual persons (living and/or dead), places or events in any sense but a coincidental one.

Greek usage is based on the usage of the period and on the social position of the characters: it is not modern Greek, nor it is the Greek of Homer. Transliterations and translations to English were done with the generous help of Dr. Alan Kazakis, and any errors in historicity or in linguistics are certainly not his. Thanks are also due, as always, to David Nee for indefatigable work in chasing down bibliographic information and references, as well as maps and similar records.

Thanks are also due to the good people at Tor Books, who have given my historical horror novels a new lease on life, if that's the right word, especially to my editor, Beth Meacham, and publisher Tom Doherty.

PART I
Belisarius

Text of a dispatch to Belisarius near Roma.

Hail to the General Belisarius on the Feast of the Holy Spirit in the Lord's Year 545.

We have scouted the villages around Roma as you have required us to do and it is agreed that siege is the intention of Totila. His forces have already attempted it with some success, which has given these barbarians a taste of success.

Drosos has taken a small party of five men and is currently foraging. The local farmers do not welcome us, claiming that we are as bad as the Ostrogoth fighters, which has already caused a few unfortunate events that we were unable to avoid. The foraging is necessary for Totila's men have reduced the game in the countryside, otherwise we would not be driven to this extremity.

There is a monastery not far from here and the monks are cenobites, and so are little help to us. We have not been able to persuade them to provide us more than a shelter from the rain, and that was granted grudgingly. Some other arrangements are necessary if we are going to be able to remain in the field for much longer, as we had intended to do. We will await your instructions before moving on.

Two days ago we encountered an Ostrogoth scouting party of considerable strength and from what we were able to overhear, they are part of a larger contingent sent to establish themselves with the peasants so that they will be supported when they strengthen their assault on Roma itself. We are trying to gain confirmation on this now, but we do not expect to have more information for some little

3

time since you specifically ordered that we were not to engage these men in combat, no matter how much we might wish to do so. It was no easy thing to have the enemy close at hand and to do little more than cower in bushes and listen like slaves at a keyhole.

We pray that God will continue to aid Roma, no matter how she has fallen into evil, and that it will be given to us to save her from the rapine and pillage of these barbarians. Surely if God can pardon all sin, He will rescue this whore of a city as He welcomed the harlot Maria into the company of Heaven.

From the hand of Captain Chrysanthos and carried by the man-at-arms Iakobos, two hours before sunset.

• 1 •

At Neapolis there was chaos as those who could flee Roma came to this port seeking escape. Carts, wagons, litters, and every beast of burden had been pressed into use for the rout, and reports from Belisarius' forces indicated that the flood of refugees ran all the way back to the walls of Roma itself.

"What has become of the Romans, that they do this?" Belisarius asked the officer who rode beside him against the surge of terrified humanity.

Drosos shrugged. "They're frightened. Small wonder."

"Romans were supposed to be made of sterner stuff than this," Belisarius said, a faint regret in his words. He shielded his eyes against the sun and squinted down the road through the dust.

"Perhaps they were once," said Drosos, dragging on the reins to keep from running into a heavily laden oxcart.

His horse quivered with dread as the vehicle lumbered by them.

"That beast of yours is as bad as the Romans," said Belisarius, doing his best to make light of the situation now that he was faced with it. "The Emperor will be disgusted to learn of this. I hope we can give him a better report of Roma itself once we arrive there."

"Do you still intend to go there?" Drosos asked, sweating with the effort to hold his mount.

"I am ordered to do so. And I confess that I want to see if any of the old Roman virtues still survive in the people. Surely they can't all be running away, can they?" Belisarius was not a big man, but he sat a horse like a giant and he carried himself like one of the most noble. There were lines around his eyes and his mouth was framed by deep creases.

Drosos was a stockier version of his General, and his junior by eight years. He was as steadfast as Belisarius was forceful and as such was an ideal subordinate and Captain. "What are the plans now?"

"We leave for Roma at first light tomorrow." He said it as calmly as if he had discussed the weather or the breed of horse he rode.

"Who rides with you?" As always when he asked such questions, Drosos had to fight the urge to hold his breath as he waited for the answer.

"You, of course, and one or two others; I haven't decided who yet." He indicated a group of monks in filthy habits. "Even they are leaving. What does that say of their faith and devotion? How can the Romans claim any right to the favor of God if His servants fly with the rest of the people?"

"Totila has not been kind to monks and priests," Drosos offered, embarrassed for the religious men whose vocation had shown itself to be so inadequate.

"And the people of Judah chose Barabbas over Our Lord," said Belisarius more sternly, not willing to excuse the cowardice he saw.

Drosos had no answer for this; he busied himself with his horse and with watching the wretched parade that wound from the gates of Neapolis to the quays.

At nightfall, when the gates had to be closed, there were many hundreds of people still on the road, and they made what little they could of this, some banding together to make a more secure camp to afford some protection from the Ostrogoths as well as from the other Romans. All along the branch of the Via Latina the way was marked with cooking fires and makeshift tents, and the sounds and odors crowded together in the air.

A delegation from the city of Neapolis visited Belisarius early in the night. They were exhausted men, most of them wary and a few angry with what had befallen their home.

"We are thankful to the Emperor for sending his aid," began the oldest, who boasted his family went back to the time of the ancient Roman Republic.

Belisarius recognized the note of disapproval in the man's tone and he raised his eyes from the report that had been handed to him only moments before. "Yes? What are your objections?"

"They are not objections, precisely, General," the man said, glancing at his companions uneasily.

"Then what are they?" Belisarius sensed that the visit would be a long one unless he brought the others to the point as soon as possible.

"Reservations," said the oldest man. "We are concerned, as you must be yourself. There are so many people leaving Roma and while we are willing to do what we can for them, we haven't the room or the supplies to care for all of them."

"And what supplies we have are already reduced," added one of the others. "We cannot continue to give out food and cloth at the rate we have been doing. It isn't possible."

Belisarius looked at the men before him and tried to find a virtue in them that reflected all he had been told of Roma in her days of glory. He could find nothing but exhaustion and the venality that was the chief complaint of most of those who dealt with Romans in these days. "What do you propose?" he asked them patiently.

The youngest scratched his head and flicked away lice. "We need to know what the situation is—what we really have on hand and how much of it we can spare. We must find out what the farmers can actually supply us and how safe the crops will be once Totila and his forces arrive."

"Wait," said Belisarius, holding up his hand to halt the stream of words. "There is no indication that you have to fear Totila will get this far, and I tell you from experience that you cannot anticipate everything that happens in a campaign."

"We must be prudent," said the oldest. "You may not think that we are putting up the kind of resistance that you and the Emperor would like, but we have families and businesses and trade to fill our time, and we're not eager to see our children starve, no matter who rules in Roma or in Constantinople, and you may tell the Emperor that. It is not treason to want to preserve our lives and the lives of our families. According to what you and the others say, that is what Justinian wishes to do." He folded his arms, revealing two long tears in the threadbare silk.

"It is what all of us wish to do," Belisarius said wearily. "Your goals are no different than those of the Emperor; we work to the same ends."

"That may be," said the youngest, his expression blank with disapproval. "But what can we do to save our children? Whether the Emperor agrees or not, we must look to our own welfare or see our families without shelter and food."

"Yes," said the one with the darkest beard.

Belisarius nodded. He had seen hungry children all over Italy. "We will do all that we must to insure that as few as possible are lost."

"Fine words," scoffed the oldest man. "But it will not feed our children or save our houses." He glared at Belisarius and did not bother to appear respectful.

"What do you wish me to do, good citizens?" Belisarius inquired, rubbing his aching eyes as he spoke. "Tell me."

This was what they had been waiting for; the youngest took a step closer and said, "We want to keep the gates closed in the morning so that we can take time to find out how much there truly is in the city. We need to discover how much food is left, where there is room for more people to be housed, where there can be more animals stalled and fed, how much water is left, what clothing is available—"

The one with the darkest beard interrupted him. "There are also slaves and servants to deal with. Most of those coming from Roma are not wealthy, but they are bringing their goods and chattels with them, and all must be considered if we are going to be able to plan for any of them."

"And," the oldest went on with a nod to the others, "there are those who need to find out what has been taken, what is missing, and where the thieves are taking their booty. The price of certain foods has already more than doubled, and I have spoken with the Guard Tribune who has said that they cannot stem the tide. With so many fleeing, all a thief has to say is that he bought an item from one of the Romans on the road; unless there is good reason to doubt him, no one will question such a statement. For one thing, no one has the time to carry on an investigation, and for another the Guard has more to do than inspect baggage for contraband and loot."

A fourth man, very lean and wearing the most elaborate palmata wound over his tunica, spoke at last. "There are slaves escaping, too. Some have killed their owners and taken treasure, confident that all they need do is remove their collars to be free of their state and the consequences of their acts."

Absentmindedly Belisarius fingered the metal torque around his neck that indicated his rank, thinking—and not for the first time—that it was oddly appropriate that his rank and a slave's should be indicated by a collar. That his was studded with amber did not alter its impact for him. "Most slaves are branded, aren't they? They can be rid of the collars, but not of the brands." Under his bracchae his legs were scarred, a General's brand, he told himself.

"But the brands are on the thigh or upper arm. It would

mean another inspection," pointed out the oldest. "I believe Lepidius is correct, that there are slaves taking advantage of this troubled time to flee, but there are others, certainly there are others legitimately seeking their owners and trying to conduct themselves according to the laws of God and man."

"It isn't practical to inspect every person coming through the city's gates," allowed the one monk in the group.

"It isn't practical to permit the kind of influx we have, but no one is concerned about that," said the one called Lepidius.

"What would be the point?" asked Belisarius. "The problem is already upon us, and there is nothing to change that. No one can ignore it, and for that reason, we must deal with it." He stretched out his legs and crossed them at the ankles, feeling the leather rub against his skin. Years ago he would have found blisters when his boots were removed, but now there were calluses on his hands and feet that prevented this. "Let me say that it would not be wise to close the city tomorrow, no matter how sensible the plan may appear to you."

"Why not?" demanded the youngest man. "Are you unwilling to spare the men to aid us?" His face darkened with the accusation.

"No," said Belisarius, although this was not completely true. "No, I am thinking of what would happen when you opened the gates once more. There would be a riot at the least, for there are those outside the gates more desperate than you. They are without homes and they are hungry. Most of them would not hesitate to seize anything they needed from what they can find here, and the longer they are denied, the more forceful they will be when the chance is afforded them."

"And you think that troops would not deter them?" asked the one with the darkest beard.

"I think that an army would not deter them," said Belisarius. "They have nothing to lose. You have much at risk. Therefore they will do more than you to get what they need. What is the threat of a lance if you have not eaten for two days? At most it ends your hunger, at least it—"

"We will close and bar our houses," the youngest assured the General.

"That will give protection of a kind for a while, until someone breaks down the door, and then there will be worse carnage than there might have been at first," Belisarius said. "I have seen this before, and I will see it again many times before I die, if God grants me life."

"Does that mean you will do nothing?"

"Lepidius," said Belisarius, grateful that he had one name he could use for this delegation. "Listen to me. Most of those who are on the road outside the gates have left all they had behind. They are tired, they are hungry and they are filled with dread for tomorrow. You cannot change that. They will not stop, they will not go away no matter how much you wish they would, and they will not listen to you should you plead with them to spare you. No matter how sensible, how reasonable your requests may be, they will mean nothing to a man who has lost his fortune and his family. Do you understand that?"

"But you are here with armed men. You can bring your army here to supervise the departure of the Romans. They are rabble, nothing more." The monk had a deep, stern voice and he used it now to good effect; the others nodded their support.

"Armed men, you say? Not prayers?" Belisarius made no effort to keep the irony out of his voice. "You are a man of God, your robes proclaim your calling, and yet you come to ask for an army to assist you."

"God favors those who are willing to act," said the monk. "God demands our faith in Him and our use of the reason He gave us through our First Parents in Eden."

The one with the darkest beard was the first to endorse the monk. "Listen to him, man. You think that you are aiding us, and yet we are facing the ruin of the city. This man—a man of God, as you say—has told us what must be done if we are to be spared, and he reminds us that

God is not bought with empty prayers, but by firm action, showing the determination of our faith in Him."

"Of course," Belisarius said. "And those outside the gates are convinced that God will approve the stealing of food to save the lives of children, or the killing of another man in order to get passage on a ship to Constantinople." He got slowly to his feet. "I cannot spare the troops to do as you wish. Tomorrow I ride to Roma myself, to find out how severe the trouble is, how many have fled and what defenses remain there."

The oldest man crossed his arms and looked outraged. "How can you do this?" he demanded.

"I have more responsibilities than this place alone," said the General with less accommodation than he had shown before. "The Emperor has entrusted all of Italy to my care, and expects that I will do all that I can to save all of it from the invasion of Totila. I must answer to Justinian and God, as you answer to your city and your families. Therefore, much as I would want to spare your city or any city misfortune, I must do as I am commanded. I leave for Roma in the morning. Those of my men I leave behind are mandated to do what they can to aid in the transport of Romans to safe ports, and that much they will do. Beyond that, you must look to your own resources. I will fail my mandate if I permit your concerns to override all that has been entrusted to me."

The monk raised his hand, making a gesture against the evil eye. "You are a tool of the forces of Hell, not of the Emperor."

Belisarius had been cursed by those more expert than this man, but he still disliked the feelings it awakened in him. "I am no one's tool, good monk. I am the Emperor's General in Italy and will remain so for as long as he honors me with the position."

"You will fall," said the monk with deep satisfaction.

"That is for God and Justinian to determine," said Belisarius with a faint smile. "I will authorize two of my Captains to do what they can to aid in controlling the people coming through the city, and if you wish, I will give them permission to deal with any disruptions in the most direct way possible." He saw the faint approval in the men's eyes and went on to warn them. "Take care. You have had near-riots here for the last several days, and now there is no doubt that these Romans will need all the aid they can get or take. If you are too stringent with them, you may lose all that you seek to preserve through your rules and limitations."

The monk lowered his eyes. "We submit to the will of God."

"Once you have troops to protect you," said Belisarius.

"And you, proud man, you are fast coming to a time when all your might and all your battles and all your honor will avail you nothing." The monk glowered at the General. "The Emperor listens to other voices than yours. Never forget that."

"He listens to his wife after God," said Belisarius, not adding that Theodora was a close friend of his Antonina; as long as the two women were close friends, Belisarius knew that his position was secure.

"If a man is led by a woman, he makes his own fall, as did Adam," said the man with the darkest beard. "It is known that these women have given themselves more to the service of Satan than of God."

"Do not let the Emperor hear you say such things," suggested Belisarius. "He says that the words of a virtuous woman are more worthy than the preaching of fools. He has gained much from his wise Empress."

It was apparent that none of the men believed this, and Belisarius was too tired to pursue the matter any further. The tallest of the delegation, a man who had remained stubbornly silent, finally said, "How many troops will you leave here, General?"

"I can leave no more than two hundred foot soldiers and fifty cavalry. The rest must follow me to Roma before midday," he said, welcoming this apparent understanding from one of the men of Neapolis. "I will be certain that the instructions are clear to these troops. You may choose one of your number to work with the men I leave behind, and that will in turn give you the opportunity to arrange the defenses you have in whatever way most suits your purposes."

"These troops—are they the best you can provide?" asked the youngest man.

"If you mean, will I leave the exhausted and the wounded behind to guard you and take with me those soldiers who are in better condition and more fully equipped, then the answer must be no, for those who are wounded are not required to fight in any sense and are with our ships in the east." He sighed. "I will be at pains to find you a Tribune you can trust to do all that you require of the soldiers without spreading them too thin or putting them at a serious disadvantage. Let me point out one thing to you, and you may then do what you wish: the soldiers can create a corridor from gate to dockside, and can keep most of the people from spilling over into your city, if you will permit them to act in that way. It would be the best use of the men you have and it would limit the amount of damage you are apt to sustain during the time the Romans are in Neapolis."

"Are those your orders?" asked the oldest suspiciously.

"No, those are my observations. You are free to do as you wish with the men so long as your orders do not contradict those of the Emperor." He stretched. "It has been more than a full day since I slept, good citizens. Perhaps you will be content to leave this for another time?"

"How can we leave this, when you will be gone tomorrow?" asked the one with the darkest beard.

"There will be other men here. Most of my officers are experienced and will do what they can to make this a worthwhile time for all of you." He moved away from the narrow table. "I will instruct them to guard the city from abuse. If you will let them do the work they are trained to do, everyone will benefit, even the unfortunates from Roma."

"And you will not have to answer for anything that goes wrong. You will be able to say that if there are problems, if there are those who are injured or in other ways harmed, that it was our actions, not yours, that brought this about. We have heard about the manner in which you of Constantinople conduct your affairs."

"Lepidius," said Belisarius, "even if everything you say is true, and everything you believe is true and everything you deplore is true, nonetheless, Justinian is the Emperor and what he orders and demands is his by right of his rule. If you question that, you question the order of the world and the word of Heaven." He reached for a small mallet and struck a small, flat bell with it. "You will be fed while you are here, if you wish. My slaves will see to it."

"And you?" asked the monk, clearly not satisfied with the hospitality Belisarius offered.

"I will be attending to my duties with my officers so that they will be prepared to act for you tomorrow." He gestured to the slave who came through the door. "These men are to be given every courtesy a guest can expect. Is Chrysanthos here, or has he already gone to his men?"

"He is still here, Master," said the slave in Egyptian-accented Greek.

"Then let him dine with these citizens," said Belisarius in Greek.

"Does this man speak Latin?" the youngest member of the delegation wanted to know.

"Yes, that is why I thought of him. You will be able to understand one another. I have three other officers who are fluent in Latin as well as Greek, and they are most in demand of the men I command in Italy." Belisarius indicated the slave. "If you follow him, he will see that you are escorted to Chrysanthos."

Most of the men were willing to depart, but the one with the darkest beard was inclined to linger, to press for more advantages than they had secured already. "I wish your assurance that if there is any trouble, you will be willing to send your troops to quell any uprising that we may have to deal with."

"You'll have to arrange that with Chrysanthos; I will abide by the terms you make with him," said Belisarius.

The other men did what they could to get their companion to leave with them, speaking a few words in low voices urging him to come with them to this new officer.

"If we are not satisfied, you will learn of it," said the oldest delegate as he left the room.

"I'm certain of that," said Belisarius, watching the door even when it was empty, as if aware of a lingering presence like an odor or the echo of a scream.

* * *

Text of a letter to Vigilius, Bishop of Roma and Pope of the Church.

On the anniversary of the election of Your Holiness to the See of Santo Pietrus, the Priest Formosus of Ostia sends this report with the deepest faith and reverence.

It has pleased Your Holiness to learn of the current state of the Church in her parent city of Roma, and it has fallen to this most unhappy of men to inform Your Holiness that the great devil and pagan Totila has made progress with his forces against this most venerable of all cities. It is his intent to tear the whole place down, or so he swears on his blasphemous gods. To this end, he has been harrying the merchants on the roads, stopping farmers bringing produce to the city, and attempting to cut the aqueducts that bring water to the people of Roma. All this has been seen and heard by many and is not the result of mere rumors and fears that are current with many of those still living within the walls of the city.

It is of particular note that those who should be most

stalwart in their duty—the religious of Roma—have fled in great numbers, and it would astonish me to find more than two hundred priests and monks in Roma to minister to the thousands of unfortunates who have remained faithful to their God and Roma.

While there are many who look to the Byzantines to succor us before Totila can break through our defenses, Your Holiness must understand that it is only through their efforts that any semblance of defense has been maintained at the present, and it would not be unreasonable to prepare for worse to come, for although the great Belisarius brings his men to our aid, the force is smaller than the one that the Emperor of Constantinople promised to provide, and they are not as well-equipped as they had been represented to be. No one wishes to think of the ruin of this greatest of cities, but there can be little doubt that no matter how vigilant we are, there are many here who will suffer, and the city will not be spared entirely.

I do not wish to make it appear that I am entirely without hope, for that would be a greater sin than the one the pagans intend to commit here. Yet I would be lax in my duty to you as a priest if I did not say it would be prudent to prepare for the worst, so that such things as sacred relics and objects of veneration may be hidden or otherwise protected from the possible ravages of the Ostrogothic warriors who are bent on destroying the city before the height of summer.

Your Holiness would do well to fortify Monte Casino against the barbarians, and to make an official request of Belisarius to give you and your company the protection that was assured you by the Emperor Justinian more than three years ago. If the Church is to survive, it must have the aid and assistance of all who are devoted to Our Lord and His Church. Whether they are of Byzantium or of Roma, surely there can be no argument that the fate of Christianity is in the hands of those willing to take up the cause of Our Lord in the face of those who are determined to bring the Church and her city to their knees.

What draws the pagans are the earthly treasures which

have been stored up out of piety and devotion. But these are not the true riches of the Church, and while the pagans seek only silver and gold, they assault far more than walls to obtain it. If we fail to defend the outward gifts of the Church, it is only too likely that we will also fail to defend the spiritual ramparts as well. I pray every hour that none of this will come to pass, but while I pray, I seek out men of experience to aid in the earthly battle, and I admonish all I see to offer up their orisons to God and the Mother Maria for the salvation of our city and our souls.

In all humility and faith, and with unswerving dedication to Your Holiness and our Church, I sign myself your most lowly Brother in Christ,

> Formosus
> Priest from Ostia
> currently with the Curia in Roma

• 2 •

By late afternoon the first contingent of soldiers arrived, making camp around the old villa in fields and orchards that were just coming into blossom. For novelty the old baths were fired up and many of the men boisterously used them, marveling at the depravity of the old Romans with their passion for bathing.

"What do you think?" Niklos Aulirios asked his owner as he stared out the windows at the camp that had grown up around them.

From her writing desk, Olivia Clemens did not answer at first; she was putting the last touches on a writ of manumission for two more slaves. Only when she had affixed both her signature and her seal did she answer. "What do I think about what?"

"These Byzantines," her Greek majordomo replied. "I'm not sure they're better than the Ostrogoths."

"They are better because they don't intend to raze the city," she pointed out, rising and coming to join him at the window.

"But look at them. And you know what they have done to half the countryside. I realize that an army must eat, and that soldiers might not have the manners of saints, but that doesn't excuse the raiding and looting they've done." He had folded his arms and was looking more stubborn than usual.

"I'm not going to argue with you," said Olivia, faintly amused by his conduct. "But this is not the first trouble we've seen, is it?"

"No," he admitted grudgingly.

"And with a little good fortune, it will not be the last." She continued to stare into the pallid afternoon. The light, softened by a faint haze rising from the Tibros, was kind to her face, making her appear younger than her years. Her soft, fawn-brown hair was braided and wrapped in the current fashion for widows, and she wore a paenula of wool embroidered with silk and gold thread that showed her wealth more than her manner.

"You have a strange way of thinking, my mistress," Niklos said, beginning to smile in spite of his own foreboding.

"It comes with the years, my friend," she said, and shook off her slight melancholy. "I want you to make sure that copies of these writs are in the hands of the monks by morning. That way, no matter what happens here, the slaves will be free and they can make lives for themselves. You'd better take the grants with you to the monks as well."

Niklos laughed cynically. "You're not seriously asking me to put money in the hands of a servant of God and expect it to go anywhere but into Church coffers, are you?"

"You may be right in that, Niklos," she sighed. "All right; I'll find a way to make sure each gets the money they've been promised, and the copies of the writs will be safe. Take one or two of the gold cups with you to make sure the good monks continue to care for the records we entrust to them. I'm not quite as trusting as you often fear I am."

"And what else?" Niklos ventured. "You have most of your belongings crated and packed and ready to be moved. Does that trouble you?"

"Of course it troubles me. Roma is my home. I drew my first breath here, within sight of the Tibros. It is part of me and I am part of it." Her expression was slightly distant as she delved her memory for the events of her long life.

"We can still arrange for you to stay in Italy," suggested Niklos. "You don't have to go as far away as Constantinople."

"Almost all those who can afford to leave have done so already and if I remain much longer, I will be exposed to more risks than the mere clash of Byzantines and Ostrogoths. So long as I must live with lions, I might as well find myself a good place in their dens." She laughed suddenly. "How unendurable! I sound worse than one of those Epicureans who ape the manner of their teacher without the least understanding of what he said."

"You don't want to go, do you?" Niklos persisted.

"No, if it were possible to remain in safety. But since it is not, then I'm . . . resigned. I will go to Constantinople, to the house that Belisarius has arranged for me, and when the army is at home, I will entertain this Drosos and do my best to be as inconspicuous as possible." She held out the parchment sheets to Niklos once again. "Please, Niklos, take these to the monks and bring me the sigil of the abbot, or whatever superior they have now, so that I can give proof of the transaction. We can squabble later, when we're safe."

"As you wish, my mistress," Niklos said, making a reverence to her that just missed being insulting. He took the parchments and strode to the door. "I'll send Kosmos to guard you while I'm gone. I don't trust those soldiers to be respectful."

Olivia chuckled. "No more do I, but they're likely to look for female slaves rather than the owner of the villa who is also known to be the hostess of their General."

"You put more store in that than I do," Niklos warned as he started across the smaller of the two atria of the villa.

It was not long before Kosmos appeared in the door, his manner as humble as his body was formidable. He lowered his head and kept his eyes averted. "Niklos sent me, great lady," he said softly.

"He said he would," Olivia agreed.

"And the General Belisarius has returned. His horse has just been taken to the stables." For Kosmos this was a long speech, and as he concluded it, he appeared to be slightly out of breath.

Olivia gave Kosmos her full attention at this. "General Belisarius. Only he?"

"There are officers with him," said Kosmos.

"I will see them shortly, in the main reception chamber. Have flowers brought there, and send Hogni and . . . oh, I guess it had better be Hogni and Beltzin, to wait on them. They will want to have wine and meat as well as washing basins." To Olivia, this seemed woefully inadequate, for when she was young, nothing less than a full bath—calidarium, tepidarium, frigidarium—and a massage with costly oils followed by a nine-course banquet would be considered a proper welcome for so august a man as Belisarius.

"Very good, great lady. But you will be left alone, and that is what Niklos required I not allow to happen." Again he was sounding breathless.

"I give you my word that I will manage, and that I will be able to fend for myself. Besides, I must do something about my clothes or I will be more improper than they are." She went briskly toward the side door. "I am going now to my private quarters, and if you will see that Fisera joins me there, that will ensure I am not alone and you will be able to complete the commission I have given you." As she watched him go, she wondered if she had made a mistake in freeing him. Kosmos was not used to living on his own, and in these troubled times, she feared he would become prey to the first scoundrel who came across him.

She stopped these ponderings as she reached the door of her private suite of rooms. Always when she stepped through the door, she felt herself on the brink of the past. It pleased her to indulge in a sense of nostalgia; this afternoon she had to admit that there was a pang of something more. She stared at the frescoes on the wall, at the furniture and the ornaments she had gathered together here, and knew that as many of them as she took with her to Constantinople, it would not be the same, and that she would not find them as appropriate, as comforting as they were here, where they belonged. They were Roman; so was she. Here she was on her native earth and there she would be a stranger. Nothing would alter that, and she knew she would have to reconcile herself to it.

There was a gentle rap on the door on the far side of the room and this brought Olivia out of her reverie. "Yes?"

"It is Fisera, mistress," said the slave.

"Enter, Fisera," she said, speaking more briskly and moving with renewed vitality. This was not the time to be distracted, she reminded herself as she admitted the slave. There was too much to do.

Fisera had brought two long pallia with her, one of a rich deep-rose color embroidered all over with golden medallions, the other a strange shade that was almost not any color—a shadow tone between gray and tan and green—ornamented with dark brown silken embroidery and with accents picked out in seed pearls. She stopped, staring at Olivia. "Oh, mistress," she said in a faltering way.

"Tomorrow I am no longer your mistress, Fisera, and you do not need to call me your mistress any longer." She gave her a heartening smile. "Come, Fisera, don't be troubled. There is no reason for me to doubt your devotion, whether you wear a collar or not."

"You have been most kind to me, mistress," said Fisera with genuine feeling.

An expression that was not quite a frown passed fleetingly over Olivia's face. "Have I? I hope so. It was my intention, but that often counts for little."

Alarmed by this sudden change in Olivia's manner, Fisera reached out and touched her arm. "Have I offended you, mistress?"

"No," said Olivia, her demeanor changing again. "No, of course not. I was remembering the past. I've been doing a lot of that recently. I must be . . . getting old."

"You are young forever, mistress," Fisera said, more in wariness than flattery.

"I have that sort of face," said Olivia.

"Perhaps more than that," murmured the slave-woman. "I have been in your household for more than eight years and I have not noticed a change in you. There are those, not close to you, who have hinted that you must practice the magical arts of the old days, when sorcery was used by the witch Messalina." She said this last with her eyes averted.

"Messalina was hardly a witch: she had the misfortune to be married to that pervert Claudius, and that—" She heard the sound of her voice and broke off. "I cannot believe that Messalina used any arts but her own woman-liness to lure her husband."

"They say that her husband wasn't all she lured," the slave said, her face more animated. "She was an infamous adulteress."

"And whose idea was that, do you think?" Olivia asked, and then, before Fisera could answer, she went on. "Well, that was hundreds of years ago, wasn't it? And I have guests who require entertainment this evening. You brought me the pallia, I see. Perhaps I ought to choose one so you may pack the other."

"It depends on what paenula you have selected." Fisera held up the rose-and-gold pallium. "This brings out color."

"So it does," agreed Olivia. "And still, do I want

color? Do I want to shout or whisper?" She fingered the two pallia. "Which is best?"

"You have the gold pectoral, and you can wear it with this. It would make a very impressive—"

"You're probably right," said Olivia, reaching for the other pallium. "But tonight, ah, tonight I believe that I will harken back to the old times. This and the paenula of pale silk, you know the one. I'll wear them over the samite dalmatica, the one with the silver threads. And there's one other thing. Instead of a tablion, get me that pectoral in silver, the disk with the raised wings."

"If you like," said Fisera, clearly disapproving.

"There's just tonight, Fisera, and then you will be free to do or say whatever you wish to me, and you will have money enough to leave here and to establish yourself wherever you wish. You have been a good and faithful servant to me. For that, your freedom is a small enough token."

The sincerity in Olivia's voice clearly startled Fisera, and she hesitated before saying anything more. "Why the pectoral?"

"Because it reminds me of a very old friend, who gave it to me many, many years ago." Olivia's smile did not quite succeed, but she went on. "He told me a few home truths that I must remember while I live in Constantinople. What a hideous thought."

"If you go, none of us will be able to live. We will be taken by soldiers or monks and we will be more slaves then than ever we have been for you." This outburst was more alarming to Fisera than to Olivia, who had been expecting something of the sort since the day before yesterday.

"I have already sent copies of your writs of manumission to the monks for their records, and I will see that every one of you has their own writ to keep." When she had been young, almost half her household slaves could read. In the intervening centuries fewer and fewer slaves had acquired the skill until now less than a dozen of her staff were literate. "As long as you and the monks have the documents, there is safety for you. But you must keep the writ with you, so that you can prove that you are truly freed. You will have money and you will have supplies. Unless you choose badly, you will have no reason to regret being freed."

"Rudis says that we are being freed so that the invaders will spend time gathering us up so that you can escape and that you have no intention of letting us remain free once the threat of Totila is over." Fisera had started to cry in the sudden and violent way that made Olivia think of a summer thunderstorm.

"Why would I free you if I intended that? Why would I bother? I would need only to tell you where you must go and you would have to comply with my wishes. If Rudis is correct, then I have done this most stupidly." She put one hand on her hip. "If you want a military escort, I suppose I could convince the General to provide you one. And speaking of the General," she said in a more hasty tone, "I suppose I ought to prepare to greet him. Get me the dalmatica and the paenula and the pallium and that silver pectoral, and then help me do something with my hair. And for the love of . . . the Saints, don't fret. You will be safe when you leave."

Fisera sniffed deeply as she began to follow Olivia's orders. Her fears had been assuaged but they had not vanished.

Some little time later, Olivia emerged from her room to seek out her guests. She was magnificent to see, though most would have been hard-pressed to say why, for she was dressed almost as mutedly as a religious. Somehow, in the colors and chaste silver ornaments, she contrived a richness that was far more impressive than the gaudy colors worn by the retinue of General Belisarius, who was arrayed in bright red and orange with bright medallions on his bracchae and his high leather boots.

"We are more grateful to you, great lady, than we can express," said the General as he made a reverence to his hostess. "Your reception of us has been princely."

"Hardly," she said with candor, recalling the splendor

of the courts of Nero and Otho and Vespasianus, half a millennium ago. "You are most welcome here, General, as are your men." She looked around the room, her eyes lingering briefly on Drosos whose hair was still wet from the baths and who wore turquoise silk and a pallium of silver and lavender.

Belisarius indicated his fourteen companions. "There are a number of us, as you see, more than we had thought there would be at first, and you are more than generous to provide for us on such short notice. From what we have seen of Roma inside the walls, you are more fortunate than most."

"And more circumspect," said Olivia. "Only a fool would think that Totila would wait for us to prepare for him before he attacked." She was very much a part of her reception room, which was a pale, faded blue with false fluted columns painted silver. Yet instead of vanishing into the walls, she seemed to make all the room an extension of herself. The men watched her with admiration and other emotions.

"They are paying the price for their foolishness now," said Belisarius. "And what little we can do, I fear, comes too late. If we had come a few months earlier, or if the supplies had been adequate, or if the Bishop of Roma had not left the city when he did, we might have a better chance of defense, but the way things stand, there is nothing left to do but to insure that the least damage possible is done while Totila holds the city."

"You believe he will succeed, then?" asked Olivia, her calm not as complete as she would have liked.

"Unfortunately, yes; for a time. And then we will roust him, for we are the stronger forces and we are not barbarians." Belisarius looked over his men. "Occasionally one of the men will forget this and then there is much cause for—"

Stamos, a powerful man with scars seaming his face and hands, looked suddenly flustered. "They were under orders not to harm anyone," he protested, although no one had accused him of anything.

"They were also without adequate care and advice, and for that if no other reason, there is much for you and the rest of those officers who have had similar incidents to answer for. You have your men submit to proper punishment, and see that it is carried out where those who were the most harmed may witness it for themselves so that they will not regard us as little better than those we are here to fight." Belisarius turned to Olivia and the harshness of his attitude faded at once. "I do not mean to distress you, great lady. These matters are for more private times, and you must forgive us for being so uncaring."

Olivia, who had heard much worse than this over the long decades of her life, waved her hand to show that she was not distressed by what she had heard. "You must attend to your work, General, as must all of us in such times as these." She clapped her hands sharply and two slaves appeared in the doorway. "Is the dining room ready?"

"Yes, mistress," said the older of the two. "And there are cup bearers waiting with wine."

"Cup bearers!" cried out one of the Byzantines. "How Roman!"

"This is Roma," Olivia reminded them all. "And I am a Roman."

As they went into the dining room, none of the men thought it strange that Olivia did not have a couch of her own, and that she did not eat with them. In Constantinople, most women did not dine with men except on very special occasions; even then, they often dined apart from their fathers, brothers and husbands, watching them from terraces and balconies instead of sitting or reclining beside them.

Only Drosos, who watched Olivia closely while he ate honied kid boiled in milk with onions, fish stuffed with garlic and poached in wine, and spiced pork baked in a bread, noticed that she showed no outward signs of hunger, treating the lavish feast with indifference. Curious, he rose while the slaves removed the platters that had held the pork buns, and walked to her chair—for unlike her guests, she did not recline on padded couches —holding out a second cup to her. "Great lady, let me pour some of this excellent vintage for you. In your generosity, you have given all to us and spared none for yourself."

Olivia looked up at him. "You are most gracious," she said with a trace of amusement that Drosos could not identify in her fascinating eyes. "But I do not drink wine."

Before Drosos could pursue the matter, Belisarius motioned him back to his couch as the slaves brought out three long spits of roasted ducks stuffed with nuts and raisins.

While Drosos went on with the banquet, Olivia watched him, a speculative lift to her brows the only indication of her thoughts.

* * *

A bill of sale sent by military courier to Belisarius outside Roma.

On the Feast of the Patriarchs, I, Andros Trachi, acknowledge the receipt of the amount of twenty-two grains of gold and thirty-seven grains of silver in total and complete payment for a domicile of nineteen rooms, with kitchen and larder attached, from the Roman lady known to General Belisarius as Olivia Clemens, a widow, who for the safety of her goods and her person has taken the advice of the General and agreed to come to the city of Konstantin.

I formally relinquish all claims on this property to the General, who has acted as sponsor of the said widow, since she is lacking in husband or father or brother to act for her in this matter. All further negotiations are agreed to be directed to her majordomo, one Niklos Aulirios, who is empowered to carry out all contractual arrangements for her, and to have the sanction of the General Belisarius for such actions. It is agreed that no member of my family, nor my heirs, nor their kindred and heirs may make claim to this property and that the transference is a permanent one.

Regarding the alterations that this widow requires, it will take the workers a period of five months to accomplish most of the construction, and until it is complete arrangements may be made for this great lady to be the guest of the family of her sponsor, that is, the General Belisarius, and this will allow the majordomo Niklos Aulirios to oversee the construction to the satisfaction of his mistress.

Witnessed by the Pope Phillipos and the Pope Alexis at Konstantinoupolis in the presence of myself, Andros Trachi, and the freedman Thalkas, who will be the one in charge of the construction to be done on the property changing hand.

Prosperity, long life, and the favor of God to our great Emperor Justinian, who defends the honor of God on earth.

An appended note, addressed to Olivia.

Great lady,

For the time you are in Konstantinoupolis, you may find that some of the customs are strange to you, and so that you do not fall into error, I, Andros Trachi, offer the advice of my wife to guide you in your first ventures here. Doubtless, since Romans are more lax than we, you have grown accustomed to a level of license that might ill-prepare you for the more decorous and dignified life of this great city. Doubtless you will not want to make yourself conspicuous with actions that are repugnant to those of breeding and distinction. What can be thought charming and eccentric in Roma could give offense in Konstantinoupolis, and lead to unpleasantness which you must wish to avoid.

I look forward to being of service to you in this matter, and I am honored to have so great a lady purchasing the property that the General Belisarius has arranged for you to own.

> In Christian friendship,
> Andros Trachi

• **3** •

Each footfall produced echoes, and both Olivia and Niklos had to resist the urge to tiptoe through the vast, empty rooms of the house that Olivia had purchased.

"And I *did* purchase it," she insisted to Niklos after they had endured the obsequious greeting of Andros Trachi. "It's barbaric, their insistence that all negotiations be done by men."

"You mean, it isn't Roman."

"Not that Roma is much better, now," Olivia said quietly. "Even a century ago, it was not so bad." She looked around the great gloomy vestibule. "I suppose I'll grow accustomed to it."

"It is austere," said Niklos with a trace of amusement.

"It is tomblike," she said, her nose wrinkling. "I expect it to smell of mold."

"But it doesn't; it smells of paint," said Niklos, indicating one of the walls where work had already begun.

"I trust that they will be finished soon; as much as I am grateful to Belisarius' cousin, I don't know how much longer I can endure to remain under the same roof with her. At least I had the opportunity of her hospitality so that I would not have to accept the kind offer"—her voice was sweet with sarcasm—"of that unctuous Trachi. I can think of few things I would have wanted less."

"And there are other considerations, are there not?" said Niklos with genuine sympathy.

Olivia did not answer at once; she paced down the room, peering at the ceiling as she went, then stopped and turned to Niklos again. "Yes. Yes, there are."

"And you are not prepared. You have done nothing to prepare yourself," said Niklos in his most blunt manner. His warm brown eyes, almost reddish in cast, bored into hers.

"There was not much time," she began, then sighed. "That's my excuse, of course, nothing more." She stared, unseeing, at the empty room. "I had such hopes for Drosos. The first time he came to me, I remembered what it was I wanted most, and for a time, I had it again." Now her face softened and she laughed once, sadly. "How rarely have my lovers cared more for me than themselves. Drosos truly enjoyed *me*, and I relished him."

"And the rest of it?" asked Niklos, with a warning gesture to her to keep her voice low.

"Ah, yes, the rest of it. For now there is no risk from the rest of it," she reminded him. "In time, there might be, but who is to say if there will be time? Drosos is still in Roma and I am here—in Constantinople." She was more adept than he at indirect speaking. "Certainly something will have to be arranged in the interim, but I am not as concerned about that as you are. It is always possible to find something that will do for a while, even here."

"You, cynical?" Niklos teased her with affection.

"I, practical. I, resigned, my friend, not cynical." She pulled the long folds of her bronze-colored paenula more closely around her. "I don't care if they say this city is hot; I am chilled. There is a darkness here, a coldness that has nothing to do with the sun."

"Olivia, mistress, be careful who hears you complain. This place is different from Roma in many, many ways," said Niklos, once again looking toward the shadowed room that joined the vestibule.

"Romans, luckily, are expected to be impulsive and capricious. Didn't that dreadful Andros Trachi tell me so at length?" She was moving restlessly once more. "Everyone knows that we can accept no city but Roma as home, and that for us she is the center of the earth."

Niklos followed her as she rushed into the larger of the two reception rooms that opened onto the vestibule. "Nevertheless," he persisted, "don't be too condemning. We are here on sufferance, and from what I can tell, we are not going to be accorded too much of that."

"Yes; yes. But from what I have seen, a mere widow, with or without a fortune, is hardly worth any attention, and one from Roma is little more than an amusement. It's our manner, you know, and our lack of propriety." There was not much annoyance in the tone of her voice, but the expression on her face was enough to make Niklos change the subject.

"Will you accept the invitation of Antonina? She is determined to fulfill her obligations to you for Belisarius' sake, if not your own. She has said she will introduce you to the best society of the city."

"And who can guess why," said Olivia as she made a swift inspection of the changes that were being wrought in the room. "I suppose we have to have those dreary Saints everywhere, don't we? I already asked for an ikonostasis in my private rooms—so it will be understood that I am pious—is it really necessary to have another, do you think?"

"The Emperor is a religious man, and his court follows his example," Niklos pointed out. "And you are a sensible woman."

"At my age, I had better be," she said, and laughed again, this time with genuine mirth. "Very well; see that we have another screen to load up with bad art, and a few more of those horrid hanging braziers for incense. And while you are being so protective, send a messenger to Antonina. I will call upon her later this afternoon if she is receiving anyone."

"And if she is not?" inquired her majordomo.

"Then discover when she is prepared to have my company for an hour or so, and we will then arrange things to that purpose." She shrugged. "I suppose I must do this eventually: why not now?"

Niklos did not answer, but his relief was apparent in the speed with which he carried out his orders.

By the time the slave had been sent as a messenger to the enormous house of Belisarius, Olivia had completed her rounds of the house she had purchased and was ready to dress for the forthcoming visit. Since her last banquet in Roma, she had continued to choose subdued clothing and modest-but-costly ornaments to wear, sensing that this would offset some of the adverse attitudes the Byzantines had toward Romans.

Still, she balked at the enclosed palanquin that Niklos had arranged for her transportation to Belisarius' house. "I don't like being enclosed," she said as Niklos assisted the slaves in drawing the draperies around her.

"You are in Constantinople, and women of good reputation do not show themselves on the street except in going to the hippodrome and the market squares. The penitential processions also require that all women show themselves, but cover their faces for the Sin of Eve and the Fall of Man." He was stern with her, needing her to use her wits more than she had been willing to do.

"I might as well immure myself and be done with it—and I have done that already and found it appalling." She pulled the silken hanging closed with her own hands. "If I do not speak to you when I return, it is your own fault, Greek."

Since Olivia only called Niklos Greek when she was displeased with him, he did not respond, but stepped back and permitted the bearers to start off with their Roman burden.

Belisarius' house was one hill over—although Olivia refused to think of such bumps as hills—and in a street that was made narrow with the extensive reconstruction and rebuilding that was the passion of Justinian. By the time the bearers set the palanquin down, they were sweating and blowing hard as dray beasts for the added effort of lifting the vehicle around the heaps of masonry and over piles of rubble that littered the streets increasingly as they neared the palace of the Emperor and his most ambitious project—the expansion of the Basilica of the Most Sacred Wisdom.

Four armed guards uniformed in the manner of Belisarius' personal soldiers flanked the door to the house as Olivia was helped from the palanquin. All the men watched her closely, each with a hand on the hilt of his sword.

"I am Olivia Clemens, a widow from Roma," she told the majordomo of Belisarius' house. "I would like the honor of spending a little time with the august lady who is wife to the great General Belisarius." She hoped that was formal enough for these ceremony- and ritual-loving Byzantines.

The majordomo, a smooth-faced eunuch in garments far richer than what most merchants could afford to wear, made her a deep reverence as he admitted her to the vestibule of the enormous house. "Be kind enough to wait here; one of the household women will escort you to the august lady."

"How good of you," said Olivia mendaciously.

The eunuch said nothing as he moved away from her, leaving her to stand by herself in the huge octagon-shaped entryroom with nothing more to look at than a series of dreadful frescoes of military Saints in battle against devils and other foreigners all in grotesque and frozen postures. Olivia found herself longing for the mosaics of her youth. Where, amid this vehement and abstracted suffering, was one dolphin, one dog worrying a bone, one cherub dangling a flute or a wine cup? These were the scenes she recalled most affectionately from those long-ago days when she grew up. In her father's villa there was one wall showing Jupiter turning into a bull, with a buxom Europa waiting for her lover with more enthusiasm than awe. There had been two swineherds in the corner of the fresco, off to the lower right-hand corner. They had been sharing a wineskin and bread, and they idly watched the transformation. One of them was forever in the act of tossing a scrap to a tabby cat. There had been nothing so everyday, so human in the art Olivia had seen here in Byzantium; even in Roma now, the touches she loved were disappearing.

"Great lady?" repeated the eunuch, who had returned.

Olivia looked up sharply. "Oh; excuse me. These pictures—" She indicated the walls.

"Antonina is a woman of much piety, and this is only the outward sign of it," said the eunuch, apparently favorably impressed by Olivia's interest. "If you will condescend to follow me, I will bring you to Antonina."

"Thank you," said Olivia, falling into step behind the slave.

"You are not the only great lady to visit Antonina today," said the eunuch. His voice was low and mature: he had been emasculated after manhood. Because he had run to fat it was hard to say if he had ever been handsome, but there was a sweetness to his round face that could once have been more attractive than it was safe for a slave to be.

"What is your name, slave?" asked Olivia.

"I am Arius," he told her, apparently surprised at the question.

"In Roma, I always wanted to know the names of those who did me service so that I would be able to leave some token of my appreciation for good service," she said, remembering how many slaves had once been able eventually to buy their freedom with those accumulated tokens. Olivia was still distressed that those laws had been changed.

"No token is necessary. This is Konstantinoupolis, great lady, not Roma, and here we give thanks to God, not to those whose place it is to serve." He had led the way down a long hall and now stopped at two tall doors. "These are the reception apartments of the august lady Antonina."

"I am looking forward to the honor of meeting her," said Olivia, doing her best not to be impatient.

Arius made his reverence as he opened the door. It was a graceful gesture, as formal and unnatural as the attitudes of the figures in the ikons that flanked the doors. "August lady, this is the great lady Olivia," said the eunuch before he stepped aside to let Olivia enter.

Antonina was seated on a silk-covered couch; she was a magnificent woman, all stark contrasts. Her hair, black as onyx, had two white streaks that only served to make the dark more impressive. Her eyes were large, rimmed with heavy lashes and accented by curving dark brows. Her skin was the lightest shade of peach that Olivia had ever seen. Her clothes were silken, the paenula so extensive that it surrounded and engulfed her in vast folds of shimmering red. At her shoulder, her tablion was the size of the palm of her hand, encrusted with garnets and gold. "Welcome to my husband's house," she said, not rising.

Olivia smiled without warmth. "I am pleased to bring you his greetings and remembrances," she said, hoping that she had come close to the proper formula.

"And this"—she indicated the other woman in the room—"is Eugenia. She is the widow of Katalinus Hyakinthos, who was the bastard of Elezaros." This name was apparently supposed to mean something to Olivia, and Antonina waited for her response.

"There was a . . . naval commander, wasn't there?" She hoped that her memory was correct; she sensed that neither woman would be forgiving of an error.

"My husband's father, yes. They were killed in the same storm." She was not as tall as Antonina, nor quite as richly dressed. Her body was rounder and softer, more yielding, and her posture was more inviting. She, too, wore an enormous paenula, hers of a deep sea-green shot with gold, and her tablion was not as large or as bejeweled as Antonina's.

"How unfortunate," said Olivia.

"My husband sends me word that you, too, are a widow." She pointed to another couch, making it clear she wished Olivia to sit there.

"For many years, yes," she answered candidly.

"Yet you are not ancient," said Antonina.

"I wear my years well," Olivia said.

"That may be fortunate," Antonina declared. "Widows are not uncommon and it is not always the most simple thing to find them proper mates. There are men who prefer women who have never been married to those who have. I was fortunate, for my husband told me from the first that he was pleased that he had found me a widow, for that meant I knew men and I knew marriage. I was most pleased that he felt that way, and I told him then, as I have continued to tell him, that no woman can appreciate a marriage until her second one." She smiled, and it was clear she expected her two guests to smile as well.

Realizing that this was likely to be more awkward than she had thought at first, Olivia said, "That may be, and certainly I have no means to tell, but let me assure you, august lady—"

"You must call me Antonina," she purred.

"You are all kindness," said Olivia, going on before she could be distracted. "Let me assure you that I have not come to you with the hope that you will supply a husband upon request. I have had such experience of marriage that I am not in a hurry to resume my married state. For a time, I am content to be a widow, and if this does not exclude me from friendships and society, I will abide as I am." She folded her hands in her lap and gave what she hoped was a trusting and guileless look to her hostess.

"No woman has a distaste of marriage," Antonina said in a manner that would clearly tolerate no disputes.

"I have, I am afraid. My husband was a man of strange appetites which he imposed upon me and that has left me with a lack of trust of marriage." She regarded Eugenia, hoping she might find an ally. "If your husband held you in respect and affection, then you have known two things I never had from my husband."

"It is not fitting to speak against the dead, let alone a

dead husband," announced Antonina, but she relented. "If what you say is true, then the Church failed you, for it is the responsibility of the priests to be certain that God's commands are obeyed on earth. As you are to be submissive to the will of your husband, so he is to give you care and comfort."

Privately Olivia thought that the last characteristic she saw in Antonina was submission, but she made no comment about it. "The priests . . . were not as apt to take a hand," she said, trusting that her vagueness would be seen as tact instead of the evasion it was.

"There are those who do not uphold the honor of their God as they ought," said Antonina, directing a hard glance at Eugenia. "I have said that your priest was wrong in permitting you to travel to Cyprus without a guard to accompany you."

"He said that since there were others in the ship who were also visiting the shrine that it would be satisfactory," said Eugenia, clearly rehashing an old argument. "My priest said that when the journey is a holy one, then it is necessary to leave all pomp behind in order to show humility in the proper manner." She smiled, her mouth turning up at the corners and making her look even more like a kitten than her angular face and pointed chin already did.

"Still, think of the insult if anything had occurred," Antonina persisted. "It may be spiritually wise to make pilgrimages, but I do not believe that it is sensible to take such extreme risks."

"You have a General for a husband," said Olivia, deciding that she might as well discover as much as she could about what Antonina's opinions were since she would have to deal with them while she lived in Constantinople.

"Yes, and a very great man. He is filled with distinction and honor, and he does not use this for anything but his service to God and the Emperor." There was a faint regret in her words, as if Belisarius' integrity was a subtle disappointment to his spouse.

Eugenia must also have been aware of the underlying lack of satisfaction in Antonina's voice, for she said, "How it must please you to know that Belisarius is as stalwart as he is, and free from the taint of manipulation and intrigue that has compromised so many others."

"It is most . . . rewarding," said Antonina in a reflective tone.

As she settled back onto the couch, Olivia said, "I am truly in your debt for your willingness to receive me, Antonina. I have come to realize that many Romans are not so well-treated here in this city, and often for excellent reason. That you have been willing to speak with me, to invite me into this house fills me with gratitude."

"My husband has said that you have donated your villa to his use while he and his men are in Roma, and that merits my hospitality." She nodded toward the ikonostasis on the far side of the room. "We know the obligations of our faith."

"Belisarius spoke glowingly of you, august lady," said Olivia, sensing a faint anxiety in Antonina. "He and his officers were always most respectful in what they said of you while they were at my villa."

Eugenia's smile was sharpened with malice. "Now the officers speak of you, Antonina."

"Only because I asked them," said Olivia, realizing her blunder almost as soon as it was spoken. "I know so little about this city and its ways, I wanted to learn how best to comport myself, and I thought that you were likely to be the best example I could have. Your husband was so proud of all you've done, and so sincere in his praises, I asked questions and had answers that truly amazed me."

"It was not correct to ask such questions," said Antonina, but her condemnation was modified by the tone of her voice. "In Byzantium we women are not eager to have our names and reputations bandied about. In Roma it might be otherwise, but here we all assume that it is not proper for a Christian woman to seek after notoriety or approbation."

"And a man placed as General Belisarius is often is

seen in the guise of his wife when he is not here to be evaluated," added Eugenia. "As some husbands are judged by their widows' conduct after the husbands are dead." She did not smirk, but it was more of an effort not to than it appeared to be.

"Then I can see why Belisarius reposes such great trust in you, Antonina." It was blatant flattery, but Olivia spoke with such skill—and Antonina was so eager to hear such praises—that if Antonina was aware of the intent, she was willing to ignore it.

However, Eugenia did not leave the issue unanswered. "It is only right for a man of Belisarius' position to rely on the good offices of his wife, and for him to know and acknowledge all that she does for him. A husband who must depend on his wife to put forth his position cannot be indifferent to her activities." From the tone of her voice, Olivia suspected that just such lapses had occurred with her and her late husband, who was the bastard of Elezaros.

"I am the helpmeet of Belisarius and his devoted servant," said Antonina in her most forceful accents. Then she regarded Olivia again. "You say he was well?"

"Well but tired," Olivia reassured her. "The campaign was hard, and the worst had not yet begun. He had been trying to find enough men to stop the raids that Totila's men had been making all around the city. It was wearing down the resistance of the peasants and farmers. Many of them wished to leave, and one of the tasks that Belisarius had set his men was convincing the farmers, as he tried to convince the citizens of Roma, not to leave, no matter how desperate their plight might seem."

"Tired. Not ill?" Her concern was without artifice; whatever else Antonina might be, she was truly concerned for the safety and welfare of her husband.

"Not while I was there, august lady. He complained of headaches from time to time, but nothing more than that. One of his officers had dislocated his shoulder and was carrying his arm in a sling while the ligaments mended, but that was the worst injury I saw, and if there was illness among them, I was not aware of it." Olivia saw the worry fade from Antonina's jet-black eyes. "Believe me, your husband is not in danger, at least he was not when I last saw him."

"May God watch over him and give him protection and guidance," said Antonina, her imperious manner returning. "I would like to know what plans he revealed, if any, for his homecoming."

"He said nothing about it while I was with him. I do not think he has made plans that are not in accord with the orders of the Emperor." This time Olivia sought to find a diplomatic way to deliver what she knew would be a disappointing message.

"It is the great honor of my husband to be high in the esteem of the Emperor and to be given the privilege of carrying out his orders." Antonina could not entirely disguise the sigh that accompanied this patriotic sentiment.

There was a discreet tap at the door and Arius opened it to admit three slaves bearing cups and plates. "As you have ordered, august lady," he said with a reverence to Antonina.

"Very good. Present the sweetmeats." She signaled the slaves with a wave of her hand.

Olivia had experienced many awkward moments of this nature and she used her abilities with the ease of long habit. "Oh, I am most upset; I did not realize there would be refreshments offered, and . . ."

"What is it?" asked Eugenia when Olivia did not go on.

"I have the misfortune to suffer from an antipathy to many fruits and some spices. They do not agree with me at all, and if I should eat them, I become horridly sick. I hope you will pardon me for refusing your gracious hospitality, but I am certain that I would prove to be a most reprehensible guest if I let myself succumb to your kindness."

"An antipathy?" repeated Antonina.

"Yes. Doubtless you know others who have similar conditions; I recall that one of Belisarius' officers becomes short of breath and flushed if he eats shellfish." She was hoping that Belisarius had taken the time to outline the failings as well as the virtues of his men to his wife.

"That would be Gregorios, I assume," said Antonina.

"The one who you introduced to me last year?" inquired Eugenia. "With the dark curly hair?"

"No, that is Drosos," said Antonina with a knowing inclination of her head. She was watching her friend and so she did not see the faint smile that flickered over Olivia's face. "Yes, Gregorios has such an antipathy, I am certain of it."

"Whichever man it was," said Olivia, "I felt for him most sincerely, for I know of my own experience how unendurable such episodes can be."

The slaves who had waited as still as monuments now moved at a signal from Antonina and placed their offerings on the low table beside their mistress' couch. They then made deep reverences and left, Arius in their wake like a whale following fishing vessels.

"Take what pleases you, and if you feel it best, touch nothing," said Antonina, making it clear that her remarks were intended for both women.

"I am hungry, and fortunately I have no antipathies that might interfere with my pleasures," said Eugenia, managing to infuse a world of meaning into her statement.

"Then you may thank God for His kindness," Antonina said as she reached for one of the wine cups.

"Oh, I do," said Eugenia, full of mischief.

Olivia leaned back on the couch and wished that this stilted, unendurable, endless afternoon would be over before either of the others had finished her wine.

"You have said," Antonina said, addressing Olivia once she had tasted some of the food set out, "that you are not interested in finding a husband, and if that is the case, I do not know what more I will be able to do for you. My area of influence is limited, as it must be for all women."

Knowing that Antonina was a close friend of the

Empress Theodora, Olivia decided that this last assertion could be interpreted very loosely. "Your civility in my welcome is more than enough. If, from time to time, you are willing to permit me to call upon you and to invite you to my house—once it is fit to be lived in—then I will think myself favored beyond my deserts."

Antonina nodded, but said, "Should you eventually change your mind, you must tell me."

"Of course," said Olivia, retreating into silence while the other two women nibbled at sweetmeats and speculated on the success of the most illustrious chariot team in the Empire.

* * *

Text of a letter from Belisarius to the Emperor Justinian.

To the most august and favored ruler, the elevated and esteemed Emperor Justinian, his most devoted General Belisarius cries "hail" on this Feast of Saint Servius.

While it is not my place to offer any criticism to you, most magnificent and knowledgeable of Emperors, I am constrained to inform you that those entrusted with carrying out your orders would appear to have been lax in their execution, for although two months have passed since our last request for additional troops, money, and supplies, little more than two or three measures of gold have been sent. Of troops and supplies we have seen nothing. I pray that this indicates that your activities are such that they require more time in order to make adequate preparation. Send me word of how many men I am to expect, and with what provisions.

This is not a request intended to impose upon your goodwill or upon your other obligations; you have entrusted me with the task of saving Roma from the forces of Totila, and it is my intention to do so, but without the aid I have already indicated, the loss of men and equipment currently available would place our risks much higher than you have indicated before was acceptable to you and to the Empire.

While we have been able to forage for half the food for men and stock, we are still not sufficiently supplied that we can march for more than a day without stopping to renew provisions. This has seriously impeded our progress and is likely to increase as we move into part of the country where Totila and his men have already raided and plundered. This would sow discontent not only with the soldiers of the army, but with the people. We have already had the gates of one monastery closed against us, and we do not wish to have this occur again.

If you will take the time to discover what is slowing the delivery of the supplies we were assured from the first would be available, then perhaps this campaign may be able to proceed in the manner you have said from the first was your preference in speed and disposition of land and peoples.

I have read Your Most August Majesty's letter to me, and I with you lament the steady stream of people from Roma into the other ports of the Empire. Sadly, unless these people are treated like slaves, there is nothing we can do to compel them to remain in their homes and within the gates of Roma. I seek your advice, for I must tell you frankly and with great reluctance that the Bishop of Roma himself, from his stronghold with his clergy at Monte Casino, will do nothing. Three times I have sent messengers to him, and once I attempted to see him myself and in all instances we were refused with only prayers to guide us. The prayers are welcome, and I am grateful even for that much, but food and arrows would be more to my liking at the moment.

It is not my intention to cause you distress, August

Majesty, but I am sure that if there is not some significant change in the manner in which this war is conducted soon, then it is not impossible that we will not make the advances here that you have said you wish. With proper supplies, the monies we needed, ships at our disposal and additional troops, we have an excellent chance to reclaim our preeminence in Italy.

Let me urge you to devote time and consideration to the plight of your men here in Italy, and to the fate of this country should it fall into the hands of that barbarian Totila. We will forfeit more than land if we cannot provide the protection and aid that is desperately needed and desired by these people as well as by Your August Majesty.

My prayers blend with your own in supplication for aid at this time, and I place myself and the lives of my men and the people of this country in the hands of God as well as in the hands of Your August Majesty.

With all duty and reverence,
Belisarius, General

• 4 •

Only one of the fountains still ran, and it was little more than a sluggish stream instead of the bright, soaring cascades that had greeted Belisarius when he first was given the right to use this villa outside the walls of Roma. He stood beside the huge marble basin, one booted foot resting on the rim, and stared into the brackish depths. His face was leaner than it had been a month ago, and the lines in it had deepened. He looked up, squinting, as he heard footsteps coming toward him.

"God's blessing this morning, General," said Drosos at his most amiable, raising his voice enough so that the greeting would carry to those nearby.

"And on you," Belisarius said with less enthusiasm than his Captain showed.

"I've finished inspection, and it should take little more than an hour for my boys to be out of here for good."

"That's fast," said Belisarius, trying to make his approval apparent to the other man. "And the others?"

"Ask their Captains, not me," Drosos chuckled, coming to stand beside the General. "I have all I can contend with to watch my own men."

"Sensible," the General nodded. "Can you venture a guess?"

"I'd say that we'll be away from here by midmorning." He indicated the villa. "It's a shame to have to give this up."

"But with Totila so close, we'd be increasing our disadvantage if we remain. This villa could easily become a trap," Belisarius reminded him. "It's a pity, but it can't be helped."

"And what do we tell Olivia? It is her villa; willed to her by an old friend, many years ago, or so she said. How do we explain that this place which she loaned to us and which we promised to care for has been left for the Ostrogoths to pick clean—which they will. Look around you: she has treasures here. The statues, the library—"

"You're impressed with books and murals?" Belisarius said with surprise.

Drosos hesitated before he answered, as if the idea were new to him. "I suppose I am." He shrugged, continuing awkwardly. "Perhaps being here, seeing all these things . . . There are over a thousand volumes in the library and there are thirty-seven statues in the villa. I've never had the chance to . . ."

"And there is Olivia," Belisarius added when Drosos did not go on.

"Yes; there is Olivia. These are her things." He broke

off, staring unseeing at the far wall. "But that's not all. She has shown me that there is worth in art and books, that they are more than the trophies of a wealthy life."

"Olivia is a woman of the old school," Belisarius said, hoping it was true. "She has some of the old Roman virtues left to her and she will not blame you or me if the barbarians get inside the compound."

"Still," Drosos objected vaguely.

"You might as well mourn for the horses she provided us—only two of them are alive now, and there were more than thirty in the stables when she left. Or the nine slaves that remained to care for us—they were gone weeks ago." He took his foot off the marble rim of the fountain. "Or for that matter, why not regret that the barbarians are here at all? and that we must meet their forces with our own or lose everything in Italy."

"You know what troubles me," Drosos said, deliberately lowering his voice to a soft growl.

"I suspect, I don't know," said Belisarius, peering into the early morning sun. Of the six hours of the day and the six hours of the night, this one was his favorite, when the world was still fresh and promising.

Drosos hitched his shoulders awkwardly. "I miss that woman. I know we had to send her away, but by the Dormition, I miss her."

"And does she miss you?" Belisarius asked without much interest.

"I hope so. When we get back to Constantinople, I intend to find out." He put one hard, square hand on his sword belt. "It will be easier then, with no battles, no war to distract us."

"You assume you will be returned to Constantinople," Belisarius said wearily. "There are other posts in the Empire, and you may find yourself at any one of them." He stretched and then tugged at the end of his pallium which was wrapped across the segmented links of his old-fashioned loricae. "Shoes of the Evangelists! I'm as stiff as a white-bearded monk this morning."

Drosos had seen this before. "It's the campaign," he

said knowledgeably. "You always sleep ready to fight the night before we break an established camp. Remember the morning we left Africa? You said it hurt to breathe." He patted the General on the shoulder once, a familiarity that was permitted few of the other Captains. "Have the farrier put some of that camphor salve on it—it stopped my roan's lameness in a day."

"If it lingers through the day," said Belisarius, knowing that the tight muscles would be eased as soon as he climbed into the saddle and finally got moving. He never felt so vulnerable as he did at this stage—when he and his men were preparing to leave, but were not yet ready to march.

Two other officers, one of them holding a chip of bone to his lips, ambled into the courtyard. They were both fresh from their morning prayers, as Nikolaos' relic showed. He lifted it toward Leonidas, and the other man also kissed what was believed to be part of the index finger of the Apostle Loukas.

"Do you think that *is* genuine?" Drosos wondered aloud. It was a question he would put to no one but the General, whose discretion was as absolute as his loyalty.

"Nikolaos believes it is, and that may be sufficient. I don't like to venture guesses. How many times have I seen scraps of Mother Maria's robes or the head of the Spear of the Crucifixion offered in the marketplace next to fresh fruit and new bread?" Belisarius shook his head. "It may be genuine. It may be all that is left of some poor creature who died walking from Jerusalem to Damascus."

"The Emperor has the Lord's Shroud," said Drosos with very little emotion.

Belisarius said nothing. He cocked his head. "Horses, coming fast."

At once Drosos' manner changed; he moved quickly and with surprising speed as he shouted to the other two officers. "Nikolaos, Leonidas, now!"

The other two responded at once, sprinting across the courtyard to the central part of the villa where they began to shout orders to the men still there.

Belisarius hurried toward the stables at the back of the second atrium. He no longer felt the stiffness in his body and he lifted his head in anticipation of news and fighting. He was almost at the stables when he heard Drosos' shout and a clarion signal. Immediately he hurried back toward the entrance to the villa.

Drosos was waiting for him, holding the steaming horse of the Emperor's messenger. He had summoned one of Belisarius' slaves to tend to the messenger and had just issued instruction for the care of the lathered horse.

"The Emperor honors me," said Belisarius as soon as he did not have to shout to be heard. There were now more than ten men in the courtyard, all gathered near the messenger.

"The Emperor tends to all those who are his subjects," said the messenger, sounding more fatigued than devoted.

"And I am to have words from him. I thank him and I thank God for this distinction." Belisarius longed to reach up and take the scroll from the man, but that would be intolerable to the man and to Justinian, so he waited until the slave finally arrived with a suitable stool so that the man could dismount in complete safety and not risk dropping the scroll he carried.

Once that ceremony had been observed, Belisarius took the scroll and retired to the dining room that now served as the officers' chapel. He broke the seals in the presence of his officers and the two priests who accompanied them, and then read the scroll.

"Leonidas, Drosos, Savas, Hipparchos, Omerion, you are all being distinguished by the Emperor Justinian, who is ever the champion of God and his people. You are ordered to return to Constantinople in forty days, at which time you are to tender a complete and unbiased report of what has taken place here in Italy. Furthermore, each of you is instructed to keep daily records from now until your time of departure, and to tell no one of the contents of those records until such time as the Imperial Censor shall examine them for the August Majesty." He sighed; such orders did not bode well.

The five officers all accepted their orders with enthusiasm, but Drosos tried to catch his General's eye as he did.

"I am required to make a catalogue of misdeeds of our soldiers here in Italy and see that it is placed in the files of the Imperial Censor, along with any record of punishment meted out for the action of the soldiers." That would cause more rancor than the daily reports, he knew, but he would not dispute a direct order from Justinian. "If there are goods, chattels and other properties to be shipped back to Constantinople, the messenger must be informed so that proper allocation of space and slaves may be made. The messenger has the Emperor's mandate to see all of you are treated with greatest respect and attention, and you are assured that nothing of value need be discarded or left behind unless you would rather not be hampered by the material, in which case access to markets in Italy will be guaranteed by Justinian." He could not imagine how the Emperor could make such promises, and having made them, fulfill them, but he knew better than to question what Justinian said and did. He held out the scroll to the messenger. "You have witnessed the notification of these officers. Is there anything more I need do while you are in my presence?"

"No, General, not at the moment," said the messenger, who looked overcome with fatigue now that his actual duties had been discharged.

"Very well. You will be escorted to quarters here, if that is your wish, although we are about to move out. We can also arrange for you to travel in a litter or—" All his life since he had become a soldier Belisarius had taken care to treat messengers well; they were far too important to ignore simply because they did no fighting.

"Any provision you make, General, will be acceptable. I am tired, but . . ." He finished the thought with a shrug.

"Then we will order a litter, so that you may rest and not have to be jostled about on a horse." He clapped his hands and was gratified when one of the household slaves hurried up. "This man needs food, and while he is eating, order a litter made ready for him, so that he can travel when we leave." He realized that in giving that order he had just pushed back their departure the better part of an hour, but he could think of no alternative.

"General?" Leonidas asked.

"Yes?" He waited while the young Captain ordered his thoughts. "What is it?"

"How long do you think we will be here? Not this place, but in the vicinity of Roma?"

"That is hard to say, but since you are returning to Constantinople, there is no reason for you to be concerned about the army in Italy." He smiled to show that he had no opinions on the matter one way or the other.

"But what will this do to the plans we have been following?" It was a question they all wanted to ask but had hesitated to bring to Belisarius' attention, for this change in officers would seriously alter the strength of his forces.

"That," Belisarius said slowly, "will depend on what Justinian decides to do in regard to our men here. If he sends the troops he has said that he would, we will be able to maintain our positions; if he does not send the troops and supplies, or if they are not sent in time, then the situation becomes a great deal more grave. As you are aware, we are not at the advantage now, and to recover it will take time and real effort."

"And the troops?" asked Drosos.

"If we have seasoned troops, good Roman and Greek fighters, we will be more likely to succeed than if the men are new to war or are from those peoples who delight in pillage. Some of the Italians are already abused by our men, and they resent this. If we continue in the same manner, then any support we might hope for will be lost." He shook his head once. "We must strive to carry out the orders of the Emperor."

"How?" was the reasonable question Drosos put forth for all of them.

"Ah, if I knew that, I would be one with the Saints and God. We will pray that if there can be victory, we will be shown the way to achieve it." He saw an odd look on the messenger's face, and then the man was following the slave into the villa.

"I say these orders bode ill for our campaign," announced Omerion, who was lean and tough as a ship's mast.

"That may be, but keep such thoughts to yourself, for your own protection," said Belisarius. "There are those in Constantinople who would turn your sentiments to your disadvantage; the court is not the army. Here we may gossip, but there a few unguarded words can endanger your life." He gave a signal. "All right. Everyone back to work. Assemble in front of the walls before midday and we will start then." That would be much later than he would have wished, but there was no chance now to move up their leaving. Cursing softly, Belisarius started away toward the stables, his attention more on the messenger than on the journey of the day.

"Belisarius," said Drosos behind him, half-running to catch up with the General.

"What is it, Drosos?" He kept walking, but slowed his pace until the Captain was abreast of him.

"I want to know what you really think about the orders. I know you can't say much in front of the men, but, by the Horns of Moses, you can say more to me."

They emerged from the hallway into haze-brilliant sunlight. Around them men were struggling to be prepared to march. The noise was tremendous, compounded of shouts and brays, of the sounds of hammers and winches and wagons. Belisarius strode along, careful to stay out of the way of the work, and Drosos dropped slightly behind him.

"Belisarius," Drosos insisted as they reached the tents where the saddlers and farriers kept their supplies.

"Yes, I know. What do I think about the orders. I don't know yet. I don't know what Justinian is preparing, but I am certain that he must be preparing something." He ducked through a tent flap and called out, "Begoz."

A gnarled old man answered the call. "Here, master. I

have been doing what I can since before dawn, but you—"

"I am not criticizing you, Begoz," Belisarius assured him. "I only want to know what progress you've made."

The old man shook his head and indicated the trunks half-filled and standing against the canvas wall. "There's not been enough time, sir. Not enough at all. I want to do you credit, but to do that, I need several more hours, and it hasn't been possible, what with all the comings and goings." As he continued his recitation, his voice took on a whine that was irritating to both Belisarius and Drosos. "You see, when someone orders something special, well, it means that I have to take extra care, and with some of these youngsters coming to me with worn girths and broken saddle-frames, what can I do? They need their tack for battle, don't they? and that means that such orders as yours must be postponed. You can see why this is so difficult for me."

"Yes," said Belisarius with more patience than he would have thought necessary. "And I know that a craftsman of your skill is not going to make a saddle that is anything less than the best you can provide. However, I think you might be a little more vigilant."

Begoz put his hands to his face. "I didn't mean anything against you, General, and I wouldn't for a moment cause you to be displeased if there were any way I could prevent it." He approached, and it was apparent that he had a severe limp; one of his feet was malformed and the leg was twisted, as if a giant hand had taken a doll and tugged the limb out of line.

"No, of course not," said Belisarius, making a motion to keep Drosos from speaking out impulsively. "But that will not prepare the saddle for Olivia, and I would like it to be sent with Drosos when he returns to Constantinople in the next few weeks. If the saddle is ready before he leaves, there will be an advantage for you." He reached into the leather pouch that depended from his wide, metal-studded belt. "This"—he held up a large gold coin with the image of the Emperor on it, his crown like a halo—"is yours if the saddle can go with Drosos to Byzantium."

The old slave stared at the coin, captivated by its size and color. "I might be able to work in the evening, when others are taking their leisure."

"If that is required, then do it," he said, keeping the gold archangel within reach for Begoz. "It is unfortunate that the widow Clemens has lost her villa to us, but we are about to lose it again. The least we can do now is to show her some sense of our appreciation. The saddle is only a token, but it is a necessary one. If you cannot aid me in this, say so now, that I may find another to undertake the task."

"No need for that," said Begoz hastily. "Grace of God, no. You need only tell me what you require and it will be yours."

"Excellent," said Belisarius dryly. "I will expect that the day after tomorrow, wherever we are camped, you will be able to report to me that you have progressed on this saddle, and will be able to say when it will be done. If you are false, and if you tell me that you are more advanced in your work than you are, then you will be flogged. Do you understand this?"

"Yes," said Begoz in a subdued voice. "Yes, I understand you, General, master."

"Then report to me at the end of the day after tomorrow and we will then determine if you are capable of completing this commission." Belisarius tossed a small silver coin. "This, for any special supplies you may need."

The old saddler caught it. "As you say, there may be supplies and you might not be free to see they are provided."

Once they were out of the tent, Drosos turned curiously to Belisarius. "You said nothing to me about this saddle."

"I wanted to be certain it could be finished."

"And do you think it will be?" They stood aside as a large cart drawn by four sweating mules lumbered by them.

"Drosos, do not concern yourself; either Begoz will

complete it or I will find another who will, and by the time you leave you will have a saddle to take to Olivia, with my compliments for all she has given us. It might take some of the sting out of learning that this villa has fared badly. I do not think that once we are gone Totila will require that his army defend the place. They have been destroying villas in the north, and they have sworn to flatten Roma herself. A saddle is a little thing compared to a villa, but it is better than nothing." He peered across the busy staging area. "Look at the orchards—more than a third of the trees are cut down, and that was only for firewood. What would it be like if we had been bent on destruction? You know that the walls would have fallen and most of the furniture would be lost." He walked slowly, speaking in an undervoice that Drosos had to strain to hear over the jostling and shouting around them. "There are not many like her left. It is not to our credit if we abuse them: we are no better than the barbarians we oppose if we make no acknowledgment of her generosity."

"She *is* a generous woman," said Drosos, a reminiscent smile on his lips.

"In more ways than the one you choose to remember," Belisarius reminded him sharply.

"But—" He broke off as three mounted bowmen clattered by. "My General, we will not be able to replace anything she has lost. I will take the saddle, or any other gift you request, and I will repeat any message, just as you bid me, but do not assume that this is recompense, even for a generous woman."

Belisarius laughed. "No, I make no such assumption. We were more fortunate than we deserved to be. It might not happen again while we are in Italy."

"What . . . what do you anticipate?" Drosos asked, reading distress in his General's eyes.

"I try to anticipate nothing. But I fear that there are not going to be more Romans like Olivia Clemens to give us their villas and their provisions as she did." He pointed away toward the distant walls of Roma, just barely visible through the dust and a wide gap in the stout fencing that surrounded the villa's grounds. "That is what we all seek; Totila and all of us. And the city is growing tired of changing hands."

"Once we strengthen our occupation, Totila will not be able to maintain his position and then he will have to withdraw to the north." Drosos said this as if he were repeating a lesson, and he was surprised to see that there was no certainty in Belisarius' expression to answer his own.

"If all we have been promised is delivered, and if all the men we need are sent, and if there is no more looting or raiding, and if Roma decides to defend herself, and if there is food enough and water enough to withstand a siege, then perhaps Totila will be discouraged, or perhaps instead he will become enraged and then the fighting will erupt with greater severity than any we have seen so far." Belisarius shook his head. "I could envy you, if it did not compromise the Emperor."

"How?" asked Drosos, surprised by this admission.

"I am the General of Justinian, and whatever he commands of me I will do. My oath binds me to him and to God. But when I look ahead, I long for soft nights and the riches of Constantinople, and the company of my wife without the promise of marches and battles." He scratched at his graying hair. "But another time, another time. Now the Emperor wants me here, and I will do all that I can to be worthy of his confidence and commission." He lifted his hand as a signal to Savas, who was supervising the loading of sacks of grain to be used as fodder for the horses.

"Why not request a posting to Constantinople, if you miss it so much?" Drosos asked, knowing the answer, and providing it before Belisarius could speak. "Because you do not want to risk losing Imperial favor, which such a transfer might entail."

"Yes," agreed Belisarius. "That's part of it. And the rest is my oath. I am bound to serve Justinian in any capacity he demands, for he is Emperor and anointed in the service of God." He summoned Savas with an impatient gesture. "Drosos, tonight we will speak again, but for now I must see what the trouble is with these carts. If we cannot carry the grain with us, we will have to make sure that it is not left behind for Totila to use." He started away from his Captain, but stopped and turned back to regard the younger, stockier man with interest. "You took an oath, too, Drosos. Never forget your oath. It is what separates us from barbarians like Totila."

"I will remember, General," Drosos promised him.

"Also, do not forget that the hottest fires of hell burn for those who betray their oaths." He then trod purposefully toward the half-laden carts.

Drosos watched him, wishing he could ask what had prompted him to give so stringent a warning. What was it that prompted Belisarius to remind him of his oath? He never doubted that he would honor his oath, for that was the duty of a soldier. As an officer, he accepted the full weight of the obligation.

"Captain," said a young soldier who approached him from the left. "Captain, there's a problem. Will you come?"

"Aren't you Leonidas' man?" Drosos inquired.

"Yes, but he is still busy with others," said the young soldier. "Someone must help us."

Drosos sighed as if to chase the glum thoughts from his mind. "Very well. Tell me what the trouble is." He set a brisk pace, permitting the soldier to point out the way.

"We have a shortage of carts and wagons," said the soldier. "We have to find a way to carry more."

"The same as everyone else," said Drosos heavily. "All right; how many mules and how many oxen do you have?"

"Not enough," the soldier said. "We lost a dozen mules in the last night-raid. We're on the perimeter of the camp, and so we're more vulnerable than some. Three of the oxen are lame and we have been told we cannot use them. Captain Leonidas has already issued orders."

"If you cannot use oxen and you are short of mules, what *do* you have for haulage?"

"Not much," said the soldier. "We have horses, but we're supposed to reserve those for riding and battle. We have been warned that they are not to be exhausted by moving camp."

"I see," said Drosos, shoving a water-carrier aside.

"We tried the goats, but they don't work well in harness," the soldier went on, becoming embarrassed.

"Holy belching angels! I should think not," said Drosos, his patience almost exhausted.

"There wasn't much else we could use," the soldier offered by way of excuse.

"I know; I know," said Drosos, clapping one hard-palmed hand on the soldier's arm. "You're doing the best you can under the circumstances. It's all any of us can do."

"We wanted to find some of those big hounds they had in the north, but no one around here breeds them. I've heard they're pretty strong." He was hoping for a word of encouragement, but he was disappointed; Drosos sighed and shook his head.

"The Emperor doesn't . . . understand. He's not aware of how strained our resources are here. He assumes that because we have come to save Italy from Totila that we are welcome everywhere and that the country is as rich as it once was. Nothing can convince him that we are not the heroes to the people that he believes we are. It is a great compliment to us, I suppose, and one that our General deserves, or would if things were not so difficult." He had almost said desperate but had stopped himself in time.

The soldier coughed. "What do we do?"

"Find the least worthy horses in your string and use them for haulage. They won't be much use to you in battle in any case and they might as well earn their hay like the rest of us." Drosos indicated the men on the far side of the camp. "You might see if Stamos' men have any spare oxen. They had one a few days ago, but you never know if they still do. Knowing that lot, they might have eaten it by now."

"Some of the men do complain about rations," the soldier agreed.

"Small wonder," Drosos concurred. "Millet cakes for four days in a row!"

"Maybe I should requisition some of the goats for food," the soldier ventured uncertainly since they were under orders to take nothing from the villa.

"Why not? If we do not eat them, Totila's men will," said Drosos, knowing that if Olivia were here she would give him the goats and anything else he might need. He would think of something to explain this to Belisarius later. "Tell your men to round up a dozen goats and take them along."

"On your authority?" the soldier asked, unwilling to risk his own neck.

"Yes, on my authority as granted by the owner of the villa." He promised himself that he would make restitution to Olivia when he saw her in Constantinople. She would understand and agree that he had done the only sensible thing in ordering the goats be taken. And if she did not, he was confident he could explain it to her.

The soldier grinned. "If that's your order, then I suppose I must obey."

"It's my order," said Drosos. He started away, then stopped. "How many men in your unit are ill?"

"Only three," said the soldier. "Why?"

"Nothing, just curious," said Drosos, and went on his way, thinking that if they continued to have men fall ill, they would not have enough to go into battle, and they were already crucially low on battle-ready troops. Briefly he resented his orders recalling him to Constantinople; Belisarius needed him and every officer and man he could get. Tired as he was of campaigning, he still was uneasy at the thought of leaving his General and friend to face Totila with depleted forces.

"Drosos!" The sharp summons of Belisarius' personal slave caught his attention and he hastened toward the General's standard, the problems of breaking camp now uppermost in his mind.

*   *   *

Text of a letter accompanying an inventory carried on the Emperor Justinian's ship Resurrection *along with military dispatches.*

To Antonina, the esteemed and august wife of the General Belisarius, on the eve of the departure of the merchantship Spairei Krohma, which sets sail on the Feast of Saint Iannis in the Lord's Year 545.

It is my honor to inform you that my vessel has been selected by your most worthy and august husband to carry the goods awarded him for his victories to you for proper installation in his home. To that purpose, the inventory he himself prepared accompanies this so that upon our safe arrival in Constantinople you can for yourself ascertain that the goods are the correct ones, shipped in good order, and received in the condition that God Himself has granted they arrive.

Of particular interest is a set of vases of fine workmanship and considerable age that are so fragile that in spite of very careful packing, I must warn you that they might not survive the sea voyage. I pray that this caution will turn out to be completely useless, but I feel that I must warn you that these more than any other items are in danger of breakage or other damage during the days at sea.

Since my ship is a simple merchantman, it will not come with the speed that the Emperor's ships travel, and I estimate that it will be twenty-three to twenty-five days for us to make the voyage, if the weather remains reasonably good.

At this time of year we often have rain but not many storms. Should we encounter a storm, then we are entirely at the mercy of the winds and in the Hand of God, as we are every day and hour of our lives.

I give you my word that I will do all in my power to see that your goods arrive quickly and in proper order. Any loss that is the fault of my slaves and ship's hands will of course be my responsibility. Those goods lost due to the elements I cannot promise to pay for, since that cost grows from acts over which I have no control.

I am sending word to Pope Sylvestros at the same time I send this to you. He may be found at the Church of the Patriarchs and he will make it his business to know where I am and how I am to be found. He will also know what the other merchant captains tell him, and if there are delays, he will send you word of it. The Church of the Patriarchs is located not far from the merchant docks, in the street where the ropemakers work.

Until I have the privilege to present you with your treasures, I sign myself your most eager and sincere servant who is honored for the distinction you and your distinguished and heroic husband have deigned to bestow on me.

> Ghornan
> ship's captain
> by the hand of the priest
> Gennarius at Santus Spiritos,
> Ostia

Between the enormous crush of people and the heat of the afternoon, Niklos Aulirios was ready to give up his task for the afternoon and return to the house where Olivia was busy establishing herself. There had been tradesmen and artisans there all morning, and now that the afternoon was fading, and the merchants had once again situated themselves in their shops, refreshed by food and sleep, Olivia decided that Niklos would have to take advantage of the time and purchase the slaves they needed.

Niklos still bristled at the orders. "How do you explain me, in this world of slaves?"

Olivia had smiled at him. "You are a bondsman—no collar, no chance of sale or . . . lending."

The memory of that smile brought one to his lips. "Slaves." He had been told that he would do best to talk to old Taiko near the Church of the Dormition. It took longer for Niklos to find it than he had anticipated because four of the streets were dug up as part of the Emperor's restructuring of the city. Niklos had to ask his way several times, his Greek halting and nearly childish.

At last a house was pointed out to him: a narrow, leaning place that bowed over the street like a curious relative. The door was thick and its iron hinges crossed most of its width. A mallet and bell were provided; Niklos used them and waited for someone to admit him to the house.

Two slaves, both fat and sleek and dressed well,

answered the door, smiling. If the old house had caused Niklos to doubt Taiko's prosperity, those two slaves banished the doubt at once. The taller of the two inquired who Niklos was and what he wanted from their master.

Once again Niklos cursed himself for the poor quality of his Greek. "I am the bondsman Niklos Aulirios," he began. "I work for the Roman lady Olivia Clemens. The wife of Belisarius told us that your master . . . he is the best in the city to buy slaves."

"This is very true, bondsman," said the taller slave, stepping aside to admit Niklos to the house. "You will find that here the best slaves are to be found, and the prices are the most equitable for everyone." He bowed and indicated his fellow. "I will inform my master that you are here and Pammez will remain here with you, to bring you whatever refreshment you require."

And to keep an eye on me, thought Niklos. "You are very kind," he said, knowing that he spoke like a child addressing his tutor.

Pammez, who was not Greek but Asian, by the look of him, indicated the smaller of the reception rooms off the vestibule. "I will attend to you." His voice was clear and high, like a boy's.

Niklos wanted to ask how many eunuchs Taiko owned, but did not know the correct way to phrase the question. He was still surprised at the number of eunuchs he encountered. There had been eunuchs in Roma, but not in the quantities he found here in Konstantinoupolis. He was not used to it and was not certain he ever would be.

Pammez made a reverence to Niklos—an extraordinary courtesy to a mere bondsman—and said, "For so august a lady as the wife of Belisarius, there can be no service my master would not perform with gladness in his heart."

So the reverence was for Antonina. "She has been good to my mistress." Niklos cocked his head to the side. "I do not know how these . . . are done. What does your master need to know from me and from my mistress?"

"He will tell you and you may rely on his discretion, for

in these matters, the position of such a lady as your mistress makes discretion necessary. Everything she requires may be accommodated, and her requirements fulfilled without any notoriety."

Niklos was not certain what notoriety there might be in purchasing slaves, but he did not know how best to inquire. He folded his hands and regarded Pammez thoughtfully. "My mistress wishes to buy several slaves."

At this, Pammez laughed aloud, though it was most impolite for him to do this. "Ah, Romans. They are so diverting. Your mistress wishes to buy slaves." He restrained himself to a chuckle.

The indignant inquiry that Niklos was struggling to form was stopped by a sound at the door. As Niklos turned, Pammez fell to his knees and ducked his head, and belatedly Niklos made a deep reverence to the lean, gray-haired man who stood there, and behind him, a lame, bearded fellow with a predatory beak of a nose and ferocious eyebrows came.

"They say," said the bearded man as the other stepped respectfully aside, "that you wanted to see me."

The lean man cleared his throat and said, "This is Taiko, master of this house, father of seventeen sons and captain of the vessel *Fishhawk*. He has consented to speak with you, bondsman of the Roman lady Clemens."

"I gather," said Taiko abruptly, "that she's the widow everyone's talking about, the one who bought the house from Andros Trachi. They say that Antonina has entertained her three times since she arrived."

"That is so," said Niklos, a trifle taken aback by the man's behavior.

"She'll need a number of slaves to run that place, and from what I hear, she's made it even more elaborate than it was. Went and installed one of those heathenish Roman baths. The popes'll have something to say about that." He grinned once. "They say she's rich."

"She is," said Niklos. "My mistress has a large fortune."

Where Pammez had laughed, Taiko guffawed. "Fortune!" he exclaimed when he could speak. "A widow with a fortune."

"Why does this amuse you?" demanded Niklos, who was growing indignant.

Taiko bobbed his head twice and then spat. "Well, I can't suppose you Romans understand that—though your name says you're Greek—and I'll explain it, but undoubtedly Antonina has already made this clear to your Roman lady. You speak as if she has money and property of her own, which belong directly and only to her. I guess they might do things that way in Roma, being so wild there. But here we are more in accord with the teachings of scripture, and we do not let women fend for themselves. Your Roman widow will have to have someone to manage her affairs for her, to purchase slaves and provide her with the housing she requires."

"What do you mean?" asked Niklos.

"I hear that Belisarius himself arranged for the house, and that's a great honor for her, but now that she's here, she'll need a sponsor, preferably a pope since she's a widow and has no father or brother living here. These are the ones who will purchase the slaves and see them installed." He motioned to Pammez. "Go and get my scribe. We will need to take down her requirements. I am sure we can see that she is given provisional purchase until something more correct can be arranged. She'll need slaves to keep that house going."

Pammez hastened to obey, making a deep reverence to his master as he left the room.

"Have a seat, bondsman," offered Taiko, and dropped onto a long couch. "This might take time."

"Why must there be a sponsor?" asked Niklos as he chose a square-backed chair.

"She's a woman. She is hardly in a position to know what is best to do." He smiled abruptly. "Maybe the Roman women have had less guidance. It wouldn't be so unusual, given what the Romans have shown themselves to be. They've permitted women to do far too many things for themselves, and look! the whole country is in disarray."

Listening to Taiko, Niklos was distressed. No wonder there had been so many difficulties since their arrival. "Why would it not be possible for Antonina to serve as sponsor in her husband's absence?" He hoped he had got the words right.

Taiko shook his head. "You Romans have no notion, have you? If the august lady Antonina were not so well-placed, I would not be able to provide even these make-shift arrangements until a churchman had approved them, but with Antonina so much a friend of Theodora, I am certain that a few changes will be overlooked if they are not too obvious or left unresolved for too long." He signaled to his majordomo, indicating Niklos and himself. "If you will bring us honeycakes and wine?"

At once Niklos held up his hand. "If you are getting this for me, I must decline. It would not be proper for a Roman bondsman to take such hospitality, because it would insult your offer. I have not learned your ways yet and keep to my own."

Taiko looked at Niklos, then shrugged. "Romans. You are an odd lot."

"You are strange to us, as well," Niklos said, doing his best to make light of this observation. "My mistress has said so hourly since we came here."

"Alone as she is, with no one to act for her and no man to guide her, it must be very sad for her. How many women can endure this without aid?" He addressed the question more to the air than to Niklos. "You are the closest thing she has to a man in this world, if what has been said is true, and a bondsman is hardly more than a slave." He took a deep breath and let it out explosively. "I suppose that I must do all that I can to assist you in this dreadful circumstance."

"I would appreciate it," said Niklos, wishing that Taiko were making a joke, and aware that he was not.

"Excellent," said the slave-merchant. "I will show you what is available for running a household like your mistress', and you will select as you see fit. I will of course be willing to accept any slave returned within two days. You may not be satisfied with a selection until you determine how the slave goes in the household. A man may deal with recalcitrant slaves by might and by his order, but women are not able to do this." He indicated Pammez. "He will see that all the slaves you select are healthy, and if they are not you will be notified. We cannot assure you that every slave is Christian, and if this is a requirement, it may take more time to staff the household to your satisfaction. Is it necessary that your slaves be Christian? I have found that some women insist that they have Christian slaves only."

"My mistress is not so fussy. In Roma we have learned to . . ." He could not think of the word for tolerate, and this annoyed him more than he wanted to admit. "In Roma," he began again, "there are many of different faiths."

"And the Bishop of Roma has said that Roma is the center of the faith," scoffed Taiko. "How can anyone believe that if there is such chaos?"

"The Bishop of Roma knows Romans," said Niklos. "And so does my mistress."

This time Taiko nodded sagely. "Yes, I understand your meaning here, bondsman. You must accommodate your mistress, and you are correct in taking such an attitude, but here in Konstantinoupolis, you need not fear for your beliefs. We protect those who are sincere, unlike the reprehensible cowardice of the Bishop of Roma, who has fled his city when it is most in danger. No wonder the world has moved to this place."

"The invaders are always a problem," said Niklos, doing his best to appear submissive.

"Come, then," said Taiko, getting up suddenly. "I will show you what I have to offer and I will tell you what the slaves will cost. You, in turn, may do as you wish in making your selection. I have a full list of the accomplishments, skills and the full records of the slaves from their previous owners."

Niklos followed him, aware that this man might easily

decide to be offended by his visitor, which would stop the negotiations for some time, and which would not be useful to Olivia. He kept his manner subdued and respectful as he entered the quarters at the rear of the house and stood while Taiko called out names.

Finally there were fourteen men and women lined up for Niklos' inspection. They ranged in age from twelve or thirteen to near thirty. Five of them were at least partly Asian, including one woman called Zejhil who had been brought from beyond Vagarshapat. There were two Egyptians, and the rest were of mixed Greek and African blood.

"This will be enough for a short time. There is no gardener, and there are only three kitchen slaves, but if it is as you say and your mistress has few requirements in that area, then these will suffice until a proper sponsor can be established for your mistress," said Taiko in his most confident manner; he had done this many times before.

"If you are willing, I would like to see two more, the Briton and the fellow from Ptolemaïs. They have skills that would be of great use to my mistress, and she wishes to have these skills in her household at once." Again he was hampered by his lack of skill with Greek, but he continued as best he could. "I will inform my mistress of the aid you have given me."

"That's good to know. All right—the Briton and the Ptolemaïsi." He clapped his hands and called out two more names. As the slaves came forward, he addressed them all. "You have been selected for the household of the Roman lady Olivia Clemens. She will have two days to install you, and if you do not give satisfaction, she will return you to me, and I will deal with you accordingly. You are to be loyal and dutiful to her. God has given you your station in life and it is for you to bow your head to your fate."

Most of the slaves made the sign of protection, but a few said nothing and remained still.

"You are to go with this bondsman, who will tell you what is required of you. Any deviation from his orders will be told to me and it will be part of your record. If you wish to live well, you will see that your record is kept clear of questions. Am I understandable to everyone?"

The Briton asked in halting Greek with a strong accent, "If we are not . . . good speakers, what then?"

Niklos answered before Taiko could. "My mistress, as this merchant has said, is Roman. She will do what she can to make all of you know what she says. And though I am Greek, I have lived most of my life in Roma, so my speech is not very good in Greek."

This appeared to be the answer the Briton was seeking, and half of the slaves looked guardedly relieved.

It took a good part of the afternoon to attend to all the business of transferring the slaves to Olivia's household, and by the time Niklos left with an escort of five of Taiko's slaves to tend the sixteen Niklos had acquired, the sun was low in the west, its copper rays slanting through the city, making sudden paths of brightness amid the shadows.

By the time they reached Olivia's house, the sky was a deep and glowing violet. At the nearest church, the sound of chanting had begun to mark the offices of the close of day. The city, suspended in silence like prayer, was hovering on the edge of night. The torches that greeted them at the house Olivia had bought were bright and festive, out of keeping with the solemn darkness around them.

Niklos gave each of Taiko's slaves a silver coin for their assistance and was startled to find that they were unfamiliar with this custom. "In Roma, it is always done for extra service," Niklos explained, adding, "My mistress keeps to her Roman ways, and so must I."

Pammez shook his head but accepted the coin. "How can slaves be trusted when they are given coins by others? It would suborn their loyalty. No wonder Roma has come on such dreadful times, if the slaves are treated so." He indicated the others. "Be wary, Roman, that you do not make your position more dangerous than it already is."

Niklos dismissed Taiko's slaves, then opened the enormous doors to admit the rest. He gathered them together in the vestibule and faced them. "In a short while you will meet your new mistress. I wish to tell you of how we conduct ourselves at this place. Olivia Clemens is a Roman lady, a widow, and she will want to continue here in the same manner that she has in Roma. You each will be permitted to accept money for service, and to keep it for yourself. You may set this aside to earn the price of your freedom, as the Roman slaves of old did. She will permit you to purchase your freedom for what she paid for you. This is also in the tradition of old Roma, and since she is part of an old and revered family, she will honor this custom. You will be assigned duties and will be expected to perform them unless injured or ill. If you are injured or ill, you will be required to report to the Ptolemaïsi for his treatment—he is a physician, according to his records—and you will follow his instructions for your recovery until such time as he informs you that you need not. If you are abused by anyone not in this household, or by any slave in this household, you are to inform me at once." He studied the faces turned toward him, noticing the expressionlessness that he had found on the countenances of most Byzantine slaves. He wanted to ask them if they understood but he could not bring himself to form the words. "If any of you are uncertain about your place here, speak with me. When you have been assigned your duties and your quarters, you will gather in the slaves' hall for your meal. All meals will be served there unless you are informed of other plans. There will be a breakfast in midmorning and a second meal at the conclusion of the afternoon repose. Fruit and bread will be available at other times, if they are needed." There had been a time, he reflected, that this was required of a slave owner, and not the strange custom it seemed to be now.

"What if the Roman lady is displeased with us?" asked the woman from beyond Vagarshapat.

"That will depend on why she is displeased," said Niklos. "If you have done wrong, you will be punished, but if you have only irritated her, then she will tell you what you have done wrong. When we are still unknown to each other there are bound to be errors and questions. While they are being settled, we must all make an effort to be alert. Once we have become more accustomed, then it will be otherwise."

There was a light step behind him and he turned to see Olivia herself standing in the door to the main hall. She was dressed in a long, dark bronze paenula that completely swathed her in silk. Her ornamentation was subdued but subtly rich, and her fawn-brown hair was coiled on her head with only three long pearl-topped pins to hold it in place. She glided into the vestibule, her deep hazel eyes moving deliberately from one slave to the next. "Niklos," she said.

"My mistress," he responded.

"So these are the slaves?" If she noticed the tension she had brought into the room, it was not reflected in her calm attitude and self-possessed air.

"As you ordered, my mistress." He stepped back to let her move closer to the men and women.

"Very good." She made a gesture of approval. "I welcome you. If you think it strange that a mistress should welcome slaves, consider this house and how it would be if I had to care for it alone." She indicated the torches burning in brackets around the room. "The task of lighting the place alone would take most of my waking hours."

"I have here the records, names, and history of the slaves from Taiko." Niklos held out a small box.

"Bring it to my apartments once you have seen these people fed and given quarters. I will want my name engraved on their collars. And do not remind me that I am not entitled to do this; I paid good silver and gold for these men and women, and I will have my name on them." Her head lifted imperiously. "This may be Constantinople, but I am a Roman, and will be until the hour when I am truly dead."

Niklos suppressed a smile: Olivia had intended to impress her new slaves and she had certainly succeeded.

It was more than her behavior, it was her quality and character that fixed the attention of the slaves so completely. He made a reverence to her. "It will be done, great lady."

At that Olivia laughed. "Long ago in Roma the proper word was domita. Then it became domina. Either will do. If you call me 'great lady' I will feel even more a stranger than I do already."

"Domita," said Niklos, his tone making it clear that the others would do well to emulate him.

"Finish your remarks, Niklos. I will not stay to hamper you. When you are through, I will look forward to speaking with you." She looked at her slaves once more. "You are welcome here; if you are not, it will be your decision, not mine." With that, she left the vestibule.

The entryroom was silent for several moments, and then Niklos took up the rest of his instructions. "Our mistress," he said, with a slight emphasis on *our*, "is very much herself. She does not live as most live, and she does not wish to. If you are able to respect this, you will have no reason to be unhappy here. If you are not able to do this, then let me know of it as soon as possible so that other arrangements can be made."

The youngest, a scrawny boy from Syracusa, said, "I have seen many Romans, but never one like her." He spoke in rough Latin, satisfied that Niklos would understand him.

"The Romans of the old Empire are not the same as those who came after. The Clemens gens goes back to the days before the conquest of the Sabines. They were of noble rank before Sulla was dictator. This is the heritage of our mistress; she lives by the code of her ancestors and the honor of her blood."

The slaves all nodded to show that they had heard; only the boy from Syracusa and the woman from beyond Vagarshapat exchanged glances.

"If you are all ready, come with me," said Niklos, indicating the hall toward the rear of the house. "I will show you your quarters."

As the new slaves followed obediently, the boy fell in beside Zejhil and murmured, " 'She lives by the code of her ancestors and the honor of her blood.' What do you suppose that means?"

* * *

Text of a letter from Eugenia to Antonina delivered by her body slave.

To the most august and excellent lady Antonina, wife of the great General Belisarius and confidante to Empress Theodora, hail on Eve of the Feast of the Annunciation.

I have your invitation for the festivities on the Feast of the Circumcision and I am eager to accept, no matter how awkward it may be for you to entertain a widow at such a gathering. You have also extended the invitation to that Roman lady Olivia, so I do not think it would be completely wrong to accept, and I want very much to accept.

You and I had so little time four days ago to enjoy the conversation we had begun, and that spurs me now to speak to you about matters we merely touched on while you and I dined together; that is, the matter of a husband.

Yes, by all means I will be most grateful for any assistance you can provide me in my search, for as you know, a widow in my position, with limited property and monies at my disposal and most of that controlled by my uncle, has little in life to find fulfilling or entertaining. Since my three children died before they were ten, I can approach my uncle for no reason other than my own position and pleasure and he is not willing to discuss either matter, nor is he of a mind to arrange a match for me, since that would place the money and property he now controls in the hands of my husband, assuming that I find another.

To be blunt, as you have encouraged me to be, I want to find a man who has some property and money of his own so that he does not entirely seek me for what I can provide. I would like him to be well enough placed in the army or the government that some advancement could be possible for him and for me, so that we could rise in position and influence through a little planning and effort. I would like him to be ambitious without being so ruthless that he will use me and then forget me. I would like him to share my interest in the life of the capital and my love of position. That way we can do much together without coming to be at cross-purposes. If he is willing to give me children, then that would be useful and would please me. If he is not willing to do that, then I will want him to let me go my way so that I will have children of another which he would recognize as his, so that there will be proper heirs for our estates as well as a source of power through advantageous alliances and marriages later in life.

If you know of such a man, or men, I am completely in your debt for bringing us together. You have always been a true friend to me, and never more than now when you have been at pains to aid me during this difficult time in my life. Be certain that if I am ever in a position to help you in any way that you may need it, you have only to ask and the thing is yours.

Once you have read this, I request that you return it to me or destroy it, for there are those who would seek reward from my uncle by disclosing the contents to him. That would not serve you or me any good, and so it is wisest to take care now that this does not fall into the wrong hands.

I know that your good offices will bring me the success I seek, and your kind words will do everything to make certain that no problems mar the resolution of my request. If you require anything more of me in this regard, send your body slave with instructions and I will provide you with more information, though I hope what I have set down *here will indicate my preferences clearly enough. I do not want to be so stringent that it becomes impossible to find what I require.*

> In all cordial duty and admiration,
> Your friend
> Eugenia

• 6 •

Rain had just started to fall when Simones left the house of Belisarius bound for the palace of the Emperor Justinian, three messages clasped in his enormous hand. He had wrapped his pallium around his shoulders and neck as well as over his head so that he would not become drenched during the short walk to the palace.

As he neared the palace, Simones took out his seal of authorization which would provide him admittance without the complicated process of verifying his identity and his owner. He had endured those procedures before, but that had been years ago and he was no longer willing to take the time required to satisfy the exhaustive demands of the court when presentation of a simple embossed piece of leather would give him the access he desired. He was prepared to deal with the men on duty as directly as they would permit.

Sure enough, the Captain of the Guard, the square-bodied Vlamos, was the one who greeted Simones with a terse order and the full weight of his authority. "Where are your permissions, slave?"

Simones held out the leather. "Heiliah eithelfei!" he

cursed mildly, "what happens here that no one remembers Simones of Belisarius' household? Is my master some unknown dog from the country who is tolerated because of his name? Is my master a merchant who seeks to buy favor? Is my master a foreigner who is known to be a barbarian? Is he not the Emperor's finest General, the man who has defeated Totila more than once and who did so much to bring order in Africa?"

"All right, all right," said Vlamos. "You have made your point, Simones. If you seek an audience with the Emperor, you may be here for a while."

"What sort of slave would I be to think such things? You see that I bear messages which I have been ordered to hand myself to the Court Censor, who in turn will evaluate them and tend to them as he sees fit. I am not one who forgets his place nor does my master expect me to behave so improperly." He drew himself up to his considerable height in his dudgeon.

"Never mind," sighed the Captain of the Guard. "Pass and perform your errand. Be certain that you need not come again this day, or we will have to regard the formalities more stringently." He signaled his men to open the gate.

Simones straightened his clothes and strode forward. Because he had been castrated at age seventeen, he did not have much of the look of a eunuch, and his voice was as deep as any man's. He had almost no beard, but there were others who were completely whole who had light beards as well. Since he was almost a head taller than most men, he was regarded with respect by those around him; he was aware of this and used it.

One of the men-at-arms followed after Simones, keeping pace with him, his expression forbidding in its blankness. There were other similar escorts with other visitors in the palace, as much to guide their charges as to guard them.

The palace of the Emperor Justinian was a maze of courtyards and corridors, wings and suites, each with its own purpose, with almost a third of the whole in various stages of construction, for Justinian was known to have a passion for building. The distant sound of saws and hammering were as familiar here as the sound of prayer and chanting.

When Simones reached the group of rooms assigned to the Court Censor, he announced himself to the Egyptian slave who sat at a long, narrow table copying texts. "I am to see Panaigios," he told the Egyptian.

"He will be here presently," the Egyptian said, irritated at having his task interrupted.

"I am Simones, and my master is the General Belisarius," he informed the slave. "Panaigios has said that he must speak with me and I do not think he would want to be ignorant of my arrival."

Reluctantly the Egyptian set his work aside. "Very well. I will inform him that you are here and return with his instruction." He made a nod that might have been intended to be polite but might also have been nothing but a last look at his copying.

Simones did not have long to wait. The Egyptian was back almost at once, and with him came Panaigios, the senior secretary of the Court Censor, and the highest ranking official that Simones, being a slave, could address directly. "I am Simones," he said to Panaigios.

"Yes; I have looked forward to this meeting." Panaigios was one of those men who are so ordinary they are almost invisible. His hair, while dark enough, was neither black nor brown and the slight wave was like that of hundreds of others. His height was average, his skin was medium olive, his eyes were ordinary brown. His pallium was good quality but simple and the slight embroidery was similar to what most other freemen wore.

"And I; it is an honor to be called to aid the Emperor in these times." Simones made a reverence as he spoke, to show his devotion to Justinian.

"Your master has caused the Emperor some concern," said Panaigios. "We must discuss it." He indicated a smaller room, and added, "We ought to be more private."

"Yes," agreed Simones as he followed Panaigios into the antechamber. He took the chair offered to him and sat very straight while Panaigios adjusted his cushions. "Hagios Vasilos," he swore, pulling at his leather slipper. "There is a pebble under my heel and it has nearly driven me mad. If you do not object . . ." He loosened the leather bindings and drew the shoe off his foot. A tiny stone fell to the floor. "To think that so little a thing could do so much hurt."

"It is often the little things that do," said Simones, pleased at the opening he had been provided. "A word here or there, a ring filled with less powder than would cover a thumbnail, and yet they are more deadly than a run-away horse."

"Sadly, you are right," said Panaigios. "Which is what has given this office so much to do."

"And why you wanted to speak to me," Simones pressed.

"And wished that it were not necessary," said Panaigios. "It saddens me to think that so fine and honorable a man as your master should have fallen in with those who plot against the Emperor."

Simones did not have to pretend to be shocked. Of all the things he had anticipated, this was the least likely. "My master?" he repeated. He had assumed that Antonina had been using her position of friendship with the Empress Theodora to gain advantages for her friends, and that the Court Censor wanted it stopped. To learn now that it was Belisarius who had attracted the attention and concern of the Censor astonished him.

"You see how insidious it is; you, his slave, have suspected nothing." Now that he had finished brushing the sole of his foot, Panaigios was once again donning his shoe.

"True. I believe there is nothing to suspect." It was daring to contradict a Court Censor, but Simones was willing to risk it—to be too quickly convinced would give rise to many questions that might not be easily or pleasantly answered—in the hope that he might discover what the Censor believed.

"That is certainly what the appearances would have you think but from what has been revealed, this is deception. There are men who have shown us that this outward loyalty and honor are nothing more than a mask worn to suit the occasion." Panaigios adjusted the drape of his pallium and settled himself more properly in the chair.

"I have never thought that my master was less than wholly devoted to the Emperor and his work," said Simones with more honesty than he usually permitted himself to show.

"That is the opinion of many, and if it were not for the devotion of others, it is what everyone would think. But certain loyal men have devoted themselves to discover what lies behind these protestations of dedication, and have discovered that there are plots to take power. No one is more active in this infamy than your master, and this is surely the most secret deception ever to be revealed. In all outward aspects this Belisarius would appear to be the most worthy of Generals, the most laudable of men. His success in this deception is astonishing." Panaigios had taken one of the folds of his pallium in his hands and was running his fingers over the embroidery.

"What has convinced you?" Simones asked, doing his best to seem uncertain.

"Many things. First has been his lack of triumphs in Italy. True, he has consistently claimed that the lack of men and supplies has hindered him, and there may be a degree of truth in this. But he has taken an inconvenience and claimed that it was a major impediment so that he could strengthen his position with the army and with the Emperor. This insistence that he must have more men and more supplies covers his determination to use the Emperor's goodwill to become above any suspicion so that he could then strike and do so with complete impunity."

There was a sudden crash and a tumult of voices from

the courtyard beyond the little room. This gave Simones a little time to compose his thoughts and to decide how to proceed. "I am aghast to think this could be true," he said when the workmen had stopped shouting, "but I cannot convince myself that it is true. It seems so unlike the virtue I have seen in the General that I am overcome."

Panaigios gave him a superior, pitying smile. "Yes. I realize that many another might be deceived, has been deceived by this. And it is appropriate that you are firm in your loyalty to your master. It is dreadful when slaves so much forget themselves and turn against their masters on a whim."

"It is," Simones agreed, his mind working furiously under his innocent frown. "But if what you say is true, then there are others who have put their trust in this man and their trust is being abused. It is wrong, very wrong."

"True enough," Panaigios stated. "How difficult it was for me to accept what was revealed. I, too, had faith in this man and I, too, wanted to find another explanation. But these good servants of the Emperor convinced me, and now it is my duty to pursue the malefactors with all the power at my disposal." He sat a little straighter in his chair. "But with so splendid a figure as Belisarius, it will not be easy to produce enough evidence to discredit him. Which is why I wanted to speak to you, Simones."

So that was it, thought Simones. He concealed the smile that plucked at his mouth. "For what reason, Panaigios?"

Panaigios cleared his throat. "You are in an enviable position, being well-placed within Belisarius' household and being trusted for your long service."

"It is too much," said Simones with a humility he did not feel. "I have done what the world and God require of me."

"And now you must do what your Emperor requires of you," said Panaigios. "It is fitting that you accept this commission and work to bring justice to this Empire. That transcends any personal loyalty you may feel to your master. The Emperor is far more worthy of loyalty than your master is, for you and he are both servants of the Emperor, or should be."

In the courtyard there was another hurried scuffle and then the sound of planking hitting the ground. Two men bellowed contradictory orders.

"It is not a decision that I desire to make," confessed Simones. "I am a slave, and if it should be determined that I am acting against the orders and good of my master, I would be lucky to escape with a life in chains. Slaves who betray their owners are not treated kindly." The degree of transgression determined the punishment, the least of which was public flogging.

"That need not concern you; I will provide you with certain guarantees from the Censor that will protect you if it appears that you may be questioned or are discovered working for us." Panaigios looked Simones directly in the eye, which only served to cause Simones to doubt him more.

"I am not certain that it would be possible for such a thing to save me." He hesitated, then said, "I am willing to undertake this because I do not wish to see any harm come to the Emperor, and if that harm were to come through my master, it would give me more shame than I could ever endure." With a gesture of resignation, he said, "I do not want to be part of this, but if you are correct and this plot exists and my master has become part of it, then I have to do all that I may to keep the Emperor and the Empire from harm."

"Admirable," said Panaigios.

"But I hope that I will discover that my master has been used by others, and that he continues to be dedicated to Justinian as his vows and station in life demand." Again he paused. "I fervently pray that this is all the plotting of evil men who are seeking to ruin my master. If I discover that he has fallen in faith and in purpose, then I will do all that I must to keep him from committing even greater wrongs." As he touched his collar, he said, "If it is true that Belisarius has turned traitor, then this collar does not bind me."

"Very good," said Panaigios. "For a man in a difficult position, you show you have good sense." He studied Simones narrowly. "You are either a very devoted or a very subtle man, Simones, and either way, your purposes march with mine. I will require regular reports from you, and if you fail to produce them, then you will find that once my protection is withdrawn that your master will know more about you than you would wish." His voice had not changed, but there was a threat in it that was more daunting for its mild tone.

"It is an honor to serve you, Panaigios, and the office of the Censor as well. You will have your reports, though there may be little of interest or of use to you." There was no change in his manner, as if the threat had made no impression. "If Belisarius is found to be a traitor, then the shame of his act will touch all his household. I do not wish to be brought down by his acts."

"You are prudent. Good." He indicated the courtyard beyond the room. "I will arrange for you to be admitted through the side gate so there will be no record of your coming and going. It will give both of us the protection we need until we are able to denounce this man for all he has done."

Simones permitted himself a brief, nasty smile. "I will need some means of getting word to you, in case what I discover requires immediate action."

"Is that so important?" asked Panaigios, taken aback at the demand.

"It is," said Simones, and he could tell from the way Panaigios hesitated, that his position with the secretary of the Censor was secure.

"Very well, I will see you are provided with seals that will gain you admittance here without delay or question, and I will work out a signal with you, so that if you must have immediate assistance, it will be provided." He appeared uncomfortable for the first time since he removed his shoe.

"Tell me, why is Belisarius suspect now? He has been on campaign for so long, he has little to do with the working of the government." It was a question he had been wanting to ask since Panaigios had described his suspicions.

"He has been on campaign, and that has made him the hero of the army. Emperors have been overthrown by their palace guards, let alone the army. Remember in Roma, back five hundred years ago when there was one year with four Emperors; they were created and deposed by the Praetorian Guard and the Legions." He tapped the arm of his chair. "Our Emperor does not attend to history except where it concerns Christians, and occasionally he overlooks the lessons of the past."

"And there is reason to think that the army intends to . . . compromise the Emperor?" He still was not certain he put any credence in what he was hearing, but he knew that the army was full of ambitious men.

"Not yet, not that we can be certain of. If we had such information, you would not be asked to do these things for us. You would only have to see the disgrace of your master." This last statement gave Panaigios satisfaction, judging from the slow half-smile he showed Simones.

"My master is still in Italy, and there is very little I can do now, from here, that would be of use to you." He watched the other man, wanting to find out if he had other reasons for his request.

"Your master regularly writes to his wife, and she advises him. You can read their communications and tell me what is revealed there, if anything." Panaigios cleared his throat as his nervousness increased.

"It would not be honorable of me to read such mail." He knew that Antonina would take a very harsh view of such activities and he feared her wrath as much as he feared Belisarius'.

"Then you must be careful and not be caught," said Panaigios. "The safety of the Empire ought to mean more to you than your hide."

"But not if that hide is wasted." He knew that it was not impossible that he had been selected to be a sacrifice, a toy to distract while others worked in the shadows.

"That is not my intention," said Panaigios. "A slave in your position, in Belisarius' household, is too valuable to waste. If we were to permit you to be a sacrificial goat, as you imply—and not unwisely—it would ruin any chances for placing others in that household to do the work we need. And no other slave has earned the power and trust that you have."

"You are very thorough," said Simones, wondering who had told the Censor so much about the household and his place within it.

"It is what I must do." Panaigios rose. "I will want to speak with you in three days. Think about what I have said, and consider the danger in which the Empire stands. You have it within your power to be of aid, and if you are willing to be the Emperor's man, then you can do much. If you are not willing, then I warn you to tread carefully, for you are in a nest of vipers and may be stricken without warning."

As Simones stood he nodded. "I will consider this, and I am grateful that you are willing to think of me in this venture. If I hesitate, it is only because I have a duty to my master and his wife, and I must—"

"It is not only your master who interests us," said Panaigios, "but there are others. Who visits there, what they do, what they discuss, how they comport themselves. All that you may learn we wish to know. It is often through his associates that a man's true sentiments are discovered. Those who are close to Belisarius are not to be overlooked simply because they seem harmless, or because they have good reason to be his friend. If there are others in this conspiracy, they must be unearthed."

Now Simones was able to relax. "I know of everyone who visits the house, how long they stay and often what is said. I know of no reason I cannot report this to you without harming my master. Rest assured that I will reveal all I learn of this to you whenever you wish to know of it."

The two men regarded each other with new understanding. "So," said Panaigios, drawing out the word.

"Very well; for a start you will report to me everyone who comes and goes from the house. You will tell me what they say and to whom, why they come and where they go when they leave. Find out what it is they want from Belisarius and his wife, and what they are offering for what they want. It is important that we learn these things."

"Important?" said Simones. "For them as well as my master."

"If you continue to think that Belisarius is blameless, you may discover that there is more than enough guilt in others to implicate him in some way. Do not withhold information from me or it might be impossible for me to continue to protect you, and once your master learns of your conduct, well—"

Simones nodded. "Of course. And you are in a position to deny anything I might claim." He accepted this with relief. He knew now that he would have to be careful in all that he did.

"You are not unintelligent, slave, and you are dedicated. All that is required of you is that you maintain your dedication but to a higher purpose." He indicated the door. "My slave will see you out. He will tell you when you will be admitted to the courtyard for your reports."

For a moment, Simones stared contemptuously at Panaigios, then changed his demeanor so that he was once again submissive. "I am in your hands, secretary of the Censor. You can shape my destiny as God controls the fate of Man."

"That could be considered blasphemy," said Panaigios, but there was a degree of delight in the warning.

"For a churchman, perhaps, but for a slave?" He stepped back and opened the door. "I will report to you soon, Panaigios, and whatever I tell you will be the truth. I care not what you do with it so long as you do not throw me to the storm."

"I can't afford to do that, in any case," admitted Panaigios. "You will come to believe that in time. Once you do, we will deal together much more effectively."

Simones made him a deep reverence that bordered on insult. "I await the opportunity to serve," he said, and left before Panaigios could say anything more.

The Egyptian slave glared at Simones, but handed him a slip of parchment with a few instructions scribbled on it. "You will receive the other items when you make your first report. Until then you must restrain yourself."

"I understand," muttered Simones. He was ready to argue with the Egyptian, but was not given the chance. Almost at once there was a household slave waiting to escort him to the main gate, and then the Captain of the Guard to send him on his way.

As he walked back to the house of Belisarius, Simones let his mind have free rein. He was determined to turn all that he had learned to his advantage. Plots and posturing, he told himself, could be made to serve his ends as well as anyone else's. But for this he would need an ally, someone who could share his risk. It would be useless to speak to Antonina, for if she ever discovered what he was doing, she would have him flogged to death without hesitation. It had to be someone close to her, someone who would listen to him. There were the two widows, and one of them might be what he wanted. Eugenia was Byzantine, and that was a tremendous advantage. She knew how the power moved and who moved it, and she was greedy for it, he could tell from her eyes. If not Eugenia, then that Roman woman, the widow Olivia might have to be used, but Simones was uncertain about her. She was too foreign and had too much power for him to be able to manipulate her as he would like.

A cart drawn by a single ox trundled by and Simones had to step to the far side of the road to avoid being injured. He called the might of heaven down on the drover's head, then resumed his progress along the noisy streets.

As he neared the house of Belisarius, he made up his mind: he would approach Eugenia first, striving to convince her that he could give her power and an access to position that he did not currently have. He liked her better than Olivia in any case, for he could sense her rapacity, and he trusted it. He did not know what it was that Olivia longed for, and was not willing to take the risks he would have to take in order to find out.

He entered the house by the side door and was informed that Antonina was waiting to speak with him, for she required his help in planning her next gathering. It was a simple matter, he decided, to make sure he remained an essential part of the household. It would satisfy both Antonina and Panaigios, which in turn would eventually satisfy Simones himself.

* * *

A letter from Pope Sylvestros to the Bishop of the Church of the Patriarchs.

> To the most reverend, sanctified and august superiors and the Bishop, Pope Sylvestros submits this most humble request on the Evangelical Feast in the Lord's Year 546.
> From my prayers and other devotions, it has come to me that there are those in Italy who yearn for the consolation of true religion, and who toil under the burdens of war and apostasy. For that reason, I am petitioning you to permit me to travel to Italy to undertake the comfort of these unfortunates. It is not unlikely that I will remain some time among those who need me, and who will be grateful to have the opportunity to find the solace of faith.
> I am known to several of the sea captains who ply the waters between here and Ostia, and it would not be a great difficulty for me to secure passage with one or another of

them. This will make my travels of little cost to the Church
as well as providing yet another chance for me to reach
those who are usually deprived of the offices of faith, for the
captains would permit me to preach to the crew and anyone
traveling with them to Italy.

We have heard of the losses and disgraces suffered by our
troops facing the forces of Totila, and it may be that the
presence of one of true religion might inspire courage and
greater dedication among the soldiers so that they will be
moved to battle with more determination for the saving of
the city of Roma as well as the rest of the countryside.

Whatever your decision, I bow my head to your wisdom
and your choice, and I profess myself wholly accepting of
anything you permit me to do.

> In the name of the Savior, the
> Father and the Sacred Spirit,
> Pope Sylvestros
> Church of the Patriarchs

• 7 •

By sundown the heat of the day faded and the first slow
night breeze moved over the Black Sea to Konstantinoupolis, its light touch heralding the coming darkness.
The voices of bells brazen as the western sky called a
farewell to the sun; the shouts and bustle from the
wharves and markets gave way to the drone of chants
from the churches.

For Drosos, this was the familiar rhythm of home, one
that he noticed only because he had so recently returned

from the chaos of Italy. That campaign was still fresh in his mind, and often he had to remind himself that it was behind him. One thing he treasured from Italy waited for him now; he smiled as he trod up the gentle hill to the house where Olivia lived. It was his second visit since his return to Konstantinoupolis three weeks ago, and this time he hoped that their meeting would be more than the formal ritual that society required. His memory burned from the three nights they had spent together at her villa outside the walls of Roma, and he hungered now for more of her.

Niklos opened the door to him, saluting instead of making a reverence. "Welcome back, Captain."

Grinning, Drosos returned the salute. "I am happy to be here, Niklos." He glanced around the vestibule and saw no sign of other guests. "What company this evening?"

"Just you, Captain," said Niklos with a knowing look.

"For the entire evening?" He was a bit surprised at the majordomo's bluntness.

"For the entire evening," Niklos confirmed, adding, "My mistress waits for you in the garden."

"Will you take me there?" He could find his way himself, but it would be taking a liberty that could easily be thought a serious breach of good conduct. "You, or one of the household slaves."

"I will take you," said Niklos, indicating the hallway they should use and following a pace behind Drosos.

"How is your mistress?" Drosos inquired, attempting to keep the tone of the evening properly reserved.

"She misses you, Captain," said Niklos, his candor putting aside the practiced phrases that Drosos expected.

"I have missed her," said Drosos, aware that it was not correct for him to discuss Olivia with her bondsman.

Niklos gave Drosos an understanding nod. "You wonder that I should say this to you, that I know so much about my mistress? It is because I have been with Olivia Clemens for a long time, and as her bondsman and majordomo, I know many things about her. She confides in me and has done so for many years." They had passed the dining room and Niklos indicated the small supper laid out for the Captain. "Refreshments are waiting for you whenever you wish for them."

"Not yet, I think," said Drosos, his appetite whetted for something other than food.

"No," agreed Niklos, and opened the door to the garden.

Olivia, swathed in soft olive-green silk shot with silver, rose from her low couch as Drosos came toward her, her hand extended to him, her lyre set aside. "Welcome, Captain."

The polite compliments died on his tongue as he touched her; his eyes darkened with emotion and he made a deep reverence to her. "Olivia."

Her smile was warm and lucid as sunlight. "How glad I am you are here." Her paenula whispered and clung as she moved. "It has been too long."

"Much too long," he said, his senses almost overwhelmed by her presence.

"It pleases me that you feel as I do." She turned to Niklos. "I will call you in a while."

"Very good, my mistress," he said, withdrawing and closing the door, leaving Olivia and Drosos alone with the lengthening shadows and the first scent of jasmine.

Drosos was used to much more complicated preliminaries, and he stood uncertainly, baffled by the directness Olivia used. "How is it with you?"

"Better now you are here." She sank back onto her couch and indicated the place beside her. "Come, Drosos; join me."

Drosos did not move for the space of two long breaths, and then, very slowly and joyously, he moved to her side. He put his hand over hers, letting them rest together. "The other time I was here," he said quietly, "I wondered if you would grant me this. . . ."

She touched his face just above his short-clipped soldier's beard. "Why would I not?"

"It has been a while." He stopped and went on with

difficulty. "You have been alone here, and you might have found another you preferred to me." His last few words came quickly and he could not bring himself to meet her eyes.

"Drosos," she said and waited until he turned to her. "I have not found anyone I prefer to you, not in many years, certainly not since I have been here." She reached out to her lyre, the strings murmuring under her fingers.

He listened to the sound, his mind drifting with it. There was a stillness around him that was as tantalizing as an embrace. He was afraid to break it with words, afraid that he would lose the joy that filled him. Finally he brought her hand to his lips and kissed her palm: he felt her lips brush his shoulder through the fabric of his dalmatica.

For some little time neither of them moved. The air around them was as quiet as they were, suspended in breathlessness and anticipation. Then a finger of air stirred the leaves; the silence turned to soft rustling.

"Drosos," whispered Olivia, moving back from him far enough from him to see his face clearly in the fading light.

He let her read his features, exulting in the yearning in her eyes. He pulled her closer. "I want you, Olivia."

"And I you," she said as she wrapped her arms around him.

"Now."

Olivia laughed low in her throat. "There is no reason to rush when there is time to savor. Pleasure is not to be squandered when it can be relished."

"But it has been so long," protested Drosos, before he kissed her mouth.

When she could speak, she said, "Be patient, Drosos. Now that we are together, we need not hurry."

He pressed close to her, urgency melding with desire. He felt her body with his need, knowing she would not deny him. He fumbled with her paenula, seeking the flesh beneath it.

"Here," she said softly, and unfastened the tablion that held the garment at the shoulder. The silk fell away, and beneath it she was naked.

For an instant Drosos stared, transfixed with wanting her. His flesh trembled, his entire being as inflamed as his organ. Abruptly he started to tug his clothes off, casting the garments around him until all he wore was his shoes.

Olivia had watched this in silence, and as he reached for her, she acquiesced.

The couch was wide enough for both of them, and they fell together in a glorious tangle, legs and arms intertwined, hands seeking. They had been apart long enough that some of their old familiarity had been forgotten; it was ineffably sweet to rediscover one another, to find once more the ways each awakened the other.

As the first rush of desire calmed, Drosos was willing to let Olivia set the pace for them, delighting in her explorations of his body and longings. She coaxed more pleasure from him than he had thought they could share, offering herself to him as wholeheartedly as she indulged him. Every caress, each kiss increased their ardor; both gave the full bounty of passion even before he entered the depths of her body.

"Lord God of the Prophets," he gasped as he felt her tighten around him. His senses swam with rapture as they moved together. Only when he had succumbed to fulfillment and released her did he feel the world return. He propped himself on his elbows and looked down at her.

She smiled up at him, her face radiant. Then she began to laugh, and he joined her. "Oh, Drosos," she said, her head pressed to his shoulder.

His laughter continued, warm and unfettered. Reluctantly he moved aside, gathering her close against him, kissing her eyes as his chuckles subsided at last.

"It is so good to have you here," she said with a long, satisfied sigh.

"I didn't remember how wonderful you are," he told her, his fingers brushing the planes of her face. "You delight me."

"Wonderful," she said, deeply content. "It's been a very long time since I have wanted anyone as I want you."

She stared up into the star-strewn night.

"So ancient you are," he teased, and was surprised when she responded quite seriously.

"Yes; so ancient I am." She touched him tenderly where her mouth had been at the height of their passion.

"You bit me," he said, amused.

"Yes." She kissed the place then kissed his mouth. "I used to think that it would not be possible to care this way again, certainly not after so long."

He was startled at her somber tone, and he smiled at her a bit uncertainly. "What is it?"

"Oh, nothing." She moved closer to him. "I'm being foolish; pay no attention."

"If this is foolish," he said, leaning over to kiss her yet again, "then I like it better than wisdom."

"So do I." There was a roguish light in her eyes now, and she pushed at his shoulder so that he rolled onto his back; she braced one arm across his chest and grinned.

He tangled one hand in her hair and drew her down to him. "You are the most awe-inspiring creature I've ever known. You're like an angel."

"An angel?" she asked, laughing again. "I thought that angels did not indulge in these things." As she said this she ran her fingers over his chest, just barely touching him; she smiled as he shivered with pleasure.

"Angels indulge in ecstasy," he said with unruffled calm. "So you are like an angel."

"I see." She kissed him on the edge of his beard. "Do all soldiers have these?"

"Most of us. It isn't convenient to be clean-shaven on campaign, though Belisarius managed most of the time I was with him." His expression darkened at the memory. "I delayed coming back as long as I could. It was hard to leave him."

"Is it bad?" She had stopped her teasing and was watching him with serious concern.

"Yes." He met her eyes. "We had to abandon your villa. I don't know what Totila's men did to it." It shamed him to admit this, and he was surprised that she waved his apology away with some impatience. "We tried to protect it as long as we could."

"You assured me that would be the case and I had no reason to doubt you. I was more concerned for you and your men than for the villa. I have lived there more years than I care to remember, and while I am fond of the place, it is only stone. Men are living flesh, which is another matter." Neither she nor Drosos assumed that she was saying this erotically.

"But it might be in ruins."

"So might Roma, so might all of Italy." She rested her head on his chest. "It is the waste of life that horrifies me."

"There are always lives wasted in war," said Drosos, trying to sound cynical and instead revealing more despair than he realized.

"I hate them for that, if nothing else." She gazed up at the sky. "And in the end, how little difference it makes."

Drosos shifted under her, his arms going around her as much to give him comfort as to embrace her. "Must we talk about war, Olivia?"

"You said you were sorry to leave. I wanted to know why," she pointed out. "But no, we need not talk about it, nor of anything else that displeases you."

"It doesn't displease me," he protested, then relented. "Yes, it does, and that is troublesome, because I am Belisarius' Captain and an officer of the Emperor. It ought not to displease me. I should be proud of the honor I have been given."

"And if you are not, what then?" Olivia asked, her voice soft and kind.

"I have failed," he said simply, with devastation of spirit.

"Oh, no," she told him, raising herself enough to be able to meet his eyes. "No, Drosos; dear dear Drosos."

"What else can it be?" He sounded lost now.

"Perhaps it is merely that you know you cannot save everyone you wish to save and this causes you anguish. You are a good soldier and a good man; you would not willingly see land lost and people killed if there were a way you could prevent it."

"It's more than that," he admitted, one hand sunk in her fawn-brown hair. "It was the futility of it all. We had not enough supplies or money or troops, and so we lost. Belisarius has done more to hold on to Italy with less than anyone—"

"Such as the Emperor?" Olivia suggested.

"He promises, but nothing comes, or not enough, or not in time," he said uncomfortably. "If he understood, if he knew, then he would not withhold what is needed."

"Perhaps," said Olivia. "Or it may be that he wishes for his forces to manage with less." She said this as gently as she could, but it did not soften the blow that Drosos felt.

"The Emperor is not like that!" He shoved her, almost throwing her off him. "He has the Empire on his mind, and that is why he does not always comprehend what one part of it is up against. He in concerned for the welfare of everyone in the Empire and that often means that he faces conflicts. Even Belisarius knows this, for he has explained it to everyone who has served with him over the last years."

"And you believe as Belisarius does?" said Olivia. "Well, I am new to Byzantium, and it may be that as a Roman I do not have sufficient knowledge to judge what I see." Inwardly she knew better—that Justinian had decided to withdraw his support of his forces in Italy—but had no desire to argue with Drosos about it.

"Women never understand these matters," said Drosos. "Although," he amended, "you have a better grasp than many; it is your Roman heritage."

"No doubt," she concurred. Her hazel eyes grew distant. "And I do miss Roma, more than I thought I would."

"Because it is your home," he said, doing his best to reassure her. "You are like all of us; you would rather be in the place you know than among strangers. That's not surprising. No one could think that it is. No matter how much more opulent and beautiful Konstantinoupolis is, you will miss Roma, because it is where you were born."

"Yes," she said very slowly dragging out the word. "Yes, Roma is my native earth, and for that reason alone it pulls me. And you do not know what it was like at the height of its grandeur. You can't imagine it, seeing it now. You don't know how glorious it was, once."

"But that was centuries ago, when the corrupt Caesars ruled," Drosos reminded her.

"The corrupt Caesars," she mused. "Well, some of them were, certainly, but others only did their best, as you have done, as Belisarius does. You might not think so now, but many of those Caesars were as revered in their time as your Emperor Justinian is now." She shook her head as if to be free of her memories. "Why are we dwelling on the past when the present is so much more enjoyable?"

He did not catch her mood quickly, but he did find a way to respond to her. "I thought all Romans longed for the past."

"If we do, then we are great fools," she said roundly, doing her best to bring him out of the unhappiness that was taking hold of him. "The past, no matter what it was, is over, and there is only the present. The future is still ahead, all unknown. We have what we have now." She kissed him on the earlobe. "Haven't we."

"Possibly," he allowed.

"Oh, Drosos, pay attention," she said, this time tweaking the edge of his well-trimmed beard. "How can I give you pleasure if your thoughts are in Roma with the army?"

"I don't know," he growled, but there was the beginning of a smile in his eyes.

"Do, please, give me your attention. Let me show you all the delights you have missed—I trust you *have* missed them?—while we have been apart." She tossed her head and her long, loose hair trailed over his chest. "You have returned to me and I want to know every joy with you."

"You're greedy, that's what it is," he told her, his expression less distant. "You want to drain me."

"Hardly," she said, her face inscrutable. "You do not understand what I want if that's what you think I'm doing."

"All right, then; what is it you want of me?" He had moved over her and had succeeded in pinning her shoulder to the couch. "Tell me."

"I want you," she said directly. "All of you, without ruse or deception."

"What?" Her serious answer took him unaware and he released her, watching her with great curiosity.

"You asked me what I want: I've told you." She remained unmoving.

"You want me?" He spoke as if the words were unfamiliar and difficult.

"Yes."

"Why?"

She hesitated before she answered. "Because you touch me, you reach something in me that has not been reached for many, many years."

"I wish you wouldn't do that," he complained softly.

"Do what?"

"Keep talking as if you were as old as the sphinx," he said. "All right, you're probably older than I am, but that doesn't mean you're my great-grandmother."

Olivia chuckled but there was a sadness in her eyes. "I'll try to remember that," she said in a remote way.

"There are times you're impossible," he said, and ended their disagreement with a long, deep kiss that left both of them breathless and wide-eyed. "If I am what you want, then I'm yours." He ran his fingers over the planes of her face, so lightly that she almost could not feel them.

This time they made love easily, with less frenzy than before. The demand they felt grew more slowly, losing nothing in being less urgent than before. Drosos was willing to permit her to take the time she wanted to bring him to a level of arousal that astonished him, for until she did this, he was certain that he would never be more stimulated and eager than he had been when he first sought her.

"Lie back," she said as her hands traced patterns of desire through his body. "There is no reason to press."

He did as she told him, luxuriating in the endless subtle caresses and kisses she bestowed on him. He returned them, taking pride in the depth of her response to him. He had known enough women to realize that Olivia's desire was more profound than any he had encountered before, and that Olivia was more vulnerable to him than any woman he had taken to bed in the past.

"Your breast was made to fit my hand," he said, demonstrating.

"There are other parts that fit as well," she reminded him, her voice low.

"Oh, Kyrios," he murmured, his need for her intensifying even more.

She drew him closer to her, her hands pressing him against the length of her body, and then into her. She arched to meet him, moving with him. The tang of him, the weight of him pervaded her senses and increased as their union deepened.

This time when it was over neither spoke; they hardly moved. Each was replete with the other, each was gratified beyond all expectation. They lay together, not quite asleep, their arms around each other no longer straining but unwilling to part more than comfort demanded.

"Olivia?" Drosos whispered, hardly more than a breath.

"Umm?"

"What if the slaves find us?"

"Niklos will bring a blanket," she said, drowsiness making her words slur.

"But you are a widow—"

"I am a Roman," she corrected him.

"But if your slaves gossip, you might be criticized for what you . . . do with me." He brushed her hair back from her face. "I don't want you to suffer on my account."

She opened her eyes and studied his face. "People will

talk no matter what. As a Roman, I will be the subject of speculation. The worst they can say of me is that I have taken a Captain of the army as my lover. If they say any more, then we can worry about it then." She kissed him affectionately. "How good of you to be concerned for me."

"Just as well that one of us is," he said, rousing himself enough to show his worry.

"If there are questions," she said as she smoothed the line that had deepened between his brows, "you need only tell anyone who has the ill grace to speculate that I am bound by my husband's will to remain a widow."

"Are you?" he asked, genuinely startled.

"No." She smiled sleepily. "But many Roman women are, for reasons of property. There was a time when it was different, when . . ." Her voice trailed off. "That was long ago, and there is no point in recalling. It only serves to make me angry at things I cannot change." She stretched her one free arm and then rested it across his chest. "If you say that I am obedient to my husband's will, no one will question it and you and I can continue as we are."

"But if it is a lie," he began only to have her stop him.

"Drosos, it is close enough to the truth that it does not matter. If you wish to remain my lover and you need some explanation, then this will do as well as any."

He took her hand in his. "And if I wish for more?"

"You are an officer in the army and your life is not wholly your own. Wait a while before you decide that you want more of me." She did her best to conceal a yawn. "In a year, if you think then that you need a different arrangement with me, we will talk about it. By then, you might prefer the way we are now."

"And I might not," he warned her.

Her smile faded as much with sleep as with apprehension. "If you insist," she said.

Drosos slid his hand over her back and drew her more close before he drifted into sleep.

*   *   *

Text of memo from Panaigios to his superior, accompanying several other memos from several of the Censor's secretaries.

To Kimon Athanatadies, from his devoted Panaigios,

The slave Simones has proven to be industrious and reliable, at least so his first two reports have led me to believe. It is my intention to subject him to another test and if he passes it as well as he has passed the first two, increase his duties and his power so that he will have more freedom of activity than has been allowed until now.

He has revealed that Antonina is actively promoting the interests of her friends as well as the returning officers of her husband Belisarius. This must be watched and guarded against for some little time until we learn one way or another how much power she has gained through the use of her influence with the Empress. It is fortunate that Simones is willing to reveal this, for it makes our dealings much more direct and useful.

You have said that you want to know what changes occur when Belisarius returns, and I have already informed Simones that he will have to be more active then. Doubtless he anticipates these developments with mixed feelings, but he will be prepared to give us the information we require to protect himself as much as to establish any fault on the part of his master.

With prayers for your continued diligence and zeal, and

with great thanks for the opportunity to serve you and our glorious Justinian, I am

> Panaigios
> secretary

• 8 •

The Hippodrome resembled the Circus Maximus, though it was not as boisterous or as crowded as the huge amphitheater in Roma had been. The stands were full, but the people behaved more decorously than the Romans. Taking her seat beside Antonina, Olivia watched the stands, her expression carefully blank.

"Is this familiar to you?" asked Antonina as she directed her body slave to arrange her pillows more comfortably.

"To a degree, but it is also very different." She looked down the length of the oblong stadium. "In Roma, everyone was more active than I have seen the people of Constantinople be."

"Yes, we do put more value on good conduct than the Romans," said Antonina with a degree of complacency that made Olivia want to argue with her.

"Your ways are different than Roman ways," she said.

"Yes," Antonina declared, clearly relieved that this was the case. "Roma was beset with strife and the presence of false gods." She was satisfied with her cushions now and waved her slave to the back of the marble-faced box in which she and her guests sat.

"But still Roma thrived," said Olivia in a light voice.

"What does that mean, but that the world of Roma was caught up in trade and that the Romans profited by the misfortunes of their neighbors." She stopped. "Not that I mean any disrespect. Your family was of the nobility, so my husband has informed me, and that certainly must mean more than a title and some estates in the country."

Olivia shook her head and said truthfully, "My family had lost most of the funds and property it had ever had by the time I came to be married, which is why they selected the husband for me that they did." Even five hundred years after, Olivia found that she could be bitter for the bargain her father had made with Cornelius Justus Silius, and all the misery that alliance had brought her in the years she was married to the senator.

"How unfortunate," said Antonina in a tone that indicated she was hardly listening at all.

The smell in the air—a combination of sweat, food, horses, and fabric—was strange to Olivia, for it was different than what she had known in Roma. The food was not the spiced pork and wine of Roma but something more exotic—grilled lamb with onions and cinnamon and pepper—than the fare of ancient Roma. The fabric, too, was cotton and silk, not linen and wool as it had been so long ago. Olivia adjusted her pillows and waved away the offer of food.

"In such a crowd," she said apologetically, "I find that eating makes me feel slightly ill."

"I had such an experience when I was pregnant," said Antonina, and waited in significant silence.

"I have been pregnant only once, and that was long ago," said Olivia. "I did not attend the Great Games then, for it was thought that the excitement might be dangerous for me."

"What of the child?" asked Antonina.

"It did not live," Olivia said, looking away across the stands toward the enormous statue of a quadriga pulled by a matched team of four horses. Unlike the Roman chariots, these harnessed all four horses to the vehicle they pulled, and the value of a perfectly matched team was enormous.

"I had two children by my first husband," said Antonina, "but both succumbed to fever before they were ten. It was a great misfortune, but I have bowed my head to the Will of God, Who gives and takes away all things."

"Truly," said Olivia, listening to the sound of the crowd. "Will the Emperor be here today?"

"He has affairs of state, but Theodora will arrive shortly." Antonina could not keep from smiling, for her friendship with the Empress had given her influence at court that many others envied, though few could emulate. "I informed her that you would be with me today and she has expressed a desire to meet you. It will be a pleasure to present you to her once the races have begun."

"That is very kind of you," said Olivia, not at all certain that she wanted to meet the wife of Emperor Justinian.

"I have given my husband my word that I would do what I could to see you properly established in the world, and I intend to honor that obligation. You are a woman alone in Konstantinoupolis and it is fitting that you gain sponsorship of more than a pope or two. You are going to need friends at court as well as friends in the Church if you are to survive comfortably in the world." She signaled her slave to bring her food, and once again offered a selection of delicacies to Olivia.

"Thank you, I had better not," said Olivia. "But do not let that stop you from enjoying your victuals."

"I confess that good food is one of my special pleasures. My confessor has warned me that this might imperil my soul, but if that is the case, then everyone alive is in some danger, don't you think?" This was clearly intended to be thought witty and Olivia managed to laugh.

"Appetite is a factor with all of us," she said and was favored with an appraising smile.

"You have a sharp mind, Olivia," said Antonina in a tone of voice that suggested that a sharp mind was not entirely admirable. What she said next confirmed this impression. "If you intend to make such comments, be sure of your company; women are expected to be circumspect."

"Of course," said Olivia.

"Ah!" Antonina turned her head at the sound of the salpinx. "The Empress is entering the Hippodrome."

Olivia listened to the sound of the ivory trumpet and decided she preferred the brazen voice of the lituus and buccina to the muffled and delicate fanfare that heralded the arrival of Theodora. She saw that everyone in the stands was standing, and she, too, rose to her feet. "Which is the Imperial box?" she asked her hostess.

"There, under the statues of the chariot and horses." Antonina did not point—that was much too rude—but indicated the direction with a nod of her head. "There is a tunnel that is used by the Emperor and Empress when they are visiting the Hippodrome, so that they will not have to walk in the crowded streets."

"I see," said Olivia, thinking that it was a sensible precaution for anyone worried about the possibility of harm or death.

"Theodora is wearing her headdress and collar of pearls. It is her most impressive jewel." Antonina again cocked her head to indicate where Olivia should look, then stood very straight, her smile widening as four women entered the Imperial box.

Olivia regarded Empress Theodora with curiosity, for doubtless Justinian's wife was the most powerful woman in all of Byzantium. There were rumors about her, attributing every vice and sin to her, just as there were rumors indicating that she was the most virtuous female ever to grace the world with her presence since Eve had smirched mankind in the Garden of Eden. Theodora stood slightly taller than the women with her, her large eyes accentuated by the enormous and elaborate headdress of pearls and jewels that adorned her, complimented by a collar large as a short cope, of pearls, some of enormous size and luminosity. The whole was worn over a paenula of rose-colored silk which in turn covered a dalmatica of gold-medallioned silk the same shade as fresh peaches.

"She is a great beauty," said Antonina, not quite free of envy.

"She certainly holds the eye," said Olivia, thinking that without the gorgeous pearls and rich fabrics, Theodora would be nothing more than a good-looking matron with a long head and slightly receding chin.

"She is the soul of the Emperor; he himself has said so many times. The woman with her, the one in dark green, is her aunt, Triantafillia. She has endowed six religious communities and has said that she will one day withdraw from court life entirely." Antonina indicated the pope who sat with them. "Have you heard that, Pope Demosthenes?"

"I have," he said, his voice low and indistinct. He had done his best to appear invisible since Antonina had admitted Olivia to her box.

"She is regarded with great respect and affection by everyone," Antonina declared. "Her conduct is not questioned by even the most censorious." She folded her hands and averted her eyes from the Imperial box. "It isn't proper to watch them too long. It then appears that they are drawing attention to themselves, which is poor behavior for a woman of merit."

"With the splendor of her garments and ornaments," said Olivia doing her best not to sound critical, "it is most amazing that the eyes do not drop out of the heads of everyone who can see her."

Antonina responded with gentle laughter. "You Romans say the most outrageous things. I have heard from my husband that everyone in Roma thinks nothing of making the most incendiary remarks, and if this is an example of Roman wit, I can readily understand why he remarked upon it to me."

"Romans have need of a little humor, like everyone else," said Olivia, taking her seat as she saw Antonina motion to the chairs once more.

"How inventive," said Antonina, but her enthusiasm

was now diminishing. "I must remember your remarks to repeat them when the General finally arrives home." She inclined her head to the pope near the back of the box. "Remind me, Pope Demosthenes."

"Yes, Antonina," said the old pope with a sour expression.

"And Olivia," Antonina went on, as if beginning a question, "when you are more familiar with our ways, let me know then what service I can be to you. I understand that you are not yet able to express those things you require since you are not able to determine what it is you ought to have to live properly in this time and place."

"You're most thoughtful," Olivia forced herself to say. "Your husband must be very proud of you."

"He has told me that before, certainly, and I do not think he has any reason to dissemble." She had adjusted the drape of her paenula so that the silk looked like water cascading over her, the most chaste and revealing caress. Her jewels were lavish hanging earrings of pearls and sapphires; her tablion holding the paenula at the shoulder was as large as her hand and was made of gold and amethysts. "For a woman to live properly and well in this city, there are certain forms you must obey. In finding a pope to sponsor the purchase of your property you have done well, for that shifts any taint of harlotry from you, and your little meetings with Captain Drosos can go on without comment or much suspicion."

"I wasn't aware it concerned anyone—Drosos stayed at my villa outside Roma for many days. Your husband and the rest of his officers were there at the same time. If anything might cause suspicions, I would have thought that this would be worse." She permitted her tone to become snide but kept her eyes wide with amazement as she regarded her hostess.

"That was Roma at time of war, which is hardly the same thing as a dalliance with an officer not active on campaign." Antonina was better at the game than Olivia was, and more patient.

"No one I knew in Roma thought anything of the arrangement, nor would they have if there had only been

Drosos—or any other officer, for that matter—who had come to me at my invitation. In Roma we understand how the will of dead husbands impose on the living, and we accept that the living will find a way to comply with the dead and with life." All her life she had hated smug women, and that word summed up Antonina so perfectly that it was difficult for Olivia to maintain her pretense of good fellowship. What about the woman had so captivated Belisarius that he could ignore this behavior and dote on her as he did? No matter how long she lived, Olivia knew that she would be baffled by what the people around her did, and with whom.

"You are severe, and I think you may be teasing me. I have heard Romans claim that on the nights of the full moon, virgins sacred to the old moon goddess cover themselves in goat dung and dance through the streets. While I was never taken in," Antonina assured Olivia with a faint, condescending smile, "I knew many others who actually believed that such things happened."

In spite of herself, Olivia laughed. "Yes, I know that such tales exist, and that no one promotes them more than Romans. It is utter foolishness, but nevertheless they continue." She saw that the first pair of chariots were being led onto the sands, and she leaned forward to look at them, studying the difference in harnessing and in the chariot—it was no longer the racing quadriga she remembered from her youth, but a similar vehicle, a little smaller in size, a little heavier in weight, and more maneuverable than the quadriga had been, which was why all four horses could be attached to it without risking spills on the tight turns of the course—as well as the manner of the charioteers, who appeared to be somewhat older than the charioteers had been in Roma.

"You enjoy the races?" Antonina asked.

"If they are done well, if the quadrigae are well-matched and the teams are paired for contest." She looked at the pair being positioned not far away from her. "The bays are a good team, but I would think that they would not last as long as that other team of chestnuts. The bays are more sprinters, judging from their rumps, and the chestnuts are runners. They will not hit their full speed until the bays are starting to tire."

"Sinhareitiryiah!" exclaimed Antonina. "I see you are no novice where horseflesh is concerned."

"I have raised them for more years than you would believe. It was one of the principal businesses of my villa. At one time we also supplied mules and hennies to the army, but that was long ago, when there was not such unrest in the land. Recently we have contented ourselves with breeding horses." She discovered that she missed her villa intensely, the sound of the place, the smells of it, the rhythms of its days.

"You mean you actually participated in the breeding of horses?" Antonina for the first time appeared to be sincerely shocked.

"Well, of course," Olivia said at her most matter-of-fact. "It was my villa and my home. What else was I going to do with my time?"

"But surely there were slaves to attend to such matters," protested Antonina.

"Certainly, and a great many freed- and freemen who were in my employ. But horses were what the villa produced, and it was my responsibility to see that the work went on as efficiently as possible." She decided to take advantage of her hostess' repugnance. "It was also my work to select which stallions would cover which mares, and which of the male foals would be gelded. We had a great reputation for the quality of our horses, as your husband will tell you, if you ask him."

Antonina had recovered her composure. "You . . . you may certainly mention these things to those you knew in Roma, I suppose, but you would do well to keep such reminiscences to yourself when you are dealing with those who live here in this city, in the Empire; you might want to be more circumspect, since here we understand that women do not participate in such things. To say that you owned a villa where horses were raised is all very well, but to add what you did in the matter would be most unwise. Because of my husband, I can understand your position a little, but there are many wives in Konstantinoupolis, believe me, Olivia, who would be so deeply distressed to learn these things of you that they would do everything they could to exclude you from the activities of the city, and that would be most unfortunate."

"I am used to living quietly on my own," said Olivia.

"Yes, that is apparent. But here we do not leave our women so rudderless. There are matters that must be tended to, and if you are not received by the women of the city, it will make your life very much more difficult for you. You were permitted to purchase slaves without sponsorship through my intervention, but ordinarily this would not be possible. Now that you have a pope to endorse you, this is better, but it still limits what you can do and where you can do it."

There was a blare of trumpets and the race began, a five-lap course between the Blue and Green teams.

Over the eruption of noise, Olivia said, "I am capable of handling my affairs for myself. I have been a widow for some time."

"Here that is not possible," Antonina reminded her.

"So I am learning," said Olivia wistfully as she watched the chariots make their first lap of the track: as she had predicted, the bays were ahead. "Those horses are very young," she said critically.

"They are most swift when they are young," said Antonina, repeating what she had so often heard.

"They are also least sensible. They are timid creatures for all their size, and it takes a while for them to learn sense and trust. Putting them in harness to race makes them more crazed than they need be." She sat back. "The chestnuts will win; they are better long-distance runners and they are older. It will give them the victory."

"You are certain of this, are you?" Antonina said, disliking the notion that Olivia might actually know more than she did about the races.

"Yes. Just watch and you will see for yourself." She looked at her hostess. "But don't be concerned. I won't mention the horse breeding unless there is no choice about it. And from what I have seen, there are few people here who think to wonder where any woman gets her wealth, so I suppose the matter will never come up."

"Even if it did," Antonina corrected her, "it would not be at all proper to speak to you about your funds and property. A man curious about such matters would correctly address your senior male relative, or, barring that, your sponsor. That way you need not be hampered by these considerations, which are not at all appropriate to you."

"Simply because I'm a woman?" Olivia marveled.

"It saves us all from much that is unpleasant." It was clear that Antonina did not intend to discuss the matter further.

Olivia was not willing to concede her position quite yet. "I see; a woman need not bother herself about her money or property. She need not know how much of either she has—which, in fact she does not have because she is not permitted to control it—or what is being done with it. There was a time in Roma, not so very long ago, that such things would be grounds for a lawsuit."

Antonina sighed. "Perhaps, in those days before the Church established itself, such protections were required. But no man who has confessed himself a Christian would profit from the labor of others, or abuse the trust of his—"

"Inferiors," Olivia interrupted her. "No wonder you have rescinded the rights of your slaves, since you have reduced your females to bonded servants." She held up her hands in mock submission. "It will take time for me to learn these things. For a little while, you must be content to have me chafe at the bit."

"You worry for no purpose," said Antonina and would have gone on, but there was a discreet rap on the entrance to her box. "Who is there?"

"Themistokles," came the answer, and since Olivia assumed it was not the ancient Athenian, she looked to her hostess.

"Who is this person?"

"The Empress' chief eunuch," said Antonina. She motioned to her two slaves flanking the door to open it. "God send you great blessings," she greeted the huge man who stepped into the box.

"God has blessed me already, more than ever I deserved." His voice was high and sweet and very strong. His face, almost completely unlined, gave no indication of his age, but there was a slight tracing of gray in his auburn curls. He made a deep reverence to Antonina and then to Olivia. "August lady, great lady," he said elegantly. "It is my privilege to serve the most serene and elevated Empress Theodora, and she has mandated that I come here to ask that you bear her company for an hour while the races are conducted."

It was a formal invitation, and as such would offer no delay in being accepted. Antonina inclined her head. "It is a great honor that so majestic a lady should deign to accept the simple company of women such as we are. We are all alacrity to attend her." She had risen as she spoke, and she signaled to Pope Demosthenes. "If it would not distress you to remain here, I will ask it of you."

"It would give me time to think," said the old pope, and he stared at the eunuch. "I petition heaven to bless your mistress every day of my life, and I recount her praises every night."

"She is humbly grateful," said Themistokles. He indicated the open doorway. "August lady? Great lady? if you will come with me?"

Antonina complied at once and gestured to Olivia to hasten when it appeared that the Roman woman was not going to leave the box at once. "We are expected, Olivia," Antonina told her sharply.

"I was only trying to gather one or two cushions," Olivia protested, doing her best not to sound sharp.

The crowd started to chant loudly, the rhythm rolling and pronounced, more compelling than any of the words they used.

"It appears that the chestnuts are overtaking the bays," said Themistokles and was puzzled when Antonina and Olivia exchanged quick glances. "There are those who risked too much money on the event."

"How fortunate that women are not permitted to gamble," said Olivia with a submissive sweetness that was completely foreign to her nature.

The sarcasm was lost entirely on the eunuch who only stood aside to allow Antonina and Olivia to step into the narrow hallway so that he could lead them to the Imperial box.

The passage was guarded at intervals by officers in the chain-ornamented loricae of the Guard. The air reeked of fish and cooking lamb and humanity. There was a hint of the tang of horses as well, but it was not noticeable in all the rest. The noise made the narrow hallway echo and moan like an enormous seashell held to the ear.

"What does the Empress want of us?" Olivia could not resist asking Belisarius' wife.

"I don't know. She did not inform me that she would want my company during the races, which is most unusual for her. I saw her only yesterday; I should have thought that she might then have said something to me. Such is her habit, you see."

Olivia was well-aware of Antonina's favored status with Theodora, but she checked the pointed observation that rose to her tongue. "It might be news from your husband."

"General Belisarius has made arrangements for me to receive my messages directly from him through the good work of his officers, and therefore it is not likely that Theodora would have any information that I lack. However, yes, there may be news of the campaign that has not yet reached me. That's very likely the case." Her unruffled calm reasserted itself and she moved more easily, her confidence apparent in every aspect of her bearing.

The Imperial box was more than twice the size of the one that Antonina occupied. It was all of pale green marble with the accents in gold. There were several marble chairs and three less imposing wooden chairs provided for those Theodora or Justinian summoned to the box. Theodora herself, resplendent in her jewels and gaudy silk, smiled at the reverence the two women offered her, then motioned to Themistokles. "See that refreshment is provided for my guests."

"How kind of you," Antonina enthused. "I was saying to Olivia that you provide the most tempting food for those you entertain."

"And I," Olivia said, doing her best to be diffident, "said that I almost envied Antonina the delight of your table, and could curse my fortune that made my liver so easily upset that I dare not eat in the company of others for fear I will become ill."

"Ill?" repeated Theodora, who was clearly not used to being refused, no matter how politely.

Olivia hesitated, trying to recall all the good advice her best and kindest lover had offered her over the centuries. He had been able to refuse food and drink so gracefully that those offering had been complimented. Olivia wished now that she could bring some of those elegant phrases to mind. "Most serene Empress," she began, "I am not yet as versed in your ways, or in your language, that I can explain to you what anguish I feel. You have provided an honor I could not have anticipated; to have to limit my participation galls me, yet it would be far worse if I was forced to withdraw from here because I could not remain without disgracing myself."

"How unfortunate," said Theodora, her dark eyes raking over Olivia mercilessly. "I am not used to such . . . intolerances."

"Then you are most fortunate, and I would thank God from my knees every hour if I could say the same thing. I pray that you never learn what I have had to learn, majestic lady." Flattery, especially such overstated and obvious flattery, appalled Olivia, but she could read a degree of approval in Theodora's narrow face.

"You must seek out an Egyptian physician; perhaps there is some medicament you have not yet encountered." She signaled to three of the young male slaves—eunuchs, also, by the look of them—to bring her meal. "Antonina," she said, some of her formality relaxing, "I decided that I did not want to pass the afternoon without company, and when I recalled that you would be here, I thought that you and your guest might be willing to spend your time here with me."

"We are overcome, Theodora," said Antonina, taking on a cozy manner. "When you made no mention of the races the other day, I naturally supposed you would have other plans for the races."

"There were others who my beloved and exalted husband wished to attend, but it has turned out otherwise, and they are all occupied with matters of state." She smiled as low tables were brought.

Below them, the chestnut team swept past the winning marker more than six lengths ahead of the bays. The crowd roared and the sound of feet thumping the stands made all conversation impossible for a short while. Theodora contented herself with watching her slaves offer food and drink to Antonina.

Finally the bray of the buccinae quieted the stands and the Captain of the City Guard presented the winner with a brass wreath made to resemble large hedge roses with exaggerated thorns.

"The people like these displays," said Theodora. "They see themselves winning. And when those they bet for lose, then it is a defeat that costs little more than the price of what was bet." She smiled at Olivia. "I understand that since these wars began, there has been little racing in Roma."

"There has been little everything in Roma," Olivia corrected her quietly.

"That is unfortunate," said Theodora. "And surely you must be overjoyed to see racing again."

"It makes me homesick," she told Theodora. "Long ago, of course, we had much more than horse racing in Roma. The Ludi Maximi were marvels that no one has equaled. Thousands participated, and they went on for three or four days." Her hazel eyes darkened with memory.

"And good Christians were killed, devoured by wild

beasts while the people of Roma shouted their approval."
Theodora looked severe now, and she glared at Olivia as
if she might have been directly responsible.

"All sorts of people were killed, some of them less
valiantly than that. To be torn apart by wild beasts is
hideous, but what of those women who were raped to
death by wild asses?" Olivia looked curiously at Antonina. "What of them?

"They were not . . ." Her words faded and she looked
at Olivia with less distrust. "What happened then could
happen again, under different circumstances. There are
those who lack all sympathy for those who insist on living
apart from the world who do so for reasons that are not
religious. And there is always great curiosity about such
strange behavior. Don't you think so, Antonina?"

Antonina held a cube of broiled lamb over her mouth,
but rather than eat, she set it aside, addressing Theodora
with her most earnest demeanor. "This is precisely what I
have been trying to warn Olivia of, my most majestic
Empress. It would appear that, so far, I have not been
heeded, and that fills me with despair, for it is necessary
that Olivia not be too lighthearted in her anticipation of
these dangers."

"She's right," Theodora said, studying Olivia. "You
don't appreciate how dangerous these matters can be, and
if you decide to ignore the danger, you are being foolish.
From what I have heard of you, you are not a foolish
creature, and so I must think that you are obstinate."

"There is some truth in that," Olivia allowed, her
opinion of Theodora changing slightly.

"A Captain of the army has told me that you are not
the sort of woman to permit herself to be taken advantage
of, either through willful malice or through inept handling." She waited for Olivia to speak, and when her
Roman guest said nothing, she continued, "I think that it
would be wise of you to take his warning to heart. He is
not one to give himself pains except where he has given
his fealty, and where that is given, it binds him unto
death."

"I am aware of that, and I treasure it more than you know," said Olivia evenly.

"I thought that it was otherwise, that he had overestimated you through the depth of his feeling, but I think now that love has perhaps cleared rather than clouded his vision." Theodora sighed. "As one who was not always where I am now, I know what dangers can stalk you. You do not wish to believe the warnings you have had. Let me tell you that they are given with affection and concern."

"Very well." Olivia turned her head so that she could meet Theodora's gaze evenly. "I will not make light of any other warning, and I will take precautions, for the sake of the Captain of the army as well as for my own. I confess that your concern surprises me."

"It is as much for the Captain as for you, Roman lady. Also, you have not sought favor as many in your position have, and this intrigues me." She raised her head. "Ah. They are about to start the second race. Watch! The grays are mine."

As the next race started, Olivia sat back and wondered what the Empress Theodora might want for her warning; the things that occurred to her troubled her more than the warning had done.

*   *   *

Text of a letter in Latin from Ragoczy Sanct' Germain Franciscus.

> *Hail to my treasured Olivia;*
> *I am relieved to learn of your decision to leave Roma. As*

difficult as it is to leave your native earth, there are times that it is the only sensible thing to do, and not simply because you are in the middle of a barbarian invasion. Remember that we cannot afford to attract too much attention to ourselves, for that often brings inquiry that is not to the advantage of those of our blood. As much as the restrictions of Constantinople infuriate you, they are preferable to being hacked to pieces by Totila's soldiers.

The reason it has taken me so long to respond to your letter is that I am moving again. Your letter finally caught up with me after almost a year in coming. I write from Poetovio; I left Pons Saravi over a month ago and have had more difficulties and delays than any I can remember for four hundred years. At the moment I am bound for Trapezus. I may remain there or go on to Rhagae in the Parthian Empire: this in case you decide to write again and are at a loss to know where to send the letter.

Your Captain sounds remarkable and I wish you much joy with him, but I warn you not to withhold your secret too long, for if he is so cherished that you are willing to share blood with him, then he deserves to know what stakes he plays for—in any sense. I know how difficult this can be; I remember my own doubts before I told you what would happen at your death. He will need to prepare, as you prepared, my love. From what you have told me of Constantinople, this may not be easily done.

Take care, Olivia. It would hurt me more deeply than you know if you should come to any harm. Know that you always may find a haven with me if I have one to offer, and know also that no matter where you are, my undying affection and care are with you.

> Sanct' Germain
> through the good offices of
> Huroghac, merchant from
> Mogontiacum traveling to
> Constantinople

• 9 •

Belisarius looked up as the fourth dispatch rider in as many hours thundered into his camp on a lathered horse.

One of his officers, an exhausted boy named Kylanthos, brought the rider to him. "General Belisarius," he said, then took up his post at the entrance to the tent.

The dispatch rider was not as scruffy as the previous three had been and this alone attracted Belisarius' attention. He rose from his narrow trestle table and came forward. "I don't know you, do I?"

"No, General," said the rider, his expression embarrassed.

"There have been so many changes of officers that I am not always sure." His apology was accompanied by a worn smile. "I hope you bring me better news than the others have done, for I am not in a good humor to sustain more disappointments."

"I bring you news from Constantinople. I landed only yesterday and have been in the saddle most of the time since then." He spoke with the zeal of a newcomer and was privately shocked when this announcement did not produce the excitement he anticipated.

"What is it this time?" Belisarius asked, hardly doing more than nodding once to show his respect for the Emperor. "Don't be upset, young man. Most of the men here have been on campaign with short rations for the last five days and we are all feeling hungry and fatigued. What message do you bring me? More delays?"

117

The rider's enthusiasm did not include a denial of the poor provisioning Belisarius' troops had experienced and he could not pretend that the General lacked reason for his behavior. He stood a little straighter and faced the older man. "I bring welcome news then; Captain Hyperion has landed at Rhegium with men, supplies and monies, and they are making their way northward to join with you in the attempt to take Roma from the invaders." He grinned, holding out his dispatches again. "Read for yourself."

Belisarius took the scrolls and broke the seals on all three of them. He read slowly, pausing once to say that his eyes hurt. "I've been on campaign too long, I think," he went on, glancing at the rider. "There are days when by sundown my eyes burn in my head. But for news like this, I am willing to have them turn into living coals."

The rider looked embarrassed. "General . . ."

"I say the same thing to my officers. Or I used to, when I could still remember who they were." He continued to read and shook his head. "More replacements. And they are all unfamiliar to me. Why does the Emperor remove my officers so frequently? How am I supposed to fight with strangers?"

"The Emperor," the rider reminded Belisarius stiffly, "does not need to account to you. If he knows that this must be done, then his will is sufficient."

"Of course," Belisarius said. "But when you have been in the field a while, you will want tested comrades beside you. All soldiers feel that, since those comrades are often all that stands between the soldier and death." He lifted the scroll. "To have eight new officers is all well and good, but nine of my staff are being recalled. They none of them have been with me longer than a year, but they are the closest thing to a cadre that I have now. To learn the ways of the new ones, and for them to learn my ways will take time, and we have little of that." He finished reading the first scroll and set it aside. "Very well, I will prepare for the new officers. This is from the Censor, and I will read the words of Justinian before the Censor's."

The rider nodded, since anything else would be intolerable. "The Censor is devoted to the Emperor."

Belisarius hardly responded; his brows had drawn together and he tensed visibly as he read. "How can! . . ." he burst out once, but read the rest in silence.

"The Emperor is not truly pleased with the progress being made here," the rider said apologetically, revealing that he knew of the contents of the second dispatch.

"That is very much apparent," Belisarius said darkly. "He has been at pains to explain to me."

The rider folded his arms. "General, the Emperor is concerned for what has been happening here."

"That, too, is obvious." He moved abruptly to the door flap of his tent. "But it is not true that I deliberately lost Roma. If I had had the men and the supplies we could have held the city and moved Totila's army back to the north. But without men and supplies my hands were tied. If Justinian believes otherwise then he has poor advisors. Every officer who came to Italy with me was dedicated to winning back all of the old Roman Empire for Justinian. I vouch for every one of them. They desired to serve the Emperor in the field and were willing to give their lives if it were necessary to gain that end. But now, I hardly know the names of the men who carry out my orders, and we have had to wage war with insufficient food and equipment. No army can continue in that way!" He paced the small confines of his tent. "I cannot accept that Justinian does not understand this, but from what he has said to me, it is clear that he does not, or that he does not know how depleted we have been." He sighed abruptly. "I should not say this, least of all to you. I am the Emperor's General, and it is my task to carry out his orders. I have not been able to, and the reasons hardly matter, do they?"

"General," said the rider, "if there has been a misunderstanding, the Emperor is a just man and he will hear you out if you petition him."

"Yes, but he has already heard out others and anything I say will have little weight now. And that does not trouble me as much as his apparent conviction that I have not done my utmost to stop the advance of Totila, given the men and materiel at my disposal." He rubbed his fingers over his brow and pinched the bridge of his nose. "That perturbs me. I have never had my loyalty and devotion questioned before. I don't know what to do to refute these charges."

"You could take Roma again," suggested the rider with a trace of sympathy.

"That is what I have been trying to do for months!" the General burst out. "Ask my men—not the officers, for they have not been on campaign long, but the cavalry and foot soldiers who have served with me since I came here—they will tell you that we have done everything possible under the circumstances. They know, because we have fought together."

"But you have lost ground. Roma is in the hands of the enemy and two ports are controlled by Totila's men." The rider stared at the peak of the tent. "The Emperor has expressed his displeasure with good cause."

"Puppy," Belisarius chided. "You've been shaving for less than a year by the look of you, and you are trying to tell me that we have not fought with determination and valor. Go outside. Look at the men. Most of them are thin because they do not get enough to eat. Half-starved soldiers make poor warriors. Our cavalry is short of mounts and there are no remounts. We have few arrows for our archers, few lances and spears. Each man should have three swords but now the soldiers count themselves fortunate if they have two. Those are the obvious problems. There are others, less visible, that beset us more keenly than hunger."

"You will have supplies when Captain Hyperion joins you," the rider assured him. "And there will be more men. He has brought also sixty horses."

"Sixty," scoffed Belisarius. "All of sixty. Gracious." He laughed. "Sixty will almost supply my men now. It will not begin to provide remounts. This is what I meant when I said that we have insufficient men and materiel."

"What of local farmers?" asked the rider.

"Picked clean months ago, and no longer pleased to help us." Belisarius dropped back into his camp chair. "We have scoured the countryside for food and mounts and equipment and slaves. At first the farmers and landholders were willing to aid us, thinking that we would give them protection and that we would be gone soon, but it has not turned out that way, and they are no longer willing to extend themselves for us. I don't blame them. We have treated them badly. Our men have foraged and raided as rapaciously as the barbarians, and they have excused themselves because it was done to benefit the ones they stole from. Now all the farmers want is for us to be gone."

With a condemning shaking of his head the rider regarded Belisarius critically. "You have not controlled your men as you should."

"If I had tried to control my men in the way you mean, they would have starved to death," countered Belisarius. "It is an easy thing for a man with six slaves in the kitchen and a full larder to condemn what we've done, but let him live with us and try to think himself satisfied on a handful of grain and a few pieces of boiled chicken, because that is what has been feeding my men for the last twelve days. For a while we had some fresh fruit as well, but the orchards are bare now."

"My uncle told me that you were using your men as an excuse to keep from waging battle."

"Your uncle, whoever he is, has no idea of what we have been enduring here," Belisarius informed the young man.

"My uncle is Captain Vlamos of the Imperial Guard," the rider said stiffly and with great pride. "I am Linos, the second son of Linos Aristrades. Captain Vlamos is my mother's brother."

"A good family," said Belisarius. "But none of them have set foot in Italy, and they can have no notion of what has transpired here."

"They are loyal to the Emperor and defend his cause,"

Linos declared, repeating a maxim.

"Yes. I am loyal and I defend him as well. Justinian wishes to restore the boundaries of the Roman Empire and that is the task he has set me. I have said from the first that if I do not succeed it not be for want of effort. If this campaign were not for the Emperor, I would have abandoned it long ago; but since it is Justinian who commands me, I will do everything I am able for as long as there is breath in my body to bring his vision to fruition." He set the second scroll with the first. "I might as well read this last one."

The scroll from the Court Censor was not as long as the other, but it contained a number of questions that the Censor requested Belisarius answer, most of them having to do with statements the General had made that might be construed as being against the wishes and orders of the Emperor. Belisarius flung the thing aside impatiently. "It's nonsense."

Linos stared in surprise. "The Censor does not deal in nonsense."

"In this instance he does," said Belisarius. "It can't be serious." He rose, stretching. "There is food of a sort, and you're welcome to eat with me, but I warn you that the fare is limited and there isn't very much of it."

"I brought my own provisions," Linos said sulkily. "I will not have to deprive anyone of a mouthful of grain."

Belisarius gave the young man a hard stare. "If that is your state of mind, you had better remain in this tent. My men are not going to be very tolerant of such temperament. Nor am I, for that matter."

"I didn't mean . . ." He flushed. "If my supplies would be of help, you're welcome to them." There was a grudging tone to this offer, but Belisarius decided to ignore it.

"Fine. Get whatever you have and give it to my slave Iakis. He's the tall fellow with the pockmarked face and a wedge-shaped scar on his shoulder." He held the flap of the tent up. "After we eat, I will confer with my officers.

You may join us if you wish. They will be relieved to hear your news."

Linos scowled, uncertain whether he was being mocked or not. "What use is that?"

"I don't know yet," Belisarius admitted. "But between your news, which will lift their spirits, and your current information they may be satisfied that the last year has not been in vain." He squinted against the sunlight, averting his head a moment. "Most of them are around that fire, over there. I used to spread my officers through the camp, but now, with so many unfamiliar faces, I need to keep them all in one place."

"Don't you trust them?" asked Linos, shocked.

"Not the way you might think; I do not know them well enough to rely on them without question. I don't know which of these officers reacts too quickly, which too slowly. I don't know who among them is best at night, and who is best before midday. I don't know if one of them is afraid of confinement, or fire, or serpents. I don't know who has a way with horses, or dogs, or peasants. I don't know which of them speaks Latin." He walked as he enumerated his points, pausing now and then to nod or wave to his soldiers. "For that reason, I require my officers to stay near me."

"Doesn't this irritate them?" Linos inquired.

"Not most of them, no, because they are as new to me as I am to them, and there are several of them who have never been on campaign before." He indicated the large fire surrounded by tents, most of them with slaves stationed in front of them. "This is where they are. You can see for yourself that half of them have new gear that has not seen much use. What they lack are horses to carry it, but that is another matter, isn't it?"

Four officers hastened forward as Belisarius approached their campfire, two of them armed with nothing more than short, wide-bladed glavi. They looked at the newcomer with Belisarius, all of them betraying some degree of curiosity.

"This is Linos," Belisarius said, raising his voice so that all would hear him. "He comes from Captain Hyperion who has landed at Rhegium with men and supplies for us."

A growl of approval met this announcement. "I know Captain Hyperion," said one of the younger officers. "He is very good in battle, so they say."

"And where has he fought?" asked one of the others, a trifle older than most of the officers. Another seven men had come up to the space near the fire, for although it was stifling in the heat, it was also the only sensible place to gather.

"He fought in Egypt," Linos said defensively. "He has had experience."

One of the men laughed unpleasantly. "If he has not had some before, he will get some now."

"Regimus," warned Belisarius, "wait until you see the man in action before you condemn him."

"You know the type as well as I do; highborn relatives, ambitious family, purchased promotion and all the rest of it. That's what all the officers are like now. They are puppets of the court." Regimus touched a jagged scar that crossed the bridge of his nose and ran unevenly down his left cheek. "None of them lifted a sword except to practice with slaves."

One of the younger officers bristled. "You don't know that. You're assuming that because you never heard of him that there's nothing to hear."

"Like you, Georgios." The speaker was wearing light-weight leather armor studded with iron.

"You're as bad as Regimus," Georgios snapped. "You and Regimus and Kyrillos and Daidalos and Urien are all the same; just because you've been here longest, you think that means you're the only ones with any knowledge of war and battle."

"That's right," said the armored man. "And you've yet to show me I'm wrong." He indicated Linos. "Is he any indication of what they're sending us now?"

"I don't know," said Belisarius. "I don't have a list of

men being sent yet. I won't see it until we join Hyperion."

"Children," scoffed another of the older men—possibly one of those Georgios had named—"they're sending us children to lead the soldiers. Is the Emperor trying to win the war with youth instead of force of arms, do you think?"

"Urien," Belisarius said sharply, "it isn't for us to question the decisions of the Emperor."

"Does that mean you never doubt the wisdom of what Justinian does?" asked Urien. "I never thought you were a fool before, Belisarius, but perhaps I was wrong. If you don't wonder what Justinian is trying to do, then you are being duped."

Belisarius was standing very straight now and his features were severe. "That is enough. Every man is entitled to his doubts, but no one is permitted to question what the Emperor does or why he does it. Do you all understand this? I do not want to have another set of replacement officers, but I will not oppose what Justinian commands. Is that clear?"

The men said nothing but their expressions were eloquent.

Linos felt suddenly very awkward, like a man who had walked into a house during an argument. He coughed once and said, "There are new officers being posted here, of course. Most of you will be sent home or to other garrisons. The Emperor is increasing the number of his troops in Alexandria."

"Alexandria," said one of the men in disgust. "Egypt! What use is that?"

"The Emperor has decided that there are dangers in Egypt. He believes that there may be attempts to end the strength of Byzantium there." Linos spoke with authority now, having spent much of the last month hearing of these things. "The Emperor wishes to increase the soldiers in Egypt so that those who might be plotting against us will see how foolish they are and desist."

"It might make them more determined," said Belisarius in a distant tone. "But there is no way to be certain of that until the action has been taken."

"Does this mean you do not think that the Emperor has been wise?" Linos was indignant at the suggestion; he glared at Belisarius. "You are his General. How can you question what he does?"

"I'm not questioning it, and I don't doubt his decisions. Christos! if I did, I would not continue this campaign under the conditions we have faced; I could not ask it of my men." Belisarius looked around him, meeting the eyes of each officer in turn. "I only wonder, occasionally, how the Emperor's decisions are seen by others, especially those around him."

One of the officers, a young man with rough bandages covering a large area of festering abrasion, looked directly at Linos with pain-hardened eyes. "If the Emperor thinks that the officers have been taking advantage of him and have used the war to increase their positions, have him come here himself and see how we fare; share our food and our tents with us."

Belisarius held up his hand to silence this objection. "I have tried in my reports to make our predicament clear, but we are not the only ones seeking the aid of the Emperor, and he must answer the needs of all his people, not just his army in Italy."

"And you never doubt him?" Linos inquired.

"Of course; I've said so. But the Emperor is the Emperor and he must be the final authority for all of us." He indicated the poor condition of his men and the camp. "If you were here, riding with us, eating with us—"

"When we eat," muttered one of the officers but Linos did not know who.

"—and living with us, you would have to question what the Emperor commanded us to do. Any sensible man would. But that does not give any of us the right to refuse what the Emperor commands us to do. Is that plain?" Belisarius was more tired than angry, and his words carried little challenge.

"I will see that your sentiments are mentioned in my report," Linos promised stiffly.

"Oh, for the Grace of Angels!" Belisarius brought his fist down on a heap of damaged saddlery. "I am not telling you this for your report. I want you to understand what we are facing here, and why there are problems and discontent, not what you may or may not have to say when you send back your impressions."

The officers moved uneasily and a number of them whispered things to each other without any inclination to include Linos in their observations.

"If you have such uncertainty, then perhaps you would recommend another man command in Italy," said Linos.

"No, I would not." His irritation was changing to wrath. "I have been entrusted with this task and—"

"Yes, entrusted, and you have failed to do what you have been ordered to do," Linos said, made bold by the young officers standing around him.

"Anyone who thinks that this is deliberate has not been here," stated one of the Captains and was seconded by nods and words from the others. "We have nothing, and we cannot go to war with nothing."

Belisarius stopped the man. "Never mind, Gnousos. There is no way to explain this to him." He turned away abruptly and strode back to his tent.

"You might have orders to question the General," said Gnousos when Belisarius was out of earshot, "but you did it as badly as I have ever seen anyone do it. What made you think that you could challenge Belisarius in front of his officers?"

"The Emperor believes that Belisarius is making a force of his own here and that the purpose of these delays is to strengthen himself so that he can march not on Roma but on Constantinople as well and attempt to bring down the government and the Emperor to his own glory and benefit. I am saying this," he went on, "so that any of you who might be aware of such a nefarious plan might clear his conscience by informing me or Captain Hyperion of this and thereby earn not only pardon for yourself but the appreciation of the Emperor for your loyalty." He had been worried what reaction this announcement might receive and was pleasantly surprised when two men gave him quick, penetrating looks. Most of the others were hostile.

"You would do well to keep such announcements to yourself, youngster," said the scarred officer, although he was not much older than Linos. "Here we do not take well to having the General compromised."

"All of you?" Linos asked sharply.

"If there are those who disagree, they know better than to speak of it."

This warning struck home. Most of the officers turned away and on one pretext or another left Linos to himself.

Gnousos asked a question for all of them when he turned back and addressed the messenger in his most casual manner. "If the Emperor did decide to post another General to Italy, who would it be, do you know?"

"It's only a rumor," hedged Linos.

"Who?"

"They say that Narses would be the one to replace Belisarius."

This was met with disbelief and derision. "Narses? The man's a eunuch. What does he know about a long campaign like the one we have here? Who suggested Narses?"

"My uncle, among others," said Linos stiffly. "Narses might not have his generative parts but there is nothing wrong with his brain."

"Narses!" The officer folded his arms and spat. "Gnousos, how would you like serving under him?"

"It's got to be a mistake," Gnousos dismissed the notion. "They might talk about it around the palace, but no one is foolish enough actually to send the fellow here."

"Narses is the first choice," Linos persisted. He looked at the men. "And the Emperor is convinced that there is a plot among Belisarius and some of his officers to seize power. You might keep that in mind when you rush to defend him."

There was a low sound from the officers like a growl,

but they all resumed their departure, taking care to pay very little attention to Linos, who gave an exasperated sigh and settled back to wait for one of the more ambitious officers to come forth with information about Belisarius' activities.

*　　*　　*

Text of a letter from Eugenia to Chrysanthos.

To the officer Chrysanthos who holds the rank of Captain at the Holy Communion barracks.

What can I have said or done that made you think I would be willing to accompany you to Africa under any circumstances whatever? What convinces you that your suit was anything more than a dalliance between us? How could you think that I would be willing to marry you?

You suggest that losing the fortune left to me by my late husband would be compensated by your battle fees and favors you believe will be forthcoming as part of the rewards of your station. How absurd you are. You have little funds now and if you should be killed in battle or maimed, then you would have nothing and I would have sacrificed what little I possess for no reason other than the dubious advantage of a bed partner. That is readily available to me; my late husband's fortune is all that stands between me and penury, and you have nothing to offer in compensation that would have any use to me.

You mention that you are planning to remain in Africa for five years. In five years any contact I have at court will be lost and whatever benefits I might be able to gain will have no more bearing than the money and glory you have yet to win.

While it is true I have enjoyed our time together and I am sorry to lose your favor, it does not pain me sufficiently for me to lose all good sense.

If you decide to continue our meetings, I will expect you to refrain from any mention of your ridiculous offer of marriage. When you return from Africa with your fame and fortune amassed, then it might be worth your while and mine to discuss marriage at that time, but certainly not before then, and not under the conditions that prevail in our lives.

Surely you will realize that you have been most capricious in your offer when you take time for sober thought. I will not be angry and will regard it as the impetuous act of an infatuated man, not a prudent officer.

From my own hand, farewell.

> *Eugenia*

• 10 •

"You should learn to call it Konstantinoupolis," Drosos told Olivia for the third time that afternoon. "You are not in Roma anymore, you are here, and it is fitting that you should learn our ways."

"Konstantinoupolis," she said dutifully. "But in my thoughts it is still Constantinople."

"In time you will change; you'll see."

From their vantage point at the crest of the hill, Drosos could point out to Olivia every part of the city. The afternoon sun turned everything gold and brass, even the ships tied up at the wharves beyond the ramparts and grounds of the royal palace on the Sea of Marmara. At the moment, it was the ships that held his attention. "That one, with the angled sail, is from Egypt. They don't often take to sea in those boats; they use them for river traffic on the Nile, but the larger ones, like that, they occasionally bring here. By the look of it, they're carrying oil and cloth."

"And the one next to it?" Olivia asked, though she tended to find ships uninteresting since she was a very poor sailor and disliked all journeys by water.

"That is from southern Gaul, from Faxinetium, judging by the way the sails are painted. You see those cages on the deck? They probably carried some livestock with them, goats or sheep, given the size of the cages." He grinned at her. "Does seeing these ships make you long for Roma, or are you longing to travel to distant lands?"

"Roma is where I was born. Nowhere else draws me as Roma does." Her eyes grew distant. "That ship beside the Gaul?"

"From Hippo Regius," said Drosos. "In Africa."

"I know where Hippo Regius is," Olivia said but without any heat. "And I have a fair idea where most other noted cities are."

"That is unusual for a woman," Drosos pointed out.

"You're used to another kind of woman," said Olivia a trifle distantly. "In Roma, it was expected that we have some education, since we would have to be able to handle our own affairs."

"Scandalous," said Drosos, teasing her.

She was used to this and refused to respond to his jibes. "It would not be so unfortunate a thing if more of your women here knew a little more of the world." She said it tranquilly and smiled at him as he reached out to touch her hair.

"Let's see: you know most of the palace grounds, don't you? And the Hippodrome is obvious enough. Hagia Sophia and Hagia Irene . . . Now, show me something in

Roma that is as splendid as the dome of Hagia Sophia. You've been down the Mese—I saw no street in Roma so fine."

"You did not see Roma at her best," Olivia reminded him.

"You were fortunate to find a house so near the Augusteum, and in so pleasant a location. For many, even those with sufficient funds, such a place would not be possible." He had mentioned this before and spoke of it now reflectively as he gazed out at the city.

Although the worst of the heat was over the day was still uncomfortably warm and the smell of the place was intense and pungent.

"Come, Drosos," Olivia said as she held out her hand. "I will agree that this is a beautiful setting and were I not a Roman I might well count myself blessed for being able to live here."

"You're shameless, that's what it is." He took her hand in his and walked with her back toward his chariot. "You ought to let me order a palanquin for you."

"Why? You could not show me your precious Constantinople if I were hidden by curtains." She used the Latin word deliberately.

"Konstantinoupolis," he corrected her.

"If you insist." She climbed into the chariot and waited while he gathered up the reins. As he set the vehicle in motion, she shifted her balance with practiced ease. "How long will it take us to get back to my house?"

"Not very long," he said. "We will be there before sunset, if that concerns you."

"Not particularly," she said, not entirely honestly. "I find the day enervating and I long for a bath." Her Roman-style tub was sunk in her native Roman earth and was especially restorative to her.

"You Romans and your infernal, eternal baths." He did not sound condemning as he spoke and he smiled in anticipation.

"You may curse all you wish if you will join me." She watched as a train of heavily laden camels went past them toward the gate that was in the west end of the city but opened on the road to the east, at the edge of the Black Sea.

"Horrible beasts. They spit." Drosos was in a buoyant mood but Olivia could also sense a restlessness, a discontent that lay under his ebullience. "I've ridden them. They sway like a ship in heavy seas."

"How delightful," Olivia said with a laugh. "I will leave them to you and I will keep to horses and chariots, if it's all the same to you."

The streets were more crowded now, and the press of humanity slowed their progress. Drosos held his team to a slow walk, remarking as he did, "These two are used to the city, God be thanked. If I brought my blacks here, I'd have to bring two slaves to lead them, otherwise they'd bolt."

"And then?" asked Olivia. "Where could they go in this crush?"

"Knowing my blacks, they'd try to go up the walls or over the men in the streets." Little as he liked to admit it, even this team of duns was fighting his control.

"Only the men?" Olivia asked with exaggerated innocence.

"Stop that," Drosos said, starting to laugh. "I can't keep my mind on what I'm doing."

The last part of their journey, once they were away from the streets feeding the Mese, went more easily and they reached her house while the sun still hung in the western sky. As Drosos turned his chariot and team over to her grooms, he pointed this out to her.

"You see, even when we must go slowly through the market, we can make good time."

"True enough." She smiled at Niklos Aulirios who opened the door for them. "Have you had any messages brought to me?" It was a regular inquiry and she did not give him her full attention.

"There was a footman from Antonina not long ago. He brought an invitation for a reception she plans to give her husband's returning officers," said Niklos. "I said that if you were able you would attend out of respect for those defending your home."

She smiled at Niklos. "You are a treasure, my friend."

Drosos, who had overheard this, looked outraged. "They have replaced his officers *again*?"

"Apparently," said Niklos, indicating the smaller reception room off the vestibule. "Will you be sitting here, great lady?"

"After bathing, perhaps," said Olivia.

"What has got into the Emperor's mind?" Drosos demanded of the ceiling. "He removes the officers again and again and again and then he becomes angry because there are no victories."

"He might not understand," Olivia suggested gently, guiding Drosos toward the rear of the house where she had had her bath built.

"He ought to understand. It's important that an Emperor understand." He stopped in the middle of the hall and turned toward Olivia, his face darkening. "Unless he is determined that Belisarius have no victories, and then everything he has done becomes sensible."

"It may be," she said, talking as if to calm an excited child. "But you yourself have warned me that there are factions at court that are so tangled in plot, counterplot and conspiracy that no one can think himself safe there." She was able to get him moving again.

"Even so, this is a military matter, not part of court life." He had made fists of his hands and he walked with such determination that Olivia hoped all the doors between here and her bath were open so that Drosos would not have the opportunity to kick them open.

"Military or court, each wields power and those who love power will embrace one as readily as another. Chide me for being Roman if you like, but admit that we Romans know something about playing with power."

"That changes nothing," Drosos declared, his brown eyes growing hot. "If Justinian seeks to restore the Empire to what it was, he'll have to do better than change Belisarius' officers every time someone at court farts."

"If you are certain that he is misled, why not petition him and ask that he hear your views?" They had reached the end of the hall that ran the length of the house, and the door leading to the bath was closed. Olivia adroitly stepped in front of Drosos and opened it.

"Don't be ridiculous," he snapped.

"I'm not being ridiculous," she protested. "Drosos, you are a Captain of the army and you have some knowledge of the whole Italian campaign. Your perspective might be needed if the Emperor is not to be swayed by those who have ambition and family interests to color their advice."

He shook his head several times. "It isn't that simple. This is Konstantinoupolis, and here there are forms that must be served if one wishes to penetrate the court. I would have to speak to the Captain of the Guard. I know Vlamos. He's not a bad sort, but his family is a nest of vipers and they are all eager to see the rest of the nephews and sons and husbands advance. He will give favor to them before he listens to me."

They had entered the main room of the bath where the holocaust warmed the water of the calidarium giving the whole chamber a haziness from steam that was faintly perfumed. There were brushes and robes set out on benches by the tall arched windows that were covered with oiled parchment. Now that it was sunset, they glowed a deep russet. There were four braziers in the room, all lit, lending their brightness to the steam.

"Would you like me to undress you?" Olivia offered.

"No," said Drosos. "I will manage." He began by tugging the end of his pallium free and starting the complicated process of unwinding it. "These things are the very devil, aren't they?"

"I have seen other garments as difficult. Remember the togas of Roma; most men hated them, in part because donning them and taking them off was so involved." She had already loosened her paenula and set the tablion aside. Her dalmatica was looser and more flowing than the Roman version of her youth had been, and she was able to pull it off over her head with ease before Drosos had finished disentangling himself from his pallium.

"You are a beautiful woman," he said, stopping his task and staring at her.

"Generous praise," she responded.

"No praise." He unwound the last part of his pallium and tossed it aside into a disordered heap. "You are lovely."

"And you are besotted." She walked to within two steps of him. "For that I am more grateful than I can say."

"If I were besotted, I would agree with you and be your slave, and I'm neither of those things." He reached out and fondled her breast. "I love your skin."

She smiled. "Just my skin?"

"Right now, just your skin. In a little while, I'll love all of you, the way I love your voice and your wit while we're out on the hills." He was content to keep the distance between them. "Do we have to bathe?"

"Magna Mater! yes, we have to bathe." She laughed but it was clear that she would not be dissuaded.

"More Roman decadence, I suppose," he sighed, mocking both of them. "How can I learn to endure it?"

"You've managed thus far," she reminded him, and went to the edge of the pool.

Her calidarium was oblong, three times her height on one side and twice her height on the other. When she stood upright, the water rose to just above her waist. There was another pool, more than twice the size of this one, a tepidarium where she swam when she was by herself. Both the calidarium and tepidarium were decorated with mosaics of Roman design and she knew that Drosos found them faintly shocking, since they were all of wholly secular subjects.

"Why do you Romans insist on baths?" Drosos asked as he dropped the rest of his clothes onto the bench.

"Because it is pleasant to be clean, and because baths are delightful."

"They glorify the flesh," Drosos said, not able to make this as condemning as he might have wished.

"Yes, they do," she said from the middle of the heated, perfumed water. "Come and glorify it with me."

"You are incorrigible," he said as he dropped into the water, splashing with gusto and embarrassment. "Why is it so necessary that you maintain your Roman ways, Olivia?"

"Do you mind?" She studied him playfully, flicking her fingers and sending a little spray at him.

"No, not really." He moved toward her. "Those tales you told me at your villa. I liked them. All those stories about Nero and Titus and Traianus, you'd think you'd been there."

"And if I were?" She said it easily, almost teasing him. "Suppose I had been there? What then?"

"You would be so old and wrinkled that . . ." His response faltered and he started to laugh. "You're doing it again, making yourself sound ancient."

"And if I were?" Behind her lightness there was firm purpose.

"Then you would not be a natural creature," he replied, sensing the underlying thrust of her question.

"In Roma I said I was not." She watched him carefully.

His laughter was less certain this time. "Are you being capricious?"

"I had not intended to be," she told him, tossing her head with a hint of defiance.

"Then why these hints? Why do you want it to seem that you are so—"

"Alien?" she interjected.

"Roman," he corrected her sternly. "In this city, being Roman is sufficient; if you tell others the outrageous things you've told me, they might not understand, and that would lead to more difficulties than you've had already."

"What I have said to you is only between us." She sighed.

"That's wise," Drosos assured her. "Others might believe your stories."

"Don't you?"

"I believe you are determined to remain as Roman as possible. I wish I knew why."

"Ordinarily I might not," she answered him seriously. "If matters were different I might strive to be much like all the others here. But my only hope of retaining even a scrap of independence is to continue to be a Roman, for if I am not, then the Church and the government will so restrict my actions that life here would quickly become . . . intolerable to me. As it is, they are willing to regard me as merely eccentric—"

"For the time being," Drosos warned her. "If you do not guard your tongue."

"—and that permits me a few . . . excuses that I would not be allowed if I were too willing to be Byzantine."

"That can be dangerous," Drosos remarked affectionately, coming toward her. "If it should be decided that you are too Roman and too eccentric, there are those who will do many things that—" He stopped just before he touched her. "Do not tell them the tales you told me, about the old days of Roma, or how you live. For me. Keep silent." He put his arms around her. "You are like a creature of the sea."

"So are you." She let Drosos and the water support her, feeling the subtle return of energy from the Roman earth that held the bath.

"But you only swim here," he said. "Only here."

"Well, I am not like some urchin, who swims in the sea," she said, making light of her own fear. Water without the protection of her native earth would sap her strength faster than the rays of the sun if she took no precautions against them.

"Nothing about you is like an urchin. You're a bit of a hoyden, riding in an open chariot through the streets where everyone can watch you, but that is Roman of you, isn't it?" He nuzzled her neck, lifting her to him. "Like this scandalous bath."

"You like all the scandalous things I do," she reminded him, and returned his kiss with ardor.

"I like you, and some of what you are is scandalous,"

he corrected her when he could, and moved her away from him a bit, not wanting to be finished with her too quickly.

"A fine distinction, but I like it," she said. Her skin was growing rosy from the heat and the light of the braziers cast a ruddy glow over the water and their wet bodies.

"The pope at headquarters would find all of this very disturbing." He sank down so that only his head was above the water.

"Then don't tell him," she suggested, pleased that he no longer resisted her Roman ways.

"Is that what they tell you in Roma; do not confess to your priests?" He flicked water at her and chuckled as she returned the favor.

"They tell us many things in Roma; they always have. It is understood by many that if confessing would put a burden on the priest, then one must trust that God will be compassionate, since He has made man the creature that he is." She slid down beside him and reached out to him. "Why talk of priests and popes?"

"You worry me, Olivia, when I come to my senses." He sounded amused but there was trouble lurking at the back of his large brown eyes. "I fear that I will bring you . . . problems."

"How could you do that? And why?" Her tone was light and playful; her hands moved over his body, darting and light as fish.

"It might happen," he said, his mood darkening. "I might say something, or someone might spy on us—that happens more than you would think—or there could be rumors."

"What rumors? Who is to start them?" She moved closer still and her touch became more insistent.

"Everyone talks, everyone whispers. And you are a foreigner, a Roman—"

"A decadent Roman," she corrected him, catching the lobe of his ear gently in her teeth.

"I'm not joking, Olivia," he said, trying to be stern without much success.

"I know that, and I am hoping to change your mind, at least for a little while." Her hair was damp now and there were soft curls forming around her face, making her seem as young as a girl. "Even if you are right, there is nothing we can do about it right now. So long as we are together, we can take pleasure in each other." She kissed his mouth softly, her lips barely parted. "Drosos?"

"We must speak of it eventually," he insisted, making a valiant last attempt to hold her off from him.

"And eventually we will. For the time being, there are other things we can do." Her kiss was deeper this time, and when their tongues touched, she slid her arms around his chest and brought her legs up around his waist.

With a happy groan he embraced her, his objections fading from his thoughts, and for some little time there were only the sounds of their passion and the splashing of the water in the low and burnished light.

When they finally emerged from the bath, languor had touched them both. They smiled as they pulled on the robes that waited for them, and they found excuses to reach out to each other frequently.

"Here; I'll tie that for you," Olivia offered as Drosos took up the long sash.

"Nothing complicated," he said, handing the long narrow band of silk to her. "That pallium was enough for tonight."

"Don't worry," she said, efficiently crossing the sash over one shoulder and then around his waist. "See? As simple as you'd find on a honey-seller's slave."

"Am I to take it that I am your slave?" he inquired with feigned hauteur.

"No; I do not want anyone who comes to me through compulsion." Her answer was serious, but her face was filled with joy.

"You could become that to me, you know." Again the worry was back in his eyes.

"Then we must take care to keep variety and novelty in what we do and how we do it," she said. "You do not want us to turn all we have into nothing more than a frenzied routine, do you?"

"You speak as if it has happened to you," he said, still troubled.

"Yes, it has," she said candidly as she indicated the door. "Come. Niklos will have supper set out for you—nothing too heavy. He said that the cooks have bought some excellent fish, and that with olives and garlic should be waiting in my private reception room." She walked a little ahead of him, turning now and then to look at him.

The house glowed with braziers; her private reception room was no exception. The promised meal waited on a low brass-topped table, and a flask of wine stood open beside the serving dishes. There were two large vases filled with flowers, and before the small ikonostasis a thread of incense curled up toward the ceiling, smelling of sandalwood.

"This is more Konstantinoupolitan than Roman," Drosos said as he sat at the single place laid. "But this refusal to dine with your guests . . . when I am the only one."

"Romans often did not dine with their guests, but served them and saw to the pleasure of those who reclined on couches at their invitation," she said, then added, "and you know my habits too well to continue to question them."

He lifted his shoulders in a gesture of resignation, but he said to her, "Olivia, think of what your slaves say."

"They say I am a Roman widow, which is entirely correct. They say that I run my household in the Roman manner, which is also true. They say that I do not live as most women in this city live, and I do not dispute that. What else can they say that might trouble you?" She poured wine into a silver cup and held it out to him. "Here."

"I prefer you to the wine," he told her, his eyes darkening with the remnants of his passion.

"If that is what you want, then you may have it, but after you have eaten, if you please."

He capitulated with an easy smile. "Are all Roman women so determined?"

"Those who have lived as long as I have are," she said, her eyes fixed on her distant memories.

"You are not going to start on that again, are you?" He was taking the flat bread on the nearest plate and stopped in the act of breaking it in half. "You always do your best to make it seem that you were around when Roma was founded."

She smiled. "Well, I won't claim that," she said, and moved the small dish of salt nearer to him.

"Good. I wish you would forget the whole thing." He dipped the edge of the bread in salt when it was broken. "You can be quite impossible."

"Thank you." She leaned back to watch him eat. "And you; how do you think of yourself, Drosos? You are fairly young to be a Captain, aren't you?"

"For a man with the few connections I have, yes I am," he said between bites. "If my family were better allied, then it might be different, but since my greatest advocate has been Belisarius, I have found my promotions in war, not in court."

"And Belisarius?" she asked.

"He is the finest General in all the Empire," Drosos said with total conviction. "He was fortunate enough to marry Antonina, and gain the good opinion of the Empress through her. Not that he did not already have the confidence of Justinian, or the marriage would not have been tolerated." He had helped himself to more of the wine.

"And what will this gain you, if the Emperor continues to deal with Belisarius as he has been doing for the last two years?"

"You are the most persistent female," Drosos chided her with laughter. "What is it that makes all you Romans think that you invented politics?"

"Didn't we?" she asked sweetly.

"The Greeks did," he corrected her. "And they knew better than to permit their women to take part in them." He broke off another section of fish. "If you continue to pursue these questions, there are questions that will be asked of you that you will not want to answer," he said, growing serious again.

"Why?"

"You are a foreign woman and you are not willing to live properly," he said. He stopped eating to look at her with great concern. "You are here on tolerance; you admit that yourself. You cannot yet return to Roma, for the war there is worse than it was when you left. What use is it to endanger yourself more than you already have?"

"I don't see that discussing politics will make my life any worse," she said, but with less determination than she had shown at first. "Are you really convinced that it could be dangerous?"

"Yes. I wish you would believe that and be careful," he replied. "I would not like to see you come to any harm, Olivia. You are much too important to me."

She leaned over and kissed him on the cheek. "All right; I'll try to control my urge to explore politics, at least for the time being."

"That's not good enough," he objected.

"As long as you are here, I will do what I can, but if you are posted to . . . oh, to Nikopolis or Patara or Syracusa, then it might become prudent for me to find other sources of information. As it is, I will fully expect you to keep me informed of anything that might impinge on me to any degree. Will you do that?"

"If you will give me your word that you will not enlist others in this project," he said, finishing the last of the wine. "I am certain that you could be very unhappy if you came under the scrutiny of the Court Censor. You may believe that or not as you wish, but I am a Konstantinou-politan and I have seen how determined the Censor can be. There are whole families living in obscurity because one member aroused too much suspicion and it tainted everything that the others said and did." He scooped up some of the fish with the bread. "You have an excellent cook."

"So I understand," she said.

"Well?" he asked after a little silence.

"I will keep everything you've said in mind," she promised, and clapped her hands to summon Niklos Aulirios with the sweetened fruit pulp offered at the close of the meal.

* * *

Text of a letter from the slave Simones to the secretary of the Court Censor, Panaigios Chernosneus.

To the most excellent Panaigios Chernosneus, secretary of the Court Censor, with full dedication and respect, hail upon the Eve of Lent in the Lord's Year 547.

True to your instruction and the good of the Empire, I have carried out your most recent instructions and have examined the books and similar writings currently in the possession of my master the General Belisarius who is at present still in Italy. The volumes I have examined are in the General's house here in Konstantinoupolis and are available to any who wishes to venture into the reading room. None of them are under lock and key and those few books that are remain so more for reasons of market value than content, as in the case of the copy of the Edicts of Constantine dating from the time when the capital was moved from Roma to this city. The texts are in Latin and as I am not familiar with that language, I can say little of the contents but that they appear to be complete and from what I can learn of Andros, the slave caring for the library, there is no reason to suspect that they contain anything other than what their titles indicate.

As to volumes that could be considered questionable, there is a text in Persian, which I am told my master does not speak but which Andros reads well, on the practical treatment of wounds in battle and at field stations. The entire purpose of the work is to provide those reading it with methods to limit the damage of bleeding, broken bones, deep injuries and infection. Andros has said that the master has looked at it from time to time and once declared that it was superior in the matter of herbs for packing fresh wounds. If there are other reasons for this interest, I do not know what they are, nor do I imagine that they are significant.

There are three books in Latin on the breeding and training of horses, with emphasis on quality of bones and hooves as compared to speed. Since General Belisarius has often expressed his opinions on the quality and condition of the horses he has purchased it is not surprising that he would keep this in his records, though the Censor has declared that the nature of the material covered is not fitting for a true Christian to read. It is my belief that if the General were aware of this, he would find less offensive texts in regard to horses.

The Censor has indicated that books originating in the lands east of the Black Sea are especially questionable, and it is my understanding that there are four books in the library that were brought along the Old Silk Road, although I do not know which was their place of origin, nor have I been able to locate such volumes, although Andros has told me that they do exist and that they are valued by our master in that they have to do with the various methods of battle used by peoples inhabiting the lands that the Old Silk Road traverses. It is his opinion that he must be prepared to counter every possible attack, and for that reason he has actively sought out all material he can find on the subject of war and its conduct. He has prided himself on discovering more material than most of those other officers of his rank who serve the Emperor. Since I do not know which these are and if I did, I would not know how to study what they say, I can only take the word of Andros and repeat to you what I have been told.

There are six Egyptian books, very ancient, on fortifications and the methods of siege which General Belisarius has had occasion to show to me in the past, and which I have asked Andros to indicate. I am aware that these are regarded as being more questionable than some of the others because of the heretical practices of the Egyptians who claim to be Christians. Since these texts are said to be older than the coming of the Lord, then it would seem to me that most of what they say is not so much colored by the vile distortions of the Egyptians as we know them today, but far more the product of the old Egyptians, who were the ones who held the people of Moses and so terribly abused the captive Israelites during the time they were made slaves of the Pharaoh Emperors, and this I can well imagine might be detrimental to true faith. Upon your order I will have these volumes removed and brought to you for examination and review so that any heresy that might have been taught in these writings may be identified and its influence expunged.

In devotion of purpose, I am always at your service and the service of the Empire which all of us, including my master, serve.

> By my own hand
> Simones
> slave of the General Belisarius

• 11 •

It was a sullen morning, with enormous dark clouds piling up over the water and crowding over the city. The air was heavy with them; the streets felt their weight.

Three Guards surrounded Niklos Aulirios as they made

their way through the breathless silence toward the grounds of the palace. They had said little since they presented themselves at Olivia's house, but it had been enough to fill the majordomo with gnawing fear.

"This is the bonded servant of the Roman woman," announced the oldest of the Guards as they brought him to one of the side gates in the palace walls.

"He is expected; bring him." The lavishly dressed eunuchs led the way into the palace, apparently taking delight in finding the darkest and most twisting corridors to reach their destination, and when they arrived at the vaulted room with an ikonostasis at both ends, they indicated the Guards should remain.

"It is always uncertain when one questions a foreigner," said the largest eunuch in a high, shrill voice.

"My name is Niklos Aulirios," he said a little too loudly. "My name is Greek."

"And you admit that you have lived in Roma since you were a boy, and that you have no sense of being Greek," said the eunuch bluntly. "It is fitting that we speak with you before we extend our inquiries to your mistress."

Niklos fell silent at once, his mind working furiously as he tried to think of some way in which to warn Olivia. He dreaded what the next hour would bring and he could think of no way to divert the attention of the Censor from her. He lowered his head and took up the position he knew the Censor's staff would regard as prayer.

"It will not be long. If you are seeking solace, your prayers had better be short ones." That was the second eunuch, who had a face so beautiful that it was a shame it was wasted on him and not given to a girl.

"Thank you," said Niklos with outward humility and concealed anger. "I have faith that God will hear my petition no matter how brief it may be."

"Indeed." The second eunuch exchanged glances with his colleague. Both nodded once and the younger one stepped up close behind Niklos. "What do you pray for?"

"Compassion," he said. "Deliverance."

"Deliverance? From the Court Censor who is the

devoted son of the Church?" mocked the eunuch, his horror tinged with malign glee.

"No, deliverance from my enemies and the enemies of my mistress," Niklos said, doing his best to keep his anger under control, remembering the many times he had given way to it and had bitterly regretted doing so later.

"What enemies does a simple majordomo have?" asked the larger eunuch.

"I do not know; that is why I pray to God to deliver me from them since it would appear there is nothing I can do alone." He kept his head bowed over his hands.

"There is nothing we can do alone, ever. They teach you heresy in Roma, you Roman with a Greek name." The larger eunuch cocked his head to the side and regarded Niklos with expectant patience. "Is your mistress similarly misled?"

"I do not speak of faith to my mistress," said Niklos, holding himself more rigorously in check.

"Too presumptuous? It might save her soul, and what then? Does not the welfare of her soul exceed the bounds of propriety?" The smaller eunuch was definitely enjoying himself now, goading Niklos with practiced ease.

"If I could be certain that what I had been taught of salvation was utterly true and that my understanding of it was perfect and my explanation of it was completely clear and without error on my part in telling of it and without error in what was heard, then I would not let the limitations of propriety keep me from addressing anyone, my mistress, any pope, the Emperor himself, with what I knew. But my knowledge is imperfect and I do not speak with the tongues of angels, and so I will remain as I am and strive to learn more that one day I might come to such understanding, if it is the will of God that I do." He wanted to rail at them, to accuse them of harassing him and his mistress, of conduct so improper that everyone would be disgusted if they knew of it, but that would only serve to put him in greater danger, as well as causing Olivia more distress than what she suffered already. He bowed his head and added, "I therefore must commend myself to God and the Holy Spirit and pray that they will read what is in my heart since I doubt I can speak it clearly enough for you to comprehend it."

"Humility, and from a Roman," marveled the larger eunuch.

"From a Greek bondsman," corrected the other. "You can tell he's Greek by the eloquence."

One of the Guards giggled.

"Greek or Roman, I observe the dictates of Christianity," said Niklos sharply.

"Curious wording," observed the smaller eunuch. "He observes the dictates of Christianity. He does not profess his faith."

"That is something that only God can know," said Niklos. "I do what I can to live as a good Christian lives, I strive to do evil to none and to aid those I can, I pray for guidance, but does that make me a Christian? Not if what I have been taught is true, and only the state of my soul—which I cannot know, being a man—reveals whether or not I am Christian." He decided he had better not continue this argument, or he might be regarded with more hostility for daring to interpret Christianity and its teachings.

"Very facile," said the smaller eunuch. "They are great politicians in Roma, aren't they? I hear that the Bishop of Roma has regular debates on doctrine, as if that were required of the popes of the Church."

"I am not privy to what the Bishop of Roma does or does not do," Niklos said. "I listen to the priest who preaches, or who preached at the villa of my mistress, and from that I try to gain understanding."

"And favor?" suggested the larger eunuch.

"I wasn't aware that such was the purpose of being a Christian, except the favor of God." It was a sharper answer than he had given before and as soon as he said it, he knew he had overstepped the bounds.

"A sharp-tongued servant is a disgrace to a household," stated the larger eunuch with a significant nod toward the Guards who remained in the room. "If you were a bondsman in this household, you would be whipped for your insolence."

"My mistress does not flog her servants except for criminal acts," said Niklos, attempting to show humility again. "It is her practice to encourage our speaking out so that complaints may be dealt with before they become so significant an issue that they cannot be resolved."

"When that happens, the slave is sold," the smaller eunuch declared. "That is how it is done here."

"But my mistress, as you have said and as I have said, is a Roman lady, and it is her practice to conduct herself as a Roman." Niklos looked at the Guards. "Have either of you served in the Italian campaign?"

The Guard with scarred knuckles answered. "I served there for a year."

"Then you will vouch for what I say," said Niklos. "The Romans are not like you Konstantinoupolitans, and they have other standards for their dealings with their slaves and servants. I am used to those ways, as is Olivia Clemens, and we are not yet accustomed to the manners of this city." He looked to the Guard once more. "You have seen Roma? You know how Romans live?"

"I have seen Roma, but the people were leaving in droves and everyone said that the times were remarkable." He cleared his throat. "Still, we heard enough and saw enough that I will agree with what you say; the Romans do manage servants and slaves in ways that we do not." He addressed the eunuchs. "He is freespoken, but it is not so strange in a Roman."

The larger eunuch glared. "You may be correct, but that does not mean that suspicion is therefore diverted from the Roman woman, or from this bondsman." With that declaration, he folded his arms and fell silent.

"Why do you seek to defend your mistress?" demanded the smaller eunuch, then stopped himself as the door opened and a tall, elegant man came into the room. He was partially bald and so thin that he appeared to be perpetually in profile, his body angling away from his hips as if he were slightly bent. His face was lined but expressionless. Both eunuchs made him a deep reverence.

The tall man paid them no heed but directed all his attention to Niklos Aulirios. "I am Konstantos Mardinopolis," he announced, as if the name carried impact.

"You are not the Censor," said Niklos.

"No, but I am his nearest associate," said the tall man. "He has entrusted me with this inquiry." He indicated the eunuchs. "You may be certain that these faithful servants will bear witness to what we discover."

"How fortunate," said Niklos, his face revealing nothing of his misgivings.

"In other circumstances we would conduct this through the eunuchs themselves, but since your mistress is a lady of dignity and fortune, it has been decided that my presence is required." He took a seat at the long table and ostentatiously unrolled a sheet of vellum. He then set out an inkstand and a stylus. "I will make notes of what is said and the eunuchs will sign what I have written if they judge it to be accurate for what has passed between us."

"May I see your record, as well?" asked Niklos.

"It will be read to you," Konstantos said. "You will find that is enough protection." He looked up, his features still set and without any feeling. "That will suffice, won't it?"

"If you put down what is said accurately and completely, I do not see why it should not be." He straightened himself and waited. "I am at your disposal."

Konstantos did not speak at once, but took his time in writing the circumstances of the examination on the sheet before him, unaware that Niklos was able to read what was there. "It has come to the attention of the Censor that your mistress has made the acquaintance of the Empress Theodora."

This was not the question Niklos had anticipated, and he was startled enough to stammer when he answered. "S-she has, through the wife of Belisarius."

"That would be Antonina," said Konstantos unnecessarily. "And we are aware that when they met, the Empress Theodora made reference to enemies that might attempt to discredit your mistress. Perhaps you will tell us who these enemies are."

"If I knew, I would. I am my mistress' majordomo, but I do not share her confidences," he lied. "If she has knowledge of enemies, she has not told me of them. I do know that she was surprised by the warning, and took it much to heart because it came from the Empress herself."

"If you do not know what enemies these are, why did your mistress heed the warning?"

"Would you not heed a warning from the Empress?" countered Niklos. "To do less would be insulting to Theodora."

"That is true. Yet since your mistress has taken no additional action, we must assume that she does not believe that the warning was genuine." He stopped speaking to write. "What can you say to that?"

"I do not know what my mistress has decided. It is not for me to question her." He made a sign of protection.

"Why do you speak so?" asked Konstantos as blandly as possible.

"To do anything else would be disrespectful and improper." He stared at the stylus as it moved over the vellum and he wanted to correct the words that appeared there, but dared not. "It is important to remember that I am her bondsman," Niklos went on, still reading upside down. "Here in Konstantinoupolis you are more stringent about these things than are most Romans; surely you know that I would be exceeding my station to require any explanation of my mistress in regard to her conduct in this or any other matter."

"Surely," murmured Konstantos.

The questioning continued for most of the afternoon, and when Niklos was finally escorted back to Olivia's house he was more shaken than his demeanor revealed. He dismissed the Guards with aplomb that was far from genuine, and took care to wait a while before seeking out Olivia, for he was convinced that at least one of the household slaves was spying for the Censor or one of his officers.

"You were gone quite a while," said Olivia when

Niklos finally answered her summons to wait upon her in her reception room.

"Yes," he agreed.

"For good reason, I suspect," she said casually, having caught his slight warning gesture as he entered the room.

"The officers of the Censor were seeking information," he said carefully.

"About me as well as you?" She was certain of it but knew enough not to make this too apparent.

"Yes, and to discourage any comments on the early life of the Empress Theodora." This had been part of the inquiry and Niklos knew he was safe discussing it.

"Oh, you mean the rumors one hears about public dancing and harlotry," said Olivia with faint laughter. "It is always thus, isn't it, when a woman who is not born noble catches the fancy of an Emperor. No one takes such gossip seriously."

"That is what I said," Niklos told her, making a sign to let her know that they were being overheard.

"I hope so. Think of all the tales you have heard about me over the years. You are my majordomo and you know how I spend my time, and with whom, and yet you have been told of my many lovers, most of whom I have never met. I trust you made it clear that I put no stock in such . . . speculations. I assume it comes from envious fools who do not know how fine a woman Theodora is, or how great is Justinian's love for her."

Niklos nodded encouragement. "I hope I conveyed some of your thoughts. There was also some concern about your life before you came here."

"The same questions as you were asked about Theodora?" guessed Olivia.

"To some extent. The Court Censor is aware that Drosos is your lover, but there has been some hint that there are many others and that you are nothing more than a loose woman who has tricked everyone into believing you are noble." It was one of the questions that Konstantos had repeated in many forms and Niklos knew that it was important to still such speculation.

"Let them go to the tombs by the Via Appia and see those of the Clemens and my husband's family; Clemens and Silius are old and exalted names in the history of Roma, and I can show documents going back to the time of the Caesars that prove my claims." She sounded more indignant than she was—her greatest emotion was cold fear.

"Sadly, there have been so many records destroyed thanks to the raids of Totila's army it may be no longer possible to produce the proofs you mention," Niklos said, lifting one brow to let her know that this was the story he had held to. "Ever since we learned that the villa had been gutted, I have lost all hope ever to find your family records again."

"Ah," she sighed, her relief more genuine than the distress she tried to show. "It is sad to see so many things lost. The villa . . . how I will miss it."

"And the material you have lost—that is important, too." He leaned forward and said in an undervoice, "Olivia, you are in danger. Be careful what you say."

"Yes, it is important," she said, cocking her head toward the door. "There are other estates that I will probably never recover. How fortunate that my late husband will never learn of this, for he was a man of great pride, as were all the Silii."

"Will you make an effort to recover the estates?" Niklos already knew the answer but wanted Olivia to answer it for the benefit of whoever was listening.

"I doubt if Totila will honor my request, but once his forces have been routed, then I hope that the Bishop of Roma will accept my petition and see that my lands are restored." She paused. "At least in Roma I may still present such petitions in person. Here I would have to wait until my sponsor chose to act on my behalf."

"Mistress, I beg you, do not challenge the order here." He made a gesture to encourage her to go on.

"It is not for you to tell me what to do, Niklos, and you would do well to remember this. I have not made it any secret that I am dissatisfied with the restrictions that have been placed upon me since I left Roma, and I will not pretend that I have come to terms with the position in which I find myself. You may be right and it might be prudent for me to make my peace with the requirements of this city, but I cannot. I am a Roman woman, I am a nobleman's widow and I am not accustomed to the hindrance I find here." She saw Niklos motion for more, and so she went on. "If there are no other means to regain my property, then I suppose I must accommodate the laws here but it galls me."

"Mistress, be cautious," said Niklos, again gesturing to her for more objections.

"Why? Because it is inconvenient for you, or for some of the Byzantines? What is it to me if there are popes in this city who believe that it is improper for women to have property of their own? You tell me to bide my time, but I wonder to what purpose. I hold your bond, Niklos, and as long as I do, you are beholden to me. I will not tolerate opposition and insolence from you." She brought her hand down on the small table beside her low chair. "Keep that in mind, you arrogant Greek."

Niklos gave her a thumbs-up as he said, "Mistress, I think only of your welfare."

"You think only of your own welfare, you mean. You are trying to curry favor with the officers of the Court Censor. I will not have it."

"You're wrong, mistress," he said, flashing her a smile. "I would never do such a—" He broke off and moved silently to the door, waiting. "Whoever it is has left."

Olivia's manner changed as abruptly as Niklos'. "How bad is it?"

"We must be very careful, and we must be always on guard. There are spies everywhere." He sat down opposite her. "They are going to make inquiries about you in Roma."

"I have no worries there," said Olivia. "There are enough people to testify that I have been living as a widow for some time, and I think that the Bishop of Roma has some of the old records on my land claims, since I have leased sections of it to the Church from time to time." She took a deep breath. "I'm glad I did that, now."

"The Court Censor is afraid that you might be part of a conspiracy," Niklos went on.

"Magna Mater, who could think such a thing?" Olivia asked the ceiling. "What would I gain from it, and who would I conspire against?"

"They think that everyone associated with Belisarius might be aiding him in overthrowing the Emperor," said Niklos with a slow shake of his head.

"That's ridiculous," said Olivia. "I can't take such ideas seriously." She hesitated. "Yes, I can."

"Then do so," warned Niklos. "And be aware that whatever you say might be reported."

"Accurately?" she asked at once.

"I don't know," admitted Niklos. "Most of what was recorded of the examination I had this afternoon was put down in more or less true form, but there was a slant to it, just in case. I think they are preparing material in case they need it."

"Why?" said Olivia.

"Because they are trying to discredit Belisarius. He is too popular with the army and the Guard. Justinian is not a fighting man, and there are those who say that if the Empire is to be restored it will be through battles and conquest. For this they will have to have a soldier on the throne. At least that is what the Court Censor appears to think." He leaned back. "These questions were slipped in between those about your genealogy and rumors about the Empress Theodora, and yet the answers I gave to them were more completely recounted than any others."

"Ah," said Olivia. Her hazel eyes grew tired. "I wonder why— Who will benefit if Belisarius is discredited?"

"Those close to the Emperor. In that I think your friend Drosos is correct. There are factions at court that strive for power that they cannot have if Belisarius remains where he is; he must be brought down so that they can gain access to the army through various officers. If the eunuch Narses does indeed replace Belisarius, then there are many who could take advantage of this change and see men of their family advance in the ranks and in military influence." Niklos rubbed his jaw. "I used to think that Roma was bad, but they are amateurs compared to these Byzantines."

Olivia got up from her chair and began to pace. "I can't let them inquire too closely. If they ever found out all there is to know about me, they would have me stoned in the marketplace, and once my spine was broken, I would die the true death at last."

"We could leave Konstantinoupolis." The suggestion lacked any conviction.

"So soon after arriving? That would attract more attention than we have already." She halted, her eyes fastened on the ikonostasis. "I wish I could find a way to profess my conversion to the religious life, but it isn't practical."

Niklos laughed. "No, a vampire is not often welcome in a religious retreat. And you would be noticed, after a while."

Reluctantly Olivia joined in the laughter. "And I doubt I could convince anyone it was my way of taking communion, although in a way, it is."

"That would be worse than the rest." He met her eyes seriously. "You must be careful, Olivia. It grows more and more dangerous for you here."

"And elsewhere," she said. "I wish we had not left Roma, but I know it was necessary."

"Yes," said Niklos. "And while we are here, I will do what I can to be alert. If I knew who in the household was spying on you, I would do what I could to keep watch over that person and be sure that the information he got was carefully controlled."

"But you don't know, and neither do I. And if we are too obvious in trying to find out, it will only serve to make matters worse for us both." She touched his arm affectionately. "We are strangers surrounded by enemies," she said softly. "We must depend on one another more than ever."

Niklos nodded gravely. "You can rely on me, Olivia."

"And you can rely on me, Niklos." She gave a sudden, fleeting grin. "What mere mortal has a chance against the two of us?"

"Do you want me to make a list?" he answered without a trace of humor.

Outside there was a sudden shouting in the street and the rush of footsteps. Both Olivia and Niklos listened with hushed alarm.

"No," she said when the footfalls were gone.

"Nor I," he agreed.

In a distant part of the house, they heard a door close softly.

* * *

Text of a letter from Antonina to Eugenia.

In anticipation of the festivities to come, Antonina sends her warmest greetings to Eugenia and wishes to tell her how pleased she is that Eugenia will be able to attend the celebration that will take place in eight days.

Naturally, most of the guests will be officers of Belisarius, recently returned from the Italian campaign. It is appropriate that they have such distinction for their action on my husband's behalf, and doubtless I will be able to learn more of what has transpired since I had my last letter from my husband.

Not to be too blatant, Eugenia, this will give you a wonder-

ful opportunity to meet men of rank and ambition who are sensible to the realities of court life and the lives of those close to the court. There are certain to be officers who are of a good age to marry who seek a woman with some skill in court matters and proper conduct for the level of society to which they all aspire. There may be a few, also, with better connections than either of us may easily boast of. Those will be of special interest to you, I am sure, and you will do well to come a trifle early so that we may see who among those who have accepted will be most interesting to you. Since you are to serve as my companion, there is no bar to your addressing any of the guests, or to being the first to speak if that is what you wish to do.

Lamentably, Empress Theodora will not be with us. Her health is not what it should be, and her physicians are forbidding her almost all public appearances. I have heard it said by certain malicious and unwise persons that she is paying the price of her early debauchery, and that the illness that is overtaking her is the result of all she did before she became the love of the Emperor. Even if this were true—and it is never wise to think the worst of the Empress, no matter who she is—it is most shortsighted of those speaking against her to do so, for if she recovers, or if Justinian learns of these allegations then the results might be severe.

On that note, let me advise you to be very circumspect in what you say about Theodora. Not only are there spies everywhere, but considering the circumstances, you will be well advised to keep your opinions to yourself, no matter what they are, for until it is established how ill Theodora truly is, no statements about her can be thought safe.

You were wise to break off with Chrysanthos when you did, but of course you will see him here at the celebration. If there should be any trace of awkwardness, you have only to seek me out and I will deal with him appropriately.

At my husband's request, I have asked Olivia Clemens to come, and she has accepted. We will do what we can for her, but she insists that she is not searching for a husband. But then, she has taken Drosos for her lover, and doubtless for the time being she has little need of one. If her sponsor should question her choice, then it might be different, for she could find her money withheld on the grounds that she is using it immorally. That might prove drastic, and all she need do then would be to marry Drosos and put her fortune in his hands instead of her sponsor's, but so far she has shown herself reluctant to do this.

I want to advise you to wear something in light red with a good deal of gold and pearls. Not only is this most fitting in terms of the occasion, but I have learned that Justinian has said that he considers wearing pearls to be a tribute to his wife, and if that is the case, we are in an excellent position to make the most of this without seeming to be courting favor. Also, have your hair dressed with restraint; it is sometimes thought frivolous of widows to be too extravagant, at least that is what Theodora told me the last time we spoke, which was ten days ago. She had some very good advice that I will pass along to you. She said that few men really admire caprice except in a brief infatuation. If a woman seeks to secure a marriage contract then she must show herself sensible and determined for the good of her husband and those around him. We have discussed this before, of course, but I think that you do not always bear it in mind, and that is a mistake, my dear Eugenia. You continue to put men to the test with sudden and outrageous demands, and this cannot help you in your search. Try to be a little less fanciful in your dealings with men, especially these men, for it serves you ill to imagine more than has been offered. You might see if Drosos is willing to become intimate with you, for if he is not going to marry Olivia, he might as well marry you, for he stands in my husband's good favor and is a man of promise as well as some little fortune of his own.

We will speak of this further when you come, and in the meantime, select your most luxurious clothes of red and gold, and let me advise you to wear the pearl-inlaid tablion, the large one with the rubies in the sigil of Christ.

This by messenger at midafternoon with my affection,

Antonina
wife of General Belisarius

• 12 •

By sunset Pope Sylvestros had reached Ostia, and as he waited to pass through the Porta Romana, he watched the carrion birds feast on the bodies of Ostrogoths hanging from the city walls.

"Name?" demanded a grizzled officer, grubby, unshaven and red-eyed.

"Pope Sylvestros," he answered. "From Constantinople."

"Business, Priest?"

"I am here to speak with a ship owner," Pope Sylvestros answered vaguely.

"Pass," grunted the officer.

At another time Pope Sylvestros might have taken time to criticize the laxness shown by the officer, but not now; he was not eager to be more closely questioned about his purpose here in Ostia. Meekly he did as he was ordered, and found himself in the narrow streets of the old port city.

At the far end of the old wharves there was a tavern known as The Seagull. It had been there more than three hundred years and had established its own particular fame among the sailors who made up its patrons.

Pope Sylvestros waited there at an evil-smelling table by the smaller fireplace. He held a cup of wine which he had been nursing long enough to earn him several nasty glances from the landlord, but he refused to buy more and fuddle his wits before his meeting with Ghornan, whose ship was supposed to have made port with the incoming tide. He felt in his sleeve for the fiftieth time for the lists he would offer the Captain.

"Food, Priest?" snarled the landlord.

"I am correctly addressed as 'Pope.'" He wished God had bestowed a more impressive face upon him, but knew that his very ordinary features aided him in his work.

"Pope or priest, you have the same appetites as the rest of us; you're as venal as the next man, but you wrap it in homilies."

"I pray God will forgive your impiety," said Pope Sylvestros, his nervousness making his words sharp.

"Impiety!" jeered the landlord. He lifted a large cup to his mouth and drank deeply. From the rosy state of his nose and cheeks, this was a habit with him. "You meeting a Byzantine ship?"

"Yes."

"Totila gives rewards to those who sink Byzantine ships," the landlord said with satisfaction, adding as he watched Pope Sylvestros bless himself, "You priests are all alike. You think that prayers and gestures make a difference. Any idiot can mumble—most of 'em do—but no one thinks that God does more than look after them in their affliction. Except for the likes of you." He started to laugh at his own bitter humor.

"In Constantinople you would not dare to speak so disrespectfully of the servants of God." Pope Sylvestros was deeply indignant and he was not willing to overlook the landlord's challenge.

"If I pour you another tot of wine, will you turn it into water to spite me?" suggested the landlord.

"That's blasphemy, even in Italy."

The landlord filled his own cup with the dark, raw wine that was standard fare at The Seagull. "Who's to report me—you?"

In order to silence the landlord—and because he was growing increasingly anxious—Pope Sylvestros tossed him a silver coin and ordered more wine.

"Been away from home long?" Now that he had money in his hand again, the landlord assumed a mendacious cordiality. He tested the coin in his teeth and counted out half a dozen dissimilar copper coins in change, flipping them in the air and showing the stumps of his teeth as Pope Sylvestros scrabbled to retrieve them. He was still hunkered down on the floor when the door to the tavern swung open and a squat-bodied sailor surged into The Seagull. He bellowed for wine and looked quickly around the room as if expecting to find armed men behind the tables and benches.

"I am Ghornan," he announced to the room, daring anyone to contradict him.

"That is your good fortune," was the landlord's laconic response. He poured wine into a large-sized cup and held it out to the newcomer. "Three standard copper pieces; I don't care where they came from if the weight is right."

Ghornan pulled the coins from the folds of the narrow pallium wound around his waist. "Here. And this had better not be watered." He slammed down the coins, and without waiting for the landlord to put them in the small scale at the end of the counter, he trod the width of the room to stare down hard at Pope Sylvestros. "Are you the one I'm supposed to meet?"

"I am Pope Sylvestros," he admitted, his voice going higher with each word.

"You've lost flesh. I was told you were portly. You ought to go home to your wife." He straddled the bench. "The Bishop of Roma doesn't like his clergy to marry. So far, he hasn't been able to stop it." He stared hard at Pope Sylvestros. "What information do you have for me?"

"I . . ." He touched his sleeve but also inclined his head toward the landlord. "If we were more private . . ."

"Oh, you needn't worry about Gordius here. He knows that if he repeats a word of what he overhears, he'll have a second smile by morning." He drew his fingers across his own throat to illustrate his meaning.

"But there might be others who would pay to know what I tell you and that could lead to . . ."

With an ostentatious display of exhaustion—a yawn, a rubbing of his large, firm belly, a scratching of his chest—the landlord left his post behind the counter and made his way out of the taproom.

"You peawit," said Ghornan. "Now he's suspicious and there's no telling what he might decide to do with what you tell me." He gestured with disgust and drank off his wine. "He'll listen now, or his slaves will. Either way, I'll have to kill him before I leave."

"I didn't intend—" Pope Sylvestros started.

"Whatever you intended, the harm's done now." He slammed his cup down. "What you have had better be worth the trouble you're causing; that's all I can say."

"It is, Captain." Reluctantly Pope Sylvestros drew his lists from his sleeve and spread the sheets out on the table. Though the light in the tavern was poor and the pope's handwriting spidery at best, the two men poured over the pages and at the end of reading the first sheet, Pope Sylvestros could see the greedy interest in Captain Ghornan's eyes. "There is something worth a risk or two here, don't you think?" he could not resist prodding.

"True," agreed Ghornan as he got to his feet and poured himself another generous serving of wine. "How far are these villas, did you say?"

"The nearest is half a day's walk, the walls are still standing, and although the north side of it was put to the torch, most of the building is intact, including everything inside it." He had lowered his voice, leaning forward so that Captain Ghornan could hear everything he said.

"Half a day," mused Ghornan. "And what is left there would make it worth our while? Where are the Ostrogoths?"

"They've been and gone. They took the livestock, not the treasure." He cleared his throat. "There isn't much furniture; I think the owners must have removed some of it when they fled. There is some jewelry, and quite a lot of personal items, such as mirrors and perfume jars. I noticed some garments in a press; I don't think any of Totila's men knew enough to look there—"

"Too personal. They might be identified," Ghornan said, dismissing them.

"There are two chariots, wood covered with brass, very fine looking. I don't know if it's practical to take them both, but if you brought mules we could harness them to one of the chariots and use it to carry some of the heavier goods."

"Such as?" said Ghornan, revising his contemptuous opinion of Pope Sylvestros a little.

"The wine stored under the kitchen floor, for example. Some of it was taken, but a great deal remains, most of it in good condition. The owner had an excellent collection. And who is to say who owns what bottle of wine?" He held out the first page for Ghornan's review and studied the second one. "This villa is not very promising, but there are one or two good paintings that might be removed. There is also a good-sized alabaster vase that could bring a very high price."

"Paintings are usually not worth much," said Ghornan, not interested. "And they're easily identified."

"These are old, and one of them shows the destruction of the lost city of Pompeii under Vesuvius. That ought to make it worth more than paint." Pope Sylvestros ran his finger down the page a little farther. "Here's something quite remarkable: three rosewood chests, all in good condition, one with brass platters in it. I found them behind the tack room in the stables; I guess the owners had intended to pack them and then changed their minds."

"That's more the kind of thing I'm looking for," said Ghornan with a speculative smile. "Chests, furniture, household goods of special quality and workmanship. The chariots are tempting, and I think that if we can find chests of good value, it might be worth a little extra." He tapped the table, his hands hard on the planking.

"There was one villa, then, east of the city. I understand that General Belisarius himself stayed there for a while. It was owned by one of those imposing Roman widows, and must have several fortunes, judging by what was left there. Even after Totila's men went through the place, I found many treasures left in it." He coughed. "It is a little farther away than you said you wished to travel, but I think you'd find it more than justifies the additional time and effort. I made a partial inventory, in case you thought you'd like to risk it."

"You know what they're doing to looters in Roma these days?" Ghornan asked. "You saw the Ostrogoths on the walls coming in, didn't you? I'd just as soon keep my hands and my skin, thank you." He glared at the smoke-blackened beams. "It would have to be really special for me to take that kind of chance." With a speculative lift to his brow, he waited for Pope Sylvestros to speak. "Well?"

"Look at the list for yourself," said Pope Sylvestros, sliding two of the sheets toward him. "Everything I found is catalogued here, and you may be sure that there is more. This is superficial. There were over two hundred volumes in the library, and she must have taken many more with her. Some of them were very old, and that might—"

"Books are dangerous," Ghornan reminded him. "No telling when they might be banned, and then they become more hazardous than a scorpion." He ran his finger down the page, his lips moving as he read. "If this plum is so ripe, what makes you think that we'll be the only one after it?"

"Most of the folk who live near the villa will not enter it for any reason. They say that it has a strange reputation. Even those who do not dislike it treat the place with the greatest respect. The owner was said to be a sybil, and some of the very old peasants insist that she had lived there since they were children." He paused. "I could say prayers for the repose of unquiet spirits. If there are ghosts, they will depart."

"We Copts," Ghornan exclaimed indignantly, "have better sense than to rely on ceremonies for all eventualities. You Byzantines have complicated worship until it is nothing more than a theatrical performance. Chalices and ikons!" He stopped his tirade with an effort. "Still, if you would rather exorcise the villa before we loot it, I will not deter you. If this place has one half the booty you show here, one industrious night might be worth everything. And if the peasants think that it is an unwholesome place, that could be to our advantage. They will attribute what we do to whatever demon they think lurks there, and we will not be hampered." He rubbed his chin. "In fact, let us take care to make it appear that there are restless spirits there. No sense in making this more risky than necessary."

"And if there are such spirits?" Pope Sylvestros could not resist asking.

"We are good Christians, aren't we?" Ghornan asked. "What have we to fear from the Devil? I'd worry more about the owners' wrath than what Hell might do."

Pope Sylvestros blessed himself. "Apostasy," he muttered. "You risk worse than anything the magistrates might sentence."

"And what of the owner?" asked Captain Ghornan with elaborate courtesy. "This widow, where is she and what will she think if we help ourselves to her treasures?"

"She has left Italy. They say that she went to Constantinople, and perhaps she did. No matter." Pope Sylvestros waved his hand to show what a minor consideration she was. "Even if we are found out, what can a Roman widow do to us? I know that her sponsor is a pope and he will not act against another member of the Church simply because a few of her things were taken."

"You're counting on a lot," grumbled Ghornan.

"No, I'm not," said Pope Sylvestros with intensity. "In the very unlikely event she discovers what has happened here, how can she trace this to us? All we have to say is that we bought the goods from a reputable merchant, and there's an end to it."

"You hope," said Ghornan at his most daunting. "And if she can convince someone that something must be done, where does that leave us?"

"Who might she convince?" asked Pope Sylvestros with genuine bewilderment.

"You said that General Belisarius used the villa. She might persuade him that something is amiss. Let me tell you right now that I have no intention of getting on his wrong side. My work is much too dependent on his—"

Pope Sylvestros interrupted Ghornan with a conspiratorial smirk. "Word has it that the General will not be in Italy much longer. The rumors are that the Emperor is displeased with the progress of the campaign and suspicious of Belisarius' motivations and is going to remove him shortly."

"I have heard those rumors; Belisarius is still here." Ghornan finished his wine. "There are others who will be on watch for contraband of all sorts. This could be a trap for us; did you ever consider that?"

"Yes, but I don't think so. There are palaces in Roma that are bound to be traps, for their contents are famous and many would recognize them if anyone were foolish enough to take them. I have no desire to have my hands cut off and my arms flayed, either. So I say that we go to this villa and take what we want from it. I doubt if anyone would be able to prove that we had taken the items ourselves, and that is what would condemn us." He made a blessing over them. "The magistrates are reluctant to accuse popes and monks of wrongdoing. If you are working with me, then you are shielded by my cloth."

"Are all popes as cynical as you?" Ghornan asked with a hint of admiration.

"Not all of them are as poor, and few know how to take advantage of opportunity when it presents itself," said Pope Sylvestros severely. "It is not as if I am helping you steal from Byzantines. These are Romans, and you know what godless pagans they are."

"And that is all the excuse we need?" suggested Ghornan.

"It is not an excuse," Pope Sylvestros insisted. "I would never assist anyone in taking goods from a true Christian, but these Romans still have temples to their gods, and they think to mislead us all by declaring that they are now churches. None of us are fooled."

"So you are actually helping the Church by seizing these goods?" Ghornan laughed. "Very well, tell me some more about this widow's villa. Is it all on the list here?" He looked over the two sheets with more care, his eyes growing large with avarice. "What's this?" He pointed to an item on the second page of notes.

Pope Sylvestros glanced at the entry in question. "Oh. Yes, that was very strange. Fourteen chests filled with earth. One of the slaves told me that twenty just like them had been shipped to the widow in Constantinople." He scowled. "I wonder what kind of pagan rites she enacts with that earth?"

"Pagan rites?" Ghornan asked, heavy brows rising.

"What else would she require it for?" Pope Sylvestros twitched with indignation. "Rites of fertility, no doubt, or some other abomination." He indicated another line on the list. "This might interest you: twenty-eight platters of silver. They were in a storeroom along with those large brass tubs. Two barrels of sweet oil, and a whole chest filled with spices, which could be worth a great deal. The chest itself is an old one, all antique lacquerwork with brass fittings. It might be as much as four or five centuries old, and there are some who would like it for that reason alone."

Ghornan rubbed his stubbled chin. "The *Spairei Krohma* already has a little cargo consigned for the voyage back to Constantinople; we can take the most salable items from this villa, and if that goes well, then we can return for more on my next trip. In the meantime, if you find any other villas that are promising, and that have not been the headquarters for the army, make a note of them. I think that we might be fortunate if we can keep from becoming too greedy, or taking too much from one place. We must loot with discrimination." He belched laughter at his own humor.

"We are not looting," said Pope Sylvestros.

"No? What would you call it?" He gave the pope a friendly thump on the shoulder. "Conversion? Donation?" This time he did not laugh. "Whatever hypocritical reason you have, embrace it if it salves your conscience. And continue to find likely sites for our activities."

Suddenly he lunged to his feet and battered open the nearest door. Beyond the landlord stood, his stained mantele caught in his hands, his face guilty. "Well, well, well, what goes on here?"

"Nothing, Captain. Nothing. I was only curious to know if you had finished your business so that I could resume business."

"For only the two of us? Your tavern isn't very popular these days. Could it be that you were hoping to augment your earnings by applying for a reward as an informant?"

"Never!" the landlord said stoutly as his ruddy face turned hideously pale.

"Ah!" Ghornan was shorter than the landlord, and not as stout, but he was strong as the trunk of an oak tree, and he flung the man across the room with less effort than most would have thought possible. "You craven. You don't even lie well." He strode over to the counter and helped himself to another cup of wine. As he drank, he regarded the landlord, saying at his most affable, "You know, I once caught one of my sailors trying to sell off part of my cargo. I took some of the rope from the sails and I had it soaked in pitch, and then I stuffed it down his gullet and up his ass. It burned quite a while."

The landlord was gulping for air, his eyes wild with terror. "I swear, Captain, by the Mother of God, that I never intended to do—"

"I think," Ghornan went on as if he had not heard the landlord, "that this time I might wrap the rope around the body a couple of times, just to speed things up."

The landlord scrambled to his feet. "You would never do such a thing, not with a priest to watch you."

"What do you think this pope would do? How could he stop me if I decided to act?" He glanced from the landlord to Pope Sylvestros and back again. "How could he stop me?"

With a choking cry, the landlord bolted from the room.

Pope Sylvestros had risen. "He will inform against us."

"Oh, no he won't. I have four crewmen waiting outside; they'll catch him for us. I'll tend to him later." He came and sat back down opposite the pope.

"What . . . what will you do to him?" he asked uncertainly.

"Do you really want me to tell you?" was the sardonic response. When Pope Sylvestros faltered, Ghornan picked up the pages from the table. "Come. Let's decide what we're going to take this time."

Numbly Pope Sylvestros nodded and turned his mind away from the landlord's fate to the prospect of possible riches.

*　　*　　*

Text of an announcement sent throughout the Byzantine Empire.

To all subjects, citizens, and slaves of the Emperor Justinian; your attention, prayers, and devotions are required to mourn the death of the Empress Theodora, who passed from worldly travail into bliss on the feast day of Saint Felix of Nola, after enduring with fortitude the ravages of disease.

Coming so soon after the Feast of the Nativity, her death in this world is seen as especially blessed and more than silences the calumnies that have been spoken of her while she lived and grew in grace as the beloved wife of Emperor Justinian. Any person so lost to faith and charity who believes and repeats all or any part of the lies that have been spread about the virtuous Empress Theodora risks his body in this life and his soul in the next. Empress Theodora rose from her obscure beginnings through her innate kindness and goodness, and it was God's approval that brought her to the throne and bed of the Emperor Justinian.

Anyone discovered defaming the memory of this most blessed Empress will face the full weight of civil and ecclesiastical justice, and the only mercy that will avail so malignant a person then will be the Mercy of God.

For one year the Byzantine Empire will mourn for Empress Theodora. Those who do not observe this period will come under rigorous scrutiny.

> By the order of
> Kimon Athanatadies
> Court Censor
> at the behest of
> the Emperor of Byzantion, Justinian I

PART II
Drosos

Text of a letter from Antonina to her husband Belisarius.

To my esteemed and beloved husband on the Eve of Good Friday, hail and embraces.

With Theodora dead, there is nothing more I can do on your behalf with Justinian. He has refused to receive either me or those officers—notably Drosos and Chrysanthos—who have continued to support you, and in fact it appears that their constancy has fed his suspicions that you are gathering men around you for the purpose of overthrowing him and assuming the throne yourself.

If you have any such plan, my husband, this is the time to act, for I would be astonished if you were permitted to remain in Italy until the end of Spring, given the Emperor's current state of mind. While you have never confided such ambitions to me, I would certainly support you in any advancement or endeavor you wish to undertake, and doubtless you have as worthy a claim to leadership as has Justinian. You have always been loyal, and I do not mean to impugn your loyalty, but there have been those in the past who have professed themselves loyal to the Empire and not to the Emperor. If this is truly the case with you, you are now at that time when action is necessary or you will lose the day and the chance you seek, should you seek it at all.

I am gratified, naturally, that you depend on my affection for your strength, and your avowal of love and continuing

175

passion is most flattering to a woman of my age, but for the moment, let us turn our attention to more pressing matters. There will be time enough later for tenderness and kisses. Now we must take care to minimize the damage that has been done so that you do not lose all credibility at court and thereby endanger yourself even more than is currently the case.

You would do well to send word to all your officers, current and former, that you are devoted to the Emperor and his vision of a New Roma. That is essential if you are not to be implicated in treason before the year is over. When you have done that, I suggest that you do your utmost to expand the area you control in Italy and show your zeal when you do. This may not do much in the long run, and it could strain your supplies and men again, but you must believe me: Justinian demands a victory or he will hold you personally responsible. Once that happens your time in his good graces is over entirely.

Let me tell you now that you are being foolish to plan to live quietly until the worst of this is past. You must not entertain such thoughts even for a moment. Without success and a great display of military prowess, all the lies that have been told of you will be accepted as true and you will be powerless indeed. If Justinian orders you back to Konstantinoupolis, you may be sure that it is to keep watch over you and to undermine any base of power you may have established.

Yes, you may be confident that my care and affection continues unabated no matter what is thought of you. I would be a poor wife if I allowed anything else to color my conduct. If you are exiled, then it is fitting that I accept exile with you, or enter the Church, which I do not intend to do. I know that you will always be a good husband to me, and will never disgrace our union in any way.

That, however, is not sufficient after all you have done for the Empire and the ungrateful Emperor who has chosen to assuage his grief for his beloved wife through measures even more stringent than ones he has taken previously. It is not wise to observe this, perhaps, but there is a severity in

*Justinian's nature that without Theodora's presence might
prove to be a trial to us all. He is a demanding man and
what he requires of his people is more extensive than most
of them realize. Without any influence with the Emperor,
you are the one he is going to vent his feelings upon, and it
is time to prepare, one way or another, for that day.*

*You have an opportunity granted to few. It is for you to
act or to fail now, not in some later time when the issues
are clearer, for then you will not have access to the men and
supplies that are around you now. Do not reject my suggestions out of hand, my husband. They are made for love of
you and the Empire.*

*By my own hand
Antonina*

• 1 •

It was a contrived meeting, one that Simones had taken
great pains to make appear both accidental and fortui-
tous. The fish market was so busy that everyone elbowed
and shouted and shoved in an effort to reach the stalls
where the various fishermen had set up slabs to show their
catch. In such a setting, two important household slaves
might expect to find each other trying to purchase the
same sole.

"You are the majordomo to the Roman widow, aren't
you?" asked Simones, feigning doubt.

"Yes; Niklos Aulirios," he said with a gesture that
indicated he was willing to permit Simones to purchase
the fish.

"Oh, that's right. You're Greek. I think the reason I didn't place you at first was that I can't remember that you aren't as Roman as your mistress." He handed over the coins to the fisherman without haggling and told the man where the sole was to be delivered. "See that you send it at once; my mistress wishes to serve it this evening and it must be properly prepared."

"You're part of Belisarius' household, aren't you?" asked Niklos as he moved away from the front of the booth. He shaded his eyes against the spring sun and watched as the eunuch made his way to his side.

"Yes. It is not so great an honor as it once was, but what slave is free to choose his master?" The philosophical tone was belied by the discontented set of his mouth.

"Or what bondsman, if it comes to that?" retorted Niklos as he indicated a booth where chilled wine mixed with honey and fruit juice was being sold. "I have a few pieces of copper. Join me."

"You're being generous to a stranger," said Simones, hardly able to believe that their meeting was going so well.

"I am the stranger here. And I am curious about your mistress. Olivia Clemens has not had the pleasure of entertaining your mistress recently, and I was curious why." He found a bench and sat down so that the shadow of the nearest wall fell across him.

"My mistress has not gone out much since . . . recent events." Simones sighed. "Even her good friend Eugenia has not been in the great lady's presence of late."

"Has the General returned yet?" asked Niklos politely, although he knew that Belisarius had come back to Konstantinoupolis more than a week ago.

"Yes; at the Emperor's insistence, there was no official welcome." Simones ran his tongue over his lips, then wiped his brow with the cuff of his sleeve.

"From the rumors, welcome would not be the word for it," Niklos suggested, raising his hand to signal one of the serving slaves of the wine merchant.

"Sadly there is a rift between the General and the

Emperor," said Simones at his most neutral. "The Emperor fears that the General has become too used to command and wishes to expand his conquests." He watched Niklos carefully. "Those who are Belisarius' friends are of interest to the Emperor, of course."

"Why of course?" asked Niklos innocently, although he knew the answer before he asked his question.

"Because the Emperor wishes to know that he is secure," said Simones, doing his best to control his impatience.

"Bring us two of your nectars," said Niklos to the slave who approached them. "And if there are any of those little cakes, one or two of them would be welcome, wouldn't they?" This last was to Simones.

"They are tasty," he said curtly, wanting to guide Niklos back to the matter at hand. "It is good of you to offer."

"Nonsense. It is good to find someone who is so cordial."

In a Konstantinoupolitan Simones would have suspected that so gracious a remark hid sarcasm, but coming from Olivia's bondsman, he was confident that there was no ulterior message in the few words. "I would be your friend, Niklos, if you would allow it. There are real advantages in my friendship."

"Are there?" He took the two cups the serving slave brought and handed the youth three copper coins. "For the drink and for your trouble."

"You Romans are always very free with money for slaves," Simones observed critically.

"It is a Roman custom, and my mistress keeps to Roman ways." He gave the larger cup to Simones. "Long life and favor to the Emperor and our mistresses," toasted Niklos, though he only tasted the nectar before he set the cup down.

"Of course," Simones seconded, taking a deep draught of his drink. He wanted to resume control of their conversation without appearing too obvious. "About your mistress. She knew Belisarius in Roma, didn't she?"

"Yes. She gave him the use of her villa when she left and she received much assistance from your mistress for this." He looked at Simones. "And surely you know this."

"Some of it. A man in my position cannot question his owner too closely." He tried to be self-effacing, but did not succeed entirely.

"Then you are aware that the friendship had its origins in Roma," Niklos declared. "And you must know that my mistress owes your master a debt of gratitude for all he has done to assist her now that she lives in this city."

"I would have thought that such an honor belonged more to Drosos," said Simones with asperity before he could stop himself.

"Well, Drosos is Belisarius' Captain, isn't he?"

"Yes," Simones agreed with polite savagery. He brought his rising temper under control. "Does that mean that Belisarius took her as a lover?"

"Saint Stephanos, no," Niklos said with a laugh, his dark, reddish eyes dancing. "My mistress rarely consorts with men who have wives. There have been very few exceptions to the rule in all the time I have been with her."

"And that has been for a while, I gather," Simones prompted smoothly.

"Longer than you would think possible," Niklos confirmed with a touch of irony in his voice.

"And . . . you must forgive me for asking this, but I do not mean disrespect." He stared down into the cup. "She is actually a widow, is she, and not simply a courtesan who has taken a convenient lie to cover her sins." His face grew sharp, almost predatory, but he did not realize that Niklos saw.

"She was widowed before I became her bondsman," said Niklos truthfully, not adding that he had been with her for more than two hundred years. "Her husband was found guilty of treason and other crimes. For that reason alone, she was not eager to marry again."

"Such acts stick to wives, don't they?" Simones said

with a contemptuous turn of his mouth.

Niklos said nothing but signaled for a second drink for Simones. "Forgive me if I do not have another," he said to Antonina's eunuch slave. "I have a poor head for wine."

"Sensible to know your limits," Simones said as if he approved; he made a note of this weakness with a sense of satisfaction.

"So my mistress tells me." He gave two more coins to the slave and waved the youth away.

"About your mistress," Simones continued ruthlessly, "how is it that she prefers to live as she does?"

"She is a Roman, my Greek friend, and she lives as a Roman woman of the highest class lives. If she would rather not be a wife, that does not make her a whore because she is not a religious." He smiled at reminiscences Simones could not share. "There were times when her life would have been religious, but these things change."

"Do not say that where officers of the Court Censor can hear you. Kimon Athanatadies is not known for his sense of humor." Now Simones took a firmer stance with Niklos. "You apparently are not aware of how different things are here in Konstantinoupolis. In Roma perhaps it is not a serious matter to question the ways of the Church. Here, the Emperor is no cynic whose faith is an act of politics. He is a man of true devotion, and his court is the same. If you wish to pass unscathed, then you will have to mend your ways."

"Is that what you have been trying to tell me?" asked Niklos with an appreciative grin. "I have been wondering what is your purpose in talking with me. You are worried that my mistress might say or do something unwise, and I am grateful that you, or more correctly your mistress, I suppose, are concerned on her behalf." As he spoke, letting himself rattle on foolishly, he watched Simones, looking for some indication of what Antonina's slave actually sought. "Yes, I suppose my mistress is a little stubborn about how she lives. Romans are like that, you know. They must always be Roman, no matter how inappropriate it might be. I have wondered myself if it would be best to keep to the old ways here, but I am a bondsman, and it is not my place to correct the behavior of my mistress. Still, if things are as you imply, then I must do something to encourage her to reconsider." He stopped and pointed to the second cup. "You're not drinking, Simones. Isn't this to your liking?"

"It is pleasant," snapped Simones, his patience almost exhausted. "You seem to think that this is nothing but an entertainment."

"Oh, no; I wouldn't make so grave an error," he said with mockery in the back of his eyes. "You are trying to give me a message that has to do with my mistress. I realize that."

Simones started to rise, then thought better of it. "You have a little of the jist of it," he said with no attempt to make his words cordial. "But you don't grasp the ramifications. If your mistress continues as she is now, she might well come under close scrutiny. Those who have been of assistance in any inquiry will escape the worst of the results of such scrutiny. If she is questioned, your prior assistance will be weighed in determining what culpability you share with her."

Niklos stared, amazed at the blatant threat Simones offered. He had expected pressure but not coercion. "I am a bondsman, and there are laws that limit what I may do," he said cautiously.

"There are laws that supercede your bond," Simones declared. "There are the laws of the Emperor and God which no bond can overrule." He faced Niklos squarely. "There are also laws that reward true service to the Emperor and God by the ending of bonds. It is something to consider."

"It is," Niklos agreed somberly. "Let me understand you; if I give information on my mistress before an inquiry is made into her actions by the Censor, that will be a factor in what treatment I, as her bondsman, receive, if judgment goes against her."

"In part, yes," Simones said, his face set in a ferocious smile.

"And, of course, if I make reports, it might increase the chance of the inquiry being undertaken at all," Niklos went on in a conversational way. "So if the judgment went in her favor, I would be the one blamed for bringing false testimony against my mistress and abjuring the terms of my bond."

Simones came close to snarling. "It isn't the way it is done here."

"Isn't it?" Niklos asked. "Well, you will have to forgive me if I require a little time to think this over. I have already spoken with a few of the Censor's officers, and your reminder, while well-meant, comes at a time that fills me with doubt." He rose abruptly. "I don't know why so many of you want to discredit my mistress, but you will not have my help in doing it."

"Consider the alternatives before you make such a rash decision," Simones warned him. "You have as much to lose as she does, and for a man of your position, the methods we use might be more than you want to endure."

Niklos' eyes were distant as he regarded Simones. "I have listened to men like you before, Simones. You cannot bear it that Olivia has her own life and her own ways. You refuse to let her be. Well, though I am only a bondsman and nothing more than her majordomo, I will not abandon her, especially to jackals like you and the men you serve." He deliberately reached down and tipped over his cup which was almost full. The contents ran over the bench and splattered onto the pavement.

"You're an arrogant fool," spat Simones.

"A thing I have learned from you," Niklos said sweetly. "I have listened to all your advice, and now I will give you some of mine: leave Atta Olivia Clemens alone. She harms no one. She is living within your laws. She has no ambition to seek power here. If you force her to change, you will regret it."

"Will I?" Simones growled. "You know nothing of it."

"And if you persist in these attempts to suborn me, I

will inform not only my mistress, but I will request that she inform yours. I do not think that Antonina would welcome so deceitful a slave in her household." He turned on his heel and strode away into the market, leaving Simones to curse him.

By the time he reached Olivia's house, Niklos was no longer satisfied that he had managed his meeting with Simones as well as he had thought he had at first. He entered his quarters in a thoughtful mood which darkened steadily with the day, so that by nightfall, he was filled with melancholy foreboding.

It was after most of the household had retired that Niklos sought out Olivia in her study where she was passing the night reading.

"You look terrible," she said as he entered the room, and her words were only half in jest.

"I'm not surprised," he said, sitting down across from her. "I fear I have done you poor service this afternoon."

"Impossible," she said affectionately as she set the old scroll she had opened aside. "What's troubling you?"

"Simones, Antonina's eunuch," he said, the words tasting spoiled in his mouth.

Olivia waited, her hazel eyes on his. She said nothing, but her attention was apparent in every line and angle of her body. Her silence was patient and unawkward, for she and Niklos had too many years together for her to need to urge him; he would speak in his own time.

Finally the story came out, a bit disjointed and with occasional digressions, but recounted accurately and without too much apprehension coloring the tale.

"The Censor and now Simones. What do you make of it?" Olivia asked when Niklos was finished.

"I don't know, but none of it pleases me." He folded his arms, sighing heavily. "I assume that if they are attempting to enlist my aid against you that there are other spies in the household."

"That's likely; we expected it," she said serenely.

"I don't like it," he said.

"Nor do I."

He lunged to his feet and began to pace. "What are we going to do?"

"What can we do? We will have to wait and find out why we are suspect, and of what, and by whom." She stared up at the ceiling. "It may be nothing more than Belisarius. Now that he has been recalled and stripped of command, there are vultures waiting to pick over his carcass. If they are seeking more ways to discredit him, they will have to find someone other than me to aid them."

"And if it isn't Belisarius?" asked Niklos.

"For the time, we will have to assume that it is," Olivia decided. "I am Drosos' lover, Drosos is Belisarius' Captain; I provided housing for Belisarius in Roma and I am here under his sponsorship. That is more than reason enough for the Court Censor. I am a Roman widow. Spying on me is a simple thing and the risks are minimal."

"Then you want me to do nothing." Niklos was growing angry. "What happens if the Court Censor decides to imprison me? What then? How do I account for what I am? And what if he imprisons you?" This last question was flung out with passion, but as soon as it was spoken, he changed, coming toward her with sympathy in his face. "By the Horses of Poseidon," he said contritely. "I didn't intend—"

Olivia had turned her face away, but now she looked at him and there was grief in her eyes. "It's all right, Niklos. You're right, I suppose. And if I am wrong, if I underestimate the risks, then you and I have a great deal to lose, and it is not merely our lives. We've already lost those once." This last was an unsuccessful joke. "Please, at least chuckle for me, or I will become as morose as you are."

"I'm . . . I'm sorry, Olivia. I can't." He looked down at her. "There are times I despair."

"And I." She got up and came to his side. "Niklos, if you think we must take greater precautions, then I will abide by your decision. You may be wiser than I about this. I dislike this place, its reek of holiness and condescension so much that I might misjudge our danger by my very dislike." She leaned her head on his shoulder. "That time in Caralis, when the ship had been blown off course."

"I remember." Now there was a hint of amusement in his response.

"I overlooked the most obvious danger because I was so utterly miserable and furious. This might be the same thing, and if it is, it would be unforgivable of me to ignore it. Only fools and cowards make the same error twice."

"Since you're neither of those, then—" He put his arm around her and patted her shoulder. "I think what we need most is our own spy in the ranks; what do you say?"

She sagged against him and then straightened. "I would like to say that I leave it up to you, but that's no answer. Very well. I agree, as little as I want to. One of the slaves will have to be taken into our confidence, at least to some degree, and we will have to find some means to establish the slave's reliability." She moved away from him. "It's all so petty, when you think of it."

"Whether it is or not, it could cost more than either of us wants to pay," Niklos reminded her.

"True." She fell into a musing silence. "Do you have any recommendations about a slave?"

"No; do you?" He had learned long ago to trust her sense about people, for her impressions were always more accurate than his. "Tell me."

She did not answer at once, and when she did, her tone was slightly remote. "That Eastern woman, I think. Zejhil is her name. The one who comes from Vagarsha-pat, if that's the place I think it is."

Niklos regarded her with interest. "Why her? The rest of the slaves treat her oddly. They don't trust her."

"That's why, in part," Olivia said. "She will be under less suspicion because she is already thought strange." She looked at him and shook her head. "You don't really understand, do you?"

"No," he admitted. "But I know that you do, and that's sufficient."

"I'm grateful for your confidence," she said lightly. "I will want to speak to her in the morning. See that she is sent to me before the first meal. I don't want the summons to start gossip."

Niklos was deeply relieved. The worry had not left him, but he no longer felt that he and Olivia were floundering, at the mercy of the shifting Imperial tides that had claimed so many others. "Very well, I'll see that she is sent to you. For what purpose?"

"Oh, to inspect my clothes. Something must need mending." She reached down and picked up the scroll. "I was hoping that we might have respite here, but I was wrong."

"Olivia—" Niklos began.

She rolled the scroll tightly. "I used to think that there would come a time when I would not have to live with . . . oh, with fear and anger around me, poisoning the world. I thought there would be good fellowship and sensible actions because we would grow wiser and more caring." She put the scroll back in its pigeon hole, then glanced over at the small ikonostasis. "I feel as if all our time is spent in terrible darkness, and that if we are fortunate, from time to time we stumble into a little light. If we are not too frightened of what we see, we huddle around it, like traders in the desert at their fires. But most are terrified or blinded, and they seek the darkness again, preferring that to—" She shook her head. "Forgive me."

"Always," said Niklos, more moved by what she had said than he wanted to admit.

This time her smile was genuine. "You're too good to me, old friend."

"Me? Never." He came to her side, kissed her cheek, and went to the door. "Zejhil, tomorrow morning."

She nodded. "I suppose I must." She turned away and did not look back again when she heard him close the door.

* * *

Text of a letter to Olivia from Sanct' Germain.

To my most cherished Olivia, hail from Perath.

Your letter reached me after five months, which is good
time, or so I am informed. For the next year I will be here
at Perath and can be reached at the House of Foreign
Scholars. I hope you will send me word of how you are, for
you seemed unhappy with your life in Constantinople, and
that saddens me. You have already endured so much, and to
have that haven denied you grieves me more than I can tell
you.

How good to know that Drosos is with you. He may not
be able to compensate for your vexation, but surely you find
some consolation in his company. Love given so honestly
is rare indeed, as you and I both have cause to know. It
has been many, many years since I knew such intimacy;
thinking back, I cannot recall such profound rapture since
you and I were lovers. Treasure your Captain Drosos,
Olivia.

You say that you suspect Belisarius will be removed from
command, and you believe that it is foolish. Of course it is.
But are you surprised, you who saw the Year of the Four
Caesars and knew Tigellinus? If Belisarius is the man you
say he is, no Emperor could tolerate having him in power;
as it is he is a living rebuke to Justinian.

This hardly provides the comfort I wish I could give you,
and for that I rely on your understanding. There are so few

things I can offer at this distance, and that distresses me.
Still, in spite of it all, this brings you my enduring love.

> *Sanct' Germain*
> *his seal, the eclipse*
> *by the good offices*
> *of Brother Petros*
> *on pilgrimage to Roma*

• 2 •

Captain Vlamos strove to hide his embarrassment. "I have to take your sword as well, General," he said to Belisarius as he and his men waited in the vestibule of Belisarius' house.

"Why? Who is there for me to use it on but myself?" Belisarius asked with a bitter laugh. "Or is that Justinian's fear? Does he think I will deprive him of my shame?"

"It isn't wise to speak so to us, General," Vlamos said stiffly. "The Emperor has given his orders and we are his sworn officers. There is nothing—"

Belisarius held up his hand to stop this confession. "I am also his sworn officer, little as he believes it." He reached down and unbuckled his sword. "Take it. It's only a symbol, but that is enough. The Emperor has already taken my personal guard, and he has restricted my movements."

"General." Vlamos held the sword as if he expected it to strike of its own accord.

"Well, he is Emperor and I am his General, no matter what he believes, and I will be his General unto death."

He pinched the bridge of his nose and rubbed his eyes. "I will do what I am able to, and I will strive to understand what it is that he wishes of me."

"He wishes your loyalty, General," said Vlamos, delivering this statement with the stiffness of one repeating a lesson by rote.

"Then he has his wish," said Belisarius, suddenly weary and out of patience with the ceremony. "I have always been loyal, and I will always be loyal. It sorrows me that the Emperor is not aware of this, but I can do little but protest. Those who have told the Emperor anything else of me lie. Those who have sought to have me removed from command for fear that I might use my position against Justinian do so without justification." He folded his arms. "Will you inform Justinian of this?"

"We are to give our report to Kimon Athanatadies, and he will present a report to the Emperor," Vlamos said, being as meticulous as he could. "I am only Captain of the Guard; I cannot address the Emperor directly."

"That's new," said Belisarius, surprised at the information. "How long has this been the case?"

"A year." He looked away from Belisarius, fixing his gaze on the murals of martyred saints. "It has been determined that the Emperor requires . . . less interference from those who are not of true importance to the Empire."

"That's a mistake, especially if the Censor thinks that the Captain of the Guard is not important to the Empire," said Belisarius dryly. "He could come to regret that decision one day."

"Is that meant—" Vlamos started.

"As a word of caution, nothing more. If a man does not think those who guard him are important, he invites problems. I was thinking of the Caesars who were overthrown by the Praetorian Guard, who watched over them."

"We are not Praetorians," Vlamos pointed out uneasily.

"No, but Justinian might err as the Caesars did," Belisarius said. "It would grieve me if that were to happen." He glanced at the other officers with Vlamos. "Is that all, or is there something more we must do before this is over?"

"I must announce to your household what is and is not permitted here now that the Emperor has removed your command and your personal guard." Vlamos coughed, the only display of emotion he permitted himself.

"Must it be the whole household, or can I limit it to the majordomo, who will give orders to the rest?" He thought it galling that he would have to face his slaves at this time; it was sufficiently degrading to be denounced before soldiers; to have the terms of his disgrace announced to his slaves was intolerable.

Although Vlamos had been told to give the orders to every member of the household, he said, "The family and majordomo will suffice." He would deal with his reprimand—and there would surely be one—later.

"Very well." He clapped his hands. "Simones! Arius!" The summons was sharp and loud as orders on a battlefield. "Come here. Bring your mistress and her aunt. And my brother." For the first time in his life, he was grateful that he had no children, and that as a bastard, he could not directly dishonor his father.

Vlamos and his men waited in silence while the summoned members of the household came to the vestibule and stood in front of the murals of the suffering holy men.

Simones and Arius stood apart from the rest, both attentive, both curious. They knew that Antonina was consumed with rage at the way Justinian was treating her husband, and both wondered if she would be able to contain her wrath during the proceedings. Both slaves waited as Captain Vlamos prepared to recite the Emperor's mandate.

"General Belisarius," Vlamos declared with almost no inflection. "You are required to give up your command and all claims to command. You are to surrender your personal guard and all personal support of those guards. You will be permitted to maintain your house and your fortune in the manner you wish as long as you do not have guards or the support of guards as part of it. You are not to receive any military officers without the presence of a pope or an officer of the Censor in attendance, and any defiance of this requirement will bring with it an assumption of treason on the part not only of General Belisarius but of the officer in question. If the General is as devoted to the Emperor as he insists, he will be at pains not to implicate his officers in any possible guilt. The members of General Belisarius' household may not consort with members of the households of other military officers but in the presence of a pope or an officer of the Censor. This restriction includes all female members of the household in their dealings with the females of other households."

Antonina gave a short, stifled cry, but said nothing more. Her aunt, a little, wizened creature in a simple dark brown paenula, reached over and put her hand on Antonina's arm.

"There is not to be written communication of any kind between General Belisarius and any military officer," Captain Vlamos went on, "except if it has been read and copied by an officer of the Court Censor. Any communication that is clandestine will be assumed to be treasonous, and will result in imprisonment of the officer involved in the communication."

"Is that all?" Belisarius asked when Vlamos fell silent.

"For the time being," Vlamos answered. "I'm sorry, General. I have to say it that way."

"I'm sorry too, Captain," said Belisarius heavily. "All right, you may tell whomever-it-is you report to that I have heard Justinian's strictures and I will abide by them, though I maintain now, as I have from the first of this regrettable misunderstanding, that there is no need for the Emperor to take these precautions, and I will pray God every day that the Emperor will come to know this for himself." He made a small reverence to Captain Vlamos. "Thank you for discharging your duty."

"You should curse me," Vlamos said with feeling.

"What would be the point of that?" Belisarius asked. "Take what you must take and leave me. I would like to spend some time alone with my family." He nodded to Antonina and his brother.

"Of course," said Captain Vlamos, and barked a command at his men. "We must post a guard at your door, so that we may know who comes here, how often, and when."

"Certainly," said Belisarius, already turning away from the soldiers. "Come into the private reception room, Lysandros; we must talk."

Lysandros set his jaw and glared at his older brother. "I have little to say to you, Belisarius."

"But I have a great deal to say to you," said Belisarius, his face darkened with sorrow. "When I have done, you may say what you like."

"And what of me?" demanded Antonina, who had contained herself as long as she could and was now filled with indignant fury.

"Let me have a short time with Lysandros, my delight. You and I have many hours to spend together; Lysandros returns to Nicaea in the morning, and who knows when we will speak face to face again?" He watched the door of his house as Captain Vlamos and the Guard soldiers left. "Arius, Simones, one of you close that, will you?"

Arius busied himself with the door; Simones went to Antonina. "Great lady, would you want a cup of honied wine?"

"I would want a cup of hemlock and gall," she said in a hate-thickened voice. "I want poison and acid and instruments of torture to exact vengeance."

"My niece," said her aunt in a small, distressed voice.

"To think that this could happen!" Antonina burst out, and then began to weep in great, angry sobs, refusing to be comforted. "I am going to my quarters," she informed the air, shrugging off the ineffective consolation of her aunt.

"Your wife is overwrought," observed Lysandros as Belisarius closed the door.

"She is also in despair, and I am the cause of it," Belisarius said.

"You are the cause of misfortune for all of us," Lysandros accused him. "You ought to have thought of that before you embarked on your schemes."

Belisarius looked steadily at his brother. Lysandros was eight years his junior, and had had a different father; the two brothers had little in common except the blood of their mother. "I had no schemes, except those aimed at running Totila's army out of Italy. Believe that or not as you wish. It is the truth."

"Then why does the Emperor confine you in this way? Why are you relieved of command and your personal guard? What sort of innocent do you think I am, brother?" Lysandros put his hands on his hips, which were already growing ample.

"I don't think you are innocent, or foolish, or any similar thing," Belisarius said carefully. "But I hope that you have some faith in me yet, for our mother's sake if no other."

Lysandros laughed and the sound was mirthless. "Then you are the one who is foolish. How could you have let this happen? I have already been told that I can no longer sell my horses to the army because of you. That accounts for more than half my earnings, and I am to lose it because you could not act in time to preserve your rank." He turned so quickly that he overset a brazier.

As the iron tripod clattered to the floor, Belisarius went to right it. "I am the Emperor's General, Lysandros. That is all I am."

"You mean you are not a husband and a brother? You're just a General?" He hurled his words like clubs and took a perverse satisfaction when they struck.

"I am all those things," Belisarius said quietly as he steadied the brazier. "And it seems I have failed at all of them."

Lysandros snorted. "Penitent, too. Doubtless I should tell you now that you are forgiven for all the misfortune you have brought down on everyone. But I am not deceived by your ways, brother. You aspired to the purple and you failed to grasp it for yourself, and now you are taking refuge in contrition. No one accepts this false front you show to the world. All the world knows you are guilty of treason and we are amazed that our Emperor should show you the clemency he does. If I were in Justinian's position, I would see you flayed on the steps of Hagia Sophia, and would hang your skin from the palace gates.''

Belisarius listened to this without interruption; only the quickening of his breath revealed his feelings. "Is that the lot?"

"How can you face me? How can you face your wife, who has been your staunchest ally at court for all the years you were in foreign lands?" He slammed his fist into his open hand. "By all the Saints in the calendar, if I were she, I would despise you."

"You despise me enough for you both," said Belisarius. "You may speak of yourself to me, but you are not to say anything for Antonina." He read astonishment and guilt in his brother's face. "You have traded on our relationship for years, and now you are about to lose that which I made possible. You are entitled to disappointment, even anger, but you are not permitted to drag my wife into this dispute."

"Belisarius—" Lysandros blustered.

"No, you have had your opportunity, and now I will have mine. I have had to listen to more accusations and calumnies in the last two months than I have heard in all my previous years, and you now will have to hear me out." He hooked a thumb into his belt. "You think—because it is the current myth bruited about the court—that I was on the verge of rebelling against the Emperor, and it was only the swift action of the Censor that prevented me from attacking Justinian. That is not and never was the truth. I have never aspired to the purple, as you claim. I have had all that I could deal with in fighting to reclaim the old Roman Empire for Justinian. I was satisfied to be the first General of the Emperor, and I was content to follow his orders to the best of my abilities and to the extent that my men and supplies made possible. I was and am now loyal to the Emperor. I am not a traitor. If I must live this way in order to satisfy the Emperor of that, then I am content to do it, and pray only that I will have the chance to show that everything I have said is true."

"And the spies will tell the Censor," jeered Lysandros.

"If there are spies they can tell whom they wish. It is the truth. Understand that, Lysandros, if you understand nothing else." He turned on his heel and went to the door. "If there is nothing else, I will leave you. I am sorry that you must suffer because of me, but you chose to prosper through our relationship, and so it haunts you now."

"Wait, Belisarius," Lysandros called less certainly.

"Why? So that you can revile me more?" For the first time there was anguish in his voice.

"I . . . If what you've told me is true," Lysandros said to his brother's back, "then I grieve for you, for you have truly been destroyed by your own honor."

"But you think otherwise," Belisarius said, and left the room. He stood in the hallway for a moment, his emotions in turmoil. This was worse than walking over a battlefield after a victory and seeing the ruined, broken men whose lives purchased it. He ground his teeth together, wishing that he trusted himself to get drunk and end the pain for a few hours.

Simones stood a little farther down the hall, and he hesitated before speaking. "Master, your wife . . . your wife desires your company."

"In a moment," said Belisarius, not confident he could remain calm with her.

"She is eager for you," Simones informed him.

"In a moment," he repeated. He indicated the door behind him. "My brother is about to depart. I pray you, give him escort."

This was not what Simones hoped for, but he made a reverence. "At once."

"See that he has an appropriate gift. Something suitable. I suppose a dozen brass cups will do." He rubbed his chin, and wished he had the excuse of shaving to postpone what he knew would be a harrowing time with Antonina. He gave a sour smile, that he who had fought armies in Italy and Greece and Africa should falter at an hour with his wife. With that thought to goad him, he went to

Antonina's private quarters.

"My husband," Antonina said when Belisarius had made his reverence to her. "My husband, what has happened to us?"

"I wish I knew," he said, thinking how beautiful she was, and how much it hurt him to see her so distressed. He went and wrapped his arms around her, saying softly, "The only comfort I can find in this is that I can be with you, beloved."

She pushed against his embrace. "What is the matter with you? Have you lost all your mettle?"

He strove to hold her, needing her nearness to assuage the other losses he had been forced to accept. "Antonina, please."

"Do not beg me, my husband. I am your wife, and yours by rights. For the Lord of Hosts, take *something,* if it is only me. You are without any steel." She broke away from him. "How dare Justinian do this to you? How dare he forget all you have done to advance him? If Theodora were still alive, this could never have happened." She dashed her hand over her face as if to banish her furious tears.

"I have asked myself that, Antonina, and I have no answer." He watched her, an ache like a festering wound burning in him. "Antonina."

"Do not speak to me! Do not do anything. I have endured all the words I ever want to hear." She reached to the nearest ikon and flung it across the room. When Belisarius reached out his hand to restrain her, she turned on him, her mouth square with ire. "What use are the Saints? What use is your precious honor if we are driven to this disgrace? Why must you be blameless? Why didn't you plot against the Emperor if this is to be the reward you have?"

"For your own sake, Anton—" Belisarius began, then broke off as Antonina threw herself on him, her hands raised and her nails poised as talons to rake his face and gouge his eyes.

"Coward!" she shrieked. "Fool! Fool! Fool!"

Striving not to hurt her, Belisarius struggled to hold Antonina and pin her arms to her sides. "Antonina," he panted. "Beloved. Wife. My most dear."

Her nails scored his neck before she was restrained. "I hate you," she hissed. *"I hate you."*

At that, the strength went out of him and he released her, standing without resistance as she scratched and struck him. Only when this gave way to high, keening wailing did he act again. Tenderly he drew her to him, holding her, smoothing her hair, whispering to her. "I can bear the rest, if I must. I will bear it. But I cannot endure to give you pain, Antonina, and your disgust of me is more than I am able to stand. Hush, hush, my dearest, my only beloved. All the rest can be borne, but not your odium. Antonina. Antonina."

Finally she recovered enough to speak without screaming vituperations. She looked at the blood on his face and shoulders, at the rents in his clothing. "Did I do that?"

"It doesn't matter," he said, kissing her brow.

"Did I?"

"Yes." He met her eyes steadily. "You were very angry."

"Yes." Some remaining fire flared in her face, then faded quickly. She let him support her and take her to her bed. "I must sleep," she murmured.

He said nothing, waiting for her invitation which did not come. As he dismissed her body slaves, he watched closely but covertly. "Do you need anything from me?"

"I have already had more from you than ever I sought," she said with consuming bitterness. "I will have to have time, Belisarius. So much has happened." This last was vague and she did not look at him.

"Antonina?" He held out his hand to her. When she did not take it, he let it fall.

"Tomorrow," she said distantly. "Tomorrow, perhaps, we will talk. When I am more myself." It was a dismissal, and he recognized this.

"Very well. Tomorrow."

As he went to the door, she said after him, "Perhaps."

*   *   *

Text of a letter from Pope Sylvestros to Captain Ghornan.

To the heretical Copt Ghornan for whom I still entertain a certain admiration, hail from Pope Sylvestros, currently in Roma.

Your information about our most recent venture has given me renewed hope in our current enterprise, and I cannot help but believe that if we continue our efforts, we might well do far more than we currently anticipate, given what we have accomplished. It seems to me that a little determination and zeal might provide the impetus your last letter had so little of. While I admire your prudence, I do not think that this is the time for hesitation. Everything has gone so well that I cannot but assume that it will continue to go well for us, no matter what you fear.

I find it ironic that you, who were so determined at the beginning of our project, are now the one who preaches caution and contentment with what we have achieved.

In this regard, let me say that there are still many valuable things to be gained in areas we have been before. We have not, by any means, exhausted the possibilities of our venture as defined in the past, and were we to continue as we have begun, there is no reason to suppose that we would not reap the rewards of our efforts. You have advised that we take time to assess what we have gained, and I concur, but you see this as a point where we might suspend our activities; I see it as the first real spur to us to be more determined than we have been.

You say you are worried at what might befall us because of our partnership, but why should anything unfortunate happen? You are concerned that some authorities could become curious about the achievements we have, and I agree that a little more circumspection about the projects would not hurt us, but I also believe that we must consider the larger benefits we stand to gain from our dealings, and weigh that against the hazards of official objections.

This is not to say that I am unaware of the risks. I know that what we do may be frowned upon by some of those in Roma, but there are those in Konstantinoupolis who will be delighted with our efforts and who will urge us to continue.

We are admonished in scripture to turn ourselves to the labor that we do best and to do it with dedication and determination. It is not unreasonable to assume that what we have accomplished thus far has been due to our determination, and if we only persevere, we might look forward to many more such successes. Before you reject the new venture out of hand, consider the possibilities in this light and you will have to come to the same conclusion I have reached, that there is enough treasure here to justify the things we must do to claim it.

Think of your well-being and you will see that I am right. I pray that you will reconsider and join with me in this expansion of our previous activities. It would pain me to think I might have to search out another to aid me in this worthy pursuit; that would merely serve to increase the danger to all of us, and I cannot think that you would want that.

I will be waiting for you at the villa where we discovered the chalcedony jars. I will be there for a period of ten days, and if at the end of that time you have not come there, I will conclude that you are no longer interested in what we have done and will at that time begin the task of seeking out other assistance.

With prayers that you will be guided by me and continue

to champion the work I have begun here, I send you my blessings and a list of those items you will find interesting.

> *Pope Sylvestros*
> *at the villa of the Gracchi*
> *north of Roma*
> *near Capena on the Via Flaminia*

• *3* •

"They denied me entrance!" Drosos fumed, his eyes hard with indignation. "They would not let me see him."

Olivia trailed her hand in the fishpond and sought for the right words to console him. "It isn't your fault, Drosos."

"Of course it's not my fault," he concurred, flinging the parchment scroll he had been given halfway across the garden. "It's the damned Censor and his clique that are to blame, and they will answer for it, believe me." He paced down the wide stone path, then came back to her. "Aren't you going to say anything more? Just that it's not my fault?"

"What can I say? I am as distressed as you are; it is a dreadful state of affairs, and I wish it were otherwise. But words do not change these things." She watched the flickering shine of the fish under the water lily pads.

"No, they don't," he agreed, trying to be fair. His disappointment lessened. "You wouldn't want to try to gain entry to Belisarius' house yourself, would you?"

She turned, not quite smiling. "I am not prohibited from seeing him, but I am not allowed to carry any messages to him, or bring any writing to the house." It was only two days since she had paid her first visit to Belisarius since his return from Italy, and she was still shocked by the reception she had received at the hands of the Guard who were posted there.

"You could tell him a few things from me, couldn't you?" Drosos suggested, putting his hand on her head and starting to loosen the pins that held her complicated hairdo in place.

"I might," she said, her voice softening as the first lock fell on her shoulder. "If I were caught doing it, I would be prohibited from seeing him again."

"You're clever. They wouldn't catch you," Drosos said belligerently. "Tsakza!" he cursed, kicking at the path, his manner changed from teasing and sensual to restless dissatisfaction in an instant. He dropped one of her hairpins and let it lie at his feet.

"But if they did," she went on, unflustered by his behavior, "I would cease to be much use to you or to him. Drosos, I do not want to see you cut off from your friend."

"My General," he corrected her, moving away from her, her hair forgotten. He paced through her garden.

"Your friend," she insisted gently. "Drosos, if you had a tail it would be lashing. Come back and let us see if there is a way we might reach Belisarius without endangering him or you or me."

"You just said there isn't," he reminded her, close to sneering.

"I said that if I were caught giving him a message I wouldn't be allowed to see him again, and that's another matter entirely." She took the last of the pins from her hair and shook it loose. "Drosos, please."

"They've made a prisoner of him, but they dare not lock him up. The people wouldn't stand for it." He folded his arms and stopped beside her fishpond.

"Whether the people would or wouldn't, the Court Censor isn't going to test his power with Justinian quite yet. As displeased as the Emperor is with Belisarius, he isn't ready to be rid of him entirely, or you can be certain that he would already be locked in a cell or have been condemned as a traitor."

"You learned that in Roma, did you?" Drosos asked her, relenting.

"It's a familiar pattern, you'll allow that." She indicated a place beside her. "Sit. We'll think of something between us."

"You're a lascivious creature, Olivia," he said, not accepting her offer.

"Yes, but right at the moment I am a political one." She sat straight, and even with her fawn-brown hair cascading down her shoulders and back, everything about her implied business and reason. "You will not be happy until we have some tenable solution, and I would rather you be happy while you are with me. So we will consider what is to be done."

Drosos went back to the fishpond. "I don't want you enmeshed in my snares," he said slowly. "I don't mind risking disgrace for myself, but I don't want to bring it on you."

"That's very kind of you," she said, her sincerity more genuine for its simplicity. "And if you were nothing to me, I would not act with you in this, for all that Belisarius befriended me in Roma. However, you are dear to me, and he is my friend, and there is no reason for me to hesitate."

"You're not Konstantinoupolitan. That is always a factor, and it puts you at a disadvantage, no matter how you want to assess this." He had changed again, becoming more determined. "Still, we might arrange something, if you're sure you are willing to do this."

"Magna Mater!" she burst out, exasperated. "Drosos!"

"All right; all right. I'll assume for the time being that you are going to aid me. But I want it understood that if we cannot think of something that is at least reasonably safe that you will stay out of it. They might hesitate at condemning Belisarius, but you're not as distinguished as he; Athanatadies would not balk at confining you. Or worse." His eyes narrowed. "I wouldn't like that, Olivia."

"Nor would I," she agreed. "And I know that you're right. We'll have to work out a prudent way to manage."

She was serious enough, but amusement tinged her voice.

"A prudent conspiracy," he said, and snorted once with laughter.

"Why not?" She rose and went to his side. "What do you want Belisarius to know?"

He looked at her, a little startled by the bluntness of the question. "Isn't this place a little . . ."

"Niklos and Zejhil are watching us, which ought to prevent anyone else from listening. We're as safe here as we're apt to be most other places. Here, if there is someone listening or watching, we will know of it." She looked at the wall enclosing the garden. "I'm not certain there isn't an urchin in the street with his ear open wide, but that might be the case anywhere, and if that is how we must think, then no one would be safe saying anything anywhere."

"You're made your point," he sighed. "Very well, if you trust your slaves, I suppose I will have to trust them, too. But don't forget that loyalty is purchased with the slave." He said this last with stern cynicism.

"Niklos is a bondsman, not a slave," she reminded Drosos. "Now, what are we to tell Belisarius?" she went on, returning them to the problem.

"I want him to know that if he has any need of his officers for any reason whatever, he has only to get word to me, and we will come to him, and the Pit take the Guard set to watch him." He spoke softly but with emphasis, each syllable rapped out as if he were giving orders on a battlefield.

"You mean that if the rumors are true and Belisarius seeks the purple for himself, you and many of his officers would support him," Olivia said.

"Yes."

"He has said all along that he has no such aspirations," she pointed out.

"I know. I also know that he never thought he would be under house arrest. Ingratitude like that can change a man." He shook his head. "It's the Censor, I know it is. Justinian would not be so unreasonable if he understood.

He's the Emperor, and he is not unjust. I am loyal to him, but I have a greater loyalty to Belisarius. The Emperor . . . the Emperor does not have men around him who recognize honor, and therefore they advise him unwisely. Justinian would not treat Belisarius this way if he had a few soldiers close to him. He would realize that Belisarius is his champion, and he would reward the service that he has been given in the past."

"But you would support an action on Belisarius' part to overthrow the Emperor?" Olivia asked.

"If nothing else were possible. I would not want to bring Justinian down. He is Emperor. But if there were no other way to remove the Censor and that clique from the Imperial Court, then I would pray to God to forgive me for acting against Justinian. I hope it never comes to that. I hope that there are ways to be rid of men like Athanatadies—he is puffed up with that name of his, thinking he is already illustrious—without having to act against Justinian."

"And if there isn't?"

"Then the sooner it is done, the better for all of us. It would be possible to depose Justinian without imprisoning him, or worse. I do not want the Emperor's blood on my hands, even indirectly. There could be no greater dishonor. It's one thing to dispose of those men who are corrupt and ambitious, but no soldier can rise against his Emperor and think himself worthy of his rank."

"He may be your Emperor, but he's not God, Drosos," Olivia said, chiding him a little.

Drosos responded seriously. "The Emperor is more than the rest of us. He would not be where he is if he were nothing more than a man. Justinian is . . . an officer of God, and for that reason alone we who are sworn to uphold his reign would imperil more than our lives if we abused his trust. The rest of the court is as fallible as we are, and they are subject to the sins of men. But the Emperor . . ." He did not finish.

"The Emperor is a man like other men, Drosos," Olivia said very quietly.

"No." He took a deep breath. "I don't expect you to understand. You Romans have had to watch your Church crumble along with the power you had. You don't see that God has taken it from you because you were not willing to find those men who could serve Him as well as the state." He moved away from her. "I know that Belisarius would tell you the same thing."

"Which is why he has not protested his treatment any more than he has?" suggested Olivia. "For those of us who remember the Caesars, this appears strange." She tilted her head and looked at him speculatively.

"They were corrupt and corrupting, men without faith and without the power of God to support them." He touched the cross that held his pallium. "The world was in terrible darkness before Christ redeemed us."

Olivia was silent, not knowing what to say. She had watched the development of Christianity with mixed emotions which in the last century had become increasingly apprehensive. She stared down into the water, watching for the movement of the fish and hoping that Drosos would not insist on discussing his religion with her, for inevitably he would disagree with her.

"You are a Roman," he said again, some little time later.

"As you are well aware," she said, trying to make her voice lighter than her heart.

"Yes. I like that in you. I can say things to you that I could not possibly say to a Byzantine." He reached out and took one soft curl in his fingers. "You do not judge me, do you?"

"Not in the way you mean," she said.

He laughed, not understanding her. "And you are not like the women I have known."

Her smile was stunning. "I should hope not."

"You are not like anyone I have known before." He let her hair go, the fine strands pulling slowly across his palm.

"I know that." She had a fleeting thought of the man she now thought of as her first lover, and recalled how he had cautioned her to keep her secret even when she assumed revelation would be welcome. "We are so easily loathed, Olivia," he had said in great sorrow. "We are feared and despised, and then it is a simple matter to . . . be rid of us. Keep your nature to yourself, for your own sake." Looking at Drosos, sensing his turmoil and his desire, she admitted to herself that Sanct' Germain had been right.

"Why is that?" Drosos' question cut into her memories.

"It's . . . my nature," she said slowly and with great care.

"Your Roman nature," he ventured.

"If you like." It was not an answer she wished to give, but one she had learned long ago. There was, deep within her, a yearning to be without guile, to tell Drosos everything about herself—her life and death, five hundred years before, her life since then, the truth of her nature—and she knew that if she did, he would be lost to her. She was amazed to discover how much that mattered to her; she saw Drosos through new eyes.

He rubbed his chin, his thumbnail rasping against his beard. "You are worried about talking to Belisarius, aren't you?"

"Not really," she said. "If he is willing to talk, then I'll know it fairly quickly and that will be all right. If he isn't, then he and I will merely talk like the friends we are. He will apologize for the ruin of my villa and I will tell him how much it saddens me to see him in his . . . predicament."

"I did mean everything I said," he told her, speaking quickly. "I want him to understand that. For him I would risk perdition, but for no one else."

"Drosos, if Belisarius is as devoted to the Emperor as you are and for the same reasons, he will not permit you to act on his behalf. He might not permit it in any case, for he is protective of his men." She wanted to move closer to him, to offer him what little comfort she could, but she remained where she was, watching him.

"Yes," he said, frowning. "But I must try; I have to find

out. You understand, don't you?" This last was a plea, and she felt his anguish.

"I understand. And I will do what I can. Trust me, Drosos. I will find out whatever you need to know, and I will not expose you or Belisarius or myself to any risk beyond the risk of speaking to a man in disgrace." She held out her hand. "Is that enough, Drosos? Will that suffice?"

"I don't know," he said ruefully. He stared at her, respect in his deep brown eyes.

"You're honest, at least," she said, waiting for him to touch her.

"You are willing to take a great chance for me," he said as if aware of it for the first time.

At another time she might have shrugged this off, finding an easy dismissal, but there was something in his face that stopped her. "I value you more than the risk, Drosos."

"I never . . ." He took three hasty steps toward her. "I didn't realize what . . ."

"Then you weren't paying attention," she teased him.

"Do you believe that?" he countered, his hands on her shoulders. "Do you?"

"You were paying attention to other things," she said, her eyes half-closed as she studied him. "You have had so many things on your mind."

"You're a sorceress," he said, his hands holding her more tightly.

"No," she said, "and that is one jest that might be dangerous."

He nodded, sobered. "I wish it weren't so. You're enchanting. Will that do?" He pulled her to him, his lips against her brow. "What is it about you? Why do you possess me this way? What makes you so much more than any other woman?"

She wondered briefly if she ought to answer him, but she could not bring herself to do much more than say, "Why are you unlike other men? Why do I prefer you to anyone else?"

He kissed her abruptly, his mouth hard on hers, his arms confining her. As he drew back, he would not release her, but kept his grip on her, as if he feared she would escape him.

"Drosos," she said softly, and kissed the corner of his mouth for punctuation. "Do not fret."

His expression relaxed a bit. "Is that what I'm doing?"

"Isn't it?" She slid her arms from around his waist and lifted them so that her hands touched at the back of his neck. "You are so mercurial."

"Me?" he said with surprise. "I'm steady as a rock. Mercurial!" he scoffed.

"You are, you know," she told him, her voice little more than a whisper.

"It's because of you. You do things to me, make me feel things, and then I don't know myself anymore." He was not desperate now, but there was a look to him that would have brought tears to her eyes had she been able to weep.

"That's a wonderful gift to give me," she said, and this time kissed him with passion, leaning into him so that she could feel his body through his clothes.

He was breathing more quickly when they moved apart, and as she stepped back, he kept one hand on her, as if parting from her was unbearable. "Which room?" he asked as she started toward the door.

"Mine, of course," she said, smiling back at him. "There are fresh roses and a vial of perfume and sweet oils in my room."

"Decadent. So decadent." He made the word an endearment.

"Roman," she concurred.

"Roses and perfume and oil," he said as they entered the hallway.

"Yes."

He stopped and drew her to him again, his lips lingering on hers, then brushing her cheek, her eyes, her hair. "Why didn't I do this when I first arrived?" he wondered aloud.

"Because you didn't want to," she said honestly.

"More fool me," he murmured, his hands fumbling with her paenula. "You don't have anything on under this, do you?"

"No," she admitted.

"Shameless, too." He nuzzled her neck, then gently caught her earlobe between his teeth.

"Careful," she warned him playfully.

"Why? you do it to me."

"That's different," she said, moving back a step and taking his hand. "Come. We don't want to entertain the servants."

He laughed aloud. "Of course not," he said, trying to sound prim and failing.

At the door of her bedroom, they kissed again, more intensely, tongues exploring, hands spread wide and moving over backs and shoulders. "For love of—"

"You," he finished for her.

"Of Aphrodite," she corrected, although it was not what she had intended to say at first. "Inside, and get out of those clothes. You are going to madden me if you make me wait too long for you."

"Will you rage and pull out your hair?" he prompted.

"No, I will seize heavy objects and throw them at you," she promised. "Inside."

Chuckling he allowed himself to be tugged through the door, and once it was closed, he reached to her tablion to unfasten it. "Let me. I want—" He could not speak of what he wanted; his eyes were eloquent, his hands explained, his mouth formed a poetry that was more sublime for its lack of words.

Olivia, carried by his passion, felt a wonderful stillness about her, a rapture that was so complete that it suspended both of them with its enormity and its tenderness. She opened all of herself to him, so that when he entered her he penetrated much more than her body. It was the sweetest delirium to move with him, to know his savor and weight, his fervor, his ecstasy. She was imbued with his ardor, discovering an awe within herself that had remained inaccessible until now.

As Drosos plunged into release, Olivia found her fulfillment, and so immense was their joy together that her special appetite was gratified almost as soon as her mouth touched him.

They remained as they had been, flesh held by flesh, now unmoving, neither willing to sacrifice their intimacy by separating even to lie in each other's arms.

Olivia looked up into his face, her desires so replete that she could say or do nothing that could add to her bliss. She could feel a thin ribbon of sweat down her ribs and another on her shoulder, and wondered idly if it might be hers as well as his. Damp tendrils of hair clung to her face and the smell of their passion blended with the scent of the roses around them.

They kissed slowly, their lips so sensitive that they barely grazed; exquisite sensations surged through them.

He started to speak, but she stopped the words with her lips, longing to sustain their glorious, prodigal delight. "I must be squashing you," he whispered some while later.

Reluctantly Olivia let herself slip from passion to contentment. "I don't mind."

"Um." He plucked a few stray hairs from his beard off her cheek. "I can't stay in anymore," he said with regret.

Finally they rolled to the side, still together, though the intoxication of their union no longer consumed them.

"Let me move my arm," she offered, shifting so that they would both be more comfortable.

They lay together, her head on his shoulder, her leg over his thigh, the hair of his chest making patterns on her skin. Their hands were joined.

"Every time I think that it cannot be better than the last, and every time it is," he said when he was starting to drift into sleep.

She turned her head so that her lips pressed his shoulder.

"Olivia?" he whispered a little later.

"Yes?"

"In two months, I am being sent to Alexandria." There was devastation in his words.

She felt her throat tighten. "Alexandria?"

"In Egypt," he explained.

"I know where it is," she said, trying to keep the hurt out of her voice.

"So anything that is going to happen has to be before then." He made an angry slash with his free arm. "I'm a toad!"

"Shhush," she admonished him.

But he could not stop. "I shouldn't have said that. It wasn't what I meant. I wanted to tell you all the things in my heart. I wanted you to know what you give to me. I didn't want to say anything about plots or Alexandria, and I did both."

Olivia moved onto her elbow and looked down at him. "It's all right, Drosos," she assured him, hoping she sounded more convincing than she felt.

"I was going to say something later, when we'd slept, when it wouldn't matter as much." His fingers sought her face, tracing the planes of it.

"It would matter whenever you said it." She bent her head and kissed his nipple. "And it doesn't change what we have together."

"It doesn't?" he pleaded.

"No. And you're right. You had to tell me sometime." There was a fine line between her brows, but otherwise her features were tranquil. "We'll have to make the best of the time we have."

"Can we?" His fingers stopped moving and he looked at her with an intensity that was so pure that it was like a light among them.

"It's what we always do," she pointed out with great gentleness. "At least we know what time we have. That makes us more fortunate than most."

"Does it?" He sighed and fought to get the next words out. "I need you, Olivia."

Only twice before had anyone said that to her, and one had been her husband, who had admitted it with abhorrence. The other had been a boy struggling into manhood. Neither had moved her as she was moved now. "I love you, Drosos."

"And I love you; but that's not the same thing," he said, clearly and softly.

"No." She lay down once more, her head tucked under the curve of his jaw. "It's been so long since I mattered that much to anyone. Thank you for—" She stopped.

"For?" he echoed.

"For you." Under her, his chest rose as he stifled a yawn. "Go to sleep. In the morning we will make our plans."

"But . . . it was so perfect. I wrecked it." He patted her shoulder, suddenly ineffective.

"Things like that can't be wrecked, Drosos, no matter what comes after." She wished she could find a way to show him that she was telling him the truth, and it hurt her more than she wanted to admit when at last he drifted into sleep with a murmured fragment of an apology.

Drosos awakened shortly before sunrise, his mood terse. After a small meal of bread and figs he was able to jest about the hour and to remark that Olivia managed better in the morning than many soldiers on campaign did. Olivia accepted the compliment playfully; she did not mention that she hardly ever slept.

*   *   *

*Text of an anonymous letter to the physician Mneno-
datos.*

To the learned Mnenodatos of the Crown of Martyrs'
Church, on the Feast of Saint Iakobis of Nisibis, hail from
one who wishes you well.

It is known of you that you have much skill in the
detection and treatment of poisons, and that is what I must
consult you about on this occasion. You certainly understand why it is that I will not reveal myself, for such
inquiries are often misunderstood. I have sent a messenger
and will send one for your answer in a day's time.

The person I am eager to have you assess is a woman of
middle years, well-born and strong, with a tempestuous and
commanding manner and a fit constitution. This woman
has often suffered from extreme emotions, as women will,
and when episodes of this sort occur, she is likely to do
herself and others an injury.

Composing draughts have sometimes been tried, and have
had some limited success, but it is apparent that they are
not sufficient to the problem, and something stronger is
needed if any lasting relief is to be obtained.

I am reliably informed that most composing draughts are
made from herbs and other substances that have elements of
poison in them, but are concocted in such a way as to
minimize the poison. Is there any way to make such
substances more efficacious without rendering them more
dangerous to the person taking them, and have them act so

214

that the woman would not be convinced that she was being poisoned? She is the sort of woman who might believe such a thing. She often assumes that others are working against her, and for that reason it is likely that she would be willing to believe that those who have her welfare most truly at heart would instead act to her distress.

If there is anything that might aid her, please present the substance, with instructions, to the slave who will call upon you tomorrow. It is of the utmost importance that we carry out this transaction in secrecy and with discretion, for not only is the woman of an uneven temper, her husband of late has had to be careful of unseen enemies, and he would be severe with those he believed were not caring for his wife as they ought.

I have taken the liberty of sending eight pieces of Egyptian gold with my request, both to insure your prompt compliance and to reward you for your silence. You may rest assured that your substance will be treated with care and respect and nothing will be permitted to cast doubts on you or your profession.

A Sincere Friend

· 4 ·

Rain scraped the walls and spattered in on the mosaic floors where the oiled parchment windows had given way under the onslaught of the storm. The room was a miserable place to sit, filled as it was with sudden, hostile draughts and the chill rattle of the rain.

Antonina offered a second cup of hot spiced wine to her

visitor, then pulled her plain wool paenula more closely around her shoulders. "I am still surprised that you came to visit me," she said to Eugenia. "From your last two notes, I thought that you no longer wished the association." Since Belisarius' disgrace the two white streaks in her hair had become more pronounced but her face, in contrast, appeared more glacially serene than it had before.

"Well," Eugenia began, accepting the hot wine gratefully; not only was the warmth needed in this dreadful reception room, but she needed a little time and help to build up her courage. "I have to be sensible, as you've told me time and time again," she began.

"And you are going to be sensible," Antonina said tonelessly.

"To a degree. I must, Antonina." She took a larger gulp than she had intended and tried to swallow it without choking. "I must be careful, being a widow with limited funds. If anything were to render me more questionable as a possible wife, I might not be able to marry again, not for years."

"I know," Antonina said, and although her voice was harsh, she did understand the predicament of her friend. "I don't blame you for doing what you must. I don't even think that you are being disloyal, for you must first be loyal to the Emperor and his rulings."

"Antonina—" Eugenia began, then stopped.

"Have some of these stuffed dates. They're excellent." There was no enthusiasm in the offer, but Eugenia obediently helped herself. "You are placed in the same awkward position as most of my husband's officers are, but you are not as much a risk as they. But if you want to place yourself well, doubtless being seen here will not help you." She poured herself more of the wine but did not drink it.

Eugenia nibbled the dates and ordered her thoughts. "I am aware that you are under constraints. Like many other Konstantinoupolitans, I believe that the treatment is unfair and unnecessary, but it will take time for the

Emperor to see this. Those close to him are determined to continue this estrangement as long as possible."

"So I understand," said Antonina.

"And for that reason, if I curtail my visits, I hope you will not be too horrified by my actions, and will not be too severe in your judgment of me." This last was in a lower tone, and she dared not look too closely at her hostess.

"In your position, I would be tempted to do the same thing," said Antonina. "You have so much to lose, and certainly I do not wish you to have to endure what we are enduring now."

Eugenia cringed under this assault, but she continued to keep herself in check. "I have hopes of a ship's captain. He has eight merchantmen. While he is not as well-placed as my husband was, he is interested in wedding me. And it does not matter to him that I am still seen here. He is not part of the court and has no aspirations to be." She sighed. "He is over fifty and has a belly like a captive bear, but it is something."

"You had your sights higher at one time," Antonina reminded her.

"I still do. But if it becomes necessary, it is rewarding to know that I am not wholly without those who admire me." She tossed her head defiantly, a gesture that had been applauded when she was young and now she did out of habit.

"I would hate to see you stuck with your captain of merchantmen," admitted Antonina. "I had such hopes for you, when I could still command some interest and some respect from those within the ranks of the Guard." She sipped the wine and glanced at the torn windows.

"You have been my staunchest supporter and friend," Eugenia said firmly. "It disgusts me that we are reduced to this when you and I had such hopes. If Theodora could rise from her place, why should not I? I am in a far better position than she was, and I have some fortune to offer a husband."

Antonina held up a warning hand. "Don't speak that way. There are those who would be eager to report what you have said to others who are not your friends. It would do you more harm than simply drinking hot wine with me." She leaned back in her low chair. "It's true, but with Theodora dead, none of us dare remember what she came from. Justinian would not like to hear such things said of her."

Eugenia lowered her eyes, chastened and worried. "Theodora never made any excuses for herself."

"That was Theodora," Antonina said bitterly. "Theodora was not like her husband in many ways. She was not shamed by her past and she appreciated her rise and the favor she attained." She turned too quickly and knocked over the wine cup that stood at her elbow.

"I'll summon a slave," Eugenia said, dabbing ineffectively at it with the edge of her rosy-beige paenula.

"No; there's no saying if we'll have any privacy if you do. Here." She took one of the soft pillows and dropped it onto the wine, watching the stain spread across the linen.

"You'll ruin the pillow," Eugenia warned.

"And who would see it that would care?" She picked up the pillow and dropped it on the floor.

"Antonina, you aren't—" Eugenia cried out.

She was interrupted. "What use for us to pretend, Eugenia? The Emperor has withdrawn the favor he bestowed and for all the position my husband now has, he might as well be posted to the most remote fort in the Empire. In fact, he would think himself lucky if that would happen." She shivered and not entirely because the storm was sniffing at the walls of her house like a hungry animal.

"You must not despair," Eugenia said, repeating what her confessor had told her so many times.

"Why not? I pray that the Emperor will escape the influence of those who are my husband's enemies, but I cannot do as Belisarius does and assume that Justinian is at the mercy of those who wish him ill. I believe—and if I were a man, the belief would be treason, I know—that Justinian is jealous of Belisarius and has decided to take away his power so that he need not fear for his throne. I believe that the Emperor is petty and ungrateful and filled with spite. I believe that he wishes to disgrace my husband and to make an example of him to those who might desire to advance themselves at the Emperor's expense. I believe that nothing my husband does or says will change this and that he would have done better to have died in battle, which is what I think Justinian prayed would happen." She stopped, breathless and flushed.

"I won't repeat that," Eugenia said.

"No matter," Antonina told her with a shake of her head. "The Emperor has spies in this house and he knows all that is said here, and most of what is invented. The slaves know that if they bring a report that further impugns my husband the reward will be greater, and so they embroider everything they hear until a chance remark becomes a flagrant threat." She reached out and gave both of them more wine. "Here. It doesn't matter now. I have already unburdened myself and there is no reason to try to keep a silent tongue in my head."

Eugenia was becoming actively alarmed by her friend's behavior, and she tried to shift their conversation. "Do you think that the mourning we must observe for Theodora will last longer than a year?"

"Who is to say?" Antonina responded. "She would have limited it, but now that she is gone, there is no one to keep the Emperor from his most rigorous demands." She took a long sip of wine and clapped twice loudly. "Simones! Another jug of hot wine."

The eunuch came into the reception room and took the empty jug from the table. "Some sweetmeats as well, great lady?"

"Anything," she answered without any inflection. "Whatever the cooks wish to serve. Just so that the wine is well-spiced and hot. And see if anything can be done about that window. It's cold as a tomb in here."

Simones made a deep, insolent reverence. "Of course, great lady. And I will have a pope petition heaven bring sunshine and balmy days at once."

Antonina straightened. "If you do not wish to find yourself on a sale block, you will never speak to me again in that manner." There was no doubt that she was in earnest, and her eyes bored into him. "And my husband will know of your conduct, so that you will be watched in future. Do you understand that?"

"I understand," said Simones, aware that he had gone too far. He knew that any value he might have existed because he was in the Belisarius household, and that if ever he was sold, he would be of use to no one, and in fact might be thought a liability for his knowledge. The prospect of what could happen then made him correct his demeanor, and he went on, "I vow before God that I will not forget myself again."

"You think that because there are Guards at the door, you may show the same contempt they do, don't you?" Antonina accused him, glad to have someone she could vent her rage and frustration on in safety.

"I forgot myself," he allowed.

"And you have assumed that no one in the household would dare to correct you because of the Guard. You are the slave of this household, not of the Guard, and as long as that is so, you will show yourself subservient and obedient." She paused, satisfied at the fright she recognized in his eyes. "If you are abusive, there is the lash."

"Abusive slaves deserve the lash," Eugenia said severely as she watched Simones. "Don't they?"

"Yes," he said softly. "And when I give abuse, I will thank God for the correction you mete out to me." It was the same formula he had been taught since he was a boy, but he no longer said it like a chastized child.

"You should also thank God that you were made a eunuch," said Antonina. "Rebellion in a whole man is regarded far more seriously than in a eunuch." She indicated the ikonostasis. "Even the Saints have said so."

"Because eunuchs are more tractable?" Eugenia suggested.

Simones bowed his head, and decided to take a chance. "General Narses"—no one in the household had dared to mention Belisarius' replacement in Italy—"is a eunuch."

"Who has nephews," Antonina said curtly. "Speak that name again, and I will assure you that you will be mining copper in Syria before the week is out."

"I did not mean to give insult," said Simones mendaciously. "But there are many who suppose that a man who lacks testicles is unable to turn traitor or be of a warlike disposition. With some this is true, but not with all. I pray that the Emperor will remember this."

"Do you?" Antonina demanded.

"Yes. We are all required to pray for the Emperor, aren't we? The pope where I worship exhorts us often to ask God's especial care for the Emperor's benefit so that he might never lose the wisdom that a ruler must have, and which must come from God." He had the knack of showing correct piety, and he now enjoyed its success again. "I am filled with fault, as man is, but the Emperor is not one who can afford similar faults."

Both women murmured the required response— "Grace of God shine over us"—and then Antonina indicated the wine-soaked pillow.

"Take this away, and bring wine and something to eat. And remember that you are not exempt from the rules that govern a slave's conduct." She waited in silence as Simones picked up the pillow and started for the door. "And Simones?" she called after him. "I never want to hear you speak out again, on any matter. If you do, I will have to send you to market or give you to . . . someone I dislike. You do understand me, don't you?"

This time his reverence was perfect. "In all things, great lady. I am grateful for your correction."

As soon as he was gone, Eugenia leaned forward. "Do you think that you ought to keep him? He seems . . . dangerous."

"In a household like this one, all slaves are dangerous," Antonina sighed. "If my husband were not so much in disfavor, then I might insist that we be rid of him at once, but any slave we purchased to replace him is almost certain to be the creature of one courtier or another.

Simones lacks respect, but he has been in this household for more than ten years and he is loyal. As things stand, that is worth more than conduct." She leaned back once more. "Oh, Eugenia, I am sorry that I have turned out to have so little use to you."

"You must not expose yourself and your husband to greater indignities," said Eugenia with a primness that did not match her look. "And it fills me with dismay that I must make the choice I must. I have consoled myself with the realization that if I were married, my husband would forbid me to come to visit you at all, if he were connected to the court. We would not have this chance to speak."

Antonina nodded. "Yes. And it might have been wiser if you had done that. But still, I am glad that you were willing to see me."

"I . . . I will not see your husband," Eugenia stipulated, her cheeks becoming flushed.

"No, of course not," Antonina concurred. "There would be no good for any of us if you did." She sneezed suddenly and wiped at her eyes. "The storm has brought illness with it."

"You should apply to one of the Greek physicians to give you a tincture for it," Eugenia advised. Greek physicians were trusted more than most, and it was fashionable to have one come to treat minor ailments. Serious disease was another matter: for that you summoned the nearest pope for his prayers and then summoned an Egyptian.

"Perhaps I ought," said Antonina. "But there are herbs here that I can use myself. I am afraid of what a physician might be bribed to give me."

"Why would anyone want to poison you?" Eugenia asked. "You have taken precautions to protect your husband, so why would anyone wish to injure you?"

"I don't know, but the Censor is a man who needs no reason beyond his whim." She coughed once and then looked up as Simones returned bearing a tray. "And hot wine. Hot wine will cure most simple ills except hangnails."

Both women were able to smile at this minor witticism, and they watched as their cups were filled again.

"I have taken the liberty, great lady," Simones said in his most neutral tone, "to request one of the cooks to make honied lamb with onions and rosemary that you like so well."

Antonina showed faint approval. "Your gesture is accepted, Simones," she said, and indicated her guest. "Be sure that there is something for Eugenia as well. My guest would not be pleased to watch me eat with nothing for herself."

"Of course," said Simones, and made his reverence as he withdrew.

"He knows he went too far," Eugenia said as soon as the slave left the room. "He's making amends, isn't he?"

"He's trying," Antonina allowed. "He also knows that if he were sold now, he would not find a master who would please him even as much as my husband does now in his current position."

Eugenia helped herself to the wine. "You must not see many visitors."

"Not welcome ones," Antonina confirmed darkly.

"Who calls on you?" She was wondering how conspicuous her own visit would be, and how much of a risk she had taken in coming.

"A few of the officers call, but they must come with a pope with the Censor's approval. Drosos has been here most often. I have seen the widows of those officers who fell in Italy and Africa." She stared at the window, angry with the storm. "The relatives who are not at court have visited me, and a few of my husband's mother's family have come. That Roman widow Olivia has been here three times. The four daughters of Aristinos Pavko have been here, but now that they are religious, they are bound by the rules of their community, and we have little we may discuss."

"That's all?" Eugenia asked, horrified at the degree to which she had exposed herself to censure.

"All that are welcome. You see how things have

changed here. A year ago I would not have been eager to listen to four young women tell me why it is heretical to believe that the nature of Christ was more divine than human." She finished the wine in her cup and filled it again.

By the time Eugenia left her hostess, she was feeling reckless and light-headed. Her visit, which seemed the most terrible folly an hour before, now felt more pleasant, an adventure that had an air of heroism about it because of what it did for Antonina. Let others hesitate and worry and keep away for fear of what the Censor might say; she, Eugenia, would not be intimidated. She would visit her old friend and show that she had the same strength of purpose as Belisarius' officers. In this frame of mind, she was almost to the door, and thinking of a few pithy things to say to the Guards, when she noticed that Simones was waiting for her.

"Come to apologize to me?" she asked, her words not quite as crisp as usual. "Or do you want me to intercede for you and get you back into your mistress' favor?"

"Neither," Simones said. "I want to arrange a few things with you."

Eugenia was too astonished to be affronted. "With me? You?"

"I have to find someone who will assist me, and you are the most promising. Antonina trusts you and she wants to see you. She believes that you will not desert her as most of the others have done, and you still can benefit from her favor, which none of her other friends could." He watched her, curious to see what her reaction would be.

"What if I go back to her right now and tell her what you have said?" There was a speculative light in her eyes and she waited to hear what Simones would say.

"That would not be wise," said Simones. "You might be rid of me, but another would come in my place and he might decide that Antonina is to be kept in isolation for the good of the Emperor."

"And you?" asked Eugenia, curious and becoming apprehensive.

"I know that my mistress is distressed and lonely, which is unfortunate. I know that no matter what she says, she is eager for your company and wishes that you might continue to visit her in spite of the risk that such visits entail. You do not know how devastating this has been, and you do not know how much she has longed for the Emperor to relax the restrictions against this household. But that isn't going to happen for some time yet." He watched her. "She depends upon you, although she does not know it."

"Why do you tell me this?" She was aware that Simones had no reason to sacrifice so much to Antonina, and she suspected the level of dislike the slave had for his mistress.

"Because I need assistance," he said bluntly. "I have been ordered"—he used the word deliberately—"to watch and make note of all that happens in this household. Certainly I do what I must because of the order of the Emperor and his Censor. I am in no position to do otherwise."

"And what if Antonina discovers your duplicity?" Eugenia asked with malice in her smile.

"Why should she know anything of it?" countered Simones with a distinct threat in his tone.

"Anything might happen. And then off to the copper mines?" She shrugged.

"If I am sent to the copper mines, there will be others with me." He folded his arms. "Why not assist one another? You could impress the Censor with your devotion and there is no reason that anything you said to me would compromise Antonina." Simones knew how to be persuasive. "You would advance yourself and not add to Antonina's discredit. Think of the advantage that you could have. This would be one way you might return some of the favor Antonina has shown you over the years. You would be able to inform her of your actions when the Court Censor is satisfied that her husband is not guilty of any conspiracy or has supported any plots against the Emperor. Your activities on her behalf would be rewarded and you would show Antonina that you are to be trusted and respected."

"You wheedle and tempt, don't you?" Eugenia asked, but there was a speculative turn to her face now and she did not move away from him or reprimand him for making such a suggestion.

"Hardly," he said. "I only mention this so that we might both benefit and aid this household during its troubles." He resisted the urge to smile, knowing that she would be offended by smiles.

"A woman in my position cannot take risks, slave. I have no one who can sponsor me if I am questioned or accused. I have little money, and my husband's family has some influence but not enough to influence anyone near the Censor."

"And so it would be sensible of you to think about acting on your own behalf so that you have some position and protection. It would give you access to the court again, and with the gratitude of the Censor, you can be confident of his aid in attaining your ends. He will see your merit and wish to thank you." Simones saw that there were three household slaves approaching them, and he abandoned his efforts at once. "I hope you will consider what I have said."

"I may," said Eugenia as she went toward the vestibule.

                              *   *   *

Text of an Imperial edict.

   To all Christians living within the boundaries of our
Empire, and to those of good conscience living elsewhere in
the world, the greetings of Justinian and the Peace of God
be with you.
   We have prayed long for divine guidance in the matter of
unchristian works, and works of heresy. We are aware that
the Christ admonished us to embrace our enemies and to be
sparing in our judgment of others, yet He also stated that
we must be free of the Devil's work if we are to be with
Him in Heaven.
   To that end, we have considered the writings that are not
of Orthodox Christian origin, which lead to dissension and
confusion in our people, and we have consulted with our
popes and metropolitans as well as other religious, and we
have realized that these works, many of them well-
intentioned, are the subtle and dangerous works that lure
men from Christ and damn the souls of many to everlasting
suffering.
   For that reason alone the works stand condemned. But
there are greater considerations: these works might easily
contribute to sedition and other traitorous acts, which marks
them as the tools of those without Grace. Books that purport
to teach and have no thought of God and salvation in them
are worse than lies and deception, for their treachery lies in
their seeming innocence.
   Therefore we are requiring that all Christians examine

*their souls and review the books they possess. If what the
books contain are not worthy of Christian study and if they
are filled with heresies and lies, we ask that you show your
devotion by burning these books and encouraging those
around you to do the same with their books. We are certain
that when this is done, much of the ambivalence that has
caused such misfortune to the Christians of this Empire will
be brought to an end, and the disputes that have led to so
many unchristian sentiments and attitudes will be lessened.
We are reminded that to aid those in need is the purpose of
charity, and so if any of you are aware of those who are
misguided and who seek to preserve their books, for whatever reason, no matter how sincere, that you attempt to
persuade them to be rid of these sources of doubt and failing
that leads inevitably to perdition and the perpetual torments
of hell.*

*With the concurrence of the Court Censor and the popes
and metropolitans, we wish all of you Godspeed in these
great spiritual acts that will purge us all of much evil.*

*By our own hand on the Feast of the Evangelists at
midsummer.*

> *Justinian*
> *Emperor of Byzantion*
> *his sigil*

Just off the Mese there were a number of smaller markets that specialized in various ways. One was filled with jewel merchants, another was the home of leather workers. This street boasted furniture from foreign ports, some brought by sea, some carried overland along the Old Silk Road.

Niklos strolled through it, mildly curious about what was being offered. He had to meet with a chariot-builder in the next street, but was pleased to have a little time to spend in this way.

One of the stalls set up was filled with Roman goods: chests, tables, chairs, braziers, benches were all piled together in confusion; two bored slaves watched over the stall, one of them more interested in the food vendors than in selling anything from the trove.

Niklos regarded the Roman goods, an amused, ironic expression in his dark, ruddy eyes. He went to examine the nearest pile, remarking to the nearest slave, "I am the bondsman of a Roman lady, and she might wish to purchase some of your stock."

"Look at what we have," the slave offered without much enthusiasm. "There is more available."

"How much more?" Niklos inquired as he picked up a small chair and examined it.

"I'm not sure. My master and the merchant Ghornan have an agreement of sorts." He waved flies away from a dish of fruit. "Every time Captain Ghornan returns, he brings more things with him, and he and my master make their arrangements."

"Captain Ghornan sails to Italy, then?" There were not many merchants willing to take the risks necessary to do this now that the Ostrogoths had increased the strength of their navy.

"Regularly," the slave said with marked indifference. "He has never encountered serious trouble and does not expect to. It must be his Coptic heresy that makes him think that way." He reached over and took a handful of berries out of the dish. As he munched them, he went on. "Captain Ghornan is one who takes advantage of secret landings, I guess."

"Secret landings or bribes?" Niklos asked as he poked around the furniture.

"Probably both," the slave said through a full mouth. "He claims that he is not bothered."

"How fortunate," Niklos said dryly. He was about to observe that bribes always became more expensive as time went on when he noticed two wooden trunks with brass fittings. "Do you know where this Captain Ghornan gets these goods?" he asked very carefully.

"He says he buys them from homeless Romans." The slave ate more berries.

"Homeless Romans," Niklos repeated as he uncovered the two chests and studied them. "More likely he has them from Roman homes," he said.

"How do you mean?" asked the slave with a signal to his companion.

"I . . ." Niklos faltered. Both slaves at the stall were now watching him with suspicion. He took a short, deep breath and plunged in. "I am afraid that these two chests belong to my mistress. They were left in her villa when we came here. At the time we were assured that they would be guarded. Now, it may be that one of Totila's men commandeered the chests and then sold them, but it may also be that your Captain Ghornan has been dealing with men who are taking goods from villas that ought to be protected."

One of the slaves laughed unpleasantly. "Your mistress wants a few Roman things, and so you make this accusation in the hope that she will not have to pay the price of the things; is that it?"

"No," said Niklos, no longer attempting to be deferent. "I think that someone has taken her goods from her villa and sold them. I do not say that your Captain Ghornan is the one, but it is clear that someone has sold my mistress' goods, and that I must inform her of it."

The two slaves exchanged looks. "You will have to speak to one of the army magistrates," said the slave who was still eating berries. "That is, if there is any justification to your absurd accusation."

"My mistress had all her goods marked, and I know that these two chests have her mark." Niklos indicated the chests. "If there are other goods from the same shipment, I will have to tell the authorities."

"Marks can be added or changed," one of the slaves said.

"These marks are in the brass," Niklos said.

"In the brass?" the other slave inquired, clearly not believing him.

"Yes; it was the custom during the time of the Caesars to mark valuable property in this way. My mistress comes from an old family and has kept to the traditions." He stepped back and noticed that a small crowd had gathered around the stall. "I do not accuse your master or even this Captain Ghornan of anything. I am willing to believe that everyone involved is acting in good faith except the actual culprit who took the goods from the villa, but I do not think that the chests wandered out on their own or that they were sold entirely by accident." He addressed the slave who had finally finished eating his berries. "I will have to tell my mistress about this, and she, I know, will want to tell the authorities."

The slave glared at Niklos. "You are a foolish man," he warned. "This is not Roma, and here we do not accept the word of a slave, or a woman, for that matter. Here we demand more proof and greater authority."

Niklos decided he would not tell Olivia about this remark; she would be irritated enough as it was and this animadversion on slaves and women would enrage her. "It will be provided. In the meantime, I want you to know that I will hold you accountable for these goods. If they have disappeared between now and the time the case is reviewed, I will testify that you were in charge of the goods and that you were instructed to have them ready for inspection."

"Slaves do not testify," the other informed Niklos haughtily.

"True; bondsmen do, however, and I am a bondsman." With that, he turned and regarded the people clustered around the stall. "Every one of you will bear witness to this, if that is necessary. This is not something that can be easily forgotten or dismissed out of hand." He pointed at the two slaves. "These men are responsible for the contents of this stall. If there is any loss or disruption, the burden of that loss will be theirs."

"You're harsh, Roman," said one of the passersby.

"I'm Greek," Niklos corrected him. "My mistress is Roman."

There was a subtle shift of sympathies in the crowd, and Niklos knew that he would not have to complain without support. He smiled at the slaves in the stall. "Remember my warning."

"Your warning means nothing to us. Our master will be told of what you have claimed. The rest is up to him." With that the slave turned away and motioned for his companion to do the same.

Niklos was far from satisfied with this answer, but did not want to press the slaves for fear that he would lose the sympathy he had gained. He moved away from the stall quickly and in a short while he reached Olivia's house. He found her in her library reading.

"You look dreadful," she said as she looked up.

"I've got good reason," he said, and dropped onto the low bench across the reading table from her.

"And what reason is that?"

Niklos did not answer at once. When he did, his manner was remote, as if he were discussing events of the distant past. "You recall those two chests of yours, the ones with the brass fittings?"

As always when they were alone, they spoke in Latin, their accents old-fashioned and elegant, their phrases slightly archaic. "Chests?"

"Yes. Pay attention, Olivia. This is important." His aggravation was mixed with fondness and he touched her shoulder in a way no Byzantine servant—slave or bondsman—would dare to touch a superior. "The chests with brass fittings."

"With camphor on the inside and two drawers on one side, the ones that were made during Caracalla's reign— yes, of course I remember them. What of it?" She had set aside the book she was reading and was now watching him closely.

"I just saw them."

"What?"

"I just saw them," he repeated. "In the market. In a stall filled with Roman goods." He looked away from her, for the first time as if he were ashamed of what he was telling her. "They were for sale."

"In a stall in the market, of course they were for sale. Isn't that the purpose of a stall in the market?" She spoke amiably enough, but Niklos was not fooled.

"Olivia—"

"My things, offered for sale here. How fortunate that I will not be put to the trouble of sending for them, or requiring some account of them." Her hazel eyes had darkened and acquired a metallic glitter.

"Olivia, you're—"

"Furious," she agreed with him, favoring him with a wide, insincere smile.

Niklos nodded. "With good reason. I was appalled."

"The chests. I wonder what else?" She stared up at the ceiling so that she could avoid looking at him. "Was that all, did you notice?"

"I don't know," he said truthfully.

"But there were other Roman things in the stall, you said."

"Yes. All sorts of furniture. I saw some vases and braziers as well, but nothing I could identify for certain." He gave a short sigh.

"Aha." She drummed her fingers on the table. "So someone has helped themselves to what was left behind."

"It seems so," Niklos agreed. "But who it is, I have no way of discovering yet—"

"We will find out in due course," she said with determination. "And when we do, there are steps to be taken." She got up suddenly and began to pace. "I have been afraid this would happen. I sensed the possibility when we left. When Belisarius was recalled, I knew that any protection the villa might have had was lost. I've almost expected it." She touched her hair, fidgeting with the ordered arrangement of pins.

"Olivia," Niklos said, sharing her indignation, "tell me what you wish me to do."

"I suppose we had best find out how to make a complaint, and to whom. And you may be certain that you or a churchman or possibly even Belisarius will have to do the thing officially, since according to the law here, I cannot own property!" She flung a small iron stylus across the room.

Niklos retrieved it and held it out to her. "You'll want this later."

She was still too angry to be chagrined, but she took it and put it back on the table. "They are so certain, aren't they, that they will look after the interests of their women, and they cannot conceive of a situation arising where their judgment is not superior. It comes from having all those male gods. And do not remind me," she went on more sharply, "that they are all aspects of one god. I know Jupiter, Apollo and Mercury when I see them, no matter how they are got up."

"I wasn't going to say anything," Niklos assured her.

This time she looked him straight in the eye. "You're very clever, my friend, and I am grateful for that."

"You're not a dolt yourself," Niklos pointed out.

"And why does Drosos have to be gone now, I ask you. Why does he have to be on his way to Alexandria. After all those weeks of wanting to do something for me and not knowing what, he would have to be gone the one time I truly need him." She went and stared out her window; the oiled parchment had been moved aside and the scent of the garden drifted into the library.

"Then what shall it be?" asked Niklos. "Do you wish me to make inquiries?"

"Yes, but first go to Belisarius. Or better yet, I will go, and I will speak with him. He was at the villa. He will want to know what has been taken in any case." She adjusted the drape of her paenula. "I suppose I must use one of the palanquins, with the curtains drawn. It's exasperating."

"I will see that one is summoned," said Niklos.

"Yes. Thank you for that. And then arrangements will have to be made to have the stall searched thoroughly, and the storehouse of the merchant as well, I guess. What else should we do? What a tremendous amount of work." She sighed.

"Would you rather accept the losses?"

She rounded on Niklos. "Magna Mater, no! And you know it."

"Then to Belisarius first?" he suggested.

"Yes. Belisarius first." Now that she was set on a task, her manner changed. She moved with determination and there was no trace of doubt in her attitude.

By the time Niklos had found a palanquin, Olivia had changed her dalmatica and paenula so that she was more formally attired. She had deliberately chosen Roman cloth and her most Roman jewels to wear on her visit. As she stepped into the palanquin, she said to Niklos, "If there are questions from the Guard, you are to make this as official as you can. I came here with Belisarius' sponsorship, and now that my goods have been seized, I am requesting his aid in reclaiming them. They won't question that."

"As you say," Niklos concurred.

The streets were still busy and it took some little time to go from one hill to the next. The noise was particularly loud near the places where the streets were being widened and old buildings were being torn down to make way for them.

"This is worse than Traianus," Olivia complained from inside the palanquin. "What is it with men in power that they have sudden impulses to remake the world?"

"It's not a bad idea," Niklos said. "These streets are far too narrow for all the traffic and the stalls and shops as well."

"And so for the next year or two, no one can move along them at all," Olivia declared, then said a bit more contritely, "If I weren't already irritated, it would not annoy me as much. Bear with me." She continued to speak in Latin.

Niklos patted the drawn curtains. "How long have I served you? Wasn't the beginning the same year that Commodus was murdered?" He had taken a more playful tone with her, and now he chuckled. "Roma was not yet a thousand years old."

"It wasn't, was it?" Olivia asked, her voice less harsh than before. "It was the last thing Sanct' Germain did before he went—" She stopped. "If he were here, he'd deal with this and there would be no reason for us to be out here on the street going to Belisarius' house. And if we were in Roma, I could take care of the whole thing myself." A little of the gruffness had returned, and she cleared her throat in a conscious effort to be rid of the sound. "But he is not here, and we are not in Roma but in . . . Konstantinoupolis, and so we must proceed as the laws require us to proceed."

"Philosophy becomes you," Niklos teased gently.

"Oh, Niklos," she said, permitting herself a rare moment of despair, "what has become of us?"

"We're almost to Belisarius' house," Niklos warned, continuing in Greek. "There are five Guards at the front of the house."

"Speak to the one who is highest in rank," said Olivia, also in Greek. "And be very respectful. They put great store by subservience here."

"It's their way," Niklos agreed, and adopted a more humble manner than he usually had. "Good Captain," he said when he had come near enough to be heard clearly, "my mistress seeks a word with Belisarius."

The Captain, a lanky young man with a narrow face and haughty attitude, regarded Niklos contemptuously. "And who is your mistress that she comes here?"

"The Roman widow, Atta Olivia Clemens. General Belisarius was her sponsor when she left Italy, and it is in that regard that she wishes to speak to him now." Niklos motioned to the chairmen to put the palanquin down. "It is a matter of some urgency, good Guardsman, and one that requires the General's attention."

The Captain laughed. "What could that be?"

"It concerns theft," Niklos said baldly. "The losses are considerable and my mistress is in need of aid and advice." He knew that this was in accord with Byzantine propriety but he disliked the unnecessary complexity of fulfilling a simple request.

"The General might not be able to do much for your mistress," warned the Captain.

"Then he will have to direct her to those who can," Niklos said, becoming impatient. "Good Captain, if you are going to refuse my mistress admittance here, then tell me at once so that we may seek out a pope at Hagia Sophia or Hagia Irene to give us the benefit of his counsel."

The Captain moved aside from the door. "What is the widow's name again?"

"Atta Olivia Clemens, widow of Cornelius Justus Silius," Niklos said accurately. He did not add that her husband had been executed during the reign of the elder Titus Flavius Vespasianus, almost five hundred years ago.

"Clemens, Clemens," mused the Captain. "Is that the one who lives alone in the house with two gardens?"

"That is she," Niklos acknowledged, somewhat surprised that the Captain of the Guard would know of her.

"And she wishes to see Belisarius about a theft?"

"Yes; I have said so already." Niklos covered his sharpness by adding, "She is very angry and has been taking out her feelings on the backs of her household."

The Captain grinned. "Romans are excessive." He indicated the door. "You and your mistress may enter, and Belisarius will be informed that you have come. If he says he wishes to see your mistress, then she will be given the chance to speak with him. Otherwise, you must leave at once. Is that understood?"

"It's understood," said Niklos, bending to assist Olivia out of the palanquin.

Simones was waiting for them just inside the door and he regarded Olivia speculatively as she came into the house behind Niklos. "Great lady, I am surprised to see you here."

"I am a little surprised to be here," said Olivia loudly enough to have her words reach the Guard outside. "But circumstances require that I speak with your master."

Simones made a belated reverence to Olivia and ignored Niklos. "I will inform him of your arrival. May I tell him why you have come?"

"It concerns my villa near Roma. He stayed there some of the time during his campaign." She gave a direct, hard stare to the eunuch slave. "That ought to be sufficient, Simones."

After a second reverence, Simones hastened away, only to return promptly with word that Belisarius would wait upon Olivia in the larger reception room. "I will claim the honor of escorting you there," he added when he had delivered the information.

"It is just down the hall on the left," Olivia said. "I am able to find it. Niklos will come with me." She did not give Simones a chance to argue, but went quickly to the room she had indicated.

Belisarius looked exhausted when he joined Olivia there a little later. "I've missed you," he said. "But with Antonina in poor health, and my condition being what it is, we do not often see anyone these days."

"Antonina is in poor health?" Olivia repeated, startled at the news. "When I saw her last, she was thriving."

"It has only been recently that she has suffered. Her pope tells her that it is the result of the continuing disfavor of Heaven, but I cannot believe it. I have brought so much misfortune on her, and if—" He stopped abruptly. "That isn't why you're here, is it?"

"No," she admitted, her concern not forgotten. "Niklos was in the market today and saw goods from my Roman villa offered for sale." She had not intended to state the problem so directly, but knowing now that Belisarius had many other troubles to plague him, she decided that speaking to the point was best.

Belisarius looked at Niklos. "You're certain?"

"If you had served Olivia as long as I have, you would know these things as if they were your own," he said. "I am certain."

"He would not have spoken to me unless he was sure," Olivia added.

"What specifically did you see?" Belisarius asked.

"Two chests, antiques, with brass fittings. They're most unusual." He paused. "I didn't look further. However, the stall in the market was filled with Roman goods."

"And so you assume that if the chests are there, other things may also be. You suspect that there has been some sort of a raid on the villa." Belisarius nodded heavily. "And doubtless you have good reason to think so. My officers have brought me tales that do not bode well."

"You mean that Totila—" Olivia began.

"Not only our enemies. There are Byzantines who want to pick the carcass before the Ostrogoths get there." His bitterness was ferocious and it was a moment before he could speak safely. "I'm sorry, Olivia. When I left Italy, I was told that my obligations would be honored by Narses and his officers, but . . . it appears otherwise."

"You've heard of other complaints?" It was not truly a question. She could read Belisarius' expression and knew that there had been others.

"Unfortunately." He lowered his head and rubbed his eyes. "I am profoundly sorry to learn of this. I'll start an official inquiry at once, of course."

"But . . ." Olivia regarded him with sympathy.

"Yes. You're right." Belisarius stared across the room at a blank spot on the wall. "But as I am under suspicion of conspiracy and treason, I can make no promises for the success of the inquiry. The Court Censor is convinced that I have acted against the interests of the Emperor, and therefore everything I do and say is scrutinized for possible hidden significance." He tugged at the end of his pallium. "It has even been implied that I have poisoned my own wife to direct suspicion elsewhere."

"Oh, my friend," Olivia said, and went to put her arm over his bowed shoulders.

He shrugged her away. "I am contaminated. Don't be tainted by me."

"But I already am," Olivia said at her most reasonable. "I came here with your assistance, and I come to you for aid. You were my guest in Roma, and I have been yours here in . . . Konstantinoupolis. Doubtless if the Censor believes that women are capable of conspiracy—which I doubt—he will have long since decided that I am not to be trusted." This time when she put her arm around his shoulder, she did not permit him to break away from her. "First, I think we must determine exactly how much has been taken from my villa, and what has already been sold."

"Didn't you hear me?" Belisarius demanded.

"Yes. And now you will listen to me." She sat beside him and kept her arm across his back. "I wish to discover what I have lost. Niklos has an inventory of the goods from the villa at my house here—which I thank you again for helping me to acquire—and a copy of this can be provided to . . . to whoever needs it."

"The magistrate for the Army," Belisarius muttered.

"Fine. Niklos, a copy of the inventory for the magistrate for the Army. Then it might be wise to inspect the stall and warehouse of the merchant where Niklos found the chest." Her strength surprised Belisarius when he tried once more to move away from her. "Don't you agree?"

Capitulating, Belisarius turned to her. "All right, Olivia. I'll try to arrange for the inspection. Is there anything else you want?"

Her laughter was sadder than any he had ever heard. "Magna Mater, yes. The list is so long—" She forced a half-smile back onto her lips. "But for the time being, tell me what is wrong with Antonina. Perhaps I can help."

Belisarius took her free hand in both of his. As he stared down at their interlaced fingers, he admitted, "Christos, I hope so. I'm frightened, Olivia: I'm afraid."

*　　*　　*

Text of a letter from the physician Mnenodatos to his unknown correspondent.

On the Feast of the Armenian Martyrs, the physician Mnenodatos sends his greetings to his continuing friend.

Your request for information regarding certain poisons, while no doubt necessary, nevertheless concerns me. Your generosity is most welcome, and I am grateful for all you have done for me, but I must inquire more closely into the use to which you have put this information, for if there has been any misuse of your knowledge gained through me, I am as culpable as you are, in fact, because I have given you the degree of information I have, I am more culpable in the eyes of the law.

While I have no wish to lose your assistance and friend-

ship, I find myself in a very awkward state, since I am now in a position where I am apt to be blamed for the misfortune of another. Not only do I not know who you are, I am in no position to know who it is you have acquired this information for and to what end it is being used, and I beseech you to tell me at least some portion of what I have requested so that I will not be entirely without protection.

Your latest request comes with a most beneficent payment, one far exceeding the worth of what I have told you, and for that reason if no other, I dread what you might do. I have a wife and children to think of, good friend, and they might easily be made beggars tomorrow if you are not acting as honorably as I pray you are.

At first, it did not trouble me that you did not say who you are or in what capacity you employ the information you have obtained from me. But that was before the riots last week, and now I am afraid that those who believe that the Empress Theodora met her end by poison might search out all of us who have some knowledge of the subject and inquire into their activity. At this time, I could not prevail if such an inquiry were made of me, and that fills me with the gravest foreboding.

Come forth, I pray you, and reveal who you are and what you are doing. I give my word on the Most Holy Spear that I will not betray you, and I will accept your vow that you will not betray me. Until some such assurance is given me, I cannot provide you any more information or assistance, and I am convinced that if you examine your conscience, you will grant my requests as the reasonable protection they are.

If you decide that you cannot do this, or that you will not contact me again, know that I have your various notes and letters which I will surrender to any officer of the court who makes any inquiry whatever of me. I might not be able to identify you for them, but I will reveal to what extent you have involved me in whatever scheme you are acting upon. Naturally I would rather not have to do this, and if you act promptly and in good faith, I will demonstrate my sincerity *by surrendering all copies of your notes and letters to you for your disposal in any way you see fit.*

Mnenodatos
Physician

• 6 •

Thekla was over fifty and revered for her years as well as her long religious vocation. Since age eight, she had lived a virtual hermit in a cell scraped out of the city battlements facing the Sea of Marmara. It was said that the Emperor Theodosius II who had ordered the extension of Constantine's seaward battlements had intended to protect the city from the land as well as the sea, and Thekla was one of many who had brought her holiness to fortify the walls.

"But most holy woman," said Panaigios, leaning nearer the wall so that he would be able to hear the few, whispered words she would vouchsafe him, "surely you know more of the dangers facing the Emperor from those who stand nearest to him."

"That is always the most dangerous," whispered the dry, ancient voice. "Judas stood nearest Christos, they say. He kissed Him."

"But who stands nearest Justinian that might do such a thing?" Panaigios demanded. His position with Kimon Athanatadies had slipped in the last year and he was growing desperate for the means to renew his situation.

Thekla laughed, or so it seemed to Panaigios who heard

the rustling sound with an emotion near awe. "You do not want to know. The righteous are vilified and the vile are exalted."

"Do you mean that the Emperor Justinian is not entitled to rule?" Panaigios gasped.

Again the laugh, and the singsong repetition: "The righteous are vilified and the vile are exalted."

"I don't know what you mean. You must speak more directly." He knew that he was challenging a venerated person who could have him imprisoned for little more than the tone of his voice. He could not stop himself from speaking. "Tell me."

"You do not want to know. You embrace your ignorance. You would not know honor if Hagios Gavrilos himself announced it to you." The old woman's wheezing words came more quickly, as if she were trying to speak her last message on a single breath. "You wallow in corruption as if you partook of the manna of Paradise. The Word of God is a whistle in the rising wind."

Panaigios glowered at the stones that separated him from the famous old anchorite and wished he had the strength of body and character to pull them down and demand that she explain herself. Instead he leaned his forehead against the stones. "Do you speak against the Emperor?"

"I speak against no one," she answered. "I speak only what God sends me to know. Leave me. You are deaf to Grace." With this condemnation she fell silent.

"Thekla." He waited and when no response was forthcoming, he repeated her name several times only to be met with silence.

"I say nothing against any man," the arid voice said as Panaigios started away from the battlements.

He paused, uncertain if he had imagined the last sounds or not, but decided at last that they were the parting words from the old holy woman. He looked up toward the walkway where the Guard patrolled, and saw two soldiers standing some distance away, apparently deep in conversation. How much had they overheard and who would they tell? he wondered.

In a short while Panaigios had reached his two Egyptian slaves who stood beside his chariot. He signaled them both to follow him as he stepped into the vehicle and took the reins from the younger slave. "I have much to think about," he told them in his most important voice.

"There was a messenger from the Censor," said the older slave. "His master wishes to see you before you return to your house."

This was a summons that Panaigios dared not ignore. "Of course," he said as if it were the most natural thing in the world that he should be sent for in this unusual way. "I intended to report there before I went home in any case."

The two slaves exchanged glances; neither was fooled by this show of sangfroid. They fell into step behind the chariot, though the crowding on the streets was sufficient to keep their progress to a slow walk.

At the house of the Court Censor—which was a palace in everything but name—Panaigios turned his horse into the courtyard and waited while one of the armed private guards came and took the chariot in control.

"Where am I expected?" Panaigios asked, doing his best to keep the shudder he felt out of his voice.

"My master will see you in the room adjoining his chapel." The guard regarded Panaigios with an expression that was very near pity. "He has a few questions to ask you."

"Excellent," said Panaigios with an enthusiasm that he was far from truly feeling. "I have a few matters to discuss with him and this will make it possible for us to cover a number of matters now." He strode into the house, praying that his knees would not give way.

The antechamber to Athanatadies' chapel was oppressively small, with high walls and only two lunette windows well above reach. There were frescoes of the hideous death of the Thirty Virgin Martyrs who had been partially flayed and then left in the sun to die. Panaigios stared at the depiction of the blessed suffering and wished he had the courage to run.

Kimon Athanatadies emerged from his chapel some while later, his dusty dalmatica and disarranged pallium revealing that he had spent part of his time at prayers prostrate. He looked sharply at his secretary and indicated the door that led into the private part of the house. "I must speak with you."

"I am pleased to have it so," said Panaigios, lying heroically.

"Are you?" Athanatadies shrugged indicating that Panaigios' opinion made no difference to him.

"Most certainly. I have wanted recently to have more opportunity to speak with you, but there has not been the occasion, and therefore—" He broke off before he became completely lost in his sentiments.

"In here, if you will." He indicated a small reception room where an armed guard waited. "Melisandos, wait at the door," Athanatadies said to the man and closed the door so that he and Panaigios were alone. "Sit. In a while I will order refreshments."

"That isn't necessary," said Panaigios, anxious not to make his social ambitions too obvious.

"I'm hungry; I've fasted since last night." He had already taken the most comfortable chair leaving two small benches for Panaigios to choose between. "I've been busy with the matter of expunging the heretical writings of Eutyches and his followers. The Monophysitism heresy is more insidious than the Nestorian heresy, for it is easy to fall into the error that Christos partook more of the divine than humanity, and that is the grossest and most pernicious error. Anyone can see the error in thinking that Christos partook more of humanity than divinity. I have never feared the Nestorians."

Panaigios knew better than to enter into any religious debate with the Court Censor; he decided to respond safely. "I have never read suspect texts."

"Very wise, although the time may come when it will be

required so that you will be able to identify heresy in its most subtle disguises, that of true faith." He leaned back. "What did you want to say to me?"

This direct question took Panaigios by surprise and he stammered as he answered. "I have taken the liberty of approaching Thekla to see if I might discover who near to the Emperor is the most dangerous."

"Thekla!" exclaimed Athanatadies. "You have been busy."

"I have been worried," Panaigios countered, not wanting to appear that he had usurped any privilege of the Censor himself. "I have spoken to officers of Belisarius in the hope that they might reveal treason or the intention to act against the Empire and I have yet to get any of them to reveal themselves."

"And so you went to Thekla. Most ingenious. And what did the venerable old witch have to say?" He laughed at his secretary's scandalized expression. "The woman might be holy but I fear she is also quite mad most of the time. And she is clever enough to say nothing that would jeopardize her situation. She is wholly dependent on the bread and water left her by religious men and women who offer charity. She will say nothing that might end that charity." He folded his hands and gazed at Panaigios apparently enjoying the man's discomfort.

"I . . . I wanted the benefit of . . . of . . ." He could no longer define what he had sought. He decided the whole day had been terribly unsatisfactory.

"Oh, I know you were hoping for some clue that might give you the key to the silence of the officers. But did it ever occur to you that perhaps the reason for the silence is that there is nothing to reveal?" He sighed. "As little as I wish to believe it, and as little as I am prepared to believe it, there is no evidence yet that there was ever a rebellion planned, or that Belisarius ever hankered for the purple. Still, he will be kept under house arrest and his men watched. They are clever men who have learned the virtue of waiting. They may wish to lull us into inattention and then act."

"Yes!" burst out Panaigios. "And that is what I have been trying to puzzle out. Thekla had a few things to say, and little as you may wish to believe them, I think there was substance in her warning."

"And what was that?" Athanatadies asked with very little curiosity.

Panaigios was driven to answer, convinced that he might still hold the answer to the mystery that had confronted them since Belisarius had returned from Italy. "She said that the vile were raised up and the righteous were cast down."

"So the Prophets have said, over and over. That's safe enough." Athanatadies clapped his hands and when Melisandos opened the door, he requested that fruit and bread be brought. "Bring something for this man as well," he added as an afterthought.

"I have assigned Yaspros to the matter," Panaigios went on. "I think that if anyone can penetrate the secret, he is the one. I have also enlisted a few slaves within Belisarius' house so that if there is anything that might require our attention we will know of it at once."

"Yes; sensible." Athanatadies smoothed the front of his garments. "I have a request to make in that respect."

"Yes?" said Panaigios, grateful for the interruption.

"Find out what poison it is that is being used on Antonina and how much longer it is likely to take." This was said so bluntly that Panaigios had to bite his tongue to keep from crying out in astonishment.

"Poison?" he forced himself to ask.

"What else? She was not ill until recently, and now she can no longer hold her food and often complains of burning in her vitals. That is very like poison. Her physician hasn't been able to relieve it as he might have if it were merely an aggravation of the gut." He sighed and shook his head sadly. "If that woman had not tried to press the advantage of her friendship with Theodora then she might not have had to endure what torments her now."

"I . . . I will make a few inquiries," said Panaigios,

recovering himself enough to appear unaffected.

"And I wish to know who within the household is doing the actual administration. I am curious to discover who it is who is willing to risk the wrath of Belisarius to do this thing. Such a person might be of great use in the future, and will bear close watching in any case, since anyone willing to poison a woman of Antonina's stature is clearly a dangerous person." He tapped the tips of his fingers together. "Do you think you can do this for me, Panaigios?"

"Of course, of course," he gushed, hoping that his forced enthusiasm did not ring as hollow to Athanatadies' ears as it did to his own. "I have already made a few inquiries in regard to the household and it is nothing to make a few more."

"You're more active than you were before," Athanatadies said reflectively. "When did this come upon you?"

"I have been active in your interests for years," Panaigios said, protesting with some emotion. "You have given me the office to pursue certain of your interests on your behalf and I have done all that I might to fulfill your mandate."

"Now, there's no need to be huffy," Athanatadies soothed, his fingertips still meeting lightly. "You are always alert to any criticism, and often this is against your better judgment. I said nothing to chide you now, merely to observe that your actions would at last appear to be gathering fruit. I assume that you have already made some inquiries into the workings of the household of Belisarius, since that was required of you many months ago. In the past you have complied with my instructions promptly and I can see no reason why this case should be any different, and I know of a great many why you might wish to be especially careful where Belisarius is concerned."

Panaigios did his best to appear studious. "You have honored me with many requests, Censor, and I have striven to comply with your requirements as best I can. Certainly there have been times when this was not easily accomplished, but there are other instances when I have done all that I might to see that your instructions were carried out to the fullest."

"Who is your man in Belisarius' household?" The demand was casual, even offhanded, but Panaigios knew that if he did not answer it honestly and at once his life might easily be forfeit.

"My man there is the eunuch Simones." He tried to meet the hard gaze of Athanatadies and did not entirely succeed. "One or two others, far less significant slaves, I assure you, are also being employed to watch in minor matters."

"This Simones, is he trustworthy?" asked Athanatadies.

"What slave is trustworthy?" Panaigios countered, buying a little time.

"I am asking about this Simones. Do you trust him?" There was no suggestion in his tone that he would permit Panaigios to avoid answering him.

"To a degree, yes I do. But that is not saying a great deal." He paused, gathering his thoughts and desperately trying to guess what it was that Kimon Athanatadies wanted to know. "I know that Antonina relies on him and that he has some power in the household. I know that he is regarded with . . . respect by other slaves in the household. He has been reasonably cooperative with me and has only hesitated when he has been pressed to act in a way against his master's or mistress' interests. How much of this is loyalty and how much is simple survival, I do not know and have no way of telling. He has brought me regular reports, and those of the other, lesser slaves have supported what he said. I am not God, and I do not read the hearts of those I employ. I am limited to assessing what they do and how well they do it, and in this case I believe that he is doing his best to accommodate me without compromising himself with Belisarius too badly."

"Serving the staff of the Court Censor does not compromise him," said Athanatadies with austerity, then added, "but I suppose he does not yet believe this. It is a complicated thing for a slave to understand. They are simple creatures, which is why God appointed them to their role in life." He hesitated, his face so blank that he might have been one of the ikons on the wall. "You know, Panaigios, a man in your position does well to show a little zeal."

Caught off-guard by this shift in conversation, Panaigios could not keep from asking, "A man in my position? Isn't it preferable that I be dedicated to the work I am given?"

"Yes, but a man of vision and zeal might find a way to take on the tasks at their widest setting. For example, a man like you with those connections into the house of Belisarius might be in a position, now that there is a tragedy about to occur there, to seize the advantage of such sorrow and unearth the truth of this conspiracy against the Emperor. A man who guards his tongue at other times, when mourning his wife might say things that otherwise he would not. A man who was present, or whose agents were present, might then have information of vast significance that would be welcomed not only by me, but by Justinian himself." He regarded Panaigios. "You have been searching for oracles: heed this one."

"I . . ." Panaigios did not grasp all that Athanatadies was telling him, but he had sense enough to address the question directly. "I . . . am to find evidence, by any means, that will at last implicate Belisarius in a conspiracy, and you suggest that I use the occasion of his wife's failing health and death as the means to secure it."

"That was not precisely what I said, but I would not stop you from interpreting my words in that way." He rose. "We are in grave danger, Panaigios. There are plotters all around us and all desire to see the Emperor cast down. He himself has said to me that he fears enemies in every corner and that he is more certain than ever that only his timely recalling of Belisarius prevented the General from acting against him."

"Yes; of course." Panaigios made himself be silent for he knew he was dangerously near babbling.

"All that is lacking is actual confirmation of these plots. Once they are in the Emperor's hands, he will be relieved for there will be necessary action required by the proofs. You do understand the problem, don't you?" He was walking away from Panaigios, his dalmatica almost dragging on the floor to hide the misshapen foot no one dared mention.

"Ah . . . I believe I do," Panaigios said cautiously. "You want some letter or other document that would disclose all the men involved, and their general aims."

"That would be useful," Athanatadies said. "As Antonina grows weaker, it is likely that Belisarius will be less careful, and a prudent slave might discover much. Find out for me how much longer we have to wait; remember."

"I will; I will." He was starting to sweat and his eyes stung. This was a morass, he feared, an abyss that he was sliding into that once in he would never escape. He recalled that all of Kimon Athanatadies' personal slaves were mutes and for the first time he felt the full impact of this. "I will send for Simones and get all the information I can out of him. I will send a report to you within two days. I will make certain that if there is any information at all about Antonina's health and the cause of her illness that I discover everything I can about it."

"You know, it is not impossible that a desperate man might attempt many desperate things, such as poisoning his own wife." This was said with an air of speculation and hopefulness that filled Panaigios with dread.

"No, Censor," he said firmly. "There are many things that Belisarius might do in his distress, but hurt his wife in any way is not one of them. You and I may think of Antonina as a difficult, demanding and manipulative woman, but Belisarius loves her to adoration, and he would rather run on his sword like a godless Roman than bring any harm to her. He is more anguished by her ailment than he is by his disgrace. There are many people who know this and you might persuade them that Zeus really brings rain more readily than convince them that Belisarius would have any part in hurting Antonina."

"It was a thought," said Athanatadies with a shrug. "Pity. It would have saved so much effort." He walked a little farther. "What about that Roman woman? The widow who's Belisarius' friend? What of her? Would she have a hand in this?"

"There is nothing to link Olivia Clemens with Antonina's poor health. In the last year, Antonina has spent very little time with Olivia, and if there is opportunity for the Roman woman to give her anything poison, I know nothing of it, and I doubt it would be possible to make it appear that this was the case. Olivia occasionally visits Belisarius and often inquires after Antonina, but the two women never developed any closeness and therefore the household would not be likely to support the notion that she would harm Antonina."

"Not even to have Belisarius for herself?" suggested Athanatadies.

"Captain Drosos is her lover. He has said that she has refused to marry him." He sighed, for he knew that Athanatadies did not like the answers he was providing.

"She was waiting for a better match," Athanatadies guessed.

"A disgraced General without soldiers, stripped of everything but rank and confined to the city?" Panaigios shook his head. "If she had been hankering for Belisarius, she had ample opportunity to pursue him in Roma, and all the officers say she did not. She has been enamored of Drosos from the first."

"But Drosos is in Alexandria now, isn't he? What if this is a subtle plot, one that requires a go-between, and this Olivia is the one who serves that purpose?" Athanatadies had folded his arms, although his wide, gold-embroidered pallium shoved his arms upward when he did.

"There are better go-betweens, and as far as the spies can tell, no one has been leaving messages with Olivia for

Belisarius or anyone else, not even Drosos." He leaned back. "It might be wiser to search for the culprits elsewhere."

"You would appear to be protecting these people," said Athanatadies sharply.

"No. But if you wish to bring others into the matter, it is essential—or so it seems to me—that they be plausible. There are others who would be more . . . acceptable conspirators than these. If Drosos were here, there might be a way, for he has often railed against what he claims is the unfairness of Belisarius' recall and restrictions. But he does not wish to go against the wishes of the Emperor or his General. If anyone was eager for a conspiracy, it was Antonina. And she . . . she—"

"Yes," said Athanatadies slowly. "Yes. I accept your reservations for the time being, but I must say that I still believe that there is proof of some sort, somewhere, of a conspiracy that will be acceptable and believable and will show that Justinian was not mistaken in his fears." He swung around and all but blocked Panaigios in his chair. "You know what is required."

"I do," Panaigios said tensely.

"Excellent. I expect to have your report in two days' time. Speak to that eunuch Simones and see what you can accomplish between you." He joined his hands prayerfully. "I repose great faith in you, Panaigios. Do not forget that."

Panaigios nodded, finding the burden almost too much to bear. "Censor."

Athanatadies stepped back. "You have much to do, haven't you? And it is time you were about your tasks." He waved his dismissal. "Pray for guidance, Panaigios," he recommended before he left his secretary.

As Panaigios made his way back to his chariot, he felt numb; the problems heaped upon him by Athanatadies seemed insurmountable, and he was left with the sinking conviction that if he failed to do as the Censor required he would meet a fate far more ghastly than the one Athanatadies had planned for Belisarius. As he reached his chariot, he realized that he had never been given the refreshments the Censor had requested, and this only served to make his apprehension more acute.

As the Guards saluted him as he left, Panaigios felt he was fleeing the firely rivers of Hell.

*   *   *

Text of an official order from the Emperor Justinian to the garrison at Alexandria.

On the Feast of the Annunciation, the Emperor Justinian through the good offices of his Court Censor sends his greetings and commendations to the garrison at Alexandria, in particular to Captain Drosos who commands there and who is known to be devoted to us in all things.

In order that the work of Christ shall spread more quickly throughout the world, we have authorized the burning or similar destruction of all texts that are not of Christian origin and thought. In Konstantinoupolis there has been a most successful extirpation of the weeds of heresy that spring up from such writings because of the willingness of the people to aid in their own salvation. Hundreds of texts, perhaps thousands, have been cleansed in the flames, and surely the smoke that rises to Heaven from such pyres must be sweet indeed.

So far we have observed and approved the progress of these acts and have said that there is much merit for the soul in pious devotion of this sort. We are assured by those *advanced in the Church that our course is in accord with the course of God.*

Therefore we have decided to extend our mandate and to require that all those living within the Empire show a similar zeal to the Konstantinoupolitans who have eradicated apostasy from their midst. Now we wish the rest of the Empire to show that it is as devout and as worthy as any soul in Byzantion. To that end, we require that the institution known as the Library at Alexandria, by which we include the Mother and all Daughter Libraries with the exception of the one Daughter Library devoted to Christian writings, be burned in order to erase the taint of godlessness more completely from the world.

It is our wish that this be accomplished at Epiphany, to show the offering we bring to Christ in as pure a heart as the Company of Kings who waited upon Him in worldly submission.

With the concurrence of the Court Censor, the popes and metropolitans of the Church, we exhort all of you of the Alexandrian garrison to be firm in your purpose and to persevere in this most Christian undertaking.

By the hand of the Court Censor and at our order.

> *Justinian*
> *Emperor of Byzantion*
> *his sigil*

• 7 •

Zejhil's hands were shaking as she heard the door open behind her. The vial she held slipped from her fingers and broke on the floor.

In the door Niklos Aulirios stood, his attitude uncertain, as he watched the slave struggle to hide her shock. "All right," he said after a moment. "What are you doing here?"

"I . . . I was sent to fetch perfume," she said lamely, and turned her large, Tartar eyes on him.

Niklos, who at first had not been very suspicious, now came into the room, closing the door behind him. "For whom?"

"My mistress . . ." As soon as she began, she knew she had made a mistake and she flushed.

"No, not your mistress, Zejhil. She keeps her perfumes with her in her sleeping chamber, and we both know it. You must be very nervous if you forgot that." He strolled over to her and looked down at her. "You're white."

"I'm startled," she said weakly.

"You're terrified," he corrected her, not as gently as he might have done under other circumstances. "Why is that?"

"No reason." She gave a jerk to her shoulders in an attempt to dismiss or minimize his question.

"I doubt that," Niklos said, and took her gently by the arm, turning her so that some of the light from the window reached her face. "You're up to something, and you don't like it."

257

"No!" She tried to pull away but found that the easy, firm grip was unbreakable.

"Yes." He could feel her tremble and he saw the sick terror at the back of her eyes. "Zejhil, tell me what you were doing in here and why."

She gave a cry and brought up her hands, palms out, as if to ward off blows. "I can't. I can't. Do not ask me!"

"Zejhil . . ." He let her name trail off. "Listen to me."

She had contrived to turn away from him, to wriggle as far as his hold would permit. "Let me go," she said sullenly.

"I can't do that," he said softly. "You were taking a vial of perfume from my mistress' chest. Perfume is valuable, and that might mean that you are a thief. Since Olivia has reposed trust in you, she must know of this, and at once." He saw a little of the dread fade from her face. "Or perhaps you weren't stealing at all; perhaps you were putting something in that was not here before." Until he spoke the words he had not considered this possibility, but as he said them, he became sure that was what he had seen.

As if to confirm this, Zejhil kicked up at his shin and let out a loud shriek.

"Something in," said Niklos as he quickly sidestepped her first attack and braced himself for the second. "You were told by someone to put something *in* the chest, weren't you? What was it and who told you?" He continued to hold her, though now he shifted his stance enough to keep her from being able to strike out at him with her fists.

"Let go!" she yelled and was turned suddenly so that her back was pressed hard against his chest and his forearm served in part to gag her.

"No, I will not," he said, still without anger. "You were supposed to be watching the household for Olivia. She requested you do this, and we thought you were doing well. And now this."

"It's not . . . not—" The words were cut off again.

"You have a great deal to answer for," said Niklos, a stern note coming into his voice.

Whatever protests Zejhil wanted to register were lost against the force of his arm.

"I think we had better go carefully. If someone has suborned you, there's no saying how many of the other slaves are taking payment from outside." He moved her toward the closed door. "When I open this, if you scream, I will knock you out and carry you. Is that understood?"

Zejhil nodded wildly, trying to signal him with one of her confined hands.

"Very good," Niklos approved. "Now stand up straight and pretend that you're feeling weak, as if you were taken suddenly ill. I don't want any more gossip than necessary about this incident." He waited while she complied, and then he pulled the door open.

The hall was empty, but before they had gone more than a dozen steps, Niklos saw one of the cook's two scrubbing boys peering around the corner. A little farther on and he found the head groom sweeping the garden steps—a task that was not his—and just beyond him, one of the gardeners pretended to be busy trimming back the ornamental apple tree.

By the time Niklos got to Olivia's private apartments, he had counted no less than eight of the household, and this made him nervous in a way it would not have done six months before.

Olivia had been sorting dried herbs, but she abandoned this task as she saw Niklos come into the room, half-dragging Zejhil with him. Dressed in her old-fashioned palla and stolae, she seemed distinctly out of place in the room. "What on earth—"

"I'm afraid we're in for difficulties," Niklos said as he closed the door and latched it.

"Zejhil, what is going on?" Olivia asked, coming around the trestle table and wiping her hands on the mantele tied around her waist.

Zejhil said nothing, but as Niklos released her, she

moved away from him, repugnance in her angular features. She rubbed at her wrists and glared down at the floor.

"Niklos?" Olivia addressed him with a hint of impatience. "I trust you plan to tell me what this is all about?"

Niklos did not answer at once. He leaned against the door and watched Zejhil, his expression detached and difficult to read. "I surprised her in the stillroom," he said at last. "She was putting a vial of . . . of something-or-another into your spice and perfume chest."

"What?" Olivia asked, clearly disbelieving. She turned to Zejhil. "Did you do that?"

For an answer, Zejhil spat and huddled against the wall, her back to Niklos. There were tears in her eyes; she dashed them away angrily.

"Zejhil?" Olivia said. When she received no response, she looked to Niklos. "Tell me." Her confusion made her tone high and sharp.

"Wait." He opened the door suddenly and looked into the hall. After a little time, he closed the door softly and once more secured the latch. "I am afraid, my mistress, that we are being spied on."

Olivia gave a breathless burst of laughter. "Again?"

"This time, it appears that Zejhil has become part of it, and that changes matters." He cleared his throat. "I have tried to find out whose orders she is following, but she will say nothing."

"Nothing," repeated Olivia, her expression becoming uncertain. "How do you account for that?"

"Whoever has given her orders has impressed her," said Niklos, his eyes never leaving the Tartar slave on the other side of the room. "She is more afraid of this person than she is of you or me."

"That is unwise of her," said Olivia, and the edge in her voice caught Zejhil's attention as nothing else had, for Olivia spoke with gelid calm.

"I went to the stillroom," Niklos continued, "for the oils you wanted. I saw the door was not quite closed, which surprised me a little, but I thought one of the kitchen staff had been careless. When I went into the room, I saw Zejhil at the spice chest with something in her hands. She dropped it—I think her hands were shaking—as I came in. She has refused to explain what she was doing there or what she was putting into the chest." His ruddy eyes grew chilly. "That doesn't bode well."

Olivia nodded and touched Niklos on the arm. "I see." Her breath went out of her slowly. "I don't suppose you could take time to find the vial."

"No," Niklos said, adding, "I know I ought to have found it and brought it with me."

"Do you suppose there's any hope that it might still be there?" she asked.

"I can go look, if that's what you wish," said Niklos. "Do you want me to summon aid while I'm gone?"

"I can manage Zejhil," said Olivia, continuing to the slave directly, "I may be a woman and no longer young, but it would be a serious error in judgment to think that I am incapable of managing this situation." She made a sign to Niklos and he let himself out of the door. Olivia put the latch in place once more and leaned back, studying Zejhil.

The slave-woman looked around her, uncertain what to do. She had been prepared for confinement and chastisement, but this treatment was new to her and she had no defense against it. She moved into the nearest corner and braced herself there.

Olivia continued to watch her, her attentive attitude unchanging. Finally she spoke again. "When I asked you to watch the household on my behalf, you assured me that you would do so, not only for the considerations this brought you, but because you were truly convinced that it was wrong for those outside the house to spy on those within. It seemed at the time that you were sincere and honorable. I showed my appreciation in a number of ways, didn't I? You have funds being held to purchase your freedom, as would any Roman slave." She did not qualify that statement by saying that such rights had disappeared three hundred years ago. "I gave you my word that you would not be punished for reporting on the activities of the others and you have my promise of manumission within five years. What has persuaded you to act against these considerations?"

Zejhil shook her head, her jaw so firmly set that the muscles stood out in ridges in her face.

"You're terrified. What is the reason?" She waited, giving Zejhil every opportunity to speak, and when the silence had dragged out between them, she went on. "I give you my word you will be protected. You will not be harmed."

"You can offer no protection against them," Zejhil hissed through her clenched teeth. "You are nothing against them."

Olivia's lips lifted at the corner but no one could mistake this for a smile. "I am? Who are these formidable beings that I can do nothing?"

Zejhil retreated once again into silence.

"So you believe they are powerful enough to hear through walls," Olivia said gently. "And you believe that they will know anything you reveal and you will be punished for that." She saw Zejhil flinch. "I know; you've said nothing. This is only supposition, though your expression tells me that I am correct." She sighed. "Which means also that you are not the only one of my slaves to be pressed into the service of these nameless others. And that is very . . . inconvenient." She turned her head to the side. "You knew I was here, and that I would probably require things from the stillroom, yet you did this, which makes me wonder if you didn't wish to be apprehended."

"No. No, that's wrong," Zejhil cried out in protest.

"Is it?"

"No!" Her voice was higher and louder, rough with fear.

"Because," Olivia went on evenly, "you knew that it was necessary for you to have an acceptable reason not to continue your work for these others, whoever they are."

Zejhil was suddenly very still and her face betrayed nothing. She slid down the wall onto her knees, the horror of her predicament making her eyes almost chatoyant.

"So." Olivia came back toward her. "You would rather serve me than these others, but they appear more powerful to you, and so you dare not displease them." She studied the Tartar woman's face. "Eventually I will learn who these puissant beings are, so you might as well tell me now. It will be easier for both of us, and we will not have to say things to each other that we might later regret."

"I will say nothing." She stared down at the floor.

"You will, you know; in time." She looked up as Niklos came in the door, something in his hand. "You found it."

"Yes." His handsome face was grave.

"I gather that it isn't welcome, whatever it is."

"It smells of bitter almonds." He held out the broken vial to her. "Try it."

"I don't have to: I can smell it from here." Olivia's face was quite somber now, and she regarded Niklos intently. "Then something of mine was to be poisoned." Her expression hardened. "Zejhil, where were you supposed to put this?"

She shook her head repeatedly, violently.

"All right," said Olivia, attempting to calm her slave. "You are afraid of telling me even so little a thing as that. You were going to the chest with spices and fine oils, so it was for food." For an instant an ironic smile touched her lips, and then it was replaced by stern determination.

Niklos made sure the door was firmly latched. "I could force her to talk, Olivia, if you wish. You don't approve, but there are times—"

"There may be," she said, cutting him short, "but this is not one of them."

"She put poison into your spice chest," he reminded her with feeling.

"No; she *tried* to put poison into my spice chest, which is a different matter altogether." She put her hand on his arm. "Niklos, she's been treated badly. If we force her to speak, we will be as reprehensible as those who have forced her to act against us. And do not pretend that you disagree." She went and drew up a small bench. "What am I going to do with you, Zejhil?" she asked as she sat down beside the woman, leaving enough room on the bench if Zejhil wanted to use it.

"Sell me," she answered flatly.

"I'd rather not do that unless it's necessary," Olivia responded. "You've given me very good service, and until now you have protected my interests within my household. That means a great deal to me. I would not like to reward you with betrayal if I can avoid it; but if I am to avoid it, you will have to give me your aid, won't you?"

"I—" She looked at Niklos as if the bondsman might have a suggestion.

"I do need to know who is attempting to act against me, Zejhil. You must see that." She had no anger in her tone, and no hint of condemnation. "You are a good and sensible person, and you have loyalty. These are very worthwhile and I am pleased to have someone in my household with your virtues, but if you cannot tell me what I need to know, then something will have to be arranged, something neither of us would like." From her manner, it appeared that Olivia was discussing the arrangements of furniture in a room or the pattern of a garden's flowers instead of a threat against her life.

"I mustn't tell you anything. They will not spare you if I do, and they will do terrible things to me." She put her knuckles against her teeth.

"Terrible things. They must be desperate, these unknown men." She glanced quickly at Niklos.

"They are very powerful," Zejhil admitted reluctantly. "They insisted."

"And you are not in a position to resist them, are you?" Olivia straightened up. "And you are convinced that there is nothing I can do to prevent them taking action against you."

"You are a foreign woman," Zejhil said in a small voice.

"So are you," she pointed out. "Or is that what you mean? that I am as much at their mercy as a slave is?"

Niklos snorted. "More fools they."

"Hush, my friend," Olivia admonished him softly. "Zejhil, do you think that these men are trying to be rid of me?"

"One way or another," the slave admitted. "Oh, mistress, I didn't want to do anything to help them. I didn't. I told them that they would do better asking someone else, but they were persistent and they said that if I did not help them, then the officers of the Censor would come here and you would be found to have possessions that are forbidden, and then you would be deprived of your house and the things that you own—"

"But if I conveniently died, that would make it possible for the household to be without taint, or something of the sort," Olivia finished for her. "They are doing this for a reason, and not simply because I am Roman."

"They think that you are aiding Belisarius. They insisted that I tell them of every visit he has made here, and what transpired during his visit." Now that she was speaking the worst of the fear was gone from her eyes. "I told them that I would do everything they required, just so that they would not do . . . what they threatened to do."

"If they harmed my slave in any way whatever," Olivia said and there was steel in her words, "they would answer for it, in law and in other ways."

"It isn't so simple," Zejhil objected. "They knew I had been watching the staff for you, and they knew that I reported to you, and that meant that they had others telling them what I was doing."

"Yes, that much is obvious." Niklos had come nearer and was watching Zejhil with curiosity. "What makes you speak now? Are you hoping to balance favor against favor until you find the best price?"

"Niklos, for the love you bear me, stop it." Olivia's gaze rested on him and it appeared to calm him, for he fell silent, but without the ill-contained fury he had shown before. "Do you have any notion as to who among my slaves is working for the Censor? And it is the Censor, isn't it?" This last was addressed not to Niklos but to Zejhil.

"I never said that!" Zejhil shrieked.

"It had to be someone high in government and by the sound of it someone who dislikes and distrusts Belisarius. Either the Emperor himself—which is very unlikely—or one of his courtiers had to be responsible. The courtier who has been most consistent in his actions against Belisarius is the Censor, who has no reason to trust me or anything of mine." She nodded as if to remind herself of her thoughts. "I've wondered if we would have trouble because of him, but I never thought it would be so extreme."

"Olivia," said Niklos in a warning tone.

"I am safe saying these things," she told him. "Zejhil is not going to give me away. Are you?"

Zejhil was now sitting cross-legged on the floor, her back against the wall. She shook her head slowly. "I will have to tell them something."

"So you will." Olivia rubbed her face with her fingertips. "You will have to make them believe that you completed your task and that there is poison in the spice chest. That must be the start." She sighed. "And then, if you are willing, find out what they are trying to prove. I wish I knew what I had done to place myself in such jeopardy."

"It may be nothing more than your friendship for Belisarius," suggested Niklos.

"Possibly, but it may also be more." Olivia stared down at her linked hands. "And in any case, we must find a way to warn Belisarius about this. He knows of other actions, but he does not know how far the machinations extend." Once again she looked down at Zejhil. "What did they threaten to do to you?"

"I . . . I can't tell you." The Tartar slave was appalled.

"Of course you can." Olivia watched her. "Undoubtedly rape. But what else?"

Zejhil shook her head, mute again.

"For the names of your ancestors, girl!" Niklos burst out. "Tell your mistress. She can do nothing if you will not let her. Tell her!"

"Niklos, don't hector her." Olivia waited, then said in a soft voice, "If you are frightened, I don't blame you. Only a fool is not frightened by real danger. But you need not be paralyzed by your fear. You can act against it." She remained still a short time, then sighed once more and got up. "Very well."

"They said they would rape me with swords and cut out my vitals and leave me in the market for the curs to eat. They would make sure I was alive." She said it quickly, as if by getting the words out swiftly their impact would lessen.

"How charming," Olivia said bitterly.

"They would. They are that sort." Zejhil got to her feet. "I was supposed to put the poison in the sweet spices, so that you would get a little of it every day. That way poison would not be suspected until it was too late. Even if you had someone sample your food, it would not prevent your death."

To Zejhil's surprise, Olivia chuckled. "Then I will have to give them some reason to think the plot was discovered without compromising you." She shook her head. "Slow poison. In food. Magna Mater, I'm glad I've found out about this."

Niklos grinned briefly. "In the food."

Zejhil was baffled, but could not bring herself to speak.

Olivia answered for her. "You must understand, Zejhil, that I have . . . a rare condition that requires I . . . limit my diet severely. If the Censor expects me to succumb to poisoned spices, he would wait a very long time. So, perhaps, it might be best to make it appear that the poison was discovered, but not the poisoner. Let me think about it awhile."

"They will want some results," Niklos warned.

"And I suppose they will have some," said Olivia. "But this will take careful planning. I will have to think about what must be done, and then be certain that . . ." The words trailed off. "If Zejhil was given poison, who knows what the other slaves being used have been given or offered. Niklos, I want you to sleep outside my door at night."

"I will," he promised her.

"And Zejhil, I want you to listen more closely than ever to what you hear." She scowled. "Why do they want to be rid of me; it keeps coming back to that."

Zejhil stood with her head down. "I know I must be punished for what I did. I accept that. But do not punish me in front of the others."

"Punish you?" repeated Olivia, startled. "Oh, for the poison, do you mean? Yes, I imagine something ought to be done."

"I'll get the whips," Niklos said without emotion.

"Don't be silly," Olivia told him. "For punishment, I will insist that you replace Pentheus as the night keeper. I will expect you to patrol the house and the garden all through the night, and during the day, I want you to clean the reception rooms and the vestibule, starting with scrubbing the floors. Every day. Until I tell you otherwise. Is that clear?"

"It is a light punishment," said Zejhil.

"Say that when ten days have gone by and I might agree." She stared at the door. "You are to return to your quarters now and remain there. You will have no meal this evening." She waited while Zejhil made a deep reverence, then motioned to Niklos to let her out of the room.

When Zejhil was gone, Niklos said, "You did give her light punishment."

"Possibly. I am giving the agents of the Censor plenty of opportunity to approach her. If she cleans the vestibule, they can find her during the day, and if she is the night keeper, they can try after dark. And then, old friend, we can find out what it is they're really after." She paced the length of the room. "For some reason, they're becoming desperate."

"And you are becoming lax," Niklos countered.

"If we weren't strangers here, I might do this another way. But we are here on sufferance, and they are already seeking reasons to be rid of us. I would prefer to be free of suspicion, but if that isn't possible, then—"

"Then we move on?" Niklos said. "But where?"

"So you *do* understand my problem," said Olivia. "Yes; where do we go if not here? What do we do?"

Niklos came and put his hands on her shoulders. "This was supposed to be a haven."

"Yes," she said sadly. "It was, wasn't it?"

* * *

Text of a letter from the physician Mnenodatos to Belisarius.

To the great General Belisarius, Mnenodatos sends thankful greetings and prayers for his well-being and the recovery of his wife.

I confess that your offer of employment has come as a shock: most pleasant and welcome, but nonetheless a shock. I am at a loss to know how so distinguished a hero as you came to know of a physician of my station, but I bless the name of that person and I praise him for taking my interests so much to heart.

It would afford me the greatest satisfaction to attend your wife and to serve as your household physician. Such em-

ployment is the dream of any man practicing the healing arts, and I am no different from any of my associates and colleagues who also long for the time they can be sure of their futures.

From what little I have learned of your wife's condition, she will require fairly constant care. Those with such symptoms are never certain when they will once again be seized by the terrible cramping that you described and which I witnessed for myself yesterday. I certainly share your concern. To be candid, I am not sure there is much I can offer to relieve her of her suffering, but what I am able to do, you may be confident I will make every effort to do. In cases such as hers it is most important to alleviate the immediate suffering, but beyond that the cause must be determined and a course of treatment reached that will not in any way increase the symptoms of this or any other disease.

Let me urge you to encourage all your household to pray for the speedy and complete recovery of your beloved wife, for as you are aware, nothing can happen without the aid of God. Such supplications may succeed where no medicine can.

That is not to say that the case is hopeless and only the intervention of Heaven will save Antonina. This is far from the case; your wife's health is not good but she is not in danger of losing her life yet, and with prompt action and good attention, she may recover in good time and enjoy a long life free of pain and attendant distresses. Let me emphasize this to you: at this time I do not fear for her life. To be sure, if she continues as she is going now, then my view of the gravity of her case will change, and of course no illness that so prostrates a woman can be regarded lightly, but there is much room for hope and I want you to think of my treatment in this light.

It is a great honor to have so distinguished a patient, but I trust you will not be offended in any way if I say that it would please me far more if there was no cause for us to meet. The illness of Antonina is not an opportunity for advancement, as many might see it, but an occasion for the best and most devoted service not only to the benefit of the *august lady herself, but the office of physician which was elevated by having the Apostle Loukas at the head of its numbers.*

At your convenience I will take up temporary residence in your house in whatever quarters you see fit to assign to me. I confess I do not know your eunuch slave Simones, but if you say that his recommendation brought me to your attention, then I will seek him out eagerly to tender my gratitude for his kindness on my behalf.

In the meantime, I ask you take what consolation you can in the knowledge that I will dedicate all my skills to ending the travail your wife currently endures, and I will strive to restore her health so that she may once again live as so august a lady ought to live.

With my prayers and thanks, by my own hand,

> *Mnenodatos*
> *physician*

• 8 •

Night hung over Alexandria, oppressive in its remoteness. There was a lazy breeze off the Mare Internum, blowing toward the swath of the Nile.

Drosos stood in the window of his largest reception room staring out into the darkness. Although it was late, he was still in his short military dalmatica and formal, highly embossed lorica. Only his mussed dark hair gave any indication of the distress that consumed him: it was the Feast of the Circumcision and Epiphany was five days away.

"Captain?" Chrysanthos had come into the room a short while before and was still waiting for Drosos to address him.

"I know," Drosos said distantly, not leaving the window.

"The Guard is waiting." Chrysanthos kept his words level and without feeling but this served only to mask his deep concern for his superior. "You requested they accompany you."

Drosos nodded, his broad back rigid under his ceremonial armor.

"It is after midnight," Chrysanthos said as tactfully as he could.

"The nights are long," Drosos remarked inconsequentially.

"It is the dark of the year," Chrysanthos agreed, staring at the whitewashed walls, noting the smudges above the braziers.

"The Copts are fasting tonight and tomorrow. They do not feast until Epiphany." He said the last word as if it were gall.

"Yes; I know."

"They say it's heretical of them." He stopped talking, his eyes fixed on the large buildings that loomed out of the jumble of darknesses that was the city. "God," he whispered. "He does not know what he is asking."

Chrysanthos suddenly found it difficult to speak. "Drosos. If it is so unendurable—"

"I am Captain here," Drosos said in a still voice that silenced the other man. "I have been given a command by the Emperor. I am sworn to carry it out."

"There are others who will do it if you give the word," Chrysanthos told Drosos, wishing that he would turn and face him.

"Would *you*?" He asked it lightly but his hands closed into hard fists at his sides.

Chrysanthos hesitated. "No."

"You are the Emperor's officer, as I am." He looked up

at the remote stars. "They say God watches the stars as He watches men, to the end of the world." Under the metal of his lorica his chest was aching.

"Your escort—" Chrysanthos reminded him.

"Yes." At last he turned away from the window and his face was blank with suffering. He crossed the room to Chrysanthos. "I am ready."

"They're in the courtyard. Four of them, armed." Chrysanthos looked closely at Drosos, seeing how much he had changed from the man he knew on campaign in Italy. "Are you all right, Captain?"

Drosos met Chrysanthos' eyes. "No."

"Is there—"

"No. Nothing." Drosos moved past him, walking directly and purposefully to the door. He stopped there, and said without looking at Chrysanthos, "If you want to leave, I understand."

"Thank you," Chrysanthos said, longing to take advantage of the offer. "I will remain here for the time being."

"Um." Drosos nodded, unable to express the painful gratitude he felt at his subordinate's loyalty. "When I return . . . share a skin of wine with me."

"If you like," Chrysanthos said carefully, thinking that he had never needed to guard his tongue as much as he did now.

"I'll need a drink by then," Drosos said, and left the room. As he descended the stairs to the ground floor, he tried to calm his thoughts. He was the Emperor's officer and he had orders to carry out and there was nothing more to be said. He walked more quickly as he approached the escort waiting in the courtyard. "Let's get this over with," he told them as he strode to the door, letting them scramble to keep up with him.

The streets were almost empty and those few, furtive men who saw the soldiers hurried away from them, wanting nothing to do with anyone from the Byzantine garrison. Neither Drosos nor his Guard paid any attention to the others, going quickly to the enormous buildings Drosos had watched from his window.

Two Greek scholars waited for Drosos at the gates to the Library, and they admitted him with deference.

"You are most welcome," the younger said to Drosos.

"Am I?" Drosos asked, his words brittle and light. "Well, I will strive to remember that."

The older scholar regarded Drosos with curiosity and puzzlement. "Captain?"

"Pay no mind to what I say," Drosos told them. "It's late and I want to get this settled as soon as possible. I must send a full report to the Censor before we . . . before we start the fires."

"May God aid our endeavors," said the younger, pious ardor in his face. "This has been a long time coming. If the vision of the Emperor is to be fulfilled, we must see that temptation is expunged from the world so that we may better serve the cause of Heaven."

"Yes. Of course." Drosos motioned to his four Guards to remain at the gates. "Show me . . ." He was not able to finish his request.

Neither scholar appeared to notice this. "Yes, there is much to see," said the older. "If you will follow us, I will be pleased to explain this place to you."

"If you would," Drosos said, trying to be polite. He let the two scholars lead the way into the largest of the four buildings that surrounded the vast central courtyard.

"This," said the younger as they approached the largest building, "is called the Mother. It is the oldest of the libraries and was built in the time before the birth of the Christ. It has two warehouses where materials not yet catalogued are stored. We have already determined that what is in them is not Christian, and so we need have no reluctance about burning them along with the Library itself." He stepped aside so that Drosos could enter ahead of them.

"On the main floor are works of philosophy from several lands. I understand that some are from lands far to the east and that there are records about the peoples in the heart of Africa." The older scholar rubbed his hands together. "These works would lead the unwary soul to great error."

"Indeed?" said Drosos. "I am only a soldier, and I do not understand how that information might hurt the faith of one who read these works."

The younger scholar shook his head. The uneven light from the braziers made his shadow dance on the walls, huge and misshapen. "The Emperor has determined that those who pursue studies of material that is not Christian often are seduced into following areas of learning that imperil the soul. You think, as most soldiers must, I suppose, that you might have strategic reasons to want to know about . . . the peoples of Africa, for example. Surely you would seek out such intelligence if you were expected to campaign there."

"That had crossed my mind," said Drosos, relieved that the scholar had provided him an excuse for his reluctance. "It would make the campaign more effective if we knew what we were getting into. The same might be said of many other areas of learning, because a soldier never knows what information might give him the advantage in battle."

The older scholar chuckled. "You soldiers are such pragmatists. But I suppose you need to be."

The younger scholar was not as amused. "And for a simple military campaign you would imperil your soul. What are scouts for, if not to obtain the information you require? And they do not lead you into doubt and error as much of these records might. Think what would become of you if you or your men should be captivated by the terrible gods of the barbarians around us. You assume that this cannot happen, but we know that it can." He was leading the way down the hall. "There are texts here on plants and animals found through the world."

"Where is the harm in studying that?" Drosos wondered aloud.

"You are not aware of the subtle ways in which these texts turn the mind from the adoration of God and the veneration of his Saints," said the older scholar. "The

Emperor is aware of this, and we must praise him for his wisdom in sparing others from the dangers that are present here."

They had entered a cavernous room that was lit by braziers. Huge pigeon-hole shelves lined the walls and stood in serried ranks down the length of the chamber. Drosos stared at the mass of rolled and fan-folded scrolls that were stored around him and the breath nearly stopped in his throat.

"You see we have an enormous task ahead of us," remarked the older scholar. "Luckily there are excellent records for this room and we can identify every work here."

"So many," Drosos said dreamily.

"Yes. The oldest scroll here is a treatise on shipbuilding from Samos. From what we have determined, it was written at the time of Perikles." The older scholar pursed his lips. "They worshipped idols, those old Greeks."

"Perikles," murmured Drosos. "Can you tell me which one it is?"

The younger scholar frowned his disapproval. "It is not important that you know that."

"I was . . . merely curious," said Drosos. "I have never seen anything but a bronze vase from the time of Perikles." He took a deep breath but still had the sensation of having insufficient air in his lungs.

The two scholars led him through the room. "There is a smaller chamber beyond this," said the younger. "It is devoted to works on botany, for the most part. It is a pity that the authors were such dreadful pagans, attributing the properties and virtues of the plants to the activities of deities and supernatural beings instead of to the Will of God."

"You can see, Captain, that the Emperor has considered this most carefully." The older scholar indicated a narrow, steep stairway. "There are medicinal texts on the floor immediately above us, and material on jewels, metals and rare earths on the floor above that. Some of those writings come from far away and their heretical content is more obvious than in works written in the Empire."

"Medicinal texts and metals. These things can be of great value to soldiers," Drosos said trying to speak in a disinterested way.

"We can show them to you, if you require it, Captain," offered the older scholar.

"That won't be necessary." He had not intended to be harsh with these two, but the words were out before he could stop them.

"No; soldier's pragmatism," said the older scholar to the younger. "You see he is a man of good sense. He leaves these matters to those equipped to deal with them, as a good officer of the Emperor ought."

The words stung Drosos like a lash; he closed his eyes so that he would not have to look at the two men accompanying him, or at the doors into rooms filled with books. "Are the others like this?" The question was out before he could phrase it properly; he mastered himself sufficiently to give the older scholar a cool stare.

"Very similar. The Daughter Library of Christian writing is on the far side of the courtyard, if you need to inspect it." The older scholar had become slightly servile and Drosos wondered if the man felt as oppressed as he did.

Before Drosos could speak, the younger scholar said, "You will have to take every precaution to be sure that the Christian Daughter escapes the flames. If any harm should come to those sacred writings, the loss to the world would be incalculable."

Drosos did not trust himself to speak. He motioned to the two men to take him out of the building. "What do the other Daughter Libraries contain?"

"Oh, works of history and literature. A few are interesting to Christian scholars, but the Emperor has rightly pointed out that the only history any Christian needs is the history of the world since His coming. The Testaments are literature enough and philosophy enough for the soul of any man, and the writing of good Christian scholars

278 • Chelsea Quinn Yarbro

have more merit and worth than all the pagan writings of
the world. What man desires to know things that will
condemn his soul to eternal torment?" The younger
scholar indicated the long rows of shelving. "Think of the
improvement in the world if one tenth of this mass were
devoted to determining the true nature of Christ. This
would be a shrine as sacred as Hagia Sophia."

"But might not there be . . ." Drosos began, then let
his thought remain unfinished.

"You forget that few men have the wisdom to know the
difference between information and knowledge, and they
often confuse one with the other," said the older scholar.
"A great pope or metropolitan might read some of these
works without danger, but there are many others who
assume they would not be led astray who would be at the
greatest risk."

"Including pragmatic soldiers," said Drosos, his neck
and shoulder aching now, and his heart.

"Most certainly," said the older scholar, his attitude
almost comradely. "It is a sign of your virtue that you
recognize this."

"Is it?" Drosos asked, feeling more desolate than he
ever had in the aftermath of battle. As they left the
building, he looked back at it.

"It will take care to burn it safely," the younger scholar
warned him. "It is just as well that the burning is being
left to you and your soldiers or it might be disastrous."

"Yes; disastrous." The lorica Drosos wore felt as if it
had shrunk, compressing his chest in its brass embrace.

"We will see that you are given every assistance," the
younger scholar promised him. "You and your men have
only to tell us what we must do and we will perform your
orders to the best of our abilities."

"How many are you? scholars who are willing to assist
in the burning," asked Drosos.

"Some have refused, which is to be expected. We have
kept a list of their names to pass on to the Court Censor
and the Emperor for whatever action they believe is
appropriate." The younger scholar cleared his throat.

"There are forty-eight of us; there are several hundred scholars here, but most of the Coptic scholars have refused to help on the grounds that this is an Alexandrian monument and they are not willing to diminish it, even at the hazard of their souls. Since they are heretics in any case, we have taken no notice of them."

"Will they resist us, do you think?" Drosos asked, hoping that he might find an excuse for disobeying the Emperor's orders in opposition from the Copts.

"They have said they will not," the younger scholar said with pride. "They have admitted that their allegiance to the Library is as much vanity as dedication and they are willing to stand aside if we agree to keep the Christian Daughter intact."

"We have spent over a month attempting to persuade them to join us, but they are not willing," said the older scholar as he led the way across the courtyard to the second-largest building. "All the documents in this Daughter are in foreign tongues—nothing in the walls is in Latin or Greek."

Drosos stared up at the stone front of the Foreign Daughter and he had to bite his lower lip hard to keep from weeping. "How many manuscripts are stored here?"

"They say there are over twenty thousand, but I assume that is a boast," said the older scholar. "Perhaps twelve thousand at the most, or so I believe. This Daughter has one small warehouse, but it is two streets away, and you will have to arrange for that to be burned at another time. It is too dangerous to try to control two fires at the same time, or so your officer explained it to me yesterday."

"Two fires—yes, two fires are much too dangerous," said Drosos, hardly hearing the words.

The younger scholar indicated the Third Daughter. "This Library has two large warehouses directly behind it, but they front on the leatherworkers' market, and so it will be tricky to keep the burning from spreading."

"My men will see to it," Drosos declared, wishing fervently he did not have to listen to any of this. "I will send a contingent of Guardsmen to you tomorrow afternoon and you can show them everything that will have to be protected." He gazed around the courtyard, thinking for a wild moment that there might be a way to protect all of it, or perhaps a few of the warehouses. Surely the loss of one building would be enough to satisfy the Censor. He imagined all the arguments he might put forth, and abandoned the notion at once. His orders were specific and if he failed to carry them out, he would be disgraced.

"Captain?" the older scholar ventured.

"I'm sorry," said Drosos, coming back to himself. "I was attempting to assess the—"

"—the magnitude of the task," the younger scholar supplied enthusiastically. "Yes, it must be a challenge to find the most effective means to burn such large buildings."

"A challenge," Drosos echoed as if he did not comprehend the word.

By the time Drosos left, the moon was down and the streets were wholly deserted. He set a brisk pace for his Guard and would not speak to them as they made their way back to the small palace where the Byzantine garrison was housed. Once there, he dismissed the soldiers and went back to his reception room, black despair in his heart.

"Captain." Chrysanthos shook his head and got unsteadily to his feet, a yawn concealed behind his hand.

"Chrysanthos," Drosos exclaimed angrily. "What are you doing here?"

"You wanted me to stay," Chrysanthos reminded him sleepily.

"And I wakened you." His face showed no emotion.

"I was drowsing," Chrysanthos admitted. "But I'm awake now."

Drosos had gone to the window, drawn by the dark mass of the Library. He stood as if transfixed by the sight, though it was now impossible to make out anything more than an irregular shape where he knew the buildings to be. "Only one will be left when we're through," he said after a little time.

Chrysanthos heard the pain in Drosos' words and had no anodyne to offer. "At least there will be one."

"They'll probably be rid of that, one day," Drosos said unhappily. "It's like that, once the burning starts."

"Captain." He was not sure Drosos had heard him, but he went on doggedly. "Captain, you asked for wine. I brought two skins with me. They're right here."

Drosos turned heavily. "Wineskins." He laughed harshly. "Why not?"

"And I have two cups," Chrysanthos said, taking them from a narrow shelf by the door. "Choose the one you wish."

"Oh, I leave that to you," Drosos said, coming away from the window at last. "Just so long as you keep it full. I want to be drunk as a barbarian whore." He threw himself down into his chair and looked at Chrysanthos expectantly.

"On good Cypriot wine?" Chrysanthos pretended to be scandalized at the suggestion.

"On any wine," Drosos said with determination. "God, God, God, I want to forget tonight." He sighed suddenly and deeply.

"Drosos—"

"Pour the wine," he ordered. "When we've drained a cup or two, I might say something. But then it will only be maundering, and it won't matter; you'll be drunk, too, and you won't care what I say." He braced his arm on the table at his side. "Hurry up there, Chrysanthos."

As Chrysanthos poured out the first generous measures of wine, he said, "Did you take that Egyptian slave to bed with you at last?"

Drosos stopped in the act of loosening the buckles that held his lorica and said, "I decided against it. She's tempting enough but . . . I never trust a slave in bed. Who knows why they're there?"

Chrysanthos held out the larger of the two cups to Drosos and lifted the other. "Well, here's to forgetfulness."

"Amen," said Drosos as he took the cup. He drank

greedily, a little thread of wine sliding down his chin from the corner of his mouth. He wiped this away on his cuff. "No, I changed my mind about the Egyptian girl."

"You miss your Roman widow," Chrysanthos said, making the suggestion a teasing one; in Drosos' mercurial mood he did not know how he would react to such a remark.

"Yes," he said after taking a second draught. "That is just what I need," he told Chrysanthos.

"The wine or the widow?"

"Either. Both." He picked up the cup a third time but did not drink at once. "She would understand."

"Then it's a pity she's not here," said Chrysanthos, feeling his way with his Captain.

"Yes, a great pity." He drank and held out his cup for more.

They sat together until the sun came up; gradually their words became slurred and indistinct and their thoughts no longer held together. But though Drosos drank with single-minded determination, the anguish remained at the back of his eyes and nothing he could do or say touched it.

*   *   *

Text of a letter from Captain Ghornan to Pope Sylvestros.

   To Pope Sylvestros, currently in Puteoli, Captain Ghornan sends greetings and thanks for his perseverance.
   The tables and chests you found for me when we last dealt together have brought a higher price than we expected,

and I have paid the monies to your wife's family, as you requested. You will find that they are more pleased with your absence now than they were a year ago.

However, I must warn you that the Emperor has ordered that more inspections for contraband be carried out on ships landing in Byzantion, and therefore I am considering marketing our goods elsewhere. There is a good market in Nicopolis which is not as profitable as that of Konstantinoupolis, but has the advantage that there are very few questions to answer and no soldiers to seize questionable items. It might mean that we do not realize as much gold, but we will have our hands and our ears which means much to me.

You mentioned that you found a villa near Vivarium that has eight fine chairs inlaid with ivory. That would be a treasure, but something that distinctive might be too risky for us just now. We've had some cargo identified as smuggled, and we had better save those until later. If you still have space in that warehouse in Ostia, it might be worth taking the chairs there and storing them for a while until a suitable market may be found for them. The same is probably true of those statues you mentioned, although shipping them is difficult. As to your suggestion that we take the last of the couches from that villa near Roma, I would recommend that you stay away from there for the time being since I have learned that the owner was able to identify some of the pieces when we offered them for sale in Konstantinoupolis.

It might be wisest if you were to return to your church in Konstantinoupolis for a short while. Your continued absence might create more questions than you or I wish to answer, and I for one do not want to come under suspicion, for then we will all have to be circumspect in a way that has not been necessary before. When you return, you need only claim that the battles in Italy were too costly for you to be able to continue your ministry without great risk. It might be fashionable to court martyrdom, but your metropolitan will endorse your prudence if you are not foolish about it.

The jewels you discovered in the villa near the Via Valeria are more promising than some of the other discoveries you have made, for they are small and it is not likely that the owners survived the onslaught of Totila's men. You can put the jewels into large barrels and fill the rest with grain or some other anonymous substance and the chances are excellent that it will go undetected through the inspections that are being imposed upon us all. You can indicate that you are bringing grain or something similar to your family or the poor who come to your church and it is certain that you will be unscathed.

Let me also remind you that once you are back with your wife and your church that it will be necessary for you to have a consistent tale to tell them all. You can prepare that in advance, but once you have decided on it, you must memorize it and hold to it, or there are those who will be prepared to leave your name with the officers of the Censor and then you would be in a very bad position. As harsh as the magistrates are being with sailors accused of smuggling, they are more severe with popes who take advantage of their cloth and calling to turn the service of their faith to profit. In your case, they might want to make an example of you. Guard yourself well, you Orthodox heretic.

As soon as it is safe, we will deal together again, but not, I think, in Konstantinoupolis. If you think of a market we might exploit, let me know of it.

This by my own hand and with the recommendation that you not keep it in your possession for more than a day or two since it would go hard for us both if it were discovered,

Ghornan

· 9 ·

When Eugenia came into the vestibule of her house she was startled to discover Simones waiting for her. "Is . . . has something happened to your mistress?" she asked, unable to account for his presence and wanting her majordomo to hear whatever it was that the eunuch had come to tell her.

"She is doing much the same," said Simones as he made a reverence to Eugenia.

"The General then? Has there been a change in his condition?" She felt puzzled and worried and when she spoke again, her words came faster than before. "You are disturbing me, Simones."

"Perhaps you might spare me a little time, great lady." He sounded so self-deprecating that Eugenia nearly called him insolent.

"I have other tasks," she said, starting to move away.

"It is important, or I would not have come." He looked at her directly, without any apology. "There are some questions that I hope you will answer for me."

"What questions are those?" Her voice was sharp.

"They are only for your welfare, great lady. You need not fear my motives." He glanced at her majordomo. "If you were to grant me a little time and privacy . . . ?"

"Oh, if you're determined," she said, her mouth turning down with irritation. "The smaller reception room is this way." She indicated the way as she said to her majordomo, "Isa, leave us alone until I send for you.

There is more than enough work for you and the others. Tend to that while I discover why this slave has come."

"As you speak it is done, great lady," said Isa, making his reverence and withdrawing quickly.

"Very well; tell me." Eugenia was following Simones down the hallway, her patience already wearing thin.

"That is my intention," said Simones as he entered the smaller reception room and closed the door behind Eugenia so that they were alone. "You have not called at the house of my master of late."

"Your mistress is ill," said Eugenia bluntly.

"My mistress is no longer influential," Simones corrected her. "If she had kept her position, you would not have let her illness keep you away."

"Of all the brazen—" Eugenia began indignantly.

"Great lady, if you insist on these performances we will accomplish little." Simones had folded his arms over his wide, muscular chest and he waited while she turned startled eyes on him and fell silent. "You have not come to see Antonina, and she finds this troubling."

"I'm sorry to hear that, but she understands my predicament. She would tell you that herself." Eugenia smiled beguilingly. "If that is what you were sent to tell me, I'm sorry to tell you that Antonina and I have—"

Simones moved a few steps closer to Eugenia. "I think it would be very wise of you to resume your visits."

Eugenia laughed in disbelief. "You think that, do you? You? A slave?"

"Yes. It would be sensible for you to write Antonina a letter, telling her that you have heard that she is not well and that you wish to spend some time with her in spite of the risk you run in terms of making the match you wish to have."

"You are not to speak to me that way!" Eugenia ordered him.

"I will speak to you as I wish," said Simones with contemptuous calm. "And you will listen to me and thank me for what I tell you."

"What nonsense are you—" Eugenia was angry and she

spat out the words quickly, her face ugly.

"And you will be rewarded for what you do." He was unperturbed by her outburst.

"By you?" she scoffed.

"By the officers of the Court Censor," said Simones, and waited while Eugenia considered his statement.

Eugenia started toward the door and then stopped. "The Court Censor?"

"Yes."

"What would a slave like you be doing to aid the Court Censor?" She had intended this to be sarcastic, but instead the tone was speculative. Her soft vixen's face grew crafty, almost predatory.

"Think of who I am, great lady, not what I am." He gave her time again. "There are many who want to know what transpires in the house of Belisarius, and there is no direct way they can find out. A man in my position knows many things and the officers of the Censor know this."

"But a slave—" she said with less certainty.

"Who better? You do not think that the Censor finds his servants only among those who are free. I might not be able to testify before magistrates, but what I learn can make investigations possible, and there are others to swear to the accuracy of what I say." He came closer to her, standing less than an arm's length from her. This was a serious breach of correct behavior and was reason enough for Eugenia to have him whipped. "Listen to me, great lady. You and I, working together, can do much. And we will be rewarded."

"If you think I would conspire with a slave, Simones," she warned him, her breath coming faster, "then you have a poor opinion of my character."

Simones laughed outright. "Be as indignant as you want; you will aid me or I will see that the shadow that falls over Antonina falls over you as well."

"You're threatening me?" Her head came up and her gentleness disappeared.

"No, great lady. A slave would never threaten one such as you. I am telling you what will happen, keeping you informed as an honorable slave ought to do." He made a malicious reverence to her. "Do not suppose that I won't, or that I will not be believed."

"You're ridiculous. If this weren't so absurd, I would have you thrashed for offending me." She moved away from him, pulling the folds of her paenula more closely about her.

"Go ahead, if you are willing to throw my assistance away," he offered her with mock generosity. "But you might reconsider, great lady. Who else is there who can aid you now? You are a widow and your means are limited. You have only your sponsor, and he cares little for what happens to you as long as your husband's estate is protected. You have no lover just now—ever since you dismissed Chrysanthos you have not had a lover for more than a few days. Your means are straitened and your prospects are not good." He revealed these unpleasant truths in a conversational way, strolling toward her as he spoke. "You could make good use of the Censor's gratitude. There would be money, undoubtedly. There would also be introductions and endorsements. You do not need me to tell you the advantages that would bring you. You are not going to be lovely forever, and you should keep that in mind when you deal with me."

Eugenia had turned slightly pale at Simones' recitation, but she rallied. "You talk as if I were about to become a pauper and a hag at once."

"Not at once," he said, speaking with great care. "But suppose you were implicated in the conspiracy that my master is suspected of leading? What then? Do you think you could find anyone but an ambitious merchant to marry you? And do you think your sponsor would continue to pay for your support if he thought you had dishonored your husband's memory?" He let his hand trail down Eugenia's arm. "What would you do then, great lady?"

"There is no conspiracy," Eugenia said, pulling away from his touch.

"If the Censor and the Emperor say there is a conspiracy, then, great lady, there is one." He reached out for her again.

"Don't," she snapped.

He sank his fingers into her upper arm. "You can earn the good opinion of the Emperor or you can lose all favor. It is up to you."

"And presumably to you," she added. "Let go of me."

"All in good time, great lady," said Simones, and he smiled at her. "They did not make a girl of me, Eugenia. There is still enough man left of me that you and I could both derive benefit from it." He held her firmly as she tried to rake his face with her nails. "That is foolish."

"Release me!" She struggled in his grip.

"Not just yet, Eugenia." His hands tightened painfully. "You will have bruises if you persist. Stand still and listen to me."

She tried to kick him, but in the long, trailing folds of her garments the impact made little impression. "You cur! You offal!"

"Eugenia," he said as he dragged her close against him. "You will be my ally or you will be nothing."

Whatever additional insults she had been about to speak were silenced. She closed her eyes. "You are humiliating me."

"Good," said Simones. "That is a start." He bent his head and kissed her. "You can do it better than that."

"Please," she begged.

"You will be my ally," he repeated. "You will do what I require of you when I require it, and in the end you will be rewarded. Think of it, Eugenia. You will have a comparatively short time of this—perhaps a year at most—and then you will be free to find yourself another husband, and to enjoy the favor and approval of the Emperor. You will not need a friend like Antonina used to be to obtain introductions and other favor." This time he kissed her with calculated fervor; he opened her mouth with his tongue and he pressed her against him. Only when he felt her respond did he stop.

"You disgust me," Eugenia said.

"You'll get over it," he informed her. "Wait and see; you may even come to like me." He slid his hand down her arm and grasped her hand, drawing it between them. "There; is that enough for you?"

She tried to pull her hand away. "You're very large."

"When they docked me, they left the best part." His expression was smug. "There are great ladies who prefer eunuchs like me. We are the safest lovers. You will never get a child off of me, and I will outlast any whole man, who eventually spurts and withers." He smiled. "Do not try to hurt me, Eugenia. If you do, I will hurt you."

Her eyes were bright with fear and another unnamed and unadmitted emotion. "Why are you doing this to me?"

"I need your help. And I have wanted you a long time." At last he let her go. "You had better consider everything I have said. Everything."

"But . . . what . . ." She rubbed her arms where his hands had been.

"Think of the advantages I offer you. Or do you think that a mere eunuch slave cannot do the things I have said?" His face darkened. "Well?"

"You are being unkind to me, Simones." She said this wistfully, a little of her languishing sensuality coming back into her manner.

"I will be worse than unkind if you refuse to work with me. I will make you regret your refusal more than you can imagine."

"Threats are not very lover-like," she said, her smile more a rictus of fear than the tantalization she intended. "If you want my aid, you might ask for it differently."

"I do not want it; I need it." He looked down at her. "You are hoping you will enthrall me as you have other men, but I am not like them. I am a slave, and I do not find captivity enjoyable. Such things are only attractive to those who are free to walk away from them."

Eugenia looked away from him. "And you will make a slave of me."

"If you care to think of it that way," he agreed. He

approached her. When she flinched, he deliberately took her face in his hands. "It will not go well if you show me your repugnance so plainly, Eugenia. Take a lesson from me and learn to appear complacent." He bent and kissed her again, this time harshly, so that she felt his teeth against her lower lip.

This time she broke away from him and chose the narrowest chair in the room to sit on. "You expect me to betray my friend. You want me to be a spy. And you want me to be your whore."

"Yes," he said baldly.

"And if I do not cooperate, you will do everything you can to destroy me." She said this very calmly, but she could not look at him as she spoke.

"Yes."

"So you are saying that it is you or the gutter." She flung the words at him, daring him to contradict her.

"Yes; that is precisely what I am saying." He came and stood directly in front of her so that she was blocked in the chair and could not escape. "You will do what I ask when I ask it and you will not question me. You will comply with my instructions, no matter what they are, and you will do so without complaint. Do you understand?"

"You're gloating." She held her paenula closed.

Simones bent down so that his face almost touched hers. "It does not matter if I am. It is my right, if I wish to exercise it."

She swallowed hard, and when she spoke, her voice trembled. "Is there nothing I can do to make you change your mind?"

"What?" He laughed as he reached out and pulled her from the chair, pinning her against him with his arms and holding her. "You will have to show me a little more emotion, Eugenia. You must make me believe you are pleased that I have taken notice of you, or I might be tempted to forget our arrangement and see you made a beggar."

"Simones, please." She was weak with dread.

"And to show you how much faith I put in you, I will

tell you something that will shock you. Antonina is dying of poison." He saw her shock. "You will say nothing to her or to anyone about it. If you do, you know what fate awaits you. I will say that I said I feared she was dying of poison, and that will be sufficient. You cannot testify and neither can I, so nothing we have to say will reach the magistrates."

"Why do you tell me this?" she whispered.

"To let you know that I can and will do all that I say," he said with such calm ruthlessness that Eugenia shuddered.

"Are you poisoning her?" She knew the answer but was filled with a hideous fascination. In a remote part of her mind she wondered if this were a dream, a convincing nightmare that would leave her melancholy and exhausted.

"Indirectly," he said.

"Christos have mercy," she murmured.

"Better to appeal to Him than to me," Simones said, releasing her just enough to have one hand free to fondle her breasts through her garments. "Where are your private chambers?"

"I—"

"Where are they?" His hand tightened.

She cringed. "Must it be today? Won't you let me prepare?"

"You are prepared enough. If you succeed in sending me away now, the next time you will think you can do it again, and it will be more difficult for both of us; I would probably have to beat you into submission—and do not doubt that I would—and that is not a good way to begin. Tell me where your private quarters are."

She had not realized how large a man Simones was, nor how strong. Her throat was tight and dry and she felt as if she might be getting a fever. "It is . . . along the hall on the left. There are two doors with golden latches. The second is the room you want."

"How plaintive you sound," he jeered as he lifted her into his arms.

"My slaves—" she began, shamed at the thought of gossip.

"I will say you are faint if anyone has the audacity to ask." Holding her easily he strode to the door, deftly working the latch open before striding into the hall.

"What if I scream?" she asked, desperation making her reckless.

"I will make you sorry you did. I will begin by throttling you until you faint. After that, I will be certain you tender me a profound apology. Slaves know about such things, great lady. I give you my word it would be a lesson you would not forget." He was moving quickly but without apparent haste.

"Why do you want to do this? Why do you degrade me this way?" She felt tears well in her eyes and she hated herself for the weakness she revealed.

"What is degradation to a slave? We are born to it, and it is our fate to die as we were born. God has mandated that we have this station in life without recourse. You say we are born degraded." He was almost at the door of her private chambers. "Have you ever considered your slaves?"

"I give them the best care I can, but I am not wealthy. I see that they are housed and fed and treated well when they give good service." She lifted her chin but was appalled at the whine she heard in her protestations.

"How good of you," he said angrily as he threw the door open. "You think you are doing well because you don't abuse your slaves."

"My pope has said that a good Christian does not mistreat slaves, for they have their purpose appointed by God just as we have ours." She repeated this in a small voice, sounding almost like a child.

"And you listen and obey." He lowered her onto the bed. "You know nothing about obedience. Not yet. You will learn, Eugenia, and you will thank me for it, for it will buy you more freedom than it will buy me."

"No—" she whispered, trying to hold on to her garments as Simones kicked the door closed.

"Another time you will do this on request," he said coldly. "This time, you require a demonstration." He took the neck of her paenula and dalmatica in his hands and with a sudden wrenching pulled both garments apart.

Eugenia shrieked, aghast at what was being done to her and at the power Simones used, for the silk and wool were not easy to tear.

"Don't resist me, Eugenia; it will be worse for you if you do." He held her with the ends of her garments, staring down at her. Then, abruptly, he tugged one end of the clothing and almost wrenched it away from her.

"No!" She tried to bring her hands to cover herself, but they were still trapped in the sleeves of her dalmatica. She squirmed and pulled, but she was quite effectively trapped.

"Very pretty," Simones approved.

"Take me if you have to, but not this," she pleaded.

"A few lunges and it's over?" he suggested sarcastically. "You forget how it is with eunuchs like me. A few lunges will accomplish very little. We take a long time to be satisfied. I will see you spitted and I will hear you scream before I am finished with you."

She struggled but to no avail.

Still holding the wreckage of her garments, Simones sat beside her, staring at her critically. "I am going to determine if you please me."

"Simones—"

"You," he went on conversationally, "will say nothing. You will do as I tell you silently." He weighed her breast in his hand as if he were selecting a cut of lamb. "Firm enough." He pinched the nipple twice. "A trifle small, but probably adequate."

"This is intolerable!" she screamed softly.

Simones struck her casually, his hand open. "I said you would be silent. If you disobey again, I will have to find some way to correct you with force."

"Don't." She was still with fright as soon as the word was out.

"That's better," he approved, and loosened the belt he wore in place of a pallium. "If you struggle, I will be rough with you. I hope that won't be necessary." He tugged his dalmatica up around his waist and moved over her.

"Not yet," she implored, her body feeling leaden and cold.

"Open your legs for me."

Shuddering, she complied.

It went on forever, his body pressing hers, his intrusion seeming to be endless. Once it crossed her mind that if she had wanted this man, if he had been a chosen lover, she would feel bliss now, for his incredible endurance would bring her more satisfaction than she had ever experienced. But it was Simones who mounted her, who pillaged her. Every thrust was like a blow and their joining like a beating.

"Eventually you will give in," he told her in deep pants. "You will not resist me."

"No."

"Yes," he insisted.

Eventually she shrieked, but it was not from fulfillment or culmination; she shrieked her outrage.

*   *   *

Text of a letter from Drosos to Olivia.

To my dearest, cherished Olivia, Drosos sends his greeting and love on the occasion of Passion Sunday, in the
Lord's Year 549.

My friend Chrysanthos will bring this to you. Destroy it
when you have done reading it, and tell no one what I have
said, or you will expose us both to great dangers and I have
brought enough grief into the world without adding to it. I
would not burden you this way, but there is no one else
who I trust enough and who is not bound by oath to report
what I say. Do not be angry with me for adding to your
risks, Olivia. I do not think I could say such things to
anyone but you, and if that is dangerous, I can think of
nothing that would make amends for doing this.

I suppose by now you will have heard about the Library.
The popes here were celebrating as if they had triumphed
over Satan himself. I have heard them offer prayers of
thanksgiving, and I cannot join with them. All those books!
When they showed them to me, I couldn't believe that
anyone could want to burn them. How I hate the look of
that word: burn. I despise it. I loathe what it means. It's all
gone, all of it; all the information, all the thoughts, all the
words, because the men who wrote them did not worship
Our Lord. What does the growing of a plant have to do
with that? The popes have tried to explain it to me, and I
have wanted to understand, oh, God, God, I have wanted to
understand. There has to be a reason that it happened. If I

296

gave the order to destroy all those books for nothing more than Justinian's whim, how can I live with honor?

The Emperor has said it was good to do this, that it would cleanse the world and would take away temptation. He is not like other men, for God has elevated him and made him our Emperor, and for that he is given wisdom to be the Godly leader of the Empire. He sees more and knows more. I have wanted to serve him and to live as a proper soldier does. Though I believe Justinian was misled by the enemies of Belisarius, I must assume that in this matter he speaks with clarity of vision and complete authority.

Then why am I unable to comprehend his intentions? Why is it that every time I look out the window and see those blackened heaps of stone I can sense the rebuke in them, and I am sickened by what I have done? Why have I no sense of victory that the others have? What is wrong with me? Why have I disgraced myself in this shameful way?

Olivia, I long to be with you. At night I dream of you, and the times we have been together. I want you with me. I long for you. I have asked to be returned to Konstantinoupolis, but so far no answer has been given to my request. It is too much to hope that you have taken no other lovers, but I pray that you have not come to prefer another to me. I hope that you will still welcome me, for when I return I will seek you out as avidly as a stag in rut. There has been no woman like you, ever. I have tried others, but all I want is you. Take me back when I come. If you turn me away, I could not endure it. I would rather the worm consume my vitals than you turn me away.

Chrysanthos will give you news of me if you ask him. He has worried and fussed over me for weeks on end. He is a good man, Chrysanthos, and he will speak plainly if that is what you wish. Do not worry that he will report what you say. He has sworn that he will never speak of what I have told him, and that he will extend this vow to you. Not even the Emperor could demand that he abjure his word, you may be sure of that.

Olivia, what purpose has the burning served? I think of

everything lost, gone. It was a stilling of voices, as if it were men we burned and not words. I will fight in battle and kill if that is my fate, but this was worse than slaughter and I fear I am a butcher or a murderer. Why is the purpose of this act hidden from me? Why do I see myself as smirched with a stain that will never leave me? The popes say that this is the greatest act of the Emperor, that we are closer to Heaven for being rid of these pernicious books. Why, then, do I feel so much closer to Hell?

Pray for me, Olivia, and let me love you when I return, no matter when it is that they will finally permit me to leave this place. Olivia, let me come to you then. I am in a wasteland here, and you are the spring in the desert. If you have chosen another lover, or if you have married, then there is nothing for me in Konstantinoupolis and I might as well be sent to the battle lines again.

I wish there were something I could fight. I am a soldier, and I might find expiation in battle. The popes say that I am wrong to feel this contrition and that I have no fault, but my soul carries a heavy burden and I do not know how to put it down. If I could vanquish an enemy, I might believe that I have restored myself.

You are all that is left to me now, until the Emperor sees fit to send me elsewhere or I come to understand what purpose I have served in ordering those damned fires lit. You are sense in an insane world, Olivia. You shine like a comet in the skies. I will love you until the blood is gone from my veins and the breath from my lungs.

Remember, destroy this. No one must see it, for your sake as well as mine.

With my devotion and passion

Drosos

• 10 •

Zejhil held out two small, golden cups. "I found them in the pantry, next to the glass vessels. I didn't recognize them and I thought you'd better have a look at them."

Niklos took the cups. "They're not ours. I wonder where they came from?" He turned them over, examining them with a critical and practiced eye. "Very good quality, about two hundred years old, I'd guess. Very definitely Roman, but I know that Olivia never had anything like them."

"Why would—" Zejhil interrupted herself. "Someone wants to implicate her."

"As being in league with smugglers, I'd guess," Niklos concurred. "Doubtless you're right." He looked down at the little cups as if he expected them to burn him. "Olivia has gone to church. She's been doing that more recently; she wants to rid herself of some of the stigma of being foreign."

"If this is what someone is doing to her, she will have to try harder," Zejhil said, trying to sound cynical.

"That she will," Niklos said without humor. "I wonder what else has been hidden about the house?"

"You don't think there's more, do you?" Zejhil was not able to conceal her shock.

"If someone wants to make a case for her having things she ought not to have, two gold cups aren't enough. Anyone might have a few things they had forgotten or misplaced, even gold cups. Therefore, if this is part of a plan, there must be other things here. Unless they have just started to act, in which case we may have a chance to surprise them in the act." He gave the cups back to Zejhil. "Put these back where you found them."

"Why?" She was surprised at the suggestion.

"Because whoever put these in the pantry will know that we are aware of what he is doing if he finds they are missing." He tapped the rims of the cups together in ironic salute.

"Are you certain it is a he?" asked Zejhil.

"No. And neither are you." He faltered. "Zejhil, if you do not want to do anything more, I would understand and so would Olivia. It was one thing to assist us in gathering information about the household, but if we have reached a point where someone is attempting to do more than that, you have very good reason not to continue to cooperate."

"I am a slave," she explained.

"You are: a slave to a Roman lady," Niklos said. "She follows the old ways."

"I don't understand."

"There was a time when slaves had rights. Olivia Clemens remembers that time." Niklos took Zejhil by the elbow and pulled her into an alcove. "If anyone comes, I will kiss you. No one will think that remarkable. Now tell me what else you have discovered."

"Very little," she admitted. "Phaon, the new gardener, has been asking questions, but there is nothing strange in a slave doing that when he comes to a household. And the cook has been doing some snooping; it may be curiosity, but it may be something more than that. The laundryman has spent more time in the house than in the washing shed, but the weather is—"

Niklos wrapped his arms around her and pressed his mouth to hers. His hands moved expertly over her and he was startled to discover he was enjoying himself. When the carpenter was out of sight, Niklos released Zejhil with reluctance.

Zejhil was breathing unsteadily. "I . . . I forgot what I

was saying." Her cheeks reddened with her admission.

Niklos ran one finger along her cheek. "It's all right; I'll wait until you remember."

She caught his finger in her hand. "No. You must not."

"Why not?" he asked. "Do I offend you?"

"It's not that," she said, looking away from him. "It would not be permitted if our mistress knew of it. Slaves are not—"

"You don't know Olivia," Niklos said, deeply relieved.

"She is mistress."

"She is also Roman." Niklos let his hands rest on her shoulders. "She will not choose for you, Zejhil, if that is what troubles you."

"She is mistress," Zejhil repeated stubbornly.

"You make her sound like a monster." He dropped his hands. "Tell me the rest. We'll talk about this later, when you've had a chance to think."

"I—"

"When you've had a chance to think," Niklos reiterated. "You don't have to decide anything now." He deliberately took a step back from her. "Have you noticed anything else in the household? Has anyone said anything to you that you find questionable?"

She shook her head slowly. "Nothing specific," she said in an apologetic manner. "There have been a few comments that might be significant, but slaves learn to keep their council."

"You gossip," Niklos reminded her.

"That's different. Everyone in the household knows that the mistress has occasional lovers but that she is most fond of that Captain who was sent to Alexandria. They say that she has strange ways, Roman ways, and a few of them have said that they worry because they have not seen her eat, ever. The rest don't care one way or another as long as we're fed, which we are." She laughed once, the sound hard and breathless.

"Is that all that matters to you?" Niklos was saddened to hear these things from Zejhil, but not surprised.

"A few are curious about her shoes. They say that the soles are too thick." She dared to look at Niklos. "Why is that?"

"She prefers them that way," Niklos answered evasively. "You think something, Zejhil. What is it?"

"I have no reason for my feelings," she warned him. "It is just a . . . a feeling I have. Sometimes it seems to me that Philetus has been too attentive to his duties, and doing all his work on the walls near where the mistress is. He does very beautiful work, and the murals he paints are lovely, but there is . . . a lack in him, as if he were hidden away behind that pious mask he paints on the faces of his Saints." Her eyes watered. "I don't want to get him into trouble for no reason."

"You won't," said Niklos, permitting himself to put a comforting hand on her arm. "When Olivia returns from church, will you come to her and tell her what you have told me? I will have to speak to her in any case, but it would be best if you were willing to answer her questions."

"And you will treat me as you did before?" She had intended this as a feeble joke, but Niklos responded with great seriousness.

"Listen to me, Zejhil: you are not to be afraid of me. I am Olivia's majordomo, and I am proud of that, but I am a bondsman, not a slave, and she would not abuse that. She would not abuse slaves, either, but you don't believe that."

"She is mistress." This time when she said it, Zejhil was less remote than before. "She is better than most, I agree, but she is mistress."

Niklos accepted this. "I will come for you when Olivia is back."

"Why do you call her Olivia and not great lady or my mistress?" Zejhil asked, as she had been wanting to for more than two months.

"We have been together a long time, and during that time, her fortunes have fluctuated. We've become . . . friends." He knew he could not tell Zejhil that his association with Olivia spanned more than three centuries.

"But she holds your bond," Zejhil pointed out.

"Yes. I don't mind. She would not have objected to my leaving her service at any time, and I can easily afford the price of my bond, but the arrangement suits us, and as long as it does, I suppose it will continue." He smiled.

"Are you her lover?" Zejhil blurted out the question before she could stop herself.

"When I first met her, I was. For three nights only." If he had not been, he reminded himself, he would be nothing more than a heap of bones in Saturnia. "She . . . she saved my life." He had only the vaguest recollection of the day he had died, but his memory of his restoration was vivid; it was the first time he had ever seen Sanct' Germain who had reanimated him.

"Oh." Zejhil looked down, as if his feet were of intense interest to her. "And now?"

"You mean are we still lovers? No, not for a long time." He slipped his hand under her chin and deliberately turned her face toward his. "And she does not require that I live like a monk. It isn't her way."

Zejhil fixed her eyes on a spot behind his head. "She is a courtesan, that is what all the household says. They whisper about the men who come here, and they talk about Captain Drosos, but—"

"My mistress is a widow," Niklos said, in his most formal tone. "I did not know her husband, but I have heard little good about him. She does not wish to marry again, and she does not want to live wholly retired from the world. If that makes her a courtesan, then you are the one who calls her that, not I."

Zejhil was more embarrassed than before. "I did not intend to"—she glanced down the hall at the sound of footsteps—"I will do as you ask. I will speak to her when she returns. And Niklos, I do not care, truly I do not care, if she is or is not a courtesan. She is a good mistress."

"That she is," Niklos agreed. He raised his hand as one of the three women employed to make, care for, and repair clothing approached. "Ianthe," he said to greet her.

"Majordomo," she responded, her face expressionless; she gave no indication that she had seen Zejhil at all.

"I don't like that woman," Zejhil muttered. "She wheezes when she walks."

"She isn't young, and her hot blood is congested," said Niklos. "One can see that from her coloring."

Zejhil shook her head vehemently. "It's more than that." She moved away from Niklos. "I will come. I'll tell our mistress what I know. You can believe me. I will not fail."

"I know that," Niklos said, hoping that his smile would give her courage. "You are a good woman, Zejhil."

"If that matters," she said, and hurried away.

By the time Olivia returned, Niklos was all but chewing on the cushions from impatience. He sought her out at once and gave her as blunt an account as he could, including his response to Zejhil.

Olivia listened to this with interest. "Good," she said after a moment. "You have done well. I want to know more about this suspect contraband. I don't want you to bring me the cups—I'll go see them for myself, later tonight. For the time being I want to know how far this has gone. As to Zejhil herself, that is encouraging."

He could not hold back a burst of laughter. "Only you would express it that way, Olivia."

"Well, it is. You were afraid that once you were restored that you would not be all that you were."

"And I'm not," he said without rancor.

"That is not because you were brought back." She gave him a roguish, rueful glance. "You ought to have tasted my blood before you faced that mob. It would have saved all of us a lot of trouble." It was an old, teasing argument with them, and Niklos shrugged elaborately.

"I was shortsighted; what else can I say?" He met her eyes, the worry back in his face. "I'm troubled, Olivia."

"Yes. Whatever we have been caught up in, it is escalating." She walked over to a large Roman chest standing next to the window. "We will have to search the house tonight, all of it. I want to find out what has been brought into this house. Perhaps then we can determine who is doing it, and why."

Niklos paced down the room. "And then what? You can't go to the magistrates, and if you did, they would pay no attention."

"I can go to Belisarius. He may be out of favor with the Emperor, and he might be kept in close check, but he is still the most respected General in the Empire, and that counts for something. He will advise me."

"You need more than advice," Niklos warned her.

She gave a helpless gesture. "I realize that. But I must begin somewhere." Her demeanor changed as there was a knock on the door; she looked now as if she were discussing nothing more important than ordering replacement parchment for the windows.

Niklos opened the door and admitted Zejhil. "You're here in good time," he said to the Tartar slave. "Don't be concerned."

Zejhil was clearly apprehensive, but she was also very determined. She spent a good portion of time answering the questions Olivia put to her and making a few observations on her own.

"I am grateful to you, Zejhil," said Olivia, handing the woman five silver coins. "You have certainly been diligent, and I appreciate that more than I can tell you."

Zejhil, who had never held so much money in her hands in her life, stared as if she expected the coins to disappear. "My mistress, I do not know—"

"It is little enough. If it were permitted here, I would happily give you your freedom, but for that, sadly, I need the approval of a pope, and they do not often agree to the freeing of slaves." She folded her arms, irritated at the degree of helplessness that engulfed her.

"My mistress—" She reached to take the hem of Olivia's paenula to kiss it, and was amazed when Olivia pulled the garment away.

"Magna Mater! What is the matter with you, girl?"

Olivia burst out, frustration showing in every line of her body. "You don't have to do this; by rights, I should show that courtesy to you." She rounded on Niklos. "By tomorrow morning I want a complete accounting of everything you find that you have any reason to suspect might have been placed here to implicate me or any member of this household in illegal activities."

"And Belisarius: do you still intend to ask him for help?" Niklos asked skeptically.

"I realize you don't approve, but he is the only ally I have while Drosos is in Alexandria, and he—" She did not go on, for the anxiety of the letter Chrysanthos had brought to her clandestinely was too keen.

"Olivia?" Niklos asked, sensitive to her moods.

"It's nothing," she said in a tone that did not convince him. "Truly, Niklos."

He said nothing; as he went to Zejhil's side, he promised himself that he and Olivia would have to discuss Drosos, for something was wrong. He took Zejhil's hand in his.

"Niklos," Zejhil said, trying without success to pull away from him.

"I'm not going to let go," he said gently.

"It isn't for you or me to decide."

"And if it were?" said Olivia. "Tell me, Zejhil, what would you want, if it were up to you? Do you want Niklos? Do not fear to speak honestly to me, and pay no attention to him."

"It isn't my choice," Zejhil said in a small voice.

"Pretend it is," Olivia suggested. "Tell me."

Zejhil gave a little shake to her head. "I don't know."

"Then, Niklos, I suggest that you give her time. She cannot be pressed," Olivia said, and indicated their hands.

He let go. "All right." There was an odd light at the back of his russet eyes. "For now."

"Oh, stop it," Olivia said, and turned her attention to Zejhil. "Do nothing you do not wish to do." She then walked away from Niklos and Zejhil. "I hope that once we find out what is being done here and why that we will have no more trouble here. I am not eager to have to move again."

"If it were permitted," Niklos said with emphasis. "You would need a sponsor, wouldn't you?"

"I would find one," Olivia said with what she hoped was confidence. "Belisarius would do that much for me."

"If it's allowed," Niklos cautioned.

"You're always so optimistic," Olivia reprimanded him, and then held up her hands. "No, I didn't mean to show contempt, Niklos. I am apprehensive, and it makes my tongue sharp."

"I know," said Niklos, and took it upon himself to change the direction of their conversation. "When do we start our search? Do we wait until all the household is in bed, or do we start now?"

Olivia nodded in a businesslike way. "You're right; we ought to settle that." She glowered at the ikonostasis. "I will go to the library now. After church it would not be thought strange for me to read. Providing I read the right books," she added dryly.

"Do you think they will have placed condemned books in the library?" Niklos asked.

"It would not be a difficult thing to do," she pointed out. "And the way things are, it would simplify the accusation—apostasy is worse than smuggling. And they could be rid of me without having to deal with Belisarius, for he would have no means to defend me."

Niklos signaled Zejhil to leave, and as soon as she was gone, he regarded Olivia thoughtfully. "Very well, are you going to tell me what has put that crease between your brows?"

"Everything," she said comprehensively.

"Drosos."

"Yes," she admitted. "His letter—I fear for him."

Niklos waited for the rest.

"We are not welcome here. Simply because we come

from Italy and have been friends of Belisarius, they want to be rid of us, and use us in some way against him." She sighed. "I suppose we had best make some arrangements that will allow us to leave Konstantinoupolis quickly and . . . without fuss."

"Also without goods and money," Niklos stated.

"We have been without goods and money before. Or have you forgot?"

"How could I?" He came and stood in front of her. "Olivia, please, I ask you for your sake as well as mine, be prepared. Have a safe-conduct. You know that Belisarius will do that for you, and there isn't a soldier who will not honor it unless Justinian countermands it. Will you do that?"

"All right," she said slowly.

"It goes against the grain?" he said fondly.

"You know it does." She made a disaster of her smile. "It has to be done, though, doesn't it?"

"It would be best."

"And it would be best to search the house, and all the rest of it; yes, I know, I know, I know." She hit her fists against her thighs.

He stopped her, confining her hands in his. "Olivia, if you'd rather remain here, I will not—"

Before he could say *object*, she cut in. "Oh, yes you will. Fortunately for me." She returned to the chest and retrieved her writing materials. "If you'll wait a bit, I'll have a note for you to carry to Belisarius. I hope you'll be permitted to give it to him. If the soldiers insist on taking it, then request to see the General. They aren't supposed to prevent that. Make sure you inquire about Antonina."

He listened, and when she gave him the note, he promised to return as swiftly as possible. "Where will you be?"

"In my reading room. With all the furor about heretical books, I can't imagine our enemies would pass up so promising an opportunity." It was the first time she had admitted that she had active enemies and it chilled Niklos to hear her use the words. "It is rare enough for women to read, and to make matters worse, most of my books are in Latin." Her hazel eyes did not shed tears, but there was a look to her that was worse than weeping would have been.

"Olivia—" Niklos said tentatively.

"Go on. Take the note to Belisarius. Do it quickly; I want this over with as soon as possible."

He had the good sense not to argue. "As you wish." He made her a reverence and left her.

She stood alone in the room after he had left, and in spite of the determination she had shown Niklos, she wavered. She was more overwrought than she was aware until that moment. All along, she told herself, she had assumed that her situation would change, that in time she would be accepted or at least tolerated by the Byzantines. Now all hope of that was gone for her and she knew she would have to look elsewhere for the safety she had so orectically yearned for. She had a brief inclination to flee Konstantinoupolis at once, to leave everything behind and set out for Olbia, or Tarraco, or Alexandria.

Alexandria. And Drosos. She steadied herself and set her jaw. She would inspect her books first, making a record of any that were not hers. Then she would confer with Niklos and together they could come up with some means of protection that would last until Drosos returned.

There were no mirrors in her room, but Olivia had long since learned to arrange her clothes and hair without them. Her fingers made minor adjustments in the arrangement of pins that held her coiffure in place, then refastened her tablion at her shoulder. Satisfied, she squared her shoulders and stepped out into the hall. It was not far to her book room but she felt as if she had crossed the desert to Aelana when she opened the door.

By the time Niklos returned with a safe-conduct hidden in the folds of his garment, Olivia had found fifteen banned texts in her shelves, and was less than a third of the way through her library.

"How bad is it?" Niklos asked, looking at the scrolls, rolled and fanfolded, a few bound in heavy leather, that were laid on the table.

"Four of these are considered worse than heretical, and this one"—she held up the largest of the leather-bound volumes—"is said to be blasphemous. The others are simply Roman, and might be questioned because they were not written by Christians. I wonder if I ought to be rid of my copy of Pliny as well?"

Niklos shook his head sadly. "I'm sorry, Olivia."

She cleared her throat. "Yes. I wish . . . I wish that I could save these, for when Drosos comes back. It isn't much, but it might help ease . . ." She made an impatient gesture. "What did Belisarius say?"

"First, that he is sad to learn of this. He feels responsible for the suspicion that falls on you. He assures you that he will do everything he can to aid you, but he isn't certain that he can do much, not anymore."

"The safe-conduct is enough," said Olivia. She looked down at the books, and said on impulse, "Hide these. There must be some place in this house that we can use safely, without the slaves knowing of it."

"Where?" He sounded reasonable enough, and that alone irritated her.

"Anywhere. Under the plants in the garden, if that would not ruin them. Under the roof. I don't know." She stared at them. "We can't simply get rid of them, for then it would be known that we had them."

Niklos gathered the books up in his arms. "I will arrange something. Perhaps in the large chariot, somewhere."

"Fine. All I ask is you leave enough of my native earth there to give me a little protection." She looked thoughtfully at the shelves. "I must finish this task tonight. I hope there are not too many more of these. The gods alone know what we'll do with them."

"Would you want me to burn a little incense?" Niklos

offered, trying to lighten her thoughts.

She gave him a look of mock horror. "Aren't we in enough trouble already?"

Neither of them laughed.

*   *   *

Text of the confession of Pope Sylvestros to the Guard of the Court Censor and the secretary of the Metropolitan Daidalos.

I, Pope Sylvestros, once of the Church of the Patriarchs, now in disgrace and ruin, do, with the good aid of the officers of the Censor, state the full extent of my crimes which only recently were brought to light by the piety of good citizens who questioned my right, under sumptuary laws, to have glass vessels in my house.

The suffering that has been meted out to me by the officers of the Guard with the advice of the secretary of the Metropolitan is surely well-deserved, for a pope who has strayed from his vows falls further than those who are not bound by oaths to Heaven. I, forgetting my sacred estate, strove to acquire wealth and goods the better to enhance my position in the world—the vainest of false hopes. Not the squeezing with knotted wharf ropes nor the peeling of the flesh from my feet suffices to make amends for what I have done, and will answer for before God when He chooses to bring me to the Throne of Judgment.

With an heretical Copt, I have worked to steal goods from houses left abandoned and ruined in Italy. I have aided in selecting these houses and in storing goods. I have advised the said Copt where the best valuables are to be found, what guard if any was on them, and where we might dispose of them to our mutual profit. For this I am deeply sorry and I repent the greed that brought me to such a loss of Grace.

During my pilfering, I noticed that many of the Romans still live with tributes to the old, pagan gods of the Caesars, and that they show these tributes honor. Incense was found in front of portrait busts of ancestors and in alcoves and niches devoted to the pagan deities that these benighted peoples worshipped and continue to worship. I believe there is not a Roman alive who is a true Christian, for all the protestations we have heard. I am convinced that they are all caught in apostasy, including the Bishop of Roma, who most certainly has shown his lack of faith in God in his flight from Roma in the face of the enemy. What true Christian would leave so sacred a place if he had any trust in God? And if he has no trust in God, he cannot call himself a Christian.

I know that I have made myself wholly unworthy of anything but the most ignoble fate, and I accept that with a willing heart, for I despise those acts that brought me away from the Love of God, and I welcome the cleansing punishments I have received and those yet to be inflicted. That I so totally rejected what I knew to be the truth is inexcusable, but I do in part account for it by the heathenish climate of Roma. I was seduced by the damned place, and thinking that I was salvaging Christian goods for Christians, I was led astray.

Beware of Romans. They are pernicious and all of them are liars. Their faith is false, their piety is deception, their devotion is nothing more than convenience. They are treacherous and forever searching out new opportunities for sin. Do not be deluded, as I was, by their subtle treachery. Be on guard at all times against them, and where you encounter them, watch with care for the sanctity of your own faith, for they are the great corrupters and will contaminate you.

I have provided a partial list of everything I have aided the Copt to steal and smuggle, as well as what monies I *have been given for my acts. The money itself must, of course, be given to Holy Church, and I surrender all my earthly goods and the goods of my wife to the Church of the Patriarchs in token recompense for the shame my actions have brought them. I know that my soul is in the Hands of God and that no act of mine will bring it again to Grace but that God wills it. For traducing the laws of the Church and the Emperor, I have doubly betrayed the sacred vows of my calling and of my nation, and for that I have erred beyond forgiveness. Yet, in the most humble emulation of the Apostles, unworthy and corrupt as I am, I beseech you to spare my life that I might end it in beggary for the Glory of God and fitting homage to the Emperor in my repentance.*

> *Pope Sylvestros*
> *(his mark)*
> *since he is unable to sign*

By the hand of the secretary of the Court Censor, Panaigios, with the signatures and marks of the witnesses, and the marks of the torturers of the Censor's Guard. Authorization is given for making ten copies of this document, and for its distribution at the discretion of the Metropolitan Superior and the Emperor Justinian.

· 11 ·

As he hurried from the small audience chamber, Kimon Athanatadies strove to conceal the trembling of his hands. He had to use all his control not to run, and for once he did not pause to speak to the Guard officers who flanked the doors. God in Heaven, what would satisfy Justinian? He closed his hands, tightening them into white-knuckled fists; his stride increased and he did his best to hide his near-panic with a scowl.

Captain Vlamos was at the Guard station at the front of the various public chambers in the palace. He glanced up at the Censor as Athanatadies rushed into the vestibule. "That was a swift conference," he said, making conversation.

"It was," Athanatadies said tightly.

"Did he give you more orders than usual?" He was used to the Censor's severe appearance, but his expression was more dire than on other occasions.

"Yes," Athanatadies said, wanting to get out of the palace and back to his own luxurious house, away from the orders and demands of the harsh man who ruled the Empire.

"He's still mourning Theodora," Captain Vlamos said. "You can't blame him for his grief."

"Of course not," Athanatadies said swiftly.

"Is there anything more you need to do here, or do you want me to send the slaves for your chariot?" He interpreted the distress of the Censor as impatience.

"My chariot, at once." He barked out the words, and

314

then did what he could to modify the tone. "There are so many things to do—"

"I don't envy you the work you do, and that's a fact," said Captain Vlamos as he signaled one of the slaves near the far door. "The Censor's chariot."

"It is an honor to labor for the Empire and the Glory of God," said Athanatadies, his emotions giving heat to this statement.

"There's many another who would not be as diligent as you are," Vlamos insisted. "The Emperor is well-served by you, no doubt about it."

Kimon Athanatadies almost demanded that Captain Vlamos tell him outright what it was he wanted rather than listen to more of this flattery, but instead he made a gesture of dismissal. "Those who wish to serve greatness must rise to the occasion."

"Just what I have said to my nephew," Captain Vlamos agreed with enthusiasm. "He is finishing his studies with the Metropolitan Odilos and is an eager young whelp. I have given my word that I will do what I can for the lad. Perhaps you have a suggestion you could give me?"

"Suggestion?" He wanted to tell Captain Vlamos to send his nephew far from Konstantinoupolis into the service of some district magistrate, to record harvest weights and trade agreements for all his life long, and be thankful for it. There was no safety, no protection at court. Anyone might fall at the Emperor's whim. "Is he ambitious?"

"He's a young man," Captain Vlamos chuckled. "He sees himself in ambassador's robes by the time he's thirty. I've told him that for such a thing to happen, another plague, like the one we had seven, eight years back, would have to come along." This was clearly intended to be amusing and the Censor did his best to smile.

"Is he capable, this nephew of yours?" He knew the answer before the Captain spoke.

"So his tutors have always said, not that I set much store in that. But the fellow does read and write Latin as well as Greek and has some knowledge of Persian."

"He would do well to keep that last to himself," Kimon Athanatadies warned Captain Vlamos. "The Emperor has recently taken a dislike to the Sassanid rulers and any reference to Persian is not welcome unless the Emperor speaks of it. Tell your nephew to confine himself to Latin and Greek."

Captain Vlamos was a bit startled. "Very well. And I thank you for your good advice."

"Tell the boy, if you wish, that in a year, if he has not found someone else to sponsor him, to come to me. He must try other routes first." And there is no telling, Athanatadies added to himself, if I will still be Censor a year from now. The way things were going, Justinian might decide to send him to the most distant outpost of the Empire, or order him to live in a hermit's cave.

"That's very good of you, Censor," Captain Vlamos said with feeling. "I didn't mean to ask for so much."

"You didn't; I offered it." He saw that the slave had returned. "My chariot has arrived." His head was beginning to throb and he could not bring himself to recite all the proper phrases of leave-taking. "I trust you will excuse me: I have much to do."

"God send you His aid," Captain Vlamos called after him, too pleased with the suggestion Athanatadies had made to be offended by his informality.

The streets were terribly congested; not far from the palace four buildings were being demolished and traffic had to find its way around these obstructions. Athanatadies swore silently and comprehensively at the delays, urging his driver to make all progress. "If you cannot go faster, I will get out and walk."

The slave holding the reins was aghast. "You cannot. A man of your position must not—"

"Then hurry," Athanatadies snapped. He had no intention of getting out of the chariot, but he felt the need to press someone—anyone—to relieve the sick dread that had taken hold of him.

"I will do everything I can," said the slave. "If you

needed to move quickly, why did you not ask for an escort of Guards?"

This petulant question was rewarded by a sharp blow on the shoulder. "I do not permit my slaves to be insolent. You will remain silent for the rest of the way."

The slave complied at once, and kept his eyes fixed just ahead of the horses' ears.

When at last Kimon Athanatadies arrived at his house, he was more exhausted than he would have been had he walked three times the distance. There were smudges of dirt on his fine silk garments and his shoes were fouled with horse and camel dung. He bellowed for his majordomo, and when that middle-aged eunuch appeared, Athanatadies issued several brisk orders. "Send for Panaigios. I want to speak with him within the hour. I will need to have several documents delivered by Guard this evening. See that the officers are ready. I want to bathe. See that a change of clothing is made ready for me. At once."

The majordomo made a very deep reverence and hastened away to do Athanatadies' bidding.

In his private chambers, the Censor stripped, shivering though the air was warm enough. His terror was like a fever, making his flesh alien to him. "Be calm," he said firmly, his hands locked together. "Think. You must think."

In a short while, the majordomo informed Athanatadies that his bath was ready. "There is a slave to assist you," he informed his master, then went on, "There has been comment on your bathing."

"Who has said anything?" Athanatadies demanded, his precarious grip on himself loosening.

"Slaves will talk," was the evasive answer.

"Who?" Athanatadies pressed. "Which one has said anything, and what has been said?"

"I don't know," the majordomo said, becoming more self-effacing with each word. "It means nothing. Slaves talk, great master, and they say silly things."

"What do they say?"

He sighed. "A few wonder why a Christian must wash so often. I don't recall who brought it up. One of the household slaves was puzzled, for his former master bathed infrequently and required the rest of his household to emulate him."

"I want the name of any slave who has remarked on this. I want the names tonight. If you do not bring them to me, they will not be the only ones I sell." He had wrapped a length of cotton cloth around him and he tugged at the ends of it for emphasis.

"Great master, it is not important what they say." His voice, already high, turned to a squeak.

"It is always important. Understand that. I will have no slave who will not mind his tongue. I have enemies. All men in high places have enemies. A slave that speaks against me, be he houseman or gardener, has allied himself with my enemies. I will not tolerate that. Tell them." He glared at his majordomo. "If you do not aid me, then I will see you gone from here, and you will serve some magistrate in Aguntum."

"That is outside of the Empire!"

Athanatadies nodded with feigned satisfaction. "It is."

"You would not do that."

"If I decided it was necessary I would," he declared, knowing that he could not allow a rebellious slave to be sold to someone who might take advantage of the knowledge the slave had of him to use against him. "Any slave sold from this household will go far from Konstantinoupolis."

"I will . . . see you have the names, great master," the majordomo said with resignation.

"Fine. And my bath?"

"It is almost ready." He stepped backward to the door, his face slick with sweat. "Great master, no one means you any disservice."

"That is for me to determine," Athanatadies countered. He rubbed his hands together and directed his gaze toward the small ikonostasis on the far side of the room. "Do you pray?"

"At the correct hours for prayers—of course." The answer was breathless; the majordomo did not know what was coming and was worried about what Athanatadies might say next.

"When you pray, ask God to reveal my enemies to me, and to show me the purpose He intends for me." He blessed himself and watched his majordomo do the same. "Give that instruction to the household."

The majordomo made his reverence and withdrew gratefully.

Athanatadies went through the inner doors of his private apartments to the chamber where his bath was waiting. As he took off the towel, he noticed with distaste that he stank. His sweat was acrid from fear, and he washed himself diligently to be rid of that odor.

By the time he was dried and dressed again, he felt less frightened. He was informed that Panaigios was waiting for him in his private reception room, and he greeted this information with satisfaction. "Excellent. I will speak with him directly. See that he has food and drink and then do not disturb us unless there is a messenger from the Emperor. And send for Konstantos Mardinopolis. I want to speak to him tonight." He dressed himself, refusing his slave's ministrations.

The reception chamber where Panaigios waited was not the littlest one adjoining the chapel, but a pleasant room opening onto the side garden of the Censor's house. The scent of flowers drifted on the air and where the garden could be glimpsed through the half-open door the shadows were lengthening, fading from stark darkness to a softer shade. The reception room itself was gloomy.

"I came as soon as I had your message," said Panaigios as he made his reverence. "I confess I was surprised at the urgency."

"So was I," said Athanatadies, trying to maintain the calm for which he was known. "I was favored by the Emperor with an audience today, to . . . to hear what he has decided must be done and to learn the means to achieve his ends."

Panaigios said nothing, but he regarded the Censor with a degree of curiosity. "What did he say? that you may repeat to me?"

"He . . . he had many new goals," Athanatadies began, striving for an air of detachment. "His zeal increases with every new day."

"How this must be pleasing to God," said Panaigios, trying to interpret the Censor's intentions. He sensed an unfamiliar tension in Athanatadies which puzzled him.

"Pleasing to God?" echoed Athanatadies. "Perhaps. It is for other men to discover what pleases God; I am sworn to please the Emperor."

"Surely their purposes are the same." To say anything else might be construed as treason, and Panaigios had the terrible sense that he was being tested in some new way.

"So we are told," Athanatadies said. "The Emperor has decided that he wishes to post certain officers away from this city, to send them into the field once again so that they may use their military skills in the service of the Empire once again."

"Belisarius?" Panaigios inquired.

"No," came the dry response. "No, Belisarius is still confined to his house and Konstantinoupolis. The Emperor believes that for all his protestations, he is part of a group of discontented men who seek to bring him down. He believes that it would be folly to permit the man more liberty than he has now. There are others, however, who might do better on campaign. And there are . . . there are a few men who are not to be spoken of again." This last came out quickly. He spun as he said it, and discovered a kitchen slave standing in the doorway.

"I have brought the refreshments you ordered, great master," the slave said, trembling at the thunderous expression he saw in Athanatadies' face.

"Present them to my guest and depart," said the Censor. He stood still while the slave carried out these orders, and it was only when the slave was gone and the door closed that he spoke again. "I want you to be on guard, Panaigios."

Panaigios nodded, holding his cup halfway to his mouth. "I will do so, of course."

"More than ever. The Emperor is a stern man, an unforgiving man of strong principles and great determination. He seeks to purify his reign." He straightened up, looking toward the door. "We are either his allies or his enemies, and he will regard us accordingly."

"I am not his enemy." Panaigios put down his cup, the wine untasted.

"I did not say you are. But you must persevere and be more stringent than ever."

Panaigios swallowed hard. "You said there are those who are not to be spoken of. What have they done that they are—"

"They have displeased Justinian," said the Censor. "They have been shown to be working against the Empire." He recalled the confessions he had read, and the petitions that had been made to the Emperor for the destruction of the families of the men.

"A great crime," said Panaigios, his tone a bit distracted. "I . . . I know we are not to speak of them, but who are they?" He faltered. "Great Censor, what am I to do to defend the Empire if I do not know who these pernicious men are?"

Athanatadies cleared his throat. "I will tell you once, Panaigios, and then you are not to speak of it again. I warn you, if you mention these men, you place yourself in great danger and there is little I can do to protect you should you have so great a transgression. The men are all Captains: Savas, Leonidas, Fortunos Ipakradies, and Hipparchos. They, and their families, are . . . expunged."

"They were Belisarius' officers, weren't they?" Panaigios asked, wishing he could call the words back as soon as he had spoken them.

"Yes; Fortunos served with him in Africa, the others in the Italian campaign." He indicated the food. "You're not eating."

Obediently Panaigios took one of the dried figs stuffed with crushed almonds, but it had no taste and no savor.

"And Belisarius? What of him?"

"The Emperor demands proof before he condemns, for he is a just man." He fell silent, then resumed. "He has found no proof that makes the General part of a conspiracy."

"But his officers—"

"They claim there is no conspiracy, but they are opposed to what the Emperor has done with the army and they do not endorse his plan to reestablish the Empire as it was in the days of Imperial Roma. That is reason enough to accuse them, and their actions have shown that they are the enemies of the Emperor, so he has declared that they are not only dead men, but men who never existed." He joined his hands, staring at his linked fingers to see if they still trembled. "The Emperor has ordered me that where treason is discovered, it is to be eradicated, the traitor and all his blood, so that the poisonous growth of conspiracy may be ended."

Panaigios paled. "The families? What . . . how . . . Are they to be enslaved?"

"That is for the Emperor to determine," said the Censor in a flat voice. He saw the dark, severe eyes boring into his once more, and heard that hard-edged voice issuing orders that made his skin prickle. "I am the devoted servant of Justinian, and I will do all that he requires of me with a grateful heart and a dedicated mind."

"Amen, and God aid us in the endeavor," said Panaigios. He chose another dried fruit but could not bring himself to eat it. The fig felt as if it was lodged halfway down his gullet and if he ate anything more, it might choke him.

"I will beseech God to do so every day," Athanatadies stated. "And I will depend upon you to be more diligent than ever. You hear many things and you have those who report to you; whatever you are told that might have any bearing on this, I must hear of it at once, so that I may inform the Emperor." There were others who would tell Justinian if Athanatadies was lax in performing his duties.

What would befall him then he did not want to think about.

"Four Captains. That is very dangerous." Panaigios watched the Censor closely, searching for a clue to what Athanatadies expected of him, what he wanted from him. "I will be certain that those whose aid I have required take extra care."

"I depend on you to do that," said Athanatadies, feeling very tired. "You are to urge those you employ to be on the alert for anything that might point to treason. Tell them that no one is exempt from his duty to the Emperor and God."

"Yes, certainly," said Panaigios, determined to send for Simones before the night was over.

"Be careful of your sources, for a false accusation can be as dangerous as a true one left unspoken. The Emperor has warned me that he will not tolerate those seeking vengeance through lies. He will deal with such trickery as he would with treason." He wondered if Panaigios could hear the fright in his voice; he could smell himself again, that civetlike odor that came from fear.

"I will take care. I will examine all my assistants with care and I will do all that I can to determine the truth of what they say before I inform you of it."

"That is good," said Athanatadies. "But do not be overcautious, or delay too long, or you and I might both be taken to task for our lack of dedication." His hands were moist; he let them drop to his sides.

Panaigios took a long sip of the wine; it was no good, the fig would not budge. "I . . . I will have to make a few arrangements, Athanatadies."

"Make them." Now that he had alerted his secretary, he wanted nothing more than to be left to pray before his next interview. He longed for the solace of his chapel, where he could prostrate himself before the altar and its jeweled and gilded ikons, to lose himself in the ritual of worship.

"At once," said Panaigios, thinking that he would have to find time to visit Thekla once again, to learn what he could from the old holy woman.

"You must discharge your commission with circumspection," said Athanatadies. "The Emperor requires this of you, and if you are his true subject, you will be unstinting in your efforts on his behalf."

"Yes." Panaigios had more of the wine.

"I will expect to speak with you the day after tomorrow. Have something of value for me then, Panaigios, and you will be well-rewarded for it."

"I will do my utmost," Panaigios assured him. He rose from his chair and made a reverence. "I will renew my purpose with every prayer." As he left, he told himself that he would have to be more demanding of Simones. There had to be more information he could glean from the slave, and he feared that if he did not provide the Censor with what he demanded, he would fall into obscurity, and perhaps join the company of those who were no longer spoken of, who had ceased to exist.

*   *   *

Text of a letter from Olivia to Chrysanthos, written in Latin.

To Captain Chrysanthos, Olivia of Roma sends her greetings and makes a request of him: I know that you are in communication with your comrade Drosos, and that you have access to routes not generally open to the rest of the world. I ask that you send him my affections and my concerns, for what he has said to me troubles me, and I am worried that he is suffering.

Please say to Drosos that my love for him is undiminished, and that while he is filled with conflict, I long only to help him end his turmoil. I do not want him to turn away from me because he is angry with himself. I feel no anger toward him, and I do not despise him, no matter what he has done. It is Drosos I love, not the acts he is compelled to do. It is Drosos I miss, not the officer of the Emperor. It is Drosos, always Drosos, who compels me, not the orders he follows. I am afraid he does not trust me enough, that he doubts I would be steadfast in the face of all that has happened. Let him know that he has no reason to question my faithfulness. He is what I love, and my love does not fail when circumstances are against us.

I know you will be prudent in what you say to him, but I ask you to give him my love and my assurances. I want him to be certain that he is welcome when he returns and that he need not fear I will desert him.

It may be that my own situation will become more difficult than it is now, and if that is the case, I ask you to tell Drosos to have patience. I will find a way to be with him once he is in this city again. Sadly, I cannot go to him, much as I would like to, for my petition for permission to establish a household in Alexandria has been denied by the Court Censor. For the time being it appears that I am confined to Konstantinoupolis. However, this house is always open to Drosos, at whatever time, in whatever circumstances, for whatever purpose he wishes.

While it would not be wise to let this be known to any but Drosos, I trust to your discretion and prudence in how you inform him of what I have said. I am not permitted to write to him directly; I hope your friendship for your comrade-at-arms will extend to me in this case, and that you will find a way to pass these words to him.

If you do not believe it is safe to write to him, or if in writing to him, you decide it is wisest not to mention me, let me know of it so that I may find another way to reach him. I dare not say much about my concern, but it is genuine and profound. There are few men who have moved me as Drosos has, and I cannot see him in travail without wanting to ease his burdens.

Whatever your decision, I am grateful that you have read these words from

Atta Olivia Clemens

PART III
Olivia

Text of a commendation addressed to Narses in Italy.

On the Feast of the Holy Dormition of the Virgin in the Lord's Year 549, the Emperor Justinian sends his greetings and thanks to General Narses, commanding the troops of Byzantion in Italy.

Know that with this commendation we deliver to you and your valiant men an additional two thousand troops, nine hundred horses, five Imperial wallets of gold coins and twelve Imperial wallets of silver in the hope that they will aid you in your campaign against the enemies of our state and religion.

In order to show our thanks more fully, we have given estates to three of your nephews, General Narses, and have increased your estates; our holdings in Adrianopolis are to be given to you in token of our gratitude for your tireless efforts on the part of the Empire.

Without your constant and diligent care, no doubt the lands you guard would have fallen prey to Totila and all the forces who accompany that barbarian. You have turned the tide, and for that you have the praise of the entire Empire, and you will be acknowledged as the savior of Italy. The complaints of those people who have claimed that your troops have been more rapacious than the godless invaders have been revealed as the calumny they are, doubtless the result of agents of the disgraced Belisarius who are attempting to discredit all you have done and give false praise to *the former commander. We are instructing you and your men to pay no heed to these carping objections. We wish to see you add victory to victory, and we are confident that your vigorous campaign will serve to restore all of Italy to the Empire.*

Your loyalty is held up as an example everywhere and we are ordering a day of public celebration with Masses and prayers as well as feasting in honor of your continuing achievements. We wish that everyone in the Empire join with us in this tribute, and we encourage your troops to show you their appreciation with favors and gifts for the superior command you show them.

May God look upon you with favor and continue to grant you the might and wisdom to restore Italy to our protection. In your valor you have no equal, neither have you any rival in our esteem. We give you every sign of our approval and gratitude.

> Justinian
> Emperor of Byzantion
> his sigil

· 1 ·

"Will you let me come in?" asked Drosos when Niklos came to the door. "Will Olivia see me?"

Niklos swung the door wide. "She'd have my skin if I kept you out. Welcome back, Captain." He kept his smile wide, although once Drosos stepped into the light of the vestibule, Niklos was shocked to see him.

"Are you certain?" Drosos asked. He had aged; there

were threads of white in his dark hair, and the fretwork of lines around his eyes was much deeper. He was both thinner and softer. His nails were ragged.

"Of course," said Niklos. "Great gods, Captain, you must have a very poor opinion of my mistress if you think she is as feckless as all that."

"I never . . ." Drosos began seriously, then broke off. "It isn't wise to know me. I am in disgrace."

"Given those in disgrace," Niklos said lightly, "I think it must be excellent company. Come with me. Olivia is in her library." He did not add that in the last month she had removed and hidden over sixty books that were no longer permitted within the walls of Konstantinoupolis. "She will be delighted that you're here." As he spoke he led the way down the hall, indicating a new fresco as they went. "It's almost finished."

"The martyrdom of Saints Adrian; that's Natalia there, with his hand after they burned him." Drosos pointed to the anaemic figure of a young woman with a haloed hand in hers.

"The artist has also done work for the Censor, so Olivia was confident that it was acceptable to hire him for this work. It's not always safe to choose someone who's unknown." He reached the door to the library and paused. "Do you want me to announce you, or would you rather do that yourself?"

Drosos hesitated. "Let me do it. If she's angry, she'll want us to be private."

"She won't be angry," Niklos promised him, his sympathy going out to the Captain.

Drosos shrugged. With a lift of his jaw he dismissed Niklos, but it took him the length of several deep breaths to work up his courage to lift the latch. At last he opened the door, stepped inside and leaned back, closing it.

Olivia was seated at a low table, an ancient scroll rolled open on the narrow table in front of her. She had her long, fawn-colored hair held back with a wide silk ribbon, and she was dressed in Roman palla and stola, both of a soft muted green. As she heard the door close, she called out without turning her head, "What is it, Niklos?"

"It isn't Niklos," Drosos answered, his voice not much more than a whisper. The sight of her was so wonderful it almost hurt him to watch her.

She turned very slowly, her hazel eyes widening as she looked at him. "Drosos." Carefully she rolled the scroll, always looking at him as she did. Then, when this was set aside, she rose, lifting her arms toward him. "Magna Mater, you are come at last!"

Drosos moved slowly, his somber expression giving way to a faint smile as he reached her. Lingeringly he touched her face with the ends of his fingers. "God and the Prophets," he whispered as he gathered her into his arms.

They stood together, hardly moving, saying nothing with words; their bodies spoke with other voices in silent eloquence. When he finally let her go, Drosos said, "Olivia, I . . ."

"I'm so glad you're back," she said when he could not go on. "I've missed you, Drosos."

"I've missed you. But it isn't wise for you to see me. I shouldn't come here, but I couldn't stay away." He stared down into her eyes. "I tried to stay away."

"Why?" She took his hands in hers. "I would have been more hurt than you can imagine if you had."

"I am not safe to know," he admitted, trying without success to pull his hands away.

"Half of Konstantinoupolis isn't safe to know," she countered. "I've never let that select my friends for me."

He shook his head, refusing to be convinced. "You're already suspect because you're Roman. Letting me come here only serves to make it worse for you."

"If you stayed away, it would not be better. This way, Drosos, my troubled love, neither of us is alone. Being alone and suspect is worse than having friends with you, even if all of you are suspect." She kissed him on the cheek. "I am pleased you are concerned for me, but not if it keeps you away from me."

His eyes flickered, shifting away from hers and moving restlessly. "You ought to tell me to go."

"Why would I do that?" she asked, her face calm though she was growing more concerned as they talked.

He broke away from her. "I did a . . . a foolish thing. If I'd thought about it, I would have realized that it was stupid to do it, but I assumed that . . . I had to do something. You see how it was."

"No, I don't. Tell me, Drosos." She went to him, standing behind him and putting her arms around his waist. "Tell me. What is the terrible thing you did? And why is it so terrible."

He bit his lip, shaking his head. "It would only make things worse."

"Drosos, please. You trusted me when you wrote to me. Trust me now." She used nothing to persuade him, no wiles or tricks that he could later blame for what he did. "I want to know because it is hurting you."

Again he resisted. "If I tell you, you might have to tell others, and that would be bad for both of us."

"Drosos, I am a Roman, and as a Roman I swear to you that I will not tell anyone what you reveal to me, no matter what they require of me. You might not believe it, but there was a time when such a vow was binding and any Roman would rest his life on his honor. My family has held to the old ways and you can depend on me to treat your confidences that way. If you still would rather not speak, very well. But believe me when I say that nothing you tell me will pass beyond these walls." She rested her head against his shoulder. "Drosos?"

He broke away from her and dropped into one of the chairs. "When I was about to leave Alexandria, there had been a storm that swept in from the sea. One of my last duties was to survey the damage and make a report about it."

"Is this the thing you—"

He went on as if she had not spoken. "Alexandria is on one of the branches of the Nile. There are many little fingers of the river, and when there is a storm—and the one we had was worse than usual—some of those little fingers get even more divided, and cut up into spits and sandbars. I was out in a good-sized boat, looking over some of these sandbars. Most of them were nothing more than isolated bits of sand." His face was nearly blank, his eyes distant as if he were standing on the deck of the boat at the mouth of the Nile. "But there was one. It had been cut off from the shore. It wasn't large—no more than twice the length of the boat at most, and very narrow, and it was being reclaimed by the water more and more every hour. The water was salty there, taking as much from the sea as from the river. Nothing grew there except a few stands of marsh grass. But on that sandbar there was a cow. Don't ask me how the poor beast had got out there; the storm must have driven it, not that it matters. It was alone on the sandbar. It had been there for at least three days. It was a black-and-white cow with dark horns; I remember it so clearly. She was bawling, but there was almost no voice left, for she was dying of thirst and starvation. She was on her knees, but she kept trying to rise and to get her head out of the water. I have never seen such despair, not in battle, not in plague, not in a slave market. There was nothing for that poor, dumb creature but her suffering. I asked for a bow, so that I could kill her, but no one had anything other than a spear, and the distance was too great to be certain. . . ."

"Oh, Drosos," Olivia said. She had taken the chair nearest his and was watching him, grief in her tearless eyes.

"I don't know what it was about that cow. I'm a soldier," he said, sitting straighter. "I have killed men, I have been wounded, I have fought in war. I know what it is to have a horse lanced out from under me; I have watched men with their guts in their hands try to reach just one more enemy warrior. I have seen widows and children after the fight. Nothing—*nothing*—moved me in the way that black-and-white cow . . ." He looked away. After the silence had stretched between them, he said in another, more remote tone, "I wrote to the Emperor, after we burned the library. I said that I was convinced that we had made a great error in burning the books and that he had been given poor advice by those close to him, who did not know the Library and the things it contained. I thought, you see, that he had been persuaded by those around him to do this, not that he wanted it done himself. I told him if he understood what was stored there, he would have realized that destroying so much knowledge was against every virtue and aim of Christianity. Well, I might as well have ordered my Guard to drag me through the streets of Alexandria behind four maddened horses. It would have spared everyone trouble."

"Don't say that, Drosos," Olivia admonished him in a low voice.

In the light from the brazier only half his face could be seen, and it was more like a mask than a face. "You have to understand that it was Justinian who wanted the books burned. It was the Emperor who had decided that the Library was dangerous and that the things in it were a hazard no Christian dared endure. He was the one who gave the orders, he was the one who decided. It was not some clique around him; it was Justinian himself." He stood up abruptly. "So they ordered me back here, where they can keep an eye on me, and watch what I do, for now the Emperor numbers me among his enemies." He came and stood beside Olivia. "Which is why I must go."

She did not rise. "No."

He dropped to his knee beside her chair and looked up into her face. "Don't you understand, Olivia? Don't you realize that if I visit you, Justinian will consider you to be as dangerous as I am, and you will be subjected to—"

"I have already been counted among those the Emperor dislikes because I am still Belisarius' friend and I have kept him as my sponsor ever since he returned from Italy. If I see you as well, it will mean little to the Emperor. It will be yet another example of Roman corruption. He is almost as disapproving of Romans as he is of books these days." She rested her hands on his shoulder. "How can I endure your being here, in this city, and not see you? How can I be cut off from everything and lose you as well?"

Drosos regarded her with concern. "You are already at risk. If you continue to see me, the risk increases, and there is nothing I can offer you as protection."

"I do not ask you to protect me, Drosos. I want you to love me."

His arms went around her and he rested his head in her lap. "I should not stay."

"But you will?" She ruffled his hair, wishing there was less white in it.

"Since you seem determined to have me, I suppose I must."

"You make it sound an unpleasant duty." She was teasing him now, for the strength of his arms told her more than his spoken denials.

"No; leaving you would be the unpleasant duty." He lifted his head and reached to pull her mouth down to his. "I dreamed of you every night I was away from you. I thought of you each day. I would sit in my reception room, staring out at the ruins of the Library, the way you stare at a soldier's empty sleeve, and I would see your face instead of the ruins. It was the only thing that kept me from going mad."

She kissed his brow. "Drosos."

"If anything goes wrong with you, I will blame myself." He said this as much to the walls as to her.

"That's absurd," she informed him, now very brisk. "You have been gone too long and you've given yourself over to gloom and melancholy. You have permitted yourself to succumb to worry and dread."

Drosos moved back from her, his hands clasping hers. "You would, were you in my place."

"Probably," she agreed. "But you are here now, and we are together again." She rose and tugged on his arms to bring him to his feet once again. "Drosos, stay here. You can stay tonight and any other time you wish. You are

welcome here as long as I am living within these walls.
You will always be welcome wherever I am."

He attempted a smile without much success. "You are a
lovely woman, and you are kind, Olivia. You make me
want to believe that nothing else matters but that you and
I are together. That isn't true, is it?"

"There are times it is and times it is not," she said, her
arm around his waist as she started toward the door. "But
think how desolate this place would be if you and I were
not ever to be together again. It would cause me—" She
pulled the door open and was startled to see one of her
household slaves standing a short distance away.

The man was flustered. "I . . . I am on an errand, great
lady."

"It must be urgent if it keeps you away from your
evening meal," Olivia said with a serenity that she did not
feel. "Do not let me detain you, Valerios." She stood
while the slave hurried down the hall.

"He was spying on us," Drosos said, agitation coming
back into his voice.

"Very likely," Olivia agreed. "And I will have to
discover why and for whom, but not just now. I have
other things, more important things to do now."

"You do not—" He started to move away from her. "It
probably is best if I leave. I will not have compromised
you too much and you and I will be able to . . ." The
words trailed off as he gazed into her face. With a soft
moan he pulled her tight against him. "I can't."

"Thank every god I've ever heard of," she whispered to
his neck. "Stay with me, Drosos. It is dark and I am
lonely. I have ached for you since the day you left me. I
do not want to give you up now."

All at once his hands were fevered, hot and urgent in
their questing and probing. "What does it matter?" he
whispered against her hair, sounding like a man in
delirium.

With effort she moved back so that they could walk the
short distance to her private apartments. Every step of

the way he touched her, his hands seeking out the flesh under her clothes. He spoke little and his words were deep and thickened, as if he had been drugged.

"Let me undress you," she offered when she had closed the door on her sleeping chamber.

"Never mind," he told her as he tore off his pallium and dragged his dalmatica over his head. He reached out for her Roman clothes and nearly ripped them off her.

"Drosos," she murmured as he swarmed over her. "We can savor this. There's no need to rush."

He paid no heed to her, his hands and mouth busy and urgent, frenzied in their quest. He pressed into her with little more than a hurried stroke to open her legs, and he rode her in ominous silence until he spasmed and pulled away from her.

Olivia lay still, her eyes fixed on the ceiling, and she caught her lower lip in her teeth until she was certain she could speak clearly. "You needed—"

"So did you," he said, not looking at her.

"Why do you want to deny us what we can have?" She did not make the question an accusation; she waited for his answer.

"What did I deny?" He meant it as a challenge, but he sounded more like a sulky boy.

"Must I tell you when you know?" she asked as she rolled onto her side and propped herself on her elbow. "You tell me you remember all the times we have been together, you have dreamed about them. And you behave as if I am nothing more than your whore."

He flinched at the word which she said so calmly. "That wasn't it," he muttered.

"Then what was it?" She studied his face. "Drosos?"

He refused to look at her. "I want you. It is worse than a fire in my bones, this wanting you."

"Then why do you—"

"You are relentless, aren't you?" He faced her, something between fury and despair in his eyes. "You will not let me go. You cannot release me."

"Release you from what? To what?" she asked, pain in her voice now.

"From you. From all you are. I . . . I haven't the strength for it anymore. I'm not . . ." He touched her hair. "Did I hurt you?"

"Yes," she admitted.

"I didn't want to. But . . . I don't know. Something within me has . . . failed. There are nights when I have lain awake and thought that I was taken with disease, that I was being consumed with some vile infection."

"Oh, Drosos," she said as she stretched her arm across his chest. "How can you condemn yourself this way?"

"Why not?" he asked her. "Think of what I am, what I have done."

"I think of who you are," she told him, soothing him, wishing the cold ache under her ribs would fade. "I hear you speak and I long to find the words that would succor you."

He laughed without hope. "There are no such words. There is nothing. I am beyond mending."

"No," she protested.

"When I followed my orders, when I honored my office and my Emperor, I destroyed my honor. It's an irony worthy of one of those banned Greek plays. If I were more than the fool I am." He shifted his weight to face her. "I want to have something left of me, something that can touch you without making me feel you have been tainted by me. If that still exists, Olivia, will you help me find it? I have no right to ask, but if you won't, then it might as well go up in smoke like the rest of my honor."

Olivia regarded him solemnly. She put her free hand over his heart. "I have lost those I love to death and time more often than I want to remember. I have seen destruction overtake things of sense and beauty so wantonly that it wrung my heart to know of it. If there is a chance to save something from the ruins, then—"

"You think to save me, as a remembrance?" He made a sound that was not laughter. "You think I am worthy to serve as a token of your time in Konstantinoupolis?"

"Stop that," she said softly. "I won't have you scorn yourself."

"Who better?" He reached out and pulled her over him. "I want to give value for—"

She wrenched away from him and he was startled at her strength. "I will not be party to your mockery. I do not permit you to denigrate someone I love, even though that person is yourself." She sat up and turned to regard him seriously. "Drosos, listen to me. I do not despise you. You cannot make me despise you."

"Why not? I despise myself." He had raised his arm as if to stop a blow and it shielded his eyes from her steady look.

She ran her finger along his jaw, feeling his untrimmed beard rasp against her skin. "You are like a man with a festering wound you will not lance, and you are poisoning yourself with the humors. I wish you were free of the pain and the anguish you feel."

He lowered his arm; tears stood in his dark eyes. "God, God, so do I. But—"

Her fingers stopped his objections on his lips. "Then we will find a way. There is a way, Drosos, if you will permit yourself to find it."

"Is there?" The tears ran down his temples and he wiped them away.

"There is a way," she repeated firmly. Then she leaned down and kissed him lightly on the mouth. "Let me help you, for my sake as well as yours."

"Why for your sake?" He was trying to recover some of the dignity he had lost. "How can—"

"You have done what you have done because you have a sense of honor; I have told you I have a sense of honor, too, and it demands that I do not desert my friends in misfortune."

He sighed, his breath ragged. "There are some hurts beyond remedy."

"This need not be one, Drosos," she said, hoping fervently that it was so.

He faced her. "All right. Do what you must. I'm grateful, I suppose." As she sank down on his chest, he threaded her hair through his fingers. "It's like living silk."

She did not respond; she was listening to his heartbeats, trying to fathom the depth of his misery.

*   *   *

Text of a letter from Eugenia to Antonina.

To my cherished friend Antonina, Eugenia sends her greetings and the hopes that Antonina might soon recover from the affliction that has caused her such misery.

It was only recently that I learned of your continuing illness, and it brought home to me how great a value I have put on the hours we have spent together, as well as how important your good opinion has always been. I know that I have been most neglectful of you and I wish I had an adequate explanation that does not cast aspersions on my character, but I fear I have been nothing more than an overly cautious woman, and I have let my concerns for my position within society interfere with the more genuine ties of friendship. I have long assumed that there would be a time when all the misunderstandings would be ended and your family would be restored to the position it deserves to occupy, but from what I have been told, this might not be the case, and I am filled with chagrin that I have let these precious days slip by without overcoming my own cowardice.

I realize there is no reason you should want to see me

again after the dreadful way I have behaved, but I hope you will show more charity than I have shown you and admit me to your company once again. It would give me great satisfaction and pleasure to have the chance to speak with you. There is no one with whom I can share confidences as you and I have, and I have missed that more than I can express to you in words.

Dear Antonina, forgive me for all my slights and my ambitions. I have been a stupid, vain woman and I have spurned a friendship that has been worth more to me than the tributes of my husband. What woman ever truly gives a man the trust that she can share with another of her sex? We pretend that this is not the case, but in our heart of hearts, the truth of it cannot be denied. For that reason if no other, I hope you will not forbid me to call upon you. I have yearned for the benefit of your good sense as well as the chance to speak plainly, which we never do with the men we know.

I hope also that perhaps you have missed my company and that you will find that my presence is welcome to you; surely there are things you wish to say that you cannot discuss with your husband, for honorable and steadfast as he is, it is not the same as the understanding I have provided in the past.

Your slave Simones will bring this letter to you and he will tell you himself how much I long to renew and restore our friendship and what great importance you hold in my life. If you do not believe what I say, then perhaps you will believe what your own slave will tell you. You should thank him for seeking me out, for until he came to me I had no idea how great was your suffering. I had attributed your retirement from the world to the misfortunes of your husband and not to your health, for which I am most heartily sorry, and I ask that you will not hold against me my lack of information, for as you know this city is alive with rumors and half-truths which distort the knowledge that would have brought me to your side long before now had I any notion of the severity of your troubles.

*Let me hear from you soon, and when you tell me I may,
I will come to you to ask your pardon face to face, and I
will do whatever you request at whatever time you stipu-
late. I pray that your answer will be swift, so that I may in
some part make amends for the lack of attention I have
given you.*

*I am your friend, Antonina, and I beg you to let me have
the opportunity to demonstrate that to you.*

Eugenia

• 2 •

Zejhil was almost out of the garden when she heard the
whisper of voices near the passage that led to the stables.
At once she paused and listened, not daring to move.

"There is money in it if you will aid me," said a voice
that Zejhil did not know.

"I am a slave," came the answer from a man; Zejhil
recognized Valerios. "If I am caught, it could mean my
life."

"You will not be caught; and if you are, you have only
to say that you were working at the behest of an agent of
the Censor to determine if your mistress is an enemy of
the Emperor, and there will be little she can do against
you."

"Who will listen to a slave?" Valerios scoffed.

"Who will listen to a woman?" asked the other. "And a
Roman woman. The Emperor has said that Romans are
not to be trusted and a Roman woman—"

"My mistress has been good to me."

The unknown man laughed. "What good is that if she is accused of treason?"

"She is not a traitor," Valerios said, but with less conviction than before.

"Have you proof of that? She associates with the disgraced Belisarius and she has kept Captain Drosos as her lover in spite of his opposition to the edicts of the Emperor in regard to the destruction of heretical texts. It may be that she is only foolish."

Zejhil put her hand to her mouth to stifle her indignant objections. Cautiously she moved a little closer to the passageway.

"Suppose you were to learn that others have found her to be a traitor," suggested the stranger. "What then?"

"It is not for me to say. I am a slave." Valerios raised his voice. "And there are severe penalties for suborning slaves."

"So there are. There are also severe penalties for slaves who participate in treasonous activities. Doesn't it trouble you that you might have the skin peeled off your body and you be left staked to the ground outside the city walls?"

"Go away," Valerios said, his voice now tinged with fear.

"I will reward those who help me, and I will see that those who hinder me are punished." There was a menace in this promise that made Zejhil shiver.

"Go away. You are nothing more than a slave yourself, and anything you say to me is only the word of a slave." There was the sound of hurrying feet, and then more stealthy footsteps and a soft closing of a door.

Zejhil remained where she was, unable to move from the dread that gripped her. She tried to reason with herself, to convince herself that the sinister unknown man was no danger to her or anyone in Olivia's household, but she could not stop the shudders that overcame her when she attempted to leave the garden. "I must warn my mistress," she whispered, as if hearing the words would goad her to action. Nothing changed. Only the sudden braying of an ass in the street beyond the walls gave her the impetus she needed, and she fled into the corridor that joined the kitchen.

She had tasks to finish and knew that she might be reprimanded if she did not do them, but her fear outweighed her prudence and she sought out Niklos, hoping to find him before she lost all her courage.

He was in the counting-room, a row of gold and silver coins set out in front of him, a small scale standing beside the coins. He scowled as the door opened. "What—" As soon as he saw who it was, he changed his attitude. "Zejhil. What's the matter, girl? You look as if you've dragged a bale of silk from Antioch to Damascus."

She shut the door firmly and took a hesitant step toward him. "You . . . you said that if I heard anything I was to tell you. . . ."

Niklos was now very attentive. "Yes. And you have been very good in that regard. What have you heard now?" He got up from the tall stool and came toward her. "Zejhil?"

"I was in the garden," she said, motioning him away from her. "I didn't think that anyone else was there, but they were."

"Who was there?" His curiosity was turning to worry. "What did you hear, Zejhil? What did you see?"

"I didn't see anything," she said. She was bent over slightly, her arms crossed over her abdomen as if she were in pain. "I only heard."

"Are you all right? Did anyone harm you?" He ignored her warning and came to her side.

"Not harm, no. I said I didn't see them. They didn't do anything to me, but I heard them. I heard them." She looked up at him. "There was a man I did not know. He was talking with Valerios."

"Valerios?" said Niklos, more puzzled than before.

"He—the stranger—was offering Valerios money for information about our mistress. He said that if there was any trouble for him, the stranger would say that Valerios was acting for the Court Censor." She began to cry from terror. "If it is so, if the Censor is trying to impugn our mistress, then there is no hope for us and we are all doomed."

Niklos put his arm around Zejhil's shoulder and held her as he would have held a frightened child. "No, no, Zejhil. If the Censor wishes to learn about Olivia, he will have to do more than spy on her slaves, or make spies of them. Even the Greek male slaves."

"The man was so . . . malignant." She trembled. "I have not heard anyone speak so, not ever."

"There are malignant people in the world, Zejhil. It is a pity for everyone, but it is so." He smoothed her hair back from her face. "But there have been no accusations made and until there are, even the Censor can do nothing. Olivia has kept to the laws; she has done what her sponsor has required of her, and if she—"

"She is a friend of Belisarius and Drosos." She said this as if she expected castigation for speaking those two names aloud.

"Yes, and she will continue to be, if I know her," said Niklos. Without seeming to do so, he guided Zejhil across the room to a wooden chair. "Sit, Zejhil."

Obediently she did. She clasped her hands together in her lap and waited for what would come next. "I am afraid," she said simply.

"I know," Niklos responded, and laid his hand on hers. "I wish you would trust us. Neither Olivia or I will let any harm befall you. Olivia does not require her slaves to suffer for her. If there are charges brought against her, she will free all of you before she answers them."

"There won't be time. She will have to ask her sponsor to do that, and if she is accused, no sponsor will permit her to do that." Zejhil started to rise, then sank back.

"It is already arranged," Niklos said quietly. "I rely on you to keep that to yourself."

Zejhil stared at him. "What do you mean, it is already arranged?"

"She has the writs with her sponsor's approval in her

documents. She has only to affix a date and sign them."
He shook his head. "I have said you could trust her. She
knows that her position grows more precarious, and if she
were permitted she would leave Konstantinoupolis."

"But she is not permitted?" said Zejhil.

"Not yet," said Niklos. There were alternate plans he
and Olivia had made, but they were to be used only when
all other means were exhausted: of these he said nothing.

"Then the stranger I heard could—"

"You have done very good work, for you have put us
on our guard before the others are aware of it." He
started to pace. "I want you to speak with Olivia later
tonight, after most of the others have gone to bed. I will
give you an order while you have your evening meal so
that none of the others will pay any attention to what you
do."

"What should I do until then?" She waited as if
expecting revelation.

"What you usually do." He read confusion in her face
and went on. "If you change what you do, there are those
who will notice, and if Valerios has truly been approached, it may be that others have, as well. In which
case, everything should appear as normal as possible to
keep any potential spy from suspecting that he has been
found out." Niklos studied her reaction. "I trust you will
aid us?"

"How could you doubt it?" She rose out of the chair
and came toward him. "If anyone tried to hurt you—"

He stopped her with a swift, kind gesture. "For that I
am more grateful than you can imagine, Zejhil."

Her angular face went crimson. "I—"

"You are a very good woman, Zejhil; before you are
anything else, you are a very good woman." He took her
hand. "Now, go about your work, and know that our
mistress and I thank you for what you have done."

She nodded, the blush fading. "I will. And when you
summon me, I will be ready."

"Excellent. Now leave me alone. I have to think." He

escorted her to the door and saw her go down the hallway; then, when she had turned the corner, he left the room and went in search of Valerios. It took some time for he was not where Niklos expected to find him.

"What—?" Valerios burst out as Niklos stepped into the small room near the kitchen where furniture was made and repaired. He was wearing a leather apron and had a leather-headed mallet in his hand. Between his legs he held one of the cooks' benches, with two new legs just being fit into place.

"I thought you would be in the vestibule," Niklos said as if the two men were in the middle of a conversation. "You were adding a new screen to the ikonostasis, weren't you?"

"Yes." He hammered the mallet down on the legs. "But the cooks needed this urgently. Since the great lady wasn't as pressed for the new screen, I decided to—" He interrupted himself with his work.

"You're an industrious fellow, Valerios. They breed you hardy in—where is it you are from?" Niklos leaned on the doorframe, arms folded.

"Thessalonica," he said, accompanying the word with two heavy blows.

"A distinguished place with a long history," said Niklos, very much at his ease.

"So I've heard." He tested one of the legs and glowered at it. "Is there something I have to do? If there isn't, I want to get this finished for the cooks."

Niklos crossed one leg over the other, resting the foot on the toe of his sandal. "Yes, come to think of it, there is something you can do: you can answer a few questions."

This time the mallet faltered in its descent. "What questions?"

"Nothing too difficult, I imagine." His mouth curved but there was no smile in his eyes. "I understand that you had an interesting offer earlier today. Would you like to tell me about it, or would you rather I guess?"

The mallet struck awry, the force of the impact almost pulling the bench from the grip between his knees.

Valerios cursed, then said, "An offer? What sort of offer?"

"I understand," Niklos said, unperturbed, "that someone was willing to pay you for information. Someone wanted to know certain things about this household and for unknown reasons was not willing to approach either our mistress or me directly." He paused, sensing Valerios' tension. "Why was that, Valerios?"

"I . . . I know nothing about that. Whoever says such things is lying." His protest was far from convincing.

"Really? You mean no one came here, saying that you would not be blamed for any ill you did because you were working for the Court Censor?" He asked this with innocence a cat would envy. "I was told you refused."

Valerios swung the mallet and then flung it to the far side of the room. "All *right*!" he shouted. "All right. There was a man, a slave. He had been here before and asked about Captain Drosos. I told him that the Captain had been here. I didn't think that there was any harm in that. Everyone in the household knew about it and it's not as if the mistress has made a secret of her dealings with him."

"Did he pay you then?" Niklos inquired sweetly.

"Two silver coins," Valerios admitted.

"You said nothing of it."

Valerios shrugged defensively. "I didn't think anything of it. There was nothing secret."

"Except the inquiry," Niklos pointed out. "Who was this man? Other than a slave?"

"I don't know. I thought when he first came here that he was merely searching for Drosos." He righted the bench and sat down heavily on it.

"Why would you think that?" Niklos asked, guessing at the answer already.

"His collar had the mark of Belisarius' household. I assumed the General was concerned, what with his former officers being sent to the distant ends of the Empire." He sighed and stared down at the earthen floor. "Or that may be what I told myself when I took the money."

Niklos' expression softened a bit. "It is a reasonable assumption."

"I thought that would be the end of it, and since Belisarius is our mistress' sponsor, I thought that there was no harm in telling the slave that."

"Since Belisarius is Olivia's sponsor, why would his slave have to ask you? Why would Belisarius not send a messenger directly to me or to Olivia herself?" Niklos asked.

"Perhaps he didn't want Captain Drosos to know he was being watched," said Valerios hopefully.

"And perhaps Belisarius has a spy in his household," said Niklos.

Valerios looked away. "There might be."

"Which slave was it? Describe him." He grew more attentive though his posture did not change.

"A eunuch. Not fat. Fairly tall. Between twenty and thirty—it's hard to guess age with eunuchs. Deep voice." He shook his head. "I should have spoken to you. I knew that at the time. But I thought it would be just the once, and the money was—"

"And this time he offered more, of course." Niklos recognized Simones and anticipated the pattern.

"Yes, more. And he wanted to know more. He said that I could keep the money no matter what." He coughed. "I don't want it, not that way."

"But you said nothing," Niklos reminded him. "Neither the first time nor the second."

"I know." This was hardly audible.

"Has our mistress been unkind to you?"

"No."

"Or made unreasonable demands?"

"No." His voice was lower.

"Or mistreated you?"

Valerios surged to his feet, kicking the bench aside. "You know she hasn't!"

"Then why did you betray her?" Niklos asked, his voice quiet and sharp at once.

Valerios shook his head and moved away from where Niklos stood. "I . . . I don't know."

"Shall I tell you?" Niklos did not wait for Valerios to answer. "You thought that you might have some power, some means to control—oh, anyone—and you wanted it. Don't you understand yet that Olivia meant what she said. You are her slave, but not in the way of Konstantinoupolis, in the way of Roma, old Roma. When I brought you here, you told how the household was to be run, and you would not believe that, and now you have compromised yourself."

"I didn't agree to help the second time." Valerios was sulking now, refusing to look toward the majordomo. "I said I would not."

"If you think that you have heard the end of it, you're very mistaken. You are a tool of the enemies of my mistress now, and that makes you dangerous." Niklos finally moved into the room. "By tonight, you will be confined to your quarters. I would do that now, but it might alert others. Certainly the rest of the slaves would talk, and that is something that my mistress cannot risk at present. So you might as well get used to my company. Until you go to the kitchen to eat, you will have it."

"And then?" There was a hardness in his voice, the rasp of long-denied anger.

"You will have your meal, of course. The others will guard you. Afterward, I will secure you." He gave Valerios a measuring look. "If you are thinking of attempting to escape, let me advise you against it. If you run away, or even try to, you will have lost any chance you might have of salvaging something for yourself. A run-away forfeits everything, and there is nothing my mistress can do to change that. You will be branded a criminal and set to hard labor—probably the copper mines or aboard ship. In either case, you will not have much left to you."

"I should have taken the money, told the slave what he wanted to know, and said nothing," Valerios grunted.

"Had you done that, you would be confined right now. Be thankful to your good angel that you did not take the money." Niklos regarded Valerios a moment, then said, "Bring the bench to the kitchen. If the cooks need it so much, they will wonder if you do not fix it for them."

Valerios obeyed, his face sullen and his movements ponderous and slow. As he left the room, he looked hard at Niklos. "I could have accused you. I could have told the slave all I know about you, and—"

"And what is that?" Niklos inquired, sounding amused in order to hide his sudden apprehension.

"I *saw* you." Valerios turned narrowed eyes on Niklos.

"Do what?"

"I saw you eat. You had a shoulder of goat. You . . . just ate it. Just the way it was." Even as he hurled this accusation, there was a tone in his furious words that hinted he did not quite believe what he was saying.

Niklos shook his head. "Have you never tested meat to be sure it was fresh and wholesome before letting the cooks have it?"

"It was *raw*." Revulsion made the last word much worse than it was."

"It certainly was," said Niklos. "But no one in this household has fallen ill to tainted meat, have they?" He waited while Valerios considered what he had said. "My ways are similar to the ways of my mistress."

"So you eat goat raw?" Valerios said, now more bewildered than challenging.

"Upon occasion." He stood aside so that Valerios could carry the bench out of the room. "Come. The cooks are waiting."

Valerios had one last crafty question for Niklos. "What if I tell . . . someone that you eat raw goat?"

"What if you do?" Niklos rejoined. "If they believed you—and the chance is they would not—they would also believe the reason for what I do. Konstantinoupolitans believe almost anything about Romans." He was able to chuckle, but it was fortunate that Valerios could not see his face.

Valerios picked up the bench. "What are you going to tell the mistress?"

"Everything. I am her majordomo." He walked close behind Valerios as they went toward the kitchen. "If I did not, I would be failing her in every way."

"What will become of me." He stopped in the entryway to the kitchen.

"That is for my mistress to decide," Niklos said, his manner expressionless. Then he indicated the kitchen. "Look. Urania is waiting for the bench."

One of the two cooks, a squat, muscular woman with a round face and rosy complexion, greeted Valerios with a shout.

"About time! Put it here. My feet ache all the way up to my innards."

Niklos nodded and Valerios, after a quick glance at him, went and put down the bench. "Next time, don't pile half the kitchen on one end of it," he admonished Urania.

She uttered a gruff oath and sank down on the bench. "How anyone is supposed to cook all day on their feet, I don't know."

Niklos indicated the two long tables on the far side of the room where the slaves were served their meals. "How much longer before the meal?"

"Not long. There are some flatbreads just coming out of the oven, if you're hungry."

"I'm not," said Niklos. "But I know that Valerios is. Let him have one and we'll wait for the others."

Urania nodded, her wide face smiling even as she grumbled. "I don't know how I'm supposed to keep up with this household." She got her baking paddle and went to the oven. Her face grew ruddy from the heat as she pulled back the door and slid the paddle in. "These are best hot."

Valerios burned his fingers when he took the flatbread Urania offered him, but he refused to drop it. He sat at the nearer of the long tables and chewed slowly on the bread, watching Niklos while the other slaves began to arrive for their food.

Only when eight of the slaves were seated and Urania was bustling among them with trays of chicken cooked with dates and olives with garlic and cracked wheat did Niklos decide it was safe to leave Valerios in the kitchen. As he hurried toward Olivia's private apartments, he wondered how many other of the household slaves Simones had approached, and what they had told him. He was most troubled that Valerios had seen him eat. The fiction he had offered might be acceptable to a slave, but there were others who would find other meaning in what he did, and that could easily lead to questions with dangerous answers and more dangerous repercussions. He set his jaw and knocked on Olivia's door, saying "It's Niklos."

She was watching him as he came into her quarters. "More trouble? Of course there is more trouble," she said for him when he hesitated.

"It might be worse," Niklos hedged.

"Indeed it might," she said sardonically. "There might be an earthquake and the house could be on fire."

"Olivia—"

She managed a rueful smile. "But fortunately, we have only to deal with spies and enemies. Tell me."

* * *

Text of a letter from the physician Mnenodatos to the person who employed him to poison Antonina.

To the man who has called himself my benefactor, the physician Mnenodatos sends his apologetic greetings and will try to explain why he must dissappoint this generous person.

You have indicated that you are not satisfied with the rate of progress of my "treatment" of the August Lady Antonina and wish that she would show more signs of debilitation. If you insist, I am able to give her more of the poison you have instructed me to use, but I warn you that there are many others who would then recognize the nature of her malady and there is an excellent chance that I would be dismissed from the service of Belisarius and be accused, if not of poisoning her myself, of being so incompetent that I did not recognize that she is suffering from such treatment. If I were taken by officers of the magistrate, or by the Guard, I would have to reveal all that I know—which is not much, I admit—about the nature of the person who has engaged and paid me to do this thing.

As to your request that a similar ill befall the General himself, I must caution you that one unaccountable illness in a household like this one occasions only sympathy; two would give rise to speculation that neither you nor I would like. It is one thing for a woman of Antonina's years and temperament to have fevers and aches and sicknesses that no *physician can treat, but if her husband should succumb to the same thing, then there are those who will ask questions, and they will not be satisfied with easy answers or vague reassurances. To make the poisoning of the General acceptable, I would have to poison the entire household, slaves and myself included, so that it would appear that the food was tainted. I do not believe that this is a reasonable solution to your problem.*

If you are eager to be rid of the General, then there are others who will do the deed in any number of ways you might like. Enough gold will purchase far more than a physician's skill and conscience.

Be aware that I am doing all that I may to keep my activities undetected. If I do more, it will go badly. Since you have been willing to wait this long, I ask you take the time required for the poison to do its work. There is no advantage to discovery for any of us, not even for Antonina, poor woman, for she has taken enough of the poison that she cannot be saved no matter what was done for her. I could leave here tomorrow, give her nothing more, and she would last for perhaps two years at the most, and they would not be pleasant years.

I urge you to reconsider your request. I have done all that I can, and to undertake to do more would imperil the entire venture. I say this with authority and I ask that you respect my assertion—you respected my ability sufficiently to engage me on this filthy business.

> *Mnenodatos*
> *physician*

• 3 •

By the time the Guard arrived to search her house, Niklos had managed to hide most of the incriminating volumes Olivia had not been able to be rid of; there were a few Roman objects that might be considered suspect, but Olivia had said that disposing of all of them might be construed as more suspicious than the possession of one or two Roman items.

"We are here on the order of the Emperor and the Court Censor," announced Captain Demitrios as he held out a scroll sealed in three places. "Your scribe will read it to you."

"My Greek is not so bad that I cannot muddle my way through your writ," said Olivia as she accepted the document. "You will watch me break the seals, Captain?"

Taken aback, Captain Demitrios exchanged glances with two of his men. "If you like. Your sponsor should be here."

Olivia regarded the Guard Captain evenly. "My sponsor is General Belisarius. If one of you will go to his house and summon him, I am certain he will come."

"General Belisarius," repeated Captain Demitrios. "He is your sponsor."

"Yes. I turned over my villa outside Roma to him during his campaign and for that he has consented to be my sponsor." She was reasonably certain that Captain Demitrios knew something of this, but she was willing to go through the ritual. "If you would rather, I will send one of my slaves to fetch him."

"He ought to be here," said Captain Demitrios uncertainly. "The General—"

Olivia clapped her hands loudly. "Niklos!"

He responded at once, coming from the smaller of the reception rooms. "My mistress?" He favored her with a full reverence that was not lost on the soldiers.

"These Guardsmen require that General Belisarius be here while they perform their duty. Will you ask him to join us. Perhaps, Captain, you will tell my majordomo what your errand is so that he may inform the General?" She did her best to keep the irony out of her voice, but did not succeed entirely. "I will ask one of my two cooks to give you wine and something to eat while you wait, Captain."

The Captain straightened up. "We will have to stand guard around the house until the General arrives. We cannot act until he has read the orders. It would be best if you did not break the seals; leave that to General Belisarius." He was clearly not satisfied with the arrangement but knew his duty.

"Just as you wish. My household is, naturally, at your disposal," said Olivia as she stepped back from the armed men. "Come with me, Niklos, and I will write a note to the General for you to deliver."

Niklos heard the anger in her tone and he hastened after her, hoping she would contain herself until they were in private. "My mistress," he said as he opened the library to her, "you have only to command me."

As soon as the door was closed, Olivia turned her blazing eyes on Niklos. "I am not allowed to authorize the searching of my own house! It is bad enough that they want to search it, but I cannot read the document! Hecate shrivel them, every one of them!"

"Hush," Niklos warned her.

"Don't you—" She broke off. "You're right," she admitted after a moment. "All right. Find me my ink tablet and something to write on. The mood I'm in, I'll settle for a torn rag." She sat down, her shoulders still angular with rage. "Hurry. I don't want the good Captain to get restive."

"Will Belisarius come?" asked Niklos.

"I hope he will send a simple authorization, if that's possible. The whole thing is already intolerable." She was working the ink cake, mixing a little water with the square block, rubbing it with a small oval section of ivory until she had enough to write with. She accepted the vellum Niklos handed her and began to write, forming the letters awkwardly since she was not entirely used to the Greek alphabet yet.

"I will tell him what's going on," Niklos promised her.

"Including, no doubt, my state of mind," she said, shaking her head slowly. "Here. Take this. Make sure you show it to that oaf of a Captain."

"I will," Niklos told her, folding the vellum once and tucking it into his wide belt. He left promptly, winking at her before he closed the door.

Olivia sat alone among her shelves, a third of them empty now that the suspect texts had been removed. She forced herself to become calm. There had been other times over the centuries when she had faced worse than this, she reminded herself sternly, and she had been able to win free. She would do it again. If five centuries had taught her nothing else, she had learned a knack for survival. Much as she felt hampered by circumstances, she knew she would find a way; she always had. By the time she left the library, she was in command of herself.

Captain Demitrios greeted her return with more respect than he had shown her at first. "We are truly sorry for this"—he paused, trying to find a delicate word for intrusion—"necessity, but a soldier is the tool of the state."

"Yes; I am aware of that," said Olivia. "Perhaps you might tell me what you are ordered to look for?"

"There are a number of things," he answered evasively. "It is spelled out in the writ. The General will explain it all to you when he gets here."

Olivia bit back a sharp retort and forced herself to say, "I trust that he will. I trust that *someone* will. For to be candid, Captain, I do not understand why I am being treated in this way. Everything I brought with me to Konstantinoupolis was on the shipping manifests, and they were approved when I arrived here. There were other items of mine that we found here being sold, which were identified as contraband. What else do you think I have?"

"Great lady, it is not for me to discuss these matters. I have no knowledge of the reason the Censor wishes to have your house searched." He sounded so wooden and formal that Olivia wanted to kick him, to find out if he would feel it at all.

"Then how will you know if you find what the Censor—" She interrupted herself. "I suppose all that is in the document."

Captain Demitrios set his jaw. "Precisely."

"Then, if it is acceptable to you, I will leave you to withdraw to my quarters. Post your guards as you must. I hope it is permissible for me to have one of my slaves attend me while my majordomo is on his errand?" She hated the sound of her own voice and wanted to scream at herself for hypocrisy, at the same time knowing it was the most sensible thing to do.

"We will strive not to disturb you, great lady," said Captain Demitrios, relieved enough to show her a slight reverence.

"You have already done that, Captain, through no fault of your own. I am now going to strive to minimize the impact of your presence on my household." She gave him a brief, hard look, then turned and went down the hall. "Zejhil!" she shouted. "I want you to come to my rooms!"

Most of the household slaves heard Olivia's order, and three of them took it upon themselves to find Zejhil for her, so that by the time the Tartar slave reached Olivia's apartments, she was worried that something more dreadful than the soldiers had happened to her mistress.

Niklos returned a short while later accompanied not by Belisarius but by Captain Chrysanthos, who was visiting the General. "He has authorization from Belisarius," said Niklos, who had already given Chrysanthos the benefit of his view of the situation.

Captain Demitrios watched Chrysanthos open the document and listened while he read aloud the items that Olivia was suspected of having including a sizable list of banned books, several of which Niklos recognized as the volumes Olivia had found added to the ones in her shelves.

"This is quite an indictment, if it is accurate," Chrysanthos said when he had finished reading.

"There are those who have sworn that it is," said Captain Demitrios grimly.

"And if they are in error?" Chrysanthos asked, adding, "I am charged by General Belisarius to discover what will be done to anyone bringing false accusations against Olivia Clemens."

"I was not informed," said Captain Demitrios. "It is not for me to know of that."

"Then perhaps you will be good enough to deliver this note from General Belisarius to the office of the Censor. As the great lady's sponsor, he is obligated to ask these things." It was one of Chrysanthos' gifts that he had a frank and open face, one that expressed good fellowship so easily that few noticed the acute, canny eyes that missed little.

Captain Demitrios took the note and looked at the seal. "I will report this to Panaigios when we return to the palace," he said, and was about to summon his men for the search when Chrysanthos detained him.

"I fear that the General has charged me with requiring you to deliver this to Kimon Athanatadies himself. You will do that, will you not?" He waited until the Captain agreed.

The search lasted until after sunset; in the end the soldiers carried away three ivory-inlaid chairs, two jeweled ikons, an antique table, a tall Egyptian lyre, four leather-bound books, two bolts of linen, and a marble portrait bust made more than three hundred years before of a man Olivia called her oldest friend.

"Things of value are always suspect," Olivia said to Captain Demitrios as he offered her a copy of the list of what had been removed. She made no attempt to hide her bitterness.

"I will provide Captain Chrysanthos with a copy of this list; he can take it to General Belisarius." Captain Demitrios paused awkwardly. "It is true that the General is not in favor now, but there are those who first served under him, and we do not like to see the way in which he is treated. I am sorry that this new disgrace had to come to him, after all the other slights and indignities he has had to endure. You will tell him that, will you not?"

"I?" Olivia asked. "Or would you prefer that Chrysanthos tell him?"

"It . . . He is your sponsor and we have taken things from your house, which he is responsible for, and it is—" He looked toward Chrysanthos. "Can you explain this to her?"

"I cannot explain it to myself," Chrysanthos said without losing his cordial manner. "I am hoping that the Censor will be able to."

The Captain of the Guard took the note as if he expected it to burst into flame. "I will deliver this. What the Censor will have to say, I cannot guess."

"He will tell you that it was necessary to do this," said Olivia. "And if it is done, then leave my house. My slaves are upset, I am upset, and you have taken some of my most treasured possessions on the pretext that they are dangerous." She indicated the door.

"The Emperor demands—" Captain Demitrios began, but Chrysanthos indicated the door.

"It is late, Captain, and there is not going to be a satisfactory justification of these seizures now. You have done what you had to do. It would be best if you departed with your men." He saw a quick gesture of approval from Niklos.

Captain Demitrios did not cavil. "I will see to your requests as if they came from Belisarius himself." He saluted Chrysanthos and left, signaling his troops to come with him as he strode away from the house.

"They're nothing more than brigands with permission!" Olivia accused the closed door.

"If you had said that to Captain Demitrios, he would have had to report it to the Censor, and that would have given him the excuse to summon you for formal questioning. I don't think that you want that to happen." Chrysanthos looked at her, waiting for her to master her temper. "I know that Drosos would not want that to happen."

She turned to him. "Drosos."

"You know what he has been like . . . " Chrysanthos said, his aplomb deserting him for the first time that day. "There has been nothing either I or Belisarius could say that consoles him. You are the only one. If I felt no obligation to you, I feel one to him, and I do not want you to fall into the hands of the Censor while Drosos is in such trouble."

Niklos indicated the hall toward the rear of the house. "I will see about getting the slaves fed. That is if Urania and Xanthos are not wholly overwhelmed by what's happened." He put his hand on Olivia's shoulder briefly. "Listen to the man, Olivia. He has good sense and he knows this place. You are a stranger here."

She closed her eyes in acknowledgment. "I will try," she said to her bondsman, and once he was gone, she indicated the smaller of the reception rooms. "Will you sit? I think there are enough chairs left for that."

Chrysanthos' easy smile had deserted him. "That was unforgivable. I will tell Belisarius to petition for the return of your goods at once."

Olivia looked weary as she sat down on the padded bench. "I have asked for permission to leave Konstantinoupolis; did you know? So far I've been refused, but I have continued to request permission."

"But where would you go? You cannot return to Roma, or Italy, for that matter."

"There are other places. I have a few friends left in the world and there are places I could go." She paused. "If you want something from the kitchen it might take a while to get it, but you are more than welcome."

He waved her offer aside. "There's no need. You have enough to do without worrying about me. But you sidestepped an answer, great lady. Where would you go?"

Olivia took a long breath. "I have thought I might go to Ptolemaïs. I have not visited Africa for a long time."

"The Copts are strong there," Chrysanthos pointed out.

"That doesn't worry me." She saw he was shocked and she said, "Your Orthodox ways are not Roman ways, no matter how hard everyone tries to deny it. The Church I . . . grew up with is not the same as the Church you have here. You are all Christians, but the . . . emphasis is different."

"But the Copts are heretics," Chrysanthos said.

"For a sensible man, Captain, you have a few blind spots—as we all do. It doesn't matter to me that there are Copts in Ptolemaïs; it is not likely that my friend's house there will be searched and looted."

"Looted is quite an accusation."

"Oh, very selectively looted, I'll give you that, but looted nonetheless, and in such a way that my objections place me in a worse position than complying with what the soldiers have done." The ire was back in her voice at last and she slammed her fist into the padded seat of the bench. "I wanted to fight them. I wanted to take one of the swords out of the stable, or the heaviest plumbatae I have and beat them, hurt them, for what they were doing."

Chrysanthos held up a hand in warning. "It isn't wise to say so, no matter how deeply you feel it, for there are times when such statements are repeated." He realized he had alarmed her, and he went on in a softer tone, "I will say nothing. I would not speak of what you say, for I am here as the deputy of your sponsor. I would not repeat your words, in any case, for the friendship I bear to Drosos."

Her expression softened. "You're almost a Roman in some things, Chrysanthos. I thought Belisarius and Drosos were the only ones, but you . . ." She reached out and picked up a small, bronze rushlight in the shape of a winged serpent. "I'm a little surprised they left this to me. I don't think they knew its value or they might have wanted it. It's Persian, very old." As she held it out, she said, "Take it, please, as a token of my thanks."

Chrysanthos was startled. "Great lady, you have no reason to do this."

"But I do," she corrected him gently. "You performed a great service for me and you've been willing to do more than you were required to do. Take the rushlight. You can use it as an oil lamp if you have a bronzeworker alter it a little."

"I would not think of changing it," said Chrysanthos as he took the rushlight. "I am . . . very, very grateful, great lady. I never thought you would make such an offer."

"It is my Roman nature," she said, shrugging off his thanks. "I was taught very young to acknowledge aid and service." She adjusted her paenula so that it enveloped her like a cloak. "It isn't cold, and yet I feel cold."

Puzzled, Chrysanthos asked, "Are you well?"

"In body, oh, yes. I am cold for other reasons. I am cold for desperation." She made a complicated gesture. "Until now, I have been able to hold off actions against me, but now, everything is different. It doesn't matter that Belisarius is my sponsor and that Drosos is my lover; the time will come when that will not stop the Censor from acting overtly against me."

"Surely it won't come to that?"

"It already has. You were here and you saw what was done. It is practice for what is to come. I will have to visit Belisarius soon and find a way to gain permission to leave." Or, she added to herself, she would have to arrange to leave everything behind and flee.

"I can understand why you think this might be the way things might go, but I assure you that we are more orderly, more civilized than that. You have seen the barbarians attack Roma, and it's understandable that you confuse them with us." Chrysanthos looked toward the door. "Your majordomo—"

Niklos was standing in the door. "We've restored some order in the kitchen and the evening meal is being served. The slaves are upset."

"*I* am upset," Olivia declared. "Thank you," she said with less feeling. "I will need to talk to them in the morning, when it is less immediate in our minds. Tell them, will you? I will speak with them tomorrow at midmorning." She almost grinned at Niklos. "Find out what they're saying among themselves that they would not want to tell me."

"Of course," Niklos answered.

"I needn't have asked," Olivia agreed.

Chrysanthos took advantage of this interruption to make a departing reverence. "You have much to attend to. I will report to Belisarius and I will tell him what you have told me, and you may be certain that it will be held in the greatest confidence. Your gift is as generous as it is unnecessary." He started into the vestibule, Niklos coming after him.

"Captain," Niklos said as he opened the door for Chrysanthos. "Do you know where Drosos is?"

A frown appeared between Chrysanthos' brows. "Not today. He has often disappeared for hours at a time. I thought he might be here, but if that were the case, there would have been no reason to send for Belisarius, would there?"

"He has not been here for three days. I'm concerned for him. My mistress is worried. If you find him, tell him what has been going on here and ask him to come soon. It would mean much to Olivia." Niklos paused. "Tell him that . . ."

"What?" asked Chrysanthos when Niklos did not go on.

"Tell him that he has nothing to fear from Olivia." He held the door open and made a proper reverence.

"Why would Drosos fear Olivia?"

Niklos opened his hands, palms up, to show his innocence in the matter. "He has claimed that he does. I don't know if that is serious or only his teasing, but—"

"Yes, I see," said Chrysanthos. "I will tell him, and I hope for his sake as well as the sake of your mistress that he does come soon. She is a woman of formidable control, but I think that she is more distraught than is apparent." He stepped out into the twilight street.

As Niklos closed the door, he turned to see Olivia standing in the door of the reception room. "You're eavesdropping."

"As is everyone else in this house, it would seem." She came toward him. "I want to rail at them. I want to call down plagues and curses on them and their offspring."

"But you won't," Niklos said with confidence.

"No; not yet." She indicated the ikonostasis. "At least not yet. Another time—"

Niklos looked around. "Do you intend that there be a formal complaint?"

"If I didn't, it would look more suspicious than anything else I could say or do. I will go to Belisarius myself tomorrow, and find out how he advises me to handle this. Chrysanthos has been very helpful—I did not mean to imply that he wasn't—but I will have to speak with Belisarius privately before I know what is best to do." She began to walk restlessly and aimlessly around the vestibule. "If I can discover what the reason is, then there might be a way to combat all the lies and innuendos, but as it is—"

"About leaving?" Niklos asked.

"Yes." She stopped and turned back toward him. "You are always such a sensible man, Niklos, and there are times I wonder how you deal with me." Her expression grew distant. "The clothes I mentioned?"

"I have them."

"Buy three more horses. Make sure they are swift but ordinary looking. Saddle horses, mind, not chariot horses. If we are to leave here on . . . short notice, we will need saddle horses as well as chariot horses." This last was for the benefit of anyone who might be listening, and Niklos caught her gesture that indicated her intent.

"Three horses. Very well." He cocked his head. "Do you anticipate needing to leave soon?"

"No, but anticipation means little in such circumstances. I will have to find a way to judge when it is best to act." She shook her head. "There was a time when I would have thrown it all away and simply headed out of trouble without a second thought. But that, my friend, would be folly. If you leave a place under suspicion, you must live with that suspicion for a very long time, and there's no telling when it might—" She stopped. "We had trouble enough in Carthago Nova. I would prefer not to have such problems again."

"I won't argue," said Niklos with feeling. "But who would have thought that smug little bureaucrat would travel so far, or remember so clearly?"

"Precisely," Olivia agreed. "And I do not want to spend another twenty-five years in Pictavi or some other equally dreadful place posing as a sybil and living in a cave. That taught me a lesson I do not need to learn twice." She attempted to make light of this. "And you would not have to spend a quarter of a century pretending to be a mute."

"Spare me that," he said with feeling. "Horses. Anything else?"

Olivia gave a warning gesture toward the doors. "Not now, not until I have spoken with my sponsor. In the meantime, I will want to have a word or two with Zejhil. Find her and send her to me, will you?"

For the benefit of anyone who might be watching, Niklos made a deep reverence. "Immediately, great lady."

She waved him away, but did not leave the vestibule at once herself; she stared at the door and wondered, as she had wondered often in the last three days, where Drosos was and what he was doing.

* * *

Text of a letter from Olivia to Sanct' Germain, written in Latin code.

To my dearest, oldest friend who ought to be in Trapezus now, Olivia sends her fond greetings.

I am sending this to your house in Trapezus in the hope that you will have returned there, or that if you have not, your servants will know where you are to be found and will send this along to you. You have been traveling more in these last several years, which is inconvenient for both of us.

But it appears that I will be doing the same thing. For some reason I have not yet discovered, I have aroused suspicions here in Constantinople and from the way things are going, I will have to leave soon or face consequences that would be unpleasant. What a simple word that is— unpleasant—when I am trying to say that I fear for my life; the life you returned to me when Vespasianus wore the purple. Was it really almost five hundred years ago? You will have to forgive me if I find that hard to believe. Five hundred years seems so long, looking at the numbers, yet how swiftly those years have gone.

I have not yet determined where I will go when I leave

here, but leave here I must. I hate abandoning my house and goods; I have already left so much behind in Roma that I know I will never see again. And leaving my friends—although there are precious few of them—is more difficult than I can tell you. No, that's not true, is it? You, of all people, know how hard it is to leave friends.

Assuming I have time enough for adequate preparation, I think I will try to move toward the edges of the Empire, or to go to those parts that are Coptic. The Copts are not as eager to question the faith of everyone around them as these damned Orthodox Christians are. Of course the Orthodox regard the Copts as heretics, which might account for some of this; so long as I have the opportunity to live and move about without constant surveillance, I will be—satisfied?—content?

Niklos is making several sets of arrangements for our departure, some of them more obvious than others. He is a treasure, and when I think of him, I think also of your Rogerian, since they are the same sort. Is it their method of restoration that creates such loyalty?

When I have established myself at wherever-I-am-going, I will send you word, and I trust you will write to me from time to time. Your letters are always so welcome, so consoling. There are times they are sad, as well, for they remind me of how you brought me into your life. There are times I miss those years, and your love, so intently that my bones hurt with it. Yes, yes, do not say that it is past and that the bond continues unbroken. I know that, and I cherish it, but that does not rid me of the longing.

I am not going to apologize for the last, incidentally. I know that our love cannot be what it was before I came into your life, but that does not mean I have to deny that I miss it.

Perhaps, when the worst of this is over, there will be time to write more fully, to tell you things that I cannot yet put down in words. Until then, have care, my precious friend, my old love. This world would be far drearier than it already is if you were no longer in it.

With my enduring love, and you alone appreciate my meaning,

Olivia
in Constantinople

· 4 ·

Panaigios was more nervous than the last time he had spoken with Simones. His fingers moved almost constantly, now at his pallium, now at the hem of his sleeves, now at the large, pearl-encrusted cross he wore around his neck. He indicated a small, unpadded bench and waited while Simones sat, then cleared his throat. "You have said that you have made a discovery?"

"Yes," Simones replied without any aggrandizement to the secretary of the Censor. "I sent you word of it three days ago."

"I have your note somewhere," Panaigios said, leafing through the sheets of vellum and parchment that lay on his writing table. There were even a few sheets of Egyptian paper which Simones found surprising. "Here it is. You say here that you"—he held up a strip of vellum—"have found material that would be of great value to me and to the Censor and the Emperor. You say nothing more about what this material is. Since you describe this as material, I have assumed that you have come upon a document of some sort that has some bearing on the investigation the Censor has been pursuing in regard to your master. Have I erred in any of these assumptions?"

"Not very much, no," said Simones.

"I have also assumed that you have some reason for withholding the material itself—would it be missed?" He braced his elbows on the table and leaned forward. "If that is the trouble, it is possible that a writ to search the house of Belisarius could be obtained from the Emperor. He is eager to learn of anything bearing on the conspiracy that Belisarius claims he has not participated in. Would this material be related to that question?" He was speaking fast and in breathless little spurts, and when he finished, he coughed once.

Simones leaned back. "I am prepared to show you something that would establish my master's role in the conspiracy. It isn't necessary to get a writ and search the house. I can put my hands on the thing at any time, and if I choose when it is to be shown, it will not be missed." He folded his hands and caught them around his knee. "I want to be certain of my position in this before I go any further. Denouncing my master is a dangerous thing, and I do not want to place myself in the position of a sacrifice." He nodded at the startled glance Panaigios threw him. "Oh, yes, I have wondered if you were going to use me as the means to be rid of Belisarius and then you would be rid of me, as well."

"It . . . it isn't the way the Censor . . . manages these things," said Panaigios with unconvincing sincerity.

"I doubt that," Simones said. "I have heard of slaves who disappear with their masters when the masters have been shown to be enemies of the Emperor. I would not say the names, for they aren't to be spoken, are they?"

"You are insolent," Panaigios snapped.

"Certainly." Simones showed his teeth. "I am serving two masters, which means that I must weigh my own interests."

"Insolent slaves suffer for it." Panaigios held up the vellum. "I have this, and it places you as my agent, if I am willing to say that you have worked on my authority. If I do not say you have my authority, then you are a slave who has betrayed his master. I will have no more insolence from you." He slammed the palm of his hand on the writing table for emphasis. There was a faint sheen of sweat on his brow.

Simones straightened up. "I have other notes from you; I have kept them. They give instructions and they have your name on them." He folded his arms. "I have two things to discuss. I have mentioned the material about the conspiracy. I also want to inform you that my mistress continues to suffer declining health and it is not likely she will live more than a year given her problem."

"Poison," said Panaigios.

"Yes. It continues to be administered. The man who gives her the poison still does not know who has required her death. He thinks it is someone in the household, but he does not suspect me. In fact, he once asked me who might wish ill on Antonina." He leaned forward. "I have enrolled the aid of Eugenia, who was once the close friend of my mistress, to observe her and learn from her."

"You said that you had the support of a friend; was this what you meant?" Panaigios tapped his fingers on the piled sheets on his writing table.

"Yes. When I reported my intentions, you encouraged me. I have tried to be useful to you." His eyes hardened. "I want you to be useful to me, as well."

Panaigios dismissed this with a wave of his hand. "When we have learned all that we require, then a decision will be made regarding you, but not until that time." He waited. "Tell me more about this material."

"It shows that my master was part of a conspiracy. I will be happy to produce it as soon as I am assured that I will not suffer the same fate as my master and his household. I want a promise of manumission and I want the assurance that I will be paid for what I supply." He leaned back. "Until these things are arranged, I will not show you this material."

Panaigios sighed. "I cannot give you any such assurance. It isn't my place to do so. If you think that you must have some guarantee, then the Censor must be the one to decide it." He started to gather up the vellum sheets. "I will speak of this to my master."

"If you do not give me the things I ask for, the material will disappear." Simones gave another of his lupine smiles.

"What?" Panaigios stopped his work and stared at Simones. "Are you threatening to destroy proof of treason?"

"Unless I obtain what I want." Simones raised his head, his strong jaw more prominent than usual.

Panaigios stacked all the sheets together, watching his hands as he did. "Let me warn you, slave, that you are placing yourself in grave danger."

Simones chuckled. "I have been in danger from the start of this. It is nothing new to me."

"Then you have not considered your role in this. You have convinced yourself that you are indispensable to our investigation, and you are not. You are a slave and you have been convinced that your assistance—assistance, not direction—is needed in order to determine what your master's part has been in any plot against the Emperor. To imagine otherwise is a grave mistake. You are not the person who guides this inquiry, the Court Censor is, and all of us are his tools." He said the last in a lowered tone, but with an expression that was both severe and desolate.

Simones heard this out with a mixture of impatience and rancor. "You are his tool as well, of course," he said at last, intending to insult Panaigios.

"Certainly. We are all his tools, and he is the tool of the Emperor." Panaigios waited a moment, then said more briskly, "If you have knowledge, not suspicion but knowledge, which can link Belisarius directly to a conspiracy, then you must give it to me at once, for to withhold it is a greater treason than the action that inspired it."

"What?" Simones said, for the first time frightened of the Censor's secretary.

Panaigios nodded twice. "If you do not produce this material, whatever it is, and do so at once, then you are knowingly aiding those who oppose the Emperor, and that is a treasonable act."

Simones drew back, disliking the firm attitude Panaigios was showing now. "I . . . I am not quite certain that I can put my hands on the material."

"You had better be, or your accusations will be relayed to your master and he can deal with your insubordination." Panaigios stood up. "You have two days to accomplish this. If you do not, then I will have to review your position with this investigation. Whatever the decision, you will not be permitted to act as independently as you have in the past, for it is obvious that like most slaves, you cannot handle any authority."

"You are wrong!" Simones said with force as he got to his feet. His face had darkened and his eyes were huge. "You came to me, and you gave me orders that required I act against my master. It was on your orders that I have done the things I've done, and you are the one who must be responsible for whatever I have done and whatever I will do." He was breathing hard, as if he had just run a long way.

"You are a slave." Panaigios stepped back. "I dismiss you until you have considered your situation closely and have made up your mind what you intend to do. I will not stop you from making any decision you wish, but I warn you now that there is very little chance you will be excused if it turns out that your allegations are false. The malice of slaves is well-known, and you are no exception to that rule." He indicated the outer door. "I hope you will not dawdle."

It took all the control Simones had learned over the years for him to leave the room without smashing his fist into Panaigios' face. He made a reverence and touched his collar in a gesture of submission, then turned sharply on his heel. "I will find the material," he vowed, wishing now that he had taken the time to plant such a document within Belisarius' house. There might not be a chance now that the Censor's men were on the alert. He cursed Panaigios and himself as he strode from the palace of the Censor.

Panaigios did not hurry to Kimon Athanatadies' quarters at once, although he was aware his duties required him to report to his superior immediately. Instead he sought out the smallest chapel in the palace and took time to pray, for he was terribly afraid. He wanted to seek out Thekla again, to listen to her strange prophecies and try to determine his course from her cryptic statements, but he knew he was being watched, and such an action now might be construed as a ploy to secure a higher position within the government, which the Court Censor would view as highly questionable. There had been too many instances lately when Athanatadies had asked Panaigios awkward things, and he knew his answers had been far from satisfactory.

By the time Panaigios rose from his knees, Simones was halfway to Eugenia's house, his thoughts growing sterner with every step he took. He was determined to show himself to be trustworthy if he had to counterfeit the proof of Belisarius' treachery himself.

At Eugenia's house he was made to wait while she prepared herself to receive him. This only served to make him more aggravated than he already was, so that when Eugenia entered her larger reception room, Simones was glowering with ire.

"Lord protect us," Eugenia said, trying to find the right note to take with Simones. "You look as if half the mules in the market had stepped on your feet."

"I don't find that amusing," Simones said, coming to her side and putting his arm around her. "Find another way to amuse me."

She became very still. "Simones, there are slaves in my house who will defend me."

"Summon them," he offered, almost eager for the opportunity to have direct conflict with someone. "I will resist, but that mustn't bother you. You would like to be fought over, wouldn't you? It would be better if those fighting weren't slaves, but that is better than nothing." He put his hand under her chin and forced her to look at him. "Go ahead; summon your help."

"Not yet," she said, fearful of what might happen.

"Disappointing, but wise." He released her. "Sit down.
I must talk with you."

"Simones—" she began in protest.

"I said sit down. Unless you want it known what you
have done at my behest." He pointed to the smaller
bench near the window. "Now."

Slowly Eugenia did as she was told. "Now what?" she
asked when she had folded her hands in her lap.

"Now I must know if you have any letters or notes
written by my master to you or to friends here?" He
braced his hands on his hips.

"I don't think so," she said, puzzled at his remark.

"Are you certain?"

Eugenia shook her head. "It would not be proper for
Belisarius to write to me, in any case, unless at the request
of his wife. Since Antonina is able to read and write, there
is no reason for her husband to send anything to me." She
fiddled with the edge of her paenula. "I can only think of
one man who received any word from Belisarius while he
was here, and he has not been . . . to visit me for well
over a year. He was one of Belisarius' officers in Italy."

"Drosos?" suggested Simones.

"No; Chrysanthos. He is going to be posted abroad
soon, or so he was told by his superiors. They're doing
that with a good number of Belisarius' former officers,
you know. Most of them are on the frontiers, but a few
have . . . disappeared entirely. They might as well have
ceased to exist." She was twisting a section of the edge of
her paenula now. "I don't remember any other—"

"Chrysanthos won't do," Simones cut her off. "He's
too well-connected for my purposes. I need someone who
is not highly placed and has few friends near the Emper-
or. It's a shame you aren't a friend of Drosos. He would
be ideal. He's regarded as a rogue ever since his protest."

"I don't know Drosos, except for the few times I saw
him at your master's house," said Eugenia.

"You might try to renew the acquaintance," Simones
said, his tone more thoughtful.

"I doubt it," she replied. "I was never able to catch his

attention. He was always enthralled by Olivia Clemens, the Roman widow who—"

"I know who she is. She occasionally visits Belisarius; he's her sponsor." He bit his lower lip as he considered. "If you were to see him again, do you think you could engage his attention, for a night?"

Eugenia shrugged. "I don't know. I don't want to. The man is dangerous to know and you, for all your talk of the Censor, cannot promise me that this would not ruin me." Her voice raised in defiance. "I have called upon Antonina, I have done what I can to find out what she knows without being too obvious. You say you do not think I've done enough, but even ill, Antonina is not a stupid woman, and if I am too persistent in my questions she will not want to speak with me. She is not going to be willing to share confidences with me forever."

"Not more than a year, in any case," Simones said with a hint of gloating.

"Don't speak of that," Eugenia pleaded.

"You could help her prepare," Simones went on, tormenting her deliberately. "You can turn her thoughts away from the world and into the realms of faith. You can urge her to be rid of the sins that plague her soul and might cast her down into the Pit. It would not be the first time that death brought truth to light."

"I hate speaking with her," Eugenia confessed. "I see her in pain and with her strength ebbing, and it is all I can do to say those things I know will please her." The fabric in her fingers had started to unravel. "She is suffering. Doesn't that bother you?"

"It bothers me that we must take such a long time or be discovered." He came to her side again. "Listen to me, great lady. I am a slave. I had half my manhood cut off when I was seventeen for no reason other than a pope preached on the joys of celibacy. Mind you, the pope was married, but he spoke of the freedom from lust that comes with the loss of the hairy eggs. So all his male slaves were castrated for their own good. You see how it has dampened my lust. I have nothing in this world. There is everything to gain and nothing to lose. Why should the death of one woman make any difference to me? Do you know how I feel when I see her lying there, her face pale and great circles under her eyes, and that pain consuming her? I know that I caused it, and that her physician doesn't know that I am the one who has suborned him. It is . . . magnificent to feel so." He laughed, and though his laughter was genuine, it held no trace of mirth. "Do not speak to me about Antonina, Eugenia. It means nothing to me that she will die."

Eugenia's head had drooped as she listened to him. Finally she started to weep. "You are worse than the barbarians who are slaughtering our troops."

"No," he said when he had considered it. "No, to be their equal I would have to have accounted for more than the death of one woman and the discrediting of a single man." He reached down and sank his hands into her arms, hauling her to her feet. "Look at me, Eugenia. Look me in the face and smile for me."

"I—"

"Smile," he ordered, his hands tightening. "I want to see you smile."

Her lips twisted into the semblance of happiness, but she could not continue for long. "Let me go."

"Not yet. Not until you agree to help me."

"What choice do I have?" she asked bitterly. "You're determined to ruin me, aren't you?"

"Of course not," he said, making no effort at sincerity.

"You want to ruin me as well as your master and mistress. You have wanted that from the first." She threw her head back. "I wish I had the courage to spit in your face."

"It is just as well you do not. I would then have to remind you who commands here." He released her so suddenly that she staggered. "You are going to find a note. That note will indicate that Belisarius wanted his officers to join with him in an effort to overthrow the

Emperor. You may choose which of the officers you like, which ones you would like to see disappear. I think that the Censor would believe Drosos was part of the plot before he would believe that Chrysanthos was, but that is for you to decide. I want this note to be phrased indirectly, and I want it to be without date, so that it might apply to any time."

"I can't do that," Eugenia said.

"You can and you will." He caught her arm. "If I have to persuade you, I will. I might do it anyway."

"Not—" Her disgust was so great that she did not trust herself to speak.

"I think that it is time you spent another hour with me. I fear you have forgot what I can do to you." His grimace was ferocious. "You will write that note in a good imitation of Belisarius' hand and you will leave it in Antonina's quarters the next time you call upon her. You will put it in an unobvious but secret place. There are three alabaster jars of scent; one of those would do very well." He would not let her move away from him.

"I don't think I can do that," she said, her eyes wide with fear.

"Be inventive. Bring her another jar of scent, or offer to anoint her wrists or her brow. That will give you the opportunity you seek."

"No," she said, her conviction faltering.

"Yes. You will do this, and then you will tell me where you have placed the note. The rest will be for me to manage. You need not be concerned with any of it." He leaned against her, taking delight in her terror. "Think of how you will benefit once Belisarius is fallen completely and Antonina is dead. You will be recognized for your service."

"I do not want such recognition," Eugenia insisted.

"Perhaps not now, when you are caught up in the danger. But once it is over, you will change your mind. You will be proud to say you helped in unmasking a traitor. The Censor will show you favor, and that is to your advantage, isn't it?" He seized her and kissed her hard.

She pushed against him trying to break his hold. "I don't want you to touch me."

"It doesn't matter what you want," he said simply. "You will do as I order or you will suffer for it."

"I suffer for it already," she said, her mouth set.

"Really?" With one hand he ruffled her hair, destroying its smooth order. "Is all this so terrible? Do I make things so difficult for you? Do I?"

She did not answer, but the loathing in her eyes was eloquent and for the time being, it satisfied Simones.

* * *

Text of a letter from Drosos to Chrysanthos, never delivered.

To my comrade-at-arms and, I hope, my friend, I send my apologies and belated greetings.

I have not set out to avoid you, Chrysanthos, though you have good reason to think that might be my intention. I know I ought to have explained to you, but I have not been able to discuss the things that you and I endured in Alexandria. I do not want to be reminded, and it is unforgivable in me that because of my cowardice I have not been willing to speak with you since that would remind me of all that transpired.

You are being posted to the frontier, or so I've been told. That's been happening to most of Belisarius' officers, hasn't it? At least you are not one of those who has disappeared forever and whose names are not spoken except when one is very private or very drunk. I hope that you will have the opportunity to show your valor and to convince the Censor and the Emperor that you are worthy of their good opinion. You have always had mine, but that means less and less every day, and never meant much.

Those bleak days in Alexandria you did more for me than I had any right to expect, and for that I am truly and deeply grateful. I have not said it, and I might not say it again, but I want you to know that all you did made my stay there a bearable torture. If it weren't for you, I might have forgot all they have taught us about sin and opened a vein or run on my sword like an old Roman.

That is one of the reasons I can almost envy you: you are going to have the opportunity to fight again, and in battle there is always the chance of a spear in the side or an arrow in the belly or a sword through the neck. I used to think that the greatest challenge, and now I see it differently; I see the release it would bring. I haven't been able to confess this to my pope, though to be honest, I haven't tried or wanted to. I would never be able to make a pope understand why I feel the shame I do, or why I seek to be rid of myself. All that is sin, and admitting it places me among the damned. But I knew that already. I knew that as I watched the Library burn.

The Emperor was wrong to order it. For whatever reason, he demanded a deed that was worse than blasphemy. It may be that he truly believes that it was a triumph of faith, and possibly it was that. I cannot grasp it, and no matter how I try, I can see no reason for it that balances what was lost. So now, on top of my heresy, I am speaking treason. Perhaps you had better not read this, or I had better not send this. I would burn it, but I have had too much of burning already. If I forget myself and send this to you, I suggest you burn it for your own protection. Or you can take it to an officer of the Court Censor, and then Kimon Athanatadies can have a chance to persuade me I am in

*error. If only someone could. If only I could convince myself
that I have not enough comprehension and that what I see
as a failing really is a magnificent accomplishment.*

The souls of the books haunt me. They are like ghosts
who cry in the night, and I hear them, so many, many
voices, all lost and wandering. That sounds like the words
of a madman, doesn't it? It may be that I am mad, and
have not realized it yet. If I am mad, then does that mean I
am condemned to live with those pitiful voices for the rest of
my life?

Pay no attention to me, Chrysanthos. There is no reason
for you to have to listen to more of this; you already
suffered more than your share of this maudlin self-
recrimination I have indulged in since I carried out my
orders. And after all, the decision was not mine, it was the
decision of Justinian to do away with the books. I was
nothing more than his instrument and by rights I have no
responsibility in the act, as you had none. It is just that I
saw the books and the flames that consumed them and I
have become sentimental about them. I do not castigate
myself for the men I maimed and killed in battle, or for the
peasants that starved because my troops took the last of
their chickens to keep from starving themselves. There is no
sensible reason to be so distressed over the scribblings on
tablets and parchment and papyrus and paper. I have indulged in useless and apostatic whining long enough and I
must have exhausted your patience and the bonds of our
friendship long since.

I pray you have a worthy campaign and that you gain the
glory and advancement you have so long deserved, and that
any stigma that remains from your association with Belisarius or with me is at last removed so that you can be
recognized as the superior officer you are. Do not hesitate to
disavow your ties to me if that will aid you. I do not want
to hinder you in any way, for you have done more than I
might reasonably expect of a friend and fellow-officer. And I
no longer deserve the loyalty you have given so unstintingly.

When I hear from you again, if I ever do, I trust it will
be to learn that you are at last given full field command and
the rights and grants that go with that promotion. Never
did a true soldier earn it more completely than you have. If
it would not compromise you, I would offer an official
commendation, but since the Emperor recalled me, a good
word from me is the same as the kiss of the plague. So
perhaps you may regard this letter as a private thanks and
appreciation from an officer who is no longer in a position
to express such things.

   If I have not wholly disgraced myself, or if there truly is
a merciful God in Heaven, I might be given the chance to
expiate my sins on campaign again. The Saints know I
would welcome it. Let me be a Captain. I do not want
higher command. Let me fight and restore some of the honor
I have lost, if that is possible.

   You are good to let me carry on this way. You have
already heard most of it. So, perhaps, I will not send this
after all. There is nothing here that is new to you and there
is no reason you should have to endure this again.

   Still, I will sign it with my good wishes and affection and
respect.

                                          Drosos
                                          Captain

5

Long seclusion had leeched the deep tan from Belisarius' skin and now he looked almost as pale as a pope or a metropolitan who spent his life in religious devotions. His eyes were exhausted but he moved restlessly as he led the way from his vestibule to the one reception room that opened onto his garden.

"I am relieved that you came," he said to Olivia when the formalities had been observed. "I have not been able to get any response from the Censor regarding the items that were taken from your house. For the last month the only comment they will give me about you is that the Censor has not yet made up his mind. I have no means to demand more from him."

"You have done what you can, and more than I have any right to expect," said Olivia, wishing she could say more safely. On her arrival she had been warned that there were many spies in his household; she would have to guard her tongue.

"It ought to be more," said Belisarius, his frown deepening making furrows in his face. "It shames me that I am unable to do more."

"There is no reason it should," Olivia told him frankly. "I am a foreigner here, and a woman. That the Censor does not choose to act is not surprising. There are other more pressing cases requiring his attention, I am certain." She looked up as a slave brought refreshments into the room. "Thank you, I will take nothing."

"You never do," Belisarius complained with a smile.

"If things were different I might be offended. Under the circumstances, I admire your prudence."

Olivia laughed sadly. "It isn't that I fear what you serve. You have no earthly reason to poison me. But there are things that cause me upset, and I wish to avoid them. You have known others with antipathies to certain foods, and I am afraid I am one such." There was, she added to herself, one thing only that nourished her and lately it had been difficult to acquire.

"You've told me that before," he said, making the most of the conversation while the slave was still in the room. "I am sorry, incidentally, that my wife is not feeling well enough to join us. Her malady continues. I had hoped she would recover but that hope is—" He could not finish.

"Before I leave, I would like to call upon her, if that is all right with her. It has been almost three months since I had the pleasure of speaking with Antonina and I would like to have a little time with her."

Belisarius was able to smile fleetingly at her request. "I will send word to her. Simones has been watching her since sunrise and doubtless he will want to have a meal and stretch his legs a bit. He's been very good to her."

"At a time like this, his devotion must mean a great deal to Antonina." She kept her voice neutral, for she did not want to distress Belisarius with her own misgivings about the eunuch.

"Yes. He was a gift, you know. His former master gave him to my household when his second son was made an officer at the start of my Italian campaign. The officer proved useless, but Simones has been a treasure." His gaze was directed out the window to the garden which was coming into flower. "I am growing nostalgic for war. That is a bad sign in an old soldier."

Olivia leaned forward and put her hand on his forearm. "You long for action. There is no harm in that."

"Action? Or battle, and the blood and the thrill? It *is* a thrill, Olivia, that first charge when it seems that you are as invincible as the waves of the sea. Later there is the clamor and the sweat and the losses, but in that first

moment, it is as marvelous as taking a beloved woman."
His expression altered. "Do you see those roses? I
planted them myself, with a rat and a fish at the roots to
make them bloom more profusely."

"They are beautiful," Olivia said truthfully, wanting to
shake Belisarius.

"You're being very patient," Belisarius said to her, and
when she started to speak, he interrupted her. "I know
you have urgent problems, and I am not doing all that I
could. You have let me speak, listening and not blaming,
and I owe you more than I can repay."

"Belisarius, you don't have to—" Olivia said, hoping to
spare him the embarrassment he was bringing on himself.

"I do have to," he said. "You are rightly concerned for
your safety, and I talk about slaves and roses. You need
my aid, and I have not given it." He cleared his throat.
"All right; I will send another petition to the Censor,
requesting the return of all goods taken from your house.
I will ask that you be given permission to leave the city
before the end of the year, and I will do all that I can to
see that the requests are granted. If you do not expect a
rapid decision from the Censor, I think that I will be able
to obtain the documents you will need. How much of your
goods I can recover is another matter."

"I don't ask the impossible, I hope," Olivia said, her
eyes softening. "You have your own difficulties."

"I suppose I ought to find you another sponsor, one in
better favor with the Censor, but to be honest, I would
miss you, and it would be a greater capitulation than I can
bear to revoke my sponsorship. As long as I am permitted
to be your sponsor, I feel I have some influence, some
credibility with the Imperial Court. If I lost that, it would
be the same as surrendering."

"I do not want any other sponsor," Olivia said.

Belisarius snorted. "You don't want a sponsor at all."

"Yes. But if I must have one, then I would rather it be
you than anyone else." She shrugged. "Do what you can.
I will not hold you responsible for what others do."

"I could request that Drosos—" Belisarius offered.

"Drosos is in more disgrace at court than you are. And he is questionable since he is known to be my lover." She frowned, hesitating. "He is also . . . very much troubled. Ever since his return from Alexandria, he has been unlike himself. I . . . I have tried, but he—"

"I know," Belisarius said. "I've talked with him, and he is overburdened."

Olivia nodded in agreement. "He is not what he was. There are times I fear I will not be able to . . . to reach him again."

"Is that so important?" Belisarius asked in surprise.

"There is nothing more important," Olivia said quietly but with so much feeling that Belisarius found it difficult to look at her.

"Yes." He rubbed his hands against his pallium. "Is there anything you would like to eat?"

"No," she said. "I would like to be able to help Drosos, but he won't permit it. When we talk, it is as if he were a stranger, an angry, guilty boy."

Belisarius made a curt gesture. "This is folly."

"He cannot reconcile himself to what he has done." Now that she said it, she saw compassion and resignation in Belisarius' face.

"And if he had not done it, he would not have been able to reconcile himself to that, either." He reached for a plum. "I do not know what more can be done for him."

"He does not want to listen to me; will he listen to you?"

"I don't know." He averted his eyes. "If I were able to speak to the Emperor, I might be able to find out all his reasons for ordering the Library burned. But as it is, I cannot answer the questions that haunt Drosos, and—"

Olivia rose. "It wouldn't matter. Even if the Emperor gave his reasons to Drosos, it wouldn't end his doubts, not now." She sighed. "What does a peasant from Macedonia know about the value of books?"

Belisarius looked up sharply, his hand raised in warning. "It isn't wise to be so outspoken in this house."

"I have said the same thing in my own house and I am

certain that there are spies." She walked toward the tall window that was open on the garden. "Your Emperor began life as a peasant. He was not much different from others, except in his ambitions."

"In his vision," Belisarius corrected her, an edge in his voice.

"Call it what you will; he aspired to more than the life of a peasant—will that do?" She shook her head. "He has no concept of the worth of those books, of the tradition he has ruined."

"If the Emperor believes that the burning was necessary, then it is not for us to question him." Belisarius spoke with conviction.

"That is what Drosos tells me, too. I can't understand. You have to forgive me," she said, turning away from the garden to look squarely at Belisarius. "You are Byzantine; I am Roman."

Belisarius strove to make light of her words. "I allow that there are differences, but we are all Christians, and we all bow to the same altars."

Olivia could say nothing in response; she stared blindly at the roses, hoping to quell the anguish she felt: Drosos, Belisarius, Antonina, Chrysanthos, herself; all of them were caught in a labyrinth. Her attention was caught by a bee that had strayed too deeply into the heart of a rose and had been entrapped by a spider. Now it lay in its filament-prison, enmeshed in bonds that were all but invisible.

Belisarius spoke, but not to Olivia. "What is it, Simones?" he said to the slave who had come to the door and made a deep reverence.

"It is your wife, General. She would like a little of your time. She apologizes for this intrusion." He lowered his head in Olivia's direction.

"Is she—?"

"She wishes to see you," Simones said, his tone and attitude wholly neutral.

Belisarius was on his feet. "I will come at once," he said, adding to Olivia, "It is most improper to leave you without escort in my house, but—"

"What nonsense," Olivia said, silencing him. "I will come with you, if you don't object, and if she is willing to see me, I would be delighted to visit with Antonina." She did not wait for him to make up his mind but followed him out of the room.

"She might be too ill—" Belisarius warned her.

"Then I will return to your reception room, or you may dismiss me." She kept pace with him, her attitude pragmatic, her words crisp.

"It isn't correct," was the only observation he made to her suggestions.

"I don't care if it is or is not," she told him. "Your wife needs your help." She halted at the door to Antonina's apartments and stopped Belisarius. "Believe me, my friend, I am sorry that you are in such travail. I am sorry that your wife is ill. You will not offend me if you give her trouble precedence over mine; if you did not, I would be displeased."

"Thank you," he said, and went through the door that Simones held open for him. "I will find out if she is willing to see you."

"Your august lady is not able to rise from her bed," Simones said to Belisarius, pointedly ignoring Olivia.

"Let me speak with her," Belisarius said, directing this to Olivia. "I will return directly."

"If you like, my master, I will bear a message," Simones volunteered.

"No," said Belisarius. "If Olivia has questions, it is for me as her sponsor to answer them." With that, he entered his wife's quarter, indicating that Simones should wait with Olivia.

"My mistress suffers much with her disorder," Simones informed Olivia in his most daunting manner.

"I understand that she has been failing; it saddens me to hear of it." What would Simones think, she wondered, if he knew how many times she had expressed similar feelings over the centuries? What would Simones do if she described all the losses she had endured in her five hundred years. "It is always difficult to lose those we love. Both your mistress and master have grief in their hearts."

Simones glared at her.

In a short while Belisarius returned. "Antonina would be pleased to speak with you for a time, Olivia. You must not be too upset by her appearance. She has lost flesh and her pain has . . . changed her." He led her through the door, closing it on Simones. "Come." In an undervoice he added, "I am grateful to you for doing this. Many of her friends have ceased to visit her and that has been as hard a burden as her illness."

Olivia nodded once. "They are afraid," she said.

"Why should they fear? If there were contagion here, others would be ill, but it is only she." He paused at the door to Antonina's room.

"They are afraid because they fear their time will come," said Olivia gently. "It isn't the illness, it is the inevitability that terrifies them."

Belisarius regarded her uncertainly. He pressed the latch and opened the door. "My dear wife," he said as he approached Antonina's bed, "Olivia Clemens has come to see you."

"You are welcome, friend of my husband," Antonina said, more cordial than she had ever been; her voice was low and harsh, no longer musical.

"God give you a good recovery, August Lady," Olivia said with formal kindness.

"It will be God and God alone who does," said Antonina. She was indeed much changed. Her dark hair was now the color of tarnished silver, with a wide swath of chalk white through it. Her skin, always pale, had turned almost lunar, and there were deep hollows in her cheeks; her eyes were sunken but enormous and shiny with fever.

"Then we will pray for you, all of those who know you and care for you," said Olivia, aware that the woman was in agony.

"We're grateful for your prayers," Belisarius said when Antonina said nothing to Olivia.

"I have heard that you had goods taken from your

house," Antonina said, making the information a challenge.

"Unfortunately I have been suspected of illegal activities and the Censor desires to clear up the matter before deciding on my petition to leave the city." Olivia watched Antonina as she spoke, a question unspoken in her eyes.

"You wish to leave Konstantinoupolis?" Antonina said with astonishment. "How can you prefer to live in another place?"

"I am a stranger here," Olivia said simply.

"Where would you not be a stranger?" Antonina inquired. She was breathing a bit too fast and a dull flush had spread over her cheeks.

"Roma, of course, but that isn't possible," Olivia said with an ironic smile. "You have been most gracious to me, Antonina, and I thank you for all you have done. Yet I know that I must find another . . . home." She moved a little nearer the bed.

"What foolishness," said Antonina, glancing to her husband for agreement. "Why have you agreed to this."

"Because she has been subjected to interferences. I know that she does not ask this capriciously." He sat on the bed beside his wife. "How are you, my dearest?"

"I endure," she said fatalistically. "The physician has given me another potion, but—" She did not bother to finish.

Olivia was more attentive than before. "Your physician? You are attended by a physician?"

"An excellent and pious man. My slave Simones found him for me and has watched over me while this Mnenodatos has administered his treatments." She leaned back against the cushions piled behind her. "I am alive today, I think, because of the skill of this man."

"Truly?" Olivia said. "That is an impressive recommendation. It takes a gifted healer to earn such praise."

Belisarius caught the hard note in Olivia's tone, and he glanced at her in surprise. "Olivia?"

"There are a few matters I must discuss with you before I leave," she said smoothly to him. "You are generous,

Antonina, to permit me to take up your husband's time. I thank you for the consideration you show me." She emphasized this with a slight reverence to the woman in bed.

"He is a comfort to me. My husband is always steadfast." She patted his hand, and then said in a very small voice, "I did not know until recently how great a strength he is."

Olivia found it hard to speak. "You . . . you are fortunate to know this now. Many another has . . ." As her words faded, she made an odd, protective motion with her hands.

"It has been solace to me," Antonina went on, speaking entirely to Belisarius. "If you were not here, I would be long in my grave."

"Antonina—" Belisarius said, trying to moderate her emotions, concerned about the hectic brightness in her eyes and cheeks.

"It is true, it is true," she said, her grip on his hands tightening with convulsive strength. "You are my good angel, and I thank God and His Mercy for making me see this at last." Her face grew more pinched, but she went on talking. "I was angry with my blessed husband, do you see? I was certain that he had failed me when he was removed from command and returned to this city. I thought that he had been part of a conspiracy and that it had not succeeded and he had been found out." She gave a dry, hacking cough.

"Dearest wife, you need not say any more," Belisarius told her, stroking her hair and overcome with regret.

"It is good that I do. I have wanted to tell someone for so long. You are this lady's sponsor and you have said that she is not one to repeat rumors and gossip. Besides, who does she talk to? You? Drosos? You both know this." She stopped, breathless.

"You need to rest," Belisarius said, looking to Olivia for support.

"If you are too tired to speak, great lady," Olivia said in response to Belisarius' unspoken plea, "I will come another time, when you are feeling better."

"That will not happen, I fear," said Antonina, resignation in every aspect of her posture.

"You cannot be certain," Belisarius insisted. "Your physician is devoted to you. He will find a way to restore your good health."

Antonina looked at Olivia. "He is still my good angel, isn't he? That is why I am ashamed when I think of how I harbored cruel thoughts of him, and when he was in greatest need, I behaved more despotically than any barbarian prince might." She was exhausting herself, but she went on, her determination growing as her strength waned. "He has done everything anyone could hope for. He has comforted me, he has cared for me, he has stayed up with me when I could not sleep, and he has seen I was not disturbed when I could. He has never flagged in his aid, and his constancy has filled my heart to bursting. How could I think this man capable of any deceit, to me or to the Emperor? What made me assume that he would ever abjure his vows, to me or to anyone else? He has shown me his love with his duty."

"My love, please," Belisarius protested affectionately.

Antonina leaned back. "I wish I could tell the Court Censor these things."

"If there are spies in your household, one of them might," Olivia said, and got the worn smile she had hoped for.

"Yes, there are uses for spies, I suppose," Antonina said listlessly. "And if they will report this to Athanatadies, I will be satisfied."

"They might," said Olivia. "It depends on who is spying." She looked at Belisarius. "I do not wish to overstay my welcome. Let me have a moment of your company and then I will leave you to your wife." She made a reverence to Antonina. "I will pray for you, great lady, and I thank you for your kindness in allowing me to take up your husband's precious time."

"Be careful, Olivia," Antonina warned, her words just above a whisper.

In the hallway, Olivia glanced swiftly to see if they were overheard. "I must speak with you. Come out to my palanquin. I do not want listeners."

Obediently Belisarius fell into step with her. "She is in great pain, you know."

"Yes," said Olivia, steel in her tone. "I am amazed she is able to endure so much."

"My wife has always been a woman of mettle," Belisarius said. "From the first time I met her, I thought that I had rarely seen such substance in a woman."

"And she has courage," said Olivia. They were almost to the door, and the vestibule was empty. "You say she has a physician: are you satisfied with his treatment?"

"He works constantly to alleviate her torment," Belisarius said as they stepped out into the sunlight.

"And what has he done about the poison that is killing her?" She said it bluntly, her intention to shock him.

"Poison?" He shook his head. "He has said that this is not poison, but a corruption of her vitals."

"It probably is, and it is caused by poison." Before Belisarius could object, Olivia went on, "Give me some credit, my friend. I am a Roman and I have seen more of plots and poisons than you can imagine. Your wife is being poisoned slowly, so that it will not be suspected by you or by others. I can understand your doubt, but I cannot understand her physician not knowing what kills her. The course of the malady is clear enough; her breath is tainted with poison, and her eyes are changed because of it. There is something very wrong and you must act if you are to save her."

Belisarius stared at her in disbelief. "I . . . I appreciate your concern, but you cannot be right. Her physician came with the highest recommendation. Simones searched him out, and would not accept any but the most skilled for her." He touched her arm. "I am grateful that you tell me what you fear, but I doubt that this case—"

"Your doubt might speed her death," Olivia said directly. "I do not want to distres you more than—"

"I know. You are a sensible woman." He indicated the

palanquin. "I will send an escort home with you."

"That isn't necessary. If you wish to please me, do something about the physician attending your wife." She accepted his dismissal with philosophical grace. "Thank you for hearing me out. I trust you will receive me again soon."

"When there is something to tell you, I will." He inclined his head in response to her slight reverence, then turned and went back into his house, his head still lowered, his steps heavy.

Olivia watched him go, remorse tugging at her; she had wanted to aid Belisarius, but now she feared she had added to his distress. She got into the palanquin, for once relieved that the curtains had to be drawn.

*   *   *

Text of a dispatch to the commanders of the Byzantine navy.

To the valiant men who captain our warships, the Emperor sends his blessings and prayers for a successful encounter with the naval forces of the Ostrogoths.

As we enter the Lenten season in the Lord's Year 551, all of the Empire puts its trust and faith in you, and prays that you will prevail over the ships that are being launched against us by the infamous Totila and his barbarians. It is fitting that at this time of the greatest sacrifice you undertake our defense, for surely in going to battle now, you emulate the courage of Our Lord in facing the trials that brought Him to the Cross.

As He was raised up to glory, we are confident that you will also be raised up. As He passed through the rigors of Hell and fled the tomb, so we are filled with hope that you will pass through the battles that must be the test of your superior purpose and might to emerge without blemish to the acclaim and praise of all men within the bounds of the Empire.

For those who have worried about the cost, fear not that this will impede you. Three new taxes have been levied and the popes and metropolitans have been urged to ask for additional donations to your efforts. If you are willing to risk your lives, then it is fitting that there are a few who will expend their wealth to aid you in your quest for victory.

We admonish all of you to be stalwart in your faith and determined in your purpose. You are brave men, all of you, and it is fitting that you should go onto the ocean with the certainty and pride that sets you apart from others and reveals to you and to the Empire that there is no price we are not willing to pay to bring about your triumph.

You are not only the officers of our Empire, you are the officers of God, for you fight against pagan barbarians who are attempting to rend the world into tatters where all will be cast into Hell. You save not only your ships and yourselves when you prevail, you save the Empire and the Kingdom of God on earth.

> Justinian
> Emperor of Byzantion
> (his sigil)

6

A full moon rode at the crest of the night sky, its pallid
shine turning Konstantinoupolis into a monochrome
sketch of domes, walls and shadows. From one of the
Basilian monasteries came the sound of chanting, and
along the walls of the city the night Guard was changed.
Those few men on the streets kept to the deepest darkness, their errands demanding concealment and surprise.

Niklos was almost to the second square tower when he
heard swift footsteps behind him. He slipped into a
shallow doorway and waited while his pursuers came
abreast of him.

There were three men, one of them carrying a wooden
cudgel and the other two holding knives. They moved
efficiently, spread out in the street, their shoes tied in rags
to muffle their sounds. The largest of the three men made
a signal to the others and they slowed down, their actions
more stealthy than before.

When the three men were past his hiding place, Niklos
stepped out and followed the men along the street; he
carried a glavus in each hand, the wide-bladed weapons
catching the shine of the moon on their newly honed
edges.

Just as the three men reached the entrance to the
Church of the Resurrection, one of them turned. He saw
Niklos and would have cried out to warn the others, but
did not dare to alert the Guard to their presence. He
crouched low, his knife swinging up as Niklos moved in,

one glavus slicing toward the thief's shoulder. Deftly he turned the blade on the quillons of his knife, and he might have been able to attack if Niklos had carried only one weapon.

As his right glavus swung away, the left cut in hard and low, catching the thief in the thigh, gouging through flesh and striking bone.

The thief shrieked, and his companions turned, prepared to fight. The first man fell to the paving, narrowly missing a pile of dung. He clutched his leg in a fruitless attempt to stanch the blood that pumped from the deep wound he had been given.

The man with the cudgel raised his weapon as he advanced, bringing it down in front of him, aiming not for Niklos' swords but for his arms and shoulders; this disabling blow ought to leave their opponent helpless.

Niklos sprang backward, out of range of the cudgel, both glavi held ready to stop an attack.

The second man with a knife was moving against the buildings on the other side of the street, sliding in the darkness, to outflank Niklos.

As the man with the cudgel swung again, Niklos leaped at him, choosing the thief's most vulnerable instant— when his cudgel was low and he had not yet been able to swing it into position for another blow. His left glavus bit deep into the man's shoulder, penetrating just under the collarbone. The man howled and staggered away from the blade.

The third man hesitated, and then, seeing his chance, rushed in, his knife held to strike Niklos low in the back. But he had forgot his comrade who lay bleeding, and in his haste, he tripped over the other's arm. Cursing, stumbling, he blundered into Niklos' right blade, taking it along his ribs.

In the next street there was the sound of running, and Niklos did not wait to discover who might be approaching. He grasped his swords and raced away from the three wounded men.

"That was an impressive display," murmured the merchant from Tyre who had agreed to meet with Niklos that night.

"I thought they might have already found you," Niklos said as he stopped to wipe the blood away.

"Are you hurt?"

"Nothing to speak of," Niklos assured him. "But I want to get off the street."

"Of course." The merchant opened the door where he had been waiting and led Niklos into a courtyard. "I have been given the use of this house by another merchant, a Konstantinoupolitan who is currently on a voyage to purchase fine cloth and copper. I have extended the same courtesy to him when he has been in Tyre."

"And when do you return to Tyre?"

"I plan to leave in little less than a month. I was told that you might wish to travel with me at that time." He indicated a bench beside a fountain. "Sit. We will discuss your requirements in comfort."

Niklos made a reverence. "You're gracious."

"It is not difficult to be gracious to a man who is willing to pay forty pieces of gold to leave the city." He smiled, his teeth blue-white in his gray-seeming face. "It must be important."

"I and my . . . companion are eager to depart. There is a question of removing certain belongings that we are prepared to abandon for the opportunity to be gone." He waited. "You have arranged such departures before, or so I have been told by those who are reliable in these matters."

"Yes," the merchant said slowly, relishing the word. "But I am curious about the risk I might be taking. It is an easy thing to say that you are being treated unjustly; it might be that you are truly a criminal." He stroked his short beard and went on, musing aloud, "It might be more sensible to inquire at the office of the Censor to learn why you are so willing to pay me to get you out of here."

"You may ask what you want, where you want. Surely I

am not the only Roman who has decided to leave this city. Romans are not welcome here, and there are many who strive to make our presence a trial for everyone. Rather than wait for the Censor to determine what of my possessions are acceptable, I prefer to abandon the lot of them and seek refuge in a place that is less unfriendly. I have fled Roma already. I am prepared to leave Konstantinoupolis on the same terms." He deliberately let his Latin accent become stronger. "There have been edicts of late that have resulted in the seizure of Roman goods. Before I have to give up what little I was able to save, I want to be away from here."

"You and your companion," said the merchant.

"Yes; I and my companion." He regarded the merchant steadily. "If you are not prepared to help me, say so, and I will have to search out another."

The merchant chuckled. "Do you believe that you will find another? Don't you realize that you are under suspicion, as are all Romans?" He toyed with a small dagger that depended from the wide leather belt that held his ample girth. "You haven't yet accepted the seriousness of your position here, and for that you are going to suffer." He shook his head. "No, no, my poor Roman friend, you have more to contend with. You say you want to leave because of a desire to retain a few possessions. If you do that, you will be fortunate indeed. You might well lose your life, and that makes our bargain a more critical one."

"Critical?" Niklos repeated as if he were unaware of the purpose of this threat.

"For one thing," the merchant went on as if Niklos had not interrupted him, "you are likely to have to leave everything behind, and so the only gain I will be able to make is the fee you pay me when I take you aboard my ship. That means that I will have to raise the price, for my risk is greater, and the punishment I would suffer for giving you aid is worse than having my nose and ears struck off." He raised his hand to tick off his other objections on his long, fat fingers. "So I must have more for my own danger. Then there is the matter of smuggling you out of the city, and that will require more effort than we had discussed before, and for that I think you would agree it is reasonable that I demand a handsome price to pay for the various arrangements I must make, the extra men I must employ and the Guards I will have to bribe. Then I might have to appear before the Censor when I return, for I will come back to this city even if you will not, and that is another risk which I think deserves recompense." He grinned. "I think that eighty pieces of gold for each of you—you and your companion—is a reasonable figure."

"It's a fortune," Niklos said flatly.

"Oh, hardly that. A high price, certainly, but we are agreed, aren't we, that there is a greater hazard than first seemed the case." He combed his fingers through his beard. "You are not thinking clearly. It is because you are afraid. Once you consider all that I can do for you, you will decide that what I ask is reasonable. And, of course, if you refuse to pay me, I will have to inform the office of the Censor that you have attempted to bribe me to take you out of the city without permission. It would be necessary for me to make such a report, for who knows what the slaves of this household might have learned, or what the master will demand when he comes back?"

"Very neat," said Niklos, who was not at all surprised at the duplicity of the merchant.

"Not neat, simply pragmatic. I have to make my business worth my time and effort. You are part of my business." He clicked his tongue. "I am a simple man, and I know very little about politics and the cause of the Church. I seek only to do my work and to obey the laws of the land. There are times when it is apparent that the law might be incorrect, and in such instances I try to make allowances, but not if those allowances place me at a disadvantage."

"Naturally not." Niklos sighed. "I have only thirty gold pieces with me. That was what I was told to bring."

"It will do for a start." He held out his hand, and when

Niklos handed over the leather case, he tucked it into his belt, making it vanish as a street entertainer would make beans vanish beneath cups.

"I will bring you more tomorrow night," he said in discouraged resignation.

"The night after; tomorrow night I am to hear Mass at Hagia Sophia." He straightened up. "I am permitted to listen to the Mass in the narthex. In another year, I will be permitted to enter the church itself with those who take Communion."

"I am sure you will receive great benefit from it," Niklos said sarcastically.

"A man must think of the future," said the merchant. "And that includes the welfare of his soul." He sighed. "I will have to have at least sixty more gold pieces then. You can give me the rest when you board my ship. We will have plenty of time to arrange this as soon as I have the other sixty pieces." He stood up. "It is very late. I must retire if I am to begin arrangements tomorrow. These things take very careful planning, and that demands time." He made a small reverence to Niklos. "You are a sensible man, Flavius. If you think about it, you will come to the most reasonable decision."

"Or you will give my name to the Censor?" Niklos added.

"I cannot endanger myself without reason," he said, making it sound as if he were a victim of fate.

"Naturally," said Niklos, getting to his feet. "And you know that I am unable to haggle, given my circumstances."

"Haggling is for the marketplace," said the merchant. "You are not here to bargain, Flavius, you are here to arrange an illegal escape." He put his hands over his paunch. "Night after tomorrow. The same time. I will be here. I hope you will not keep me waiting, for I am a man who needs his sleep."

"Of course." Niklos started for the door in the wall. "I trust I haven't inconvenienced you in coming tonight, since you tire so easily."

"What an amusing fellow you are, Flavius," said the merchant with a low, popping laugh. "No, a bag of gold is always soothing to me. Doubtless if you can supply what I need next time I will be content." He held the door ajar as Niklos slipped into the street. "Be careful; there are thieves abroad."

"What would they take from me?" Niklos asked as the door was closed.

Olivia was in her book room, reading by the light of three Roman oil lamps when Niklos returned to her house. He closed the door and made a sign to her as he approached her, watching her set a volume of Petronius aside.

"They would not approve of this," she said, one hand on the first page. "I'm sure that Athanatadies would want to burn this himself."

"Athanatadies or Justinian," Niklos suggested. They were both speaking Latin, aware that none of the household slaves knew the language. "Both those men—"

"Justinian does not like to soil his hands," Olivia said with distaste. "He prefers others do the deeds." She leaned back in her chair, slipping the poems inside a ledger of household accounts. "Well?"

"The merchant will be delighted to fleece us and if I am not mistaken, he will then go to the Censor or one of his officers and inform them that one of the exiled Romans is trying to leave the city illegally. That way he will collect the monies I have paid in addition to the rewards offered to those who inform against criminals." He leaned back, bracing his shoulders against one of the large cabinets. "The ploy is obvious but neat. Any complaint against him would constitute a confession."

Olivia nodded. "Did you pay him?"

"Of course. You told me to. I wanted to throw the . . . gold in his face."

This time when she spoke, she had a suggestion of a smile in her eyes. "How much gold did you give him, really?"

"Nine pieces, in case he opened the wallet. Under the

nine pieces there are leaden coins." He gave her an answering grin. "He thinks he has duped Flavius, but—"

"Was that the name you used? Flavius?" She raised her brows, "Why on earth?"

"I remember you lived when the Flavians ruled. Nothing more." He put his hands on his hips. "He will inform, make no mistake. If there were a Flavius here, we would have to warn him."

"So what do we do now?" She frowned. "That man was our last lead."

"We'll find others." He moved away from the cabinet and came over to the table beside her. "You might speak to Drosos."

"If I knew where he was."

In the silence, Niklos shook his head. "No word still?"

"No."

He said nothing as he moved one of the small benches to the other side of the table. "Do you want me to find him?"

She was staring into the middle distance, seeing nothing. "If he doesn't want to be here . . ."

Impulsively Niklos reached across the table and put his hand over hers. "Olivia—"

"He's bleeding," she said in a small, distant voice. "He is wounded and bleeding." Her focus came back to the room and to Niklos. "Oh, not literally. For him that would be no real problem. He's a good soldier and he expects to be injured from time to time. This is something else, much worse. Nothing he has done before has . . . damaged him."

"And you can't leave him in pain, can you?"

"No. Not after—" She brought her hand up to shield her eyes, as if the little wisps of flame from the lamps were suddenly too bright.

"But what can you do for him?" His concern made his words rough, but the touch of his hand became more gentle.

"I don't know," she admitted. "But I cannot abandon him. I have his blood in me. There is an obligation in that, for he has loved me knowing . . . what he loved. I . . . I am no longer entirely separate from him."

Niklos lowered his head. "Is there anything I can do?"

She shook her head. "No."

"You have only to ask it." When his warm brown eyes met her hazel ones he repeated, "You have only to ask."

"I wouldn't know what . . ." Her sigh was as much from aggravation as from hurt. "The blood binds me, Niklos, but you are not bound."

Niklos chuckled once, mournfully. "No, blood does not bind me; I am not as you are. But *life* binds me, Olivia. If it were not for you, I would be nothing but a pile of bones. You were the one who restored me."

"No," she corrected him. "Not I; Sanct' Germain restored you."

"But you asked it. You were the one who—" He broke off and when he spoke again, it was in a different, tender tone. "I was nothing more than a horse trainer. You had no reason to intercede for me. I wasn't your lover any longer, only a freedman in your household. But you saved me when I was dead."

"Sanct' Germain saved you," she insisted.

"Because you asked it." He looked directly at her. "It isn't a debt, not as other debts are, because it can never be paid. I am not grateful, not as gratitude is understood. I am . . . beholden to you."

"I don't—" she began, trying to move her hand away.

His grip tightened. "No, you don't require it. I remain where I am because I wish to. It isn't *your* bond, it's *mine*." He let her hand go, but she did not move. "So. Do you want me to find Drosos for you?"

"Not yet." She bit her lower lip. "I am hoping that he will come of his own accord. If he does not, then I suppose we must act."

"As you wish," he said, letting go of her hand at last. "I will try the wharves again, if you like, and see if there is anyone willing to carry two people out of this impossible place, no questions asked."

"I suppose it will be necessary," she said, rising. "It's

foolish, but I have a foolish desire to be cleared of suspicion. I want to be . . . exonerated. It offends me to have so many ill things said of me, for no reason other than I am a Roman woman."

"If they knew what else you are . . ." Niklos made a cutting gesture with his fingers.

"Then we must hope that they never learn. I am not ready to die the true death yet." She took the ledger with Petronius concealed in it, replacing it in its pigeonhole.

"Do you think Drosos might—?"

"Might speak against me?" she finished for him. "It is possible, I suppose. He could decide that he needed to purge himself, and this would be one way." She linked her hands behind her neck and rolled her head back. "If he does, then there will be more trouble than—"

"You have a house on Kythera," Niklos said, deliberately stopping her.

"Yes," she said, a bit surprised that he mentioned it. "I haven't been there in centuries."

"It is still standing, although it needs some work." He folded his arms. "I spoke to a fisherman from there, and he told me all about the house; all it took was a few leading questions and he recited everything that is known about the place, including the local conviction that the place is haunted. The monks in the monastery above the harbor have records of the house, so you would not have any difficulty claiming it."

"If it is still unoccupied, then . . ." She turned to him. "What made you think of that house?"

"Honestly?" he asked. "Seeing that fishing boat and hearing the men speaking with the Kythera dialect." He turned his hands over, palms up. "I'd like to say it was inspiration or some such thing, but it was nothing more than chance. You haven't been there in a long time. The last time you were there," he went on more somberly, "was while I was learning to live with the . . . . changes of my restoration."

She nodded. "I remember."

"That raw chicken?" Suddenly he laughed, a great,

unfettered sound. She could not resist him, and in a moment they were laughing together.

"Do you recall that peasant with the two spotted goats?" He could hardly speak, but he gasped out the words. She nodded helplessly as he guffawed.

When they had recovered, and even the residual giggles had faded, Olivia folded her arms and regarded Niklos thoughtfully. "Perhaps a fisherman is the answer. We wouldn't get as far away as I might like, but Kythera could be the answer, at least for a little while. It would remove us from danger, and I doubt anyone would think of looking for us there. Who hides on Kythera?"

"You would be visible there," he warned her. "And the people would talk."

"Then we will have to take some precautions. I think that for a time I will have to be aged and ugly. That ought to keep all but the most curious away. Is there any of the walnut-juice tincture left, do you know?"

"Darkening your hair again?" he ventured. "On that island they won't notice dark hair in the way they'd notice light brown."

"You approve?"

"Certainly, if that matters." He watched her. "What about a limp? You would only have to have it when you were outside the walls of the house." He cocked his head to the side. "Unless you want a large staff for the place; then it becomes riskier."

"We'll need some staff. Anything else would be suspicious. And there are other problems, I agree." This last was said in a harder tone. "I will have to make arrangements."

Niklos studied her. "How?"

"I can always appear as a pleasant dream. That way there is no knowledge and no danger. At most the dreamer will recall a face, a touch, nothing more than that. It isn't—"

"Do not tell me that it isn't hazard; there is always the chance that someone will become curious, or will denounce you out of . . . guilt, I suppose."

"I try to avoid such men," Olivia said in her most sensible manner. "There are times, Niklos, that you're as bad as Sanct' Germain—not that he has any claim on avoiding risks, after what he did for me."

Niklos got to his feet. "Well, shall I talk to the fishermen, then?"

"Yes. Make it seem that we are destitute, that we had to leave almost everything behind in Roma, and that we cannot afford to remain here, nor can we afford the cost of filing a departure petition. The fishermen will be sympathetic at that. Oh, and add that I have been ill. That will account for my poor aptitude for sailing." Now that she had made up her mind, she showed her customary energy and clarity of thought.

"And Drosos?"

She faltered. "I don't know. I wish I did."

"Would you remain here if . . . if it were necessary?" The concern was back in his face and his words were sharp.

"You mean if he required it of me? How could I refuse, after what has passed between us? I might as well try to swim naked to Kythera." She indicated her shoes with the thick, earth-filled soles.

"How much of your native earth is at the house on Kythera?" asked Niklos.

"Enough, if the place has been undisturbed. There are three chests of it, as well as what is under the floor. It will suffice for a time." She stretched. "So it will be Kythera."

Niklos came up behind her and put his arms around her waist. "I know you will honor the ties of blood, and I cannot and would not fault you for it, but you will have to pardon me for my concern, and for—"

"For being my loving friend?" Olivia chided gently.

"Among other things." He turned her to face him. "In all the time I have known you, I have never seen you as . . . attached to anyone as you are to Drosos. With the exception of Sanct' Germain, of course."

"Yes, he always is the exception," she said, then went on. "There is something in Drosos that moves me. When he became my lover, he did it so . . . so wholeheartedly. There was no reservation, no guardedness. He was like a clear stream. Now—I don't know. But I cannot . . ."

Niklos put his hand to her hair, holding her head close to his shoulder. "I know, Olivia." He kissed her brow.

"If you would rather go to Kythera ahead of me and wait, it would—"

"No it wouldn't," he told her.

* * *

Text of a letter from Mnenodatos to Belisarius.

To the most esteemed and noble General Belisarius, the physician Mnenodatos sends his most abject apologies and sympathy upon the death of the august lady Antonina, and begs that the General will be able to forgive.

This is a most difficult letter to write to you, not only because as a physician I have failed to render the necessary treatment to save your wife, but because I permitted myself to be party to the plan that led to this eventuality.

I have not always felt this way. When I was first approached, little as I liked the notion, it had little meaning for me, for my family was hungry and I did not have the means to support them, no matter how great my skill.

Sadly, I had other skills as well, and someone found them out and turned them against me, and against you. I do not know for certain who the person was who paid me to do this reprehensible deed, but I am convinced, after examining the events that have taken place, that the person is known to you and very likely attached to your household in some capacity.

My other skills, I must confess to you, and to God, Who already knows this, is in the area of poisons, the treatment and detection of them, and their administration. It was in the latter capacity that I was paid to act, and I am dismayed to tell you that I did not question the person or the motive of the person who hired me. At the time I was willing to believe that there was good basis for the request and that you were indeed guilty of conspiring against the Emperor, and that you and your wife were enemies of the Empire and of God.

I am aware that this is not the case, and I have thought for some time that the charges against you were at best misdirected. I have assumed that you were involved with conspirators but were not one yourself, and that for reasons of honor you would not reveal the names of those who acted against the Empire because you had fought with them and would not willingly expose them to the punishment such acts would require. Your wife said many times that you had had the chance to take action and had not done so, and that she respected you for your integrity while she also doubted your wisdom in holding off from such action.

Women are strange creatures, General, made frail by God, and subject to the lures of sin more than men. I did not realize that your wife was so much in the throes of ambition that she attributed desires to you that were her own, although I ought to have suspected something of that nature when you were at such pains to conduct yourself with propriety.

None of this can excuse my actions, or my willingness to cooperate with those who were eager to pay me to administer small doses of poison to the august lady Antonina with the intention of bringing about her death. I have accomplished that, but I can take no pride in it. I am shamed and appalled at what I have done, and I pray that you will not hold me accountable for her death, but will recognize that I was merely the tool of others who are more your foes than I *will ever be. The money promised me has been paid and I have turned it over to the uncle of my wife with instructions that he is to administer it for her benefit and the benefit of my children.*

I have decided to make one last display of my ability with poisons: I have made a preparation that is both quick and not too painful. When I have finished this letter, I intend to bring about my own death. I pray that God will not regard this as the act of one lacking in faith, but will understand that I am not anxious to see what little I have taken by the courts so that my family would be left with no means of support. It is not that I wish to spare myself suffering—I will encounter enough of that in the next world so my pope assures me. At least if I end my own life in this manner, my wife and children will not be destitute. The punishments meted out by God to those guilty of the death of another will be more than anything the Censor might order, or any death the Emperor could require. Even your own sword, General, cannot equal what God will demand of me when I face Him, as soon I must.

Your wife died very bravely. She was a woman of fortitude and determination, and under other circumstances I would have the most profound respect for her and her abilities. It distressed me to have a part in her death. I beseech you to believe this, and to believe that I would rather have blasphemed in church than been party to her demise, but the temptation at first was so great that I surrendered to it. Later, my fear accomplished what my yearnings could not do. I dreaded discovery and denouncements, and I am convinced now that the one who is within your household and has been party to this will not stop his working until you are felled by the same fate that touched your beloved wife.

If you can bring yourself to pray for me, do so, for I will need the prayers of all good Christians. I am as contaminated as a house with plague and I will die knowing that there is no succor for me in this world nor the next. Pity me if there is any room in your heart for anything other than grief. I was compelled and I was weak; I did not and could not resist. You are made of sterner fibers and you have stood fast where others could not.

I have sent a confession to the secretary of the Court Censor and I have said that someone in this household is responsible for your wife's death. It is little enough, but it may aid you in attaining some justice for the great injury you have endured.

If I have a last wish, it is that the one who has brought you and me to this sorry place should be discovered and made to assume the entire burden of his villainy. If God listens to the prayers of sinners, this will come to pass. If the Emperor is just, he will exact vengeance on behalf of you, your wife, and me. Truth, we are promised, will be known, and when it is there is nothing that can spare me, but it will also bring down the one who has ordered this done, either in the Emperor's tribunal or in God's, and in either case, I am content.

Until we meet again at Judgment Day before the Father, Son, and Holy Spirit, I beg you will be more merciful than I had the strength to be.

> *Mnenodatos*
> *physician*

• 7 •

Earlier that day Belisarius had sent over some of the bounty of his garden; now a profusion of roses stood in vases and urns throughout Olivia's house. In the vestibule the air was heady with the scent of the flowers; only the kitchen and the latrine did not succumb to the fragrance.

"Smells like a church at Easter," Drosos complained when Niklos admitted him to the house that night. He had been drinking; his customary neatness had deserted him and there were three days' whiskers above the line of scraggly beard. His pallium was wrapped beltlike around his waist and knotted once without artistry. The lines in his face looked as if they had been cut with a hatchet.

"The roses are from Belisarius," said Niklos in an emotionless way.

Drosos flushed. "Oh." He stood in the vestibule, looking around as if uncertain where he was. "Will she talk to me, do you think?"

"Of course," said Niklos.

"I've been lax in visiting her. I ought not to have. I knew I ought to see her, but there are times when . . ." He made a complicated gesture.

"She has been waiting for you," Niklos said, indicating the hall that led to Olivia's quarters.

"Don't know why," he grumbled. "Not worth her while, not now." He stumbled as if to make a point, but he followed Niklos down the dim hallway, muttering to himself as he went.

"Drosos is here," Niklos announced when he had

414

knocked on Olivia's door. His voice held a warning to her, a note he knew she would not miss. "Captain." He stood aside so that Drosos could enter.

Olivia had been combing her hair, using an antique treasure the Guard had missed. She looked up, expectation in her face and worry in her eyes. "Drosos," she said, rising and coming toward him.

He accepted her embrace unsteadily and when he had his arms around her, he used them as much for support as for affection. "Sorry to come like this."

"Why? You are welcome at any time, in any way." She had seen at once what his trouble was, and she set to work dealing with it. "Niklos, I know it is late, but will you see that my bath is filled? Hot water, mind, and bring me a tea of rose hips and pepper."

"At once," said Niklos, leaving her alone with Drosos.

"I won't stay, but I had to see you," Drosos said as Olivia began to work his pallium loose. "I'm not fit to be here."

"It doesn't matter, Drosos," she said as she finally dropped the pallium to the floor. His dalmatica was stained, and stank. "What have you been doing, love?" she asked him without accusations.

"Been with my men, mostly. Soldiers' taverns." He hawked and spat, then looked at her apologetically. "I shouldn't have done that here, should I?"

"Don't worry," she said, starting to pull the dalmatica over his head. "You'll have to bend over, Drosos, if I'm to get this off you without tearing it."

He obeyed, but had to grab her waist to keep on his feet. "I slept in my clothes last night. Night before, too."

"I can tell that," she said gently. The dalmatica came off at last and she dropped it in an odorous, untidy heap near the door. "I think that I ought to send for a razor and shave you before we do anything else," she suggested, knowing it would take time for the bath to be readied.

He rubbed his cheeks. "Is it too bad?"

"No, not too bad. I have seen much worse," she said honestly, her mind cast back to other times and places.

"Still," he went on, "I ought to have shaved before I saw you. The General wouldn't like knowing that I had come here in this way. Very particular, Belisarius. He wants his men to take proper care." For the first time he realized he was naked. "God of the Prophets, I smell like a sewer."

"That's one of the reasons the bath is being readied." She was patient with him, not hurrying him.

He ambled over toward her dressing table, frowned at it, then said, as much to himself as to her. "That's right; you don't have mirrors, do you?"

"No," she said.

"Vanity, that's what mirrors are for. The pope said so."

"Which pope?" asked Olivia, glad to have found something to distract him.

"The one at the tavern, last night I think it was. He said that mirrors were evil, and showed visions of Hell." He puzzled over this. "He was drunk when he said it."

"Very likely," Olivia said, taking him by the hand and leading him toward her bath. "I will shave you. How would you like that." There was a determination about her that indicated she would do this whether he approved or not.

"I need a shave," he said uncertainly as he went with her. "And a wash, even if it is vanity." He stopped, watching the two spouts that led from the hypocaust to the bath where the first streams of hot water were starting to pour. "Roman, isn't that?"

"Yes, but then, so am I." She guided him to a bench in the alcove and there she opened a small chest where a number of razors, oil jars and scrapers were stored. She selected one and found the honing block. She worked quickly and expertly to put the proper edge on the razor.

"We could have used you in the army," Drosos said as he watched her. "Most slaves aren't good at that. The swords lose their edges at once. You know how to do it. That'll stay sharp." He reached up to test it with his thumb and gave himself a small cut for his trouble. As he sucked the blood away, he looked at her speculatively.

"Would you rather do this?"

"Not especially," she said, preparing a mixture of oil and soap. "I need more than just blood."

He laughed deep in his throat. "I know what you need."

"I need more than hard flesh inside me, if that is what you think," she said, irritation showing for the first time. "I need . . . openness. Oh, for me the blood is part of it, but it is little more than bread and water if there is nothing else. It is the touching that gives it . . . richness." She stopped what she was doing and looked down into his face. "You have given me so much."

The intensity of her words startled him and he looked at her in astonishment. "You . . . you need that of me?"

"If you are willing to give it. I can't demand it." She began to smooth the oily lather over his face. "Hold still."

He obeyed, his eyes on her face as she shaved him. "Never had a woman shave me before. Do you know what you're doing?" he said when she wiped the razor on a linen cloth.

"Yes," she said, continuing with her task.

"They're sending me away again," he told her a little later. "I'm being posted to the frontier in Italy. I have two more weeks, and then off I go."

"So soon?" In spite of herself, she stared at him in dismay. "Do we have so little time left?"

"Two weeks," he repeated. "I wasn't going to tell you that." His expression darkened as she finished her work and brought wet cloths to rinse his face. "I was going to leave, that's all, and have Belisarius tell you."

"Why?" she asked.

"Why not? There's nothing for me here anymore. Why stay? Why drag you down with me?" He set his jaw. "I shouldn't have come here tonight. I don't know why I did."

"You came because you missed me." She dried his face and looked at him. "Better."

"I miss many things," he said darkly. "I miss . . . pride. I miss everything." He leaned forward, his forehead touching her arm. "But I had to see you. I couldn't help myself. Please believe me, Olivia."

"I'm glad you've come," she said, brushing his matted hair with her hand. "The bath is nearly ready."

He got to his feet slowly. "I . . . I'm a disgrace."

"Not to me," said Olivia as she shed her paenula and the Roman palla she wore under it. "The bath is hot," she warned him as she stepped into the steaming water.

"Christos!" he swore as he joined her. "You want to cook me as well as bite me?"

"Not at the same time," she said lightly, hoping he would take it as a joke.

But his attention had wandered, and he merely smiled as he rubbed his cheeks. "Very close. Not bad."

She had reached for a sponge and was filling it with water when he came up to her, touching her breast with eager, fumbling hands. "Drosos, wait just a bit."

"Why?" He took the sponge from her hands and pulled her into his arms, his mouth hard on hers.

There was only urgency in his movements, no care and no tenderness. He pillaged with his hands, probing and grasping.

Olivia wrenched herself away from him. "Drosos! Stop that."

"I don't want to." He started toward her, a beast after prey. "You want me; I want you."

"Not this way." She reached the edge of her bath and started to pull herself out of the water, but he caught her ankle and dragged her back. She cried out in protest and the side door opened at once.

"Get out of here!" Drosos shouted at Niklos. "This doesn't concern you."

Niklos came into the room with a tray that held a single cup. "If you harm my mistress, you will learn otherwise," he said implacably. He set the tray down beside the pool and looked at Olivia, who had moved away from Drosos. "Do you want me to remain?"

"Bring two drying sheets from the chest by the door,"

she said, knowing that Niklos would use that time to assess the problem.

Drosos had consumed half the contents of the cup before he realized it was not wine but the mixture Olivia had ordered earlier. He emptied the last of it into the water. "What is this dreadful stuff?"

"It might help you feel more yourself," Olivia said with care.

"I am fine," he protested, and then his whole demeanor changed. "No." He lowered his head and began to sob deeply, wrenchingly. When Olivia started toward him, he pushed her away. "Don't."

From the edge of the pool, Niklos gave Olivia an inquiring look, and accepted her sign to leave her alone with Drosos. He withdrew silently, remaining in the hall, ready to answer any summons.

At last Olivia was able to get close enough to Drosos to take his hands in hers. "Oh love," she said, kissing his hands, holding them when he tried to pull away.

"Why don't you leave me alone?" he demanded when he could speak at all.

"Because I love you; because part of you is part of me." She said it evenly, calmly, all the while watching his eyes.

"God and the Angels, you're not pregnant?" he protested.

"No. No, that isn't . . . possible."

He sighed, his breath shuddering. "Well, we're spared that." He took her by the shoulders and shook her, but gently. "I am disgraced. Can't you understand that? I am unworthy."

"Not to me." She kissed him, just his lower lip. "You are Drosos. That is enough."

"Am I? Is it?" He moved away from her. "I must have been more drunk that I thought I was to come here. I swore I wouldn't visit you."

She did not move after him. "Why? To make yourself more miserable than you are?"

"To save you from sharing my disgrace," he said. "I don't want you to be—"

"Yes, you've told me before," she said as she came to his side. "But that means little to me. I am suspect already. You can make little difference in that." She took his hand again. "Drosos, stay with me tonight."

He scowled. "So you can get what you want from me?"

"Yes; because you will have what you want from me." She ignored the bark of angry laughter he gave. "If you want this to be the last, so be it. I will be sad, but that would be the case whenever you left me, however you left me."

His dark eyes could not meet hers. "What is the point? I will be gone soon."

"There are a few things I want to say to you," she told him, swallowing hard against the grief that was chilling her.

"You mean the tales you told me before, about living after I've died? That fable about the blood being the elixir of life? You're as bad as the popes, with their promise of life everlasting if you drink their wine." He launched himself out of the bath and reached for a drying sheet. "Lord God, how I have missed your body." He stared down at her. "All right. I'll stay. We'll have this one last time."

His tone and his attitude were not promising, but Olivia got out of the bath and wrapped herself in the other drying sheet. "If nothing else, you can rest in a clean bed."

"So I can. That's a luxury I won't have again once I reach the north of Italy." He let her lead the way back to her bedchamber. "You're as fine a woman from the back as from the front," he said, patting her rump.

Olivia glanced back at him, not knowing how to evoke the response she longed for. She nodded toward her bed. "I'll take what you have on."

Drosos tossed it across the room, on top of his dalmatica. "Let the slaves tend to it, or that arrogant bondsman of yours." He reached out, pulling her drying sheet off her. "I will miss you, Olivia," he said as he stared at her. "You could use a little more breast—but they come with children, don't they?" As he said this, he brushed his hands over her nipples. "They're pretty; it doesn't matter that they aren't very big."

Olivia listened to him in growing apprehension. She caught one of his hands in hers. "Is that all you want of me?"

"Bigger dugs? No, not all." He grabbed her. "It would be the best thing in the world to get lost in you and stay lost. That's what I want. But I will settle for what I can have." This time his kiss was more skillful, and Olivia let herself respond, hoping to feel a similar accessibility in him. He took her face in his hands and held her for his second kiss. "I never knew any woman like you and I will never know another."

By the time they sank together onto the bed, Olivia had been able to evoke a sporadic contact with him, but she felt him flee this intimacy even as his frenzy for her body increased, and her passion for him was tinged with despair. There had been so much between them, and now he eluded her, shut her out of his soul as his body covered and entered hers.

His release came quickly, seizing him like a palsy. His fingers clutched her as if her flesh would save him from being shaken to bits. He rolled off her and away as quickly as he could, and huddled in the folds of the soft woolen blanket.

Olivia lay with the taste of him on her lips and abjection in her heart. She knew that he would not permit her to reach him again; he would never offer the wholehearted access he had once given unstintingly. She knew, also, that it was not contempt for her, but detestation of himself that held him back, and the pain of that knowledge was cold and keen as a knifeblade.

Drosos sat up suddenly, his hand clapped to the little thread of blood that ran over his collarbone and down his chest. "Christos! You did it again!" He rounded on her, his other hand closed in a fist.

"Drosos?" She was fighting off the anguish that threatened to take hold of her.

"You *bit* me! You drank my blood!" He heaved himself out of the bed.

She raised herself on her elbows. "But I've always—you haven't objected—"

"You're unnatural!" he bellowed.

"Drosos—"

"Monster! *Monster!*"

Seriously alarmed, she got out of her bed and took a hesitant step toward him, one arm out.

"Keep away, monster!" He reached for the heap of his clothes and drying sheet and flung them at her. "Stay back!"

"I won't—"

"Monster!" His voice had risen to a shriek. *"Vampire!"*

She stopped. "But you know that," she said softly. "From the first you knew that."

"Fiends of Hell, I did!" He reached the door latch and yanked it open. "Keep off me, you, or I'll dash your brains out." Naked, he went into the hallway, tugging the door closed behind him.

Olivia stood alone as she listened to his hasty footsteps outside the door. He would find another place in the house to sleep, and later she would see that he was covered. Terrible desolation swept through her, and she went down on her knee to gather up the cloth he had thrown at her. Slowly, automatically, she made a bundle of it and placed it by the door so that it could all be washed in the morning. She moved the way a doll might move, her tragic eyes blank, her thoughts in such turmoil that she could not sort them out yet. She added the bedding to the other bundle, and then sat on the uncovered mattress, trying to keep from capitulating to the despair that clawed at her heart.

"There have been worse times," she whispered, the words making no sense to her. There had been awakening in her own tomb. There had been the day that Regius discovered her with his son. There was the time that she had been trapped in a burning cottage, when she was sure that she would die the true death. There had been Zaminian who had run her through with his sword six times, but never touched her spine. All of them had been more dire than this. But they were in the past; the immediacy of her debacle overwhelmed her. The loss of Drosos engulfed her.

Some little time later she was shocked out of her misery by a loud crash from somewhere near the front of her house.

Gathering one of her bed-curtains around her, Olivia rushed out into the hall. Her sight, keener than others at night, let her find her way quickly and easily to the reception room off the vestibule.

Drosos had come there to drink the wine kept for visitors, and he had consumed two amphorae of it. Now he lay where he had fallen, amid spilled wine and overturned roses.

* * *

A commendation from the Emperor Justinian to his naval fleet.

To the men who have achieved so great a triumph over the ships of Totila, we send our grateful commendation for the superb triumph you have achieved.

The Ostrogothic ships are vanquished and you all share in this victory. Each of you will know the extent of our gratitude in our prayers and our public thanks. For every man who participated in this great campaign there will be a *commemorative coin struck and distributed. To all officers there will be greater rewards, which will be heaped upon them and their families.*

All those who have been in this battle will be honored in a great Mass at Hagia Sophia, and upon the consecration of the entire great basilica, another Mass will be offered, so that the building will be made a more holy monument by the addition of the names of these valiant men who have defended our land from the predations of Totila and have discharged their duty to the Empire with greater valor than has ever been shown before.

There are many tributes that an Emperor values above the riches and treasures of his realm, and a victorious navy is one of them. You have given us more than any Emperor could want, and for that we bless your names and give thanks to God for your courage and might.

From this time on, all men who set out to sea to conquer the ships of Totila may count themselves excused from taxes levied for the benefit of our warriors, either on sea or land, for a greater measure than gold has already been paid, and we disdain to require more of you. Every officer who was part of this undertaking is relieved of taxes on all chariots, palanquins, and boats owned by his family in recognition of the officer's service in our cause.

In this, the Lord's Year 551, we offer up praises to God, His Son and the Holy Spirit for the success of the enterprise, and admonish all loyal subjects within the bounds of the Empire to join with us in this celebration, for surely we are delivered for the purpose of Christian vindication throughout the world.

> *Justinian*
> *Emperor of Byzantion*
> *(his sigil)*

• 8 •

The reception hall in the Censor's house was three times the size of the vestibule, and lined with benches and writing tables. There were three other benches at the center of the room reserved for those about to be questioned by the Censor, for this clearly was not a room intended for anything so frivolous as social entertainment.

Both Panaigios Chernosneus and Konstantos Mardinopolis were waiting for the Guard escort to arrive. Between them huddled a figure more like a collection of sticks held together with rags than a man. One of his eyes was fever-bright, the other was missing entirely. His hands were wrapped in strips of filthy cloth, but the shape of these improvised bandages suggested that part of his fingers were missing.

"When is Captain Vlamos supposed to be here?" Konstantos asked, irritated at being kept waiting. It was one thing for Panaigios to suffer these delays; he, Konstantos, was of too high a position to warrant such treatment.

"His slave said that he was leaving the house immediately. He said there had been no resistance." Panaigios folded his arms. "I suppose there is some reason they are not here yet."

"There had better be," Konstantos said, his eyes hot.

"Perhaps there has been another procession for the returning ships," Panaigios suggested.

"Then Captain Vlamos should use other streets." He

lifted his head as one of his eunuchs came to the door. "What is it?"

"The Guard escort has turned the corner, master. They will be here shortly. Are the Guards to be offered refreshments?"

"Later," Konstantos said, waving the eunuch away.

The slave made a deep reverence and left.

Panaigios hoped that Konstantos might offer him a glass of fruit juice or wine, or even a little water, but he knew better than to ask for it. He concealed a sigh and leaned back, bracing himself against the wall. "Do you think this will take long?"

"Not very long. We have this worthy pope's sworn statement, and he will confront the woman," said Konstantos, nudging the pathetic creature between them. "You will not require long, will you?"

Pope Sylvestros rolled his one eye toward the ceiling. "I have called to Heaven from the depth of my agony and I was shown the path of retribution. I was shown the way of righteousness and my soul rejoiced."

"Will that be enough?" Panaigios asked.

"If the Emperor is satisfied, you and I are not entitled to question him." Konstantos drummed his fingers on the table. "The Censor requests that we deliver our findings to him personally, so that there will be little gossip. There are those whom the Censor does not wish to know of these proceedings."

"Of course," said Panaigios, more fretful than before.

"Be pleased you are serving here," Konstantos recommended. "You and I both stand to advance through this investigation."

Panaigios nodded, feeling sweat gathering on his chest and under his arms. "It is always an honor to serve the Emperor."

Both men heard the front door open and the sound of many voices. Pope Sylvestros started to wail and slid back against the wall as if seeking to make himself invisible.

Captain Vlamos was the first into the enormous reception room. "In the name of the Emperor Justinian, we have carried out our duty," he announced formally.

"Where is the culprit?"

Olivia Clemens stepped around the Captain. "I am not a culprit and I will be grateful if you will not use such words until you have some basis for them." She was dressed in Roman splendor and her carriage was confident and regal.

"She! It is *she!*" screamed Pope Sylvestros, raising his covered hands as if to ward off a blow.

"Who is that unfortunate wretch?" Olivia asked; if his behavior caused her any alarm, there was no outward sign of it.

"He is among those who accuse you," said Konstantos, distaste in his long features. "And it is most improper for you to address any of us directly."

"Since I have been forbidden the right to summon my sponsor, I can think of no alternative. Incidentally, why have I been forbidden to have Belisarius here?" She glanced from Konstantos to Panaigios. "Or am I not allowed to have answers, either? If I am not, then these proceedings are apt to be difficult for all of us."

"Your deportment is shameful." Konstantos had half-risen and was pointing his stylus at her.

"You expect that of me, from what the Captain has told me. Was it that poor creature beside you, or another who said I was without virtue?" She dared not speak Drosos' name for fear that her calm would desert her. He had been gone for over a month, but she had learned a little of him from Belisarius, most of which distressed her as much as their final night together had.

"You flaunt your godlessness in our faces?" said Konstantos in outrage.

"No," Olivia replied, and sat on one of the hard benches. "I flaunt nothing."

"You come here in Roman dress—" Konstantos began.

"Because I am a Roman. I understand that is part of the reason I am here." She touched the fibula on her shoulder before folding her hands in her lap.

"You are here because you are guilty of great and

terrible crimes." Konstantos thundered the accusation before he resumed his seat. "This good pope knows much of you."

"Does he?" Olivia asked. "I wouldn't have thought it." So it was not Drosos who had brought her here, she realized. It had to be another. "What am I supposed to have done?"

"There are three charges," Panaigios said, his voice higher than usual. He cleared his throat and read from the sheet in front of him. "You are implicated in crimes against the Church, witnessed by this pope who vows that he has seen you make pagan sacrifices, and that within your villa in Roma there are objects of pagan worship."

"Which have undoubtedly been looted by now, and so do not exist; very convenient for you, no doubt." Olivia warned herself that she must not be too reckless. These men were capable of condemning her to a slow and painful death that would be as fatal to her as to anyone else. She lowered her eyes and listened.

"There are accusations, brought by those who cannot give witness, that you smuggled goods into the Empire without paying taxes or declaring their worth. Further, it is said that you have kept illegal books in your house, knowing they were banned and aware of the implications of their presence." Panaigios read this in a fast, flat tone, head bowed.

"Again, I must ask what proof you have." Olivia kept her manner subdued. "You say that the accusations are brought by those who cannot testify. That would mean another woman or a slave, or a foreigner who is not part of the Empire. The motives of all such persons are questionable, had they the right to speak out, which they have not."

"The third charge is the most serious," Panaigios went on, glancing once at Konstantos. "It is claimed that you provided and administered the poison that brought about the death of the august lady Antonina."

Olivia was on her feet. "Ridiculous!"

"Be silent!" shouted Konstantos.

"The charge is absurd!" Olivia insisted, but she sat down as she felt Captain Vlamos lay his hand on her shoulder. "What reason would I have for such a terrible deed?"

"You are a widow," said Konstantos. "You have been a friend of the General Belisarius since his campaign in Italy."

"So it follows that I would kill his wife?" Olivia asked in disbelief.

"If you planned to take her place," Konstantos stated.

"I have refused Captain Drosos when he offered marriage." She saw the way Panaigios started at Drosos' name. "Is he among the nameless ones now?" she asked, saddened.

"Captain Drosos was an officer of General Belisarius. He would be willing to serve his General in many ways," Konstantos averred. "It would not be the first time a man held a woman for another man."

Olivia could find no words at first. "You mean that you think Drosos was my lover so that I would be able to marry Belisarius once I killed his wife? Why would Drosos help his General if he knew what I was doing? Unless," she went on more carefully, "you are looking for a way to implicate Belisarius in Antonina's death. That would be laughable."

"You have a fortune." Panaigios refused to raise his head.

"Which Belisarius controls. He has no reason to ally himself with me. He already is in a position to take every coin and all property he has secured for me." She felt the first stirring of panic and forced herself to ignore them.

"In Roma, this pope saw your villa, and in it he found certain compounds that can be used as poisons." Konstantos plucked at Pope Sylvestros' ragged sleeve. "Tell her what you saw."

"I saw Angels descending from Heaven, and each one carried a gem of a different color. All of them had wings of fire and they flew over me—" Pope Sylvestros said in a sing-song.

"Stop him," Konstantos ordered Panaigios, who tugged ineffectively at the man.

"—and their wings made the sound of great whirlwinds, and—"

"Surely you do not expect me to take these accusations to heart, do you?" Olivia tossed her head. "What purpose do you think any of this serves? You bring that . . . wreck of a man here, who knows nothing but that Angels have come to him. You let him speak. You mention things that have been said by those who are not permitted to testify as if that could have some bearing on the matter. Am I supposed to be so contrite that I offer a confession to you?"

"You are not to speak at all," Panaigios said, his voice going up again.

"You are a woman of dangerous repute." Konstantos pointed at her again, his arm quivering. "You are not simply a Roman whore who has traded on her profession to come to this city; you are—or you claim to be—of noble background, of a gens that would be horrified to see what you have done."

"But I tell you I have done nothing wrong," Olivia said in a reasonable manner. "I am a widow and I do not seek to marry again. My husband's Will is specific about that. I have had one lover since I came here, who was my lover before, and that is Captain Drosos, who has been posted back to the Italian frontier. You seek to make this seem disrespectful when it is nothing of the sort."

"You have herbs and spices in your house," Konstantos said.

"In that I am no different than any other house holder in Konstantinoupolis." Olivia was finding it difficult to remain in unruffled control of herself; her indignation was increasing with every word Konstantos addressed to her. "As to my few remaining Roman goods, there is nothing significant in them, unless you wish to claim that anyone with a bust of an ancestor is worshipping pagan gods." This last was a deliberate slight to Konstantos, who was known to keep portraits of his grandfathers in his private apartments next to his ikonostasis.

"You are clever, and you have Roman guile." Konstantos turned to Panaigios. "The accusation about the poisons; you have it there?"

"I do," said Panaigios, taking care not to look at Olivia, who captivated him.

As Konstantos took the pages from the Censor's secretary, he held them up, showing them to Olivia, who was too far away to read them. "Here we have a report from one who works for the Censor and the good of the Empire."

"You mean a paid spy in a household, probably Belisarius' or mine," said Olivia evenly.

"That is what a dishonest person might believe," Konstantos allowed. "This person states that you have often visited Belisarius' house."

"Of course I have; he's my sponsor." For all her outward scorn, Olivia was listening carefully, aware that this was the only accusation that might cause her trouble.

"And nothing more, or so you claim." Konstantos cleared his throat. "This person describes the number of times you have been at the house, and remarks that you have paid visits to Antonina while you were there."

"Not every time," Olivia corrected him. "I was permitted to speak with her only when she felt well enough to have a visitor, and that was rarely, since she was so ill."

"Doubtless," Konstantos said smoothly, and Olivia wondered what trap she had entered. "You." He poked the demented pope at his side. "What have you seen?"

"I saw at the house of this Roman woman, at her villa outside the walls of Roma, vials and jars and other containers of many substances that were known to be dangerous. There was Purple Slipper and Wolfsbane and hemp as well as Armenian poppies. It was said that she was known to be expert with these herbs, and that there were many who came to her over the years." He recited his information as if he had memorized it badly. "I learned from monks at a nearby monastery who keep to the teachings of Saint Ambrose of Milano. They informed me that the great lady who owned the villa was a sorceress." He fell silent, then cried out, "I am treading the way, Holy Spirit. I am reaching out to You so that You may see what I have done to make amends for my sins and crimes. I am repentant, Holy Spirit. Bear witness to my deeds."

"Yes, yes," said Panaigios, patting Pope Sylvestros' arm and trying to quiet him. "Yes, we know how you strive."

"To make amends," he insisted, his one eye fixing on Konstantos. "You promised me that I would not have to beg if I would bear witness to what I saw in Italy."

Konstantos was so angry that he found it hard to speak. "You will be silent now," he ordered through his teeth.

"In effect, this miserable man has been offered a bribe if he will speak against me," said Olivia, turning toward Captain Vlamos. "What do you think of this, Captain Vlamos? You have heard the allegations and you say nothing."

"It's not for me to say, one way or another. I am here to carry out the commands of the Censor, his officers, and the commands of the Emperor." He spoke woodenly, and he refused to look at Olivia.

"Tell me," Olivia said, addressing Panaigios, "when you questioned my bondsman, did anything he said cause you to think that I might be as sinister a person as this . . . this pope has said?"

"Your bondsman is your bondsman." Konstantos would not permit Panaigios to answer.

"And your witness is demented," Olivia said, her control slipping away. She dug her nails into the palms of her hands and concentrated on the pain in order to master herself. "My bondsman has served me many years. He—if he were allowed to speak here, which he is not—might tell you otherwise. I admit I know some of the lore of herbs, as do most owners of villas in the country. Your own citizens probably have similar supplies, and for similar reasons. If you have decided that this is significant, there are many, much closer to the Emperor and the

Censor, who must share suspicion with me." She thought, as she said it, that she might have inadvertently touched on the truth.

"You are being questioned now," Konstantos shouted. "And you are not permitted to speak."

"Then send for my sponsor and let him know of your suspicions. Or would that interfere?" Olivia got to her feet again. "Belisarius is required by law to be present if there are formal charges laid against me, since he is responsible for me. Yet you refuse to send for him. Therefore you are not making formal charges. Or if you are making formal charges, you do so illegally." She looked at the three men in turn. "You need to find someone to blame, and I am safest, for I have no family and I am a foreign woman. How convenient that I also have money that you will be entitled to claim." She turned to Captain Vlamos. "Well?"

"I must not speak with you, great lady," the Captain said in some embarrassment.

"Don't these proceedings seem irregular to you?" When she received no answer from him, she went on, "I know from Belisarius himself that you are considered an honorable soldier. I ask you now to inform him or my bondsman of what has taken place here, so that one or the other of them may begin to seek remedy for this . . . this travesty." She gave her attention to Konstantos once more. "That is part of your purpose, isn't it? You want to find someone guilty for the death of Antonina so that there will be no more questions about it. You think that if you accuse me, Belisarius will ask nothing about me, and you will never have to answer for your acts." She wondered if perhaps Konstantos had guessed correctly, and Belisarius, overcome with grief, would refuse to pursue her interests.

"I have heard too much from you," Konstantos said in a low, deadly tone. "You have been permitted more leeway because as a Roman we know you do not understand proper conduct. We will enter the testimony of Pope Sylvestros in our records, and we will send all to

Belisarius for him to reply to the accusations. But you, you are to be detained until it is decided that there are grounds enough to review your case." He slapped the tabletop.

"O Lord, You strike in wrath and in thunder," intoned Pope Sylvestros, his hands pressed together. "I listen and I hear the sound of Your destruction promised to the sinful world."

"Make him be quiet!" Konstantos shouted, rounding on Panaigios, who had dropped the vellum sheets he held.

"I . . . I . . ." Panaigios began, then said nothing more as he pulled on Pope Sylvestros' arm in a futile attempt to get his attention.

"The thunder of destruction and the thunder of creation fill all Heaven and shake the earth," Pope Sylvestros exulted. "The tread of the Lord shakes the world and the cities fall before Him."

"If it is proven that you are a sorceress," Konstantos went on, doing his best to ignore Pope Sylvestros, "then you will be tied in a sack and thrown in the sea, which is the fate of all sorcerers and sorceresses."

"Tied in a sack and thrown in the sea," Olivia repeated with fascination and horror. Water would not kill her, and she could not drown, but she would be immobilized until her flesh gave way or she was eaten. And for however long that took, she would be conscious. "You condemn me to Hell," she said softly, with great feeling, for to her it was no more than the truth.

"It is your action that condemns you to Hell," said Konstantos with satisfaction, misunderstanding her. "We are only instruments of the Emperor who seeks to emulate God on earth with wisdom and judgment."

"That might be thought prideful," Olivia said in a thoughtful voice. "And as I recall, pride is a sin."

"You are not one to speak against the Emperor or the Lord God," Konstantos warned Olivia. He was about to go on when another man entered the room and approached him.

Both Panaigios and Konstantos made a reverence to

Kimon Athanatadies, and Panaigios held out the list of charges that he had read earlier.

The Court Censor took the sheet and looked over them. "Atta Olivia Clemens," he said. "I recall we have had some questions about her. Sorcery. A grave charge." He looked at Pope Sylvestros. "Who is that?"

"A witness." Panaigios had the grace to look chagrined at this admission. "He is Pope Sylvestros."

"I recall that name. He has been shown to have committed criminal acts." Athanatadies tapped the edge of the sheet. "I trust that he is not your only witness."

The cold expression in the Censor's eyes subdued Konstantos' zeal. "We are trying to find others. We have information from those who cannot testify, and in time we will obtain access to those who can."

"See that you do," said Athanatadies. "I must defend every decision made by my staff to the Emperor." He stared blankly at the far wall. "The Emperor is determined to root out all wrongdoing in the Empire. We are mandated to act for him. But if we abuse his authority, then we are culpable." He slid his fingers over his moist palms. "Have care that you do not exceed your authority, Konstantos. And you as well, Panaigios. If you do, you will have to answer for it." He handed the vellum back to Panaigios and looked toward Olivia. "Where is your sponsor, woman?"

"That is a question I have been asking since I was brought here, Censor," Olivia answered with asperity.

"Her sponsor is Belisarius and there is reason to think that this woman poisoned the General's wife," Konstantos said, not quite defiantly.

"Is that any reason not to have him here?" Athanatadies asked, thinking what Justinian might require under these circumstances. "He should be sent for."

"At once?" Panaigios said.

"How do we explain to him?" Konstantos said at the same time.

Athanatadies did not want to make any more decisions; he had been upbraided for the last two and he was afraid of the Emperor's demands. He stared in silence at a place on the floor about halfway between him and Olivia. At last he said, "Detain her."

"What?" Olivia cried out, her reserve gone. "By what right do you 'detain' me?" She did not want to be kept in a cell again, lost to the world and conveniently forgotten. This had happened to her in the past, and in many ways it was worse than awakening in her tomb. In a cell, she had become ravenous, not only for blood but for intimacy, for the exchange that satisfied more than simple hunger.

"By right as the Court Censor," said Athanatadies, his expression rigid. "You have been accused of serious acts. Until we have more to support these accusations, I remand you into the custody of Captain Vlamos. There are quarters in this building for those accused whose cases are being investigated; we maintain them for such as you." He studied Olivia for a little while. "It will not be too unpleasant, if that is what troubles you."

"Locked up and isolated is always unpleasant, Censor," she said with hard intent. "The trappings—" She shrugged.

"There is the dungeon, if you prefer," Konstantos offered, gloating.

Olivia ignored him, keeping her attention on Kimon Athanatadies. "You will see that my sponsor is notified of your investigation and the charges against me."

"Yes; in due time." He cleared his throat and moved away from her.

"When is this 'due time' you speak of?" Olivia asked, making no attempt to disguise her sarcasm.

"It is when it is," Athanatadies said without looking around, and spoke next to Konstantos and Panaigios. "I want to be kept abreast of your findings. Do not think you are being excused from your work here. Something must be found, something more than that disgusting pope. He would be unreliable at best."

"Yes, Censor," said Konstantos. "We will continue our work."

"And see that you find testimony from those who can

give it; the gossip of slaves will not be welcome, even as supporting reports. Slaves always think ill of foreign masters, and you know that as well as I do." He started toward his side door, then turned back. "You may be sure that Belisarius will begin asking questions in a few days. You had better have some answers. He may be in disgrace with the Emperor, but he is still a General and he has some authority."

"Of course, Censor," said Konstantos.

"You are not to do anything hasty. This charge of sorcery is the most worrisome. Be certain you have proof, or drop it." He did not want any of the decisions he had made regarding heretics and sorcerers called into question now, for Justinian had already indicated that he wanted to be rid of all of them at once, as he had been rid of the pernicious books at Alexandria. As Censor, it would be his task to carry out such a command, but he feared that the confusion that would result, the charges and countercharges, would lead to an unrest that the Emperor did not appreciate, and he would be unable to explain. "I do not want to be told that you have heard rumors, or that there are those who think she might be enchanting cats. Is that understood. You must be able to demonstrate your charge or you must remove it."

From her place on the bench, Olivia said, "You sound almost Roman, Censor."

"You do yourself no good speaking to me that way," Athanatadies told her, though he continued to look at Konstantos. "In ten days, I will want to have word about this woman. If there is no word, you will have to give reason why you have not done what is required of you. And if you cannot, then you will have to answer to Belisarius." With that last ominous promise, he was gone.

The reception chamber was silent; Panaigios shuffled papers.

"The earth shows worship and reverence to God," called Pope Sylvestros. "In homage to the Might of God, the people are silent."

"Then you be silent, too," snapped Konstantos. He

438 · *Chelsea Quinn Yarbro*

signaled to Captain Vlamos. "You know where the detention rooms are. See that she has one of the better ones, with a good bed." He favored Olivia with a malicious smile. "That is in case you wish to entertain friends."

Olivia had been expecting some attack, and she did not respond to it. "Captain Vlamos, lead the way."

"I'm sorry, great lady," he said, "but I must bind your hands and keep hold of the thongs."

"Of course." She held out crossed wrists. She wanted to lash out with her feet and hands, then flee, but that was worse than folly. "Not too tight, I pray."

As Captain Vlamos secured the thongs, he asked, "Will this be too bad?"

"No," she said honestly. As she was about to be led away, she glanced at the three men. "When the day comes that this happens to you—and do not think that impossible—remember me." Then she nodded to Captain Vlamos and went out of the chamber toward the detention rooms at the other end of the enormous building.

* * *

Text of a letter from Niklos to Belisarius.

To the distinguished General who is sponsor to my mistress Olivia Clemens, my greetings and supplications.

Six days ago my mistress was taken by the Guard to answer questions of the Censor's officers. She has not returned home since then, and all attempts to discover what has become of her have met with nothing.

Since I am a bondsman and my mistress is a Roman

there is little I can do beyond what has already been done. Therefore I have to ask that you act to find out what has happened to her and to take all measures to see that she is restored at once to her house and to your protection.

I had a few words with a Captain Vlamos, who was one of those who came to take her to the Censor, and he told me that the Censor has an accusation of sorcery against my mistress, which is not only a defamation of her character, but it places her in gravest danger with no means to refute such a charge.

Should you require it of me, I will place the resources of this household at your disposal to aid in any and all ways possible to secure the release and total exoneration of my mistress as well as demanding and receiving damages for what she has had to endure on these false and mendacious charges.

It is my belief that those who have brought these charges did so with malicious intent, for everything they have said has served to divide her from her household, her goods, and your protection. Since you have not been called, I have assumed that you are likely to be implicated by these charges or be found to be the victim of what is alleged.

Captain Vlamos has said that he will speak with you if you require it of him, for that is his responsibility as an officer of the Guard, since you are my mistress' sponsor here. I urge you to do so as soon as possible, for there is no telling what indignities might have been forced upon my mistress, who has already suffered enough in coming to this city. If the Captain will tell you what we need to know, then I will take action at once and do my utmost to save my mistress from any more travail.

I must warn you that I have been informed that sorcerers are executed by being put into a sack and thrown into the sea. I do not want to make demands of you, great General, but I am certain that neither of us wish to have that happen to Olivia. Since those executions are carried out in secret, I am afraid that we have less time to discover her whereabouts and take action than we might have under other circumstances.

While it pains me to intrude on your mourning and grief, I would rather do this than add to your losses, for that is what is likely to happen if you will not insist on some resolution of this dreadful business at once.

The Censor's officers Konstantos and Panaigios are pursuing the case for the Censor and the Emperor. They will not answer me, but they must answer you. I beg you to approach them at once, for to tell truth, I fear for my mistress more than I ever have in my life.

> Niklos Aulirios
> bondsman to
> Atta Olivia Clemens

P.S. The slave Zejhil has asked to be permitted to aid you in any way she can. She carries this letter, and I have given her permission to remain with you and to act in any capacity you deem necessary. Certainly you may do so as Olivia's sponsor, but in case the Censor decides that there is a valid charge and attempts to seize all of my mistress' household and goods, you will be able to retain Zejhil. Listen to her, Belisarius. She has been a great help to us. With this, I include Olivia's endorsement of Zejhil's writ of manumission, along with a request that she be given thirty gold pieces when she is freed. I trust you will honor my mistress' decision in regard to this slave.

• 9 •

Shortly after Captain Vlamos left Belisarius' house, Simones requested permission to be gone for an hour, and so was not present when Eugenia arrived and begged to speak with the General.

The eunuch slave Arius admitted her and told her that his master was not to be disturbed.

"I have to speak with him," Eugenia said, her eyes brimming with tears. "He is my only hope, and if he won't see me, I have no other chance to save myself."

Arius knew Eugenia from her friendship with Antonina, and for that reason he faltered. Belisarius might want to see this old friend of his dead wife, but then again, the presence of Eugenia might recall his loss. Weighing these two considerations only became more puzzling, and so at last he said, "Wait here, great lady, and I will speak with my master."

Eugenia looked about the vestibule a little wildly. "Let me sit in the smaller reception room," she said, precariously near begging. "I don't want . . . anyone to know I am here. The matter is confidential." She held out a silver coin. "You must tell no one but your master that I have come. No one. No other member of this household."

Arius took the coin, more out of surprise than greed. "Of course, great lady." He tucked the coin under his belt and went to Belisarius' study.

"Tell her I'm busy," said Belisarius, who was deep in conversation with the Tartar slave from the Roman woman's household.

441

"She is weeping, General," said Arius, who assumed he owed Eugenia that much for the coin.

Belisarius sighed. "Where is she?"

"In the smaller reception room." Arius made a reverence to his master. "She is very . . . upset."

Zejhil rose and made her reverence. "I have more than enough to do. I will be busy for the rest of the afternoon with the tasks you have set me. You must attend to your guest, of course." Without any fuss, she withdrew.

"All right," Belisarius said with a resigned hitch to his shoulders. "Show me to her, Arius."

Eugenia was seated in the darkest corner of the room, her back to the door, hunched over. She had dressed plainly and without any of her customary ornaments and jewels. As Arius came into the room, she started, then recovered herself and rose. "I am very sorry to disturb you at this terrible time, General," she began with proper formality.

"If you disturbed me, it must be for something more than a consolation call," he said tersely, motioning to Arius to leave them alone. "You have something you wanted to say to me."

"Yes," she said, color mounting in her face. "It's very difficult. I don't know where to begin." She was hardly audible at these last words.

Belisarius took his place on the padded bench. "Shall I send for some refreshments?"

"No!" Her protest was a wail. "No. I don't want anyone to know I am here, no one in your household." She caught the edge of her paenula and began to twist it in her fingers. "I tried to tell you this before. If I could bring myself to write, it might have been easier to set it down, for I would not have to see your face while I told you." She cleared her throat, then coughed; neither effort raised her voice or her confidence. "I . . . I've tried to do this before, but I have been afraid."

"Why didn't you speak to your sponsor?" Belisarius asked her reasonably.

"My sponsor?" Her features crumbled under her emotions. "Oh, I could not. I would be cast out for what has happened, and he would never believe that I was telling the truth. He would not be able to do anything. He would not want to. There would be too much shame, and for that he would want me to suffer, not to find the answer for me." This tangled protest caught a little of Belisarius' interest.

"Are you saying that you must speak to me about one of my officers?" He knew of her unsatisfactory dalliance with Chrysanthos, but was reluctant to think that his officer would behave badly to a former lover.

"No, not . . . not officers. Someone . . . someone in your household." She put her hands to her face and wept, trying to keep from making a sound.

Belisarius rose and went to her. "Let me summon one of the slaves to—"

"No. No slaves. No." She pushed him away from her with repugnance. "No slaves!"

Now Belisarius was both troubled and curious. He knew that he had interpreted the reason for Eugenia's visit incorrectly and he was beginning to think that there was something to be learned from her. "Come. I will not insist you be aided if you would rather not." He indicated a place on the other bench, but she retreated back into the shadows once more. "What is it, Eugenia?"

She shook her head, shuddering with tears and fright. "I can't."

"But if you came here to tell me something—" He approached her slowly, with care, as if she were an animal that was only half-tame.

"I have to tell you," she whispered. "I have to."

He watched her face, seeing the shine of her eyes and the gleam of tears; the rest was indistinct. "Then tell me, Eugenia."

"It's . . . very difficult." She trembled. "But it has to end. It has to. I can't . . . go on." She bowed over, her head caught in her hands and pressed to her knees.

Belisarius waited, trying to keep his imagination from building hideous scenarios to account for Eugenia's behavior. "When you are able, tell me. I will listen."

"Oh, God and Saints!" she screamed, the sound muffled by her hands. "I can't. If he finds . . . out. Don't tell." She looked up imploringly. "Give me your word you will not tell him."

"Tell whom?" Belisarius asked, assuming she meant either her sponsor or Chrysanthos. Her answer astonished him.

"Simones."

"Simones?" He repeated the name as if it were unfamiliar. "Why should it matter what . . ." He did not go on for a short while, and when he did, his words were sharper. "What about Simones?"

"He . . ." She found a reserve of discipline she did not know until then she had. "He came to me, oh, some time ago. He said that he would see you condemned as a traitor, that he was being paid by the officers of the Censor to find the means to discredit you completely. He said that if I confessed this to you, you would not believe me, and he would deny it."

"Simones," said Belisarius.

"He . . . demanded I be . . . I be his lover." Her voice sank and her courage nearly failed her. "He boasted of how he would bring you down, and all those who were close to you. He said he had bribed Antonina's physician to—"

"To poison her?" Belisarius asked in a low, soft voice.

Eugenia blinked. "Yes."

"There was a letter from the physician. He left it . . . in Antonina's room. For me." He clasped his hands together in front of him as if they were holding a sword.

"And?" Though she was frightened, for the first time Eugenia had hope that she might not be dismissed. "Was there something in the letter?"

"The physician was paid to poison Antonina," Belisarius said heavily. "I informed the Guard but nothing has happened. Now, with the other—" He stopped abruptly. "Tell me about Simones."

"He said he had to have my help, but . . . I don't know." She felt her face turn scarlet. "I think he wanted to have someone to command, someone he could bully and threaten. He liked that better than anything else between us." She put her hand to the neck of her paenula. "I . . . I thought I had to do as he ordered. I thought he would say I was consorting with a slave, and my sponsor would hear of it, and then I would be cast out for what I had done. I was afraid. You understand that, don't you?"

"I understand," said Belisarius, and for the first time, he did.

"I didn't dare refuse him. He said he would accuse me of conspiring against Antonina, that I would be judged guilty. I cannot speak for myself, and although he cannot speak against me, he could implicate me, and—" It took an effort but she stopped her rush of words. "He told me he had arranged for the poisoning of your wife. He said that he had done other things as well. He wants to bring down everyone associated with you. He is determined to . . . to ruin you, to destroy you. He wants to know that he arranged your downfall." She turned to Belisarius. "I am sorry. I am so very, very sorry that I let any of this happen, and that once it happened that I permitted it to continue, but truly, I did not know what to do. I didn't want to participate in what he was doing. I thought I wasn't . . . important enough. But—"

"But Antonina is dead," Belisarius said heavily. "And she died because of poison. I should have seen what was happening. I should have suspected. Oh, Lord God, how could I not have seen it?" He lunged away from her, his arms crossed over his body. "How could I not have known."

"General—"

"I *did* know. Christos, I knew." He blundered into the wall and swung around toward Eugenia. "Why didn't you come to me when it might have done some good? Why didn't you tell me when she could have been saved? *Why?*" He brought his arm up, and then held it, seeing

Eugenia cower, her face white, her eyes glazed with fear. "I won't hurt you," he said dully, stepping back from her. "It wouldn't change anything."

"But I tried," Eugenia protested in a small voice. "I tried once to talk Simones out of what he was doing; it was the third time he came to me, and I spent as much time as I could telling him why he ought not to do what . . . he was doing." She said this tentatively, like a child unsure of an angry parent.

"And? What happened?" He was exhausted. All his energy seemed to have run out of him, leaving him listless and numb.

"He . . . exacted vengeance. He made certain I would not do that again." She lowered her voice. "He used me. I have never been used so by a man before. I . . . was sick, afterward."

"Simones," Belisarius said.

"He is an angry, dangerous man," Eugenia said, reciting a litany she had told herself since her subjugation had begun.

"Simones." He nodded slowly. "So efficient, so dependable. So devoted. I assumed—" He lowered his head. "Antonina trusted him. She liked him better than any other slave in the household. Whenever she . . . she had had a . . . a bad night, she would send for Simones, for he cheered her." Without warning he hurled one of the small tables across the room; it smashed and broke against the opposite wall. "Of course he cheered her. He was enjoying his handiwork."

Two slaves appeared at the door of the reception room, one of them visibly frightened.

"Leave us alone!" Belisarius ordered. "And tell those Guards watching my house that I am going to the house of the Censor. I want them to be ready." He lurched to his feet. "I have let too much get beyond me. I have not done all that I need to do."

"What . . . what will happen to me?" Eugenia pleaded, her terror returning.

"You will be safe; I give you my word on it. If I am

betrayed, then that may be another matter." His smile was hard, cynical. "Who knows what Fallen Angels have flocked to the Censor's standard? It may be that I am already too late." He went to the door, saying to her as he left, "Have one of my men escort you back to your house. I think that you had better not still be here when Simones returns."

"Belisarius!" The force of her cry stopped him.

"What is it?"

"Say you forgive me. I never meant to be such a coward, I never thought it would go this far. Please. Forgive me." She reached out to him, suddenly very vulnerable and fragile.

"Forgive you? How can I do that while Simones breathes? Once he is gone, ask me again." With that he was gone from the reception room, striding toward his chambers, moving in a way that his soldiers knew better than his household. "Arius! I want my white dalmatica and my gold pallium set out. At once. I want a basin to wash and I want oil for my hair. Now!"

The eunuch slave hurried after him. "I will have it done, master. At once."

"Order the roan harnessed to my triumphal chariot and have two of the horsemen accompany me. Mounted. On the matched bays. Give the order while I prepare." He slammed his private door closed on Arius and began to undress.

In less than an hour, he was ready to leave his house. Since he was no longer permitted to bear arms, he had arrayed himself with every honor presented to him for his military achievements. His chest flashed and glowed with jewels and gold. He had donned his golden wreath presented to him for his victories in Africa, and he carried the three bound staves that were the sign of his rank. As he climbed into his chariot, he nodded to the two mounted slaves who flanked him. "Don't get ahead of the Guard. They'd be insulted."

The older of the two, a grizzle-haired veteran from Emisis, touched his left shoulder with his right hand in salute. "Do we go ahead of you, master?"

"Either side of the chariot." Belisarius indicated the places. "Don't hurry. Give them plenty of time to know I'm coming." There was a grimness about his mouth and his eyes narrowed as he spoke.

The two slaves exchanged glances, but said nothing, putting their mounts into movement at the walk, taking care to observe the form their master required.

Little as the two Guards liked it, Belisarius ordered this small procession to go past two of the largest markets and the front of Hagia Sophia where the workers were laboring to complete the new basilica on the foundations of the old. From within the building came the sound of chanting that faltered as Belisarius passed the open narthex. Behind them hundreds of people followed, but at a safe distance.

The Guards at the gate of the Censor's palace blocked the way with their spears until Captain Vlamos was found. He came out of the main doors, a sword in his hand, and looked up at the chariot and Belisarius.

"What is your purpose for coming, General?" he asked with respect; Belisarius might be out of favor with the Emperor, but the Byzantine soldiers regarded him as their greatest hero.

"I must speak with the Censor or with his officers. At once. It concerns a crime, and a . . . negligence on the part of his staff." He looked directly at Captain Vlamos. "Will you let me pass? As you see, I am unarmed."

"The Censor is at prayers," the Captain said, for the first time disappointed in the Censor.

"I will wait. I do not wish to interrupt his devotion." He secured the reins of his chariot and stepped out of it. "If one of your stablehands will see to my horse?"

"Yes." Captain Vlamos clapped his hands sharply, and as soon as one of the Censor's slaves responded, he issued a number of orders. Then he stood while Belisarius came up to him. "It is an honor to be of help, General."

Belisarius' face had grown craggy in the last few years, and his hair was almost white; in his splendid dress he was as imposing as a metropolitan at the high altar. His attitude was stern as he spoke to Captain Vlamos. "There have been accusations laid here that I have information to disprove. What is troubling is that no one told me of the accusations, though they concerned both my dead wife and the Roman woman I sponsor. The Censor owes me a little of his time and some clarification." He was no taller than Captain Vlamos, but he seemed to tower over the Guard officer.

"I . . ." He looked around, then motioned to the Guards who had accompanied Belisarius to step back out of hearing. "I know something of this."

"Tell me."

"I . . . I heard the accusations brought against the Roman lady." He looked around hastily, to be certain they were not overheard. "One of the articles against her stated that she . . . she had a hand in your . . . wife's death."

Belisarius gave an impatient wave to his hand. "I know she did not; I know precisely who is responsible, and I have a statement to support what I say." He moved, standing now with his feet apart and braced, as if he were preparing to attack. "I require some explanation about all of this. I have to know who suborned one of my slaves to work against me."

"It's a bad business," Captain Vlamos said, his lorica feeling much too tight.

"And it must be settled."

"Yes." He indicated the door. "I will summon an escort. It is necessary; you understand." This last was an apology and both men realized it.

The reception room was neither the grandest or the meanest; it had two tall ikonostases flanking three narrow windows that looked out on a sluggish fountain. Three padded benches were arranged around a low, square table. Neither Belisarius nor the three Guards who accompanied him sat down.

Captain Vlamos had spoken to the majordomo, informing him that the General's task was urgent. He doubted that he could hurry the Censor, but he felt obliged to try. When the majordomo suggested that wine and fruit be brought for Belisarius, Captain Vlamos declined. He remained with Belisarius and the two officers who served as the General's escort, saying nothing, growing more agitated as time dragged on.

When Kimon Athanatadies finally entered the reception room, Captain Vlamos was prepared to upbraid him for the long delay, but he was held in check by Belisarius, who saluted the Censor.

"I am sorry to have to disturb you, Censor," he said as if the wait had not been insulting. "I know you are busy on the Emperor's behalf."

Athanatadies gave a guarded nod. "I strive to discharge the tasks he sets me."

"Yes; I know from my campaigns how strict his expectations can be," Belisarius went on, as if greeting a foreign envoy. "It is one of the demands made on those willing to rise as high as you have."

"What is your intention?" Athanatadies asked, trying to gain control of their encounter.

"Why, to assist you in one of your investigations," he said blandly. "If you had notified me of it, I would have been able to spare you time and effort, and perhaps you would have apprehended a criminal before he could do more damage." He looked around the room, indicating the Guards. "Would you rather speak privately? I am not permitted to carry weapons."

This last, instead of reassuring Athanatadies, made him more restive. He knew that if Belisarius wished, he could dispatch him with nothing more than his hands. "Captain Vlamos, dismiss your men, but remain with me."

When the two Guards were gone, Captain Vlamos posted himself at the door, protecting the Censor and the General from spies and each other.

"What is it you wish to say?" Athanatadies inquired as he sat down on the largest of the padded benches.

Belisarius went to the windows, positioning himself between the ikonostases, the light behind him so that the

Censor could not see his face clearly. "I want," he said in a light, neutral tone, "to see justice done for once."

"For once?" the Censor demanded.

"Let's not waste time in debate, Censor. You have accused the Roman lady I sponsor of several crimes, including the murder of my wife. The physician who was responsible for her death left a confession—a copy of it was sent to you—that indicated he had been corrupted by a member of my household, a slave. I have learned which slave it is, and that he claims to be working at your request. He believes that he cannot be blamed or punished for any of the wrongs he has done because he has been assured that you will protect him."

Kimon Athanatadies smoothed the loose ends of his pallium. "I am not certain I understand you."

"I thought I spoke plainly," said Belisarius. "Is this slave of mine spying for you, or one of your officers? If so, did you give him permission to have my wife killed? Because if you did"—his voice was suddenly soft and cold—"I will see you die for it."

"I would never authorize such a sinful thing," Athanatadies protested smoothly. "If your slave thought he would be allowed to act in that way, he was mistaken. If he did anything at all." The last was an afterthought.

"The physician said he did."

"Oh, yes, the confession you claim was sent here. I do not recall seeing it. I will have to ask my officers; they deal with so much that occasionally something is overlooked." He hoped that Belisarius was far enough away from him not to smell the sharp sweat that betrayed his fear.

"Such as a murder confession." Belisarius made his tone light again. "I am certain that if you search for the document, you will find it. Then you can start to dismiss the charges brought against Atta Olivia Clemens. And when that is done, you will tell me what punishment will be given to my traitorous slave."

Athanatadies coughed delicately. "Which would you rather have: the Roman woman free, or the slave condemned and punished?" For the first time since he entered the room, Athanatadies felt he had some power, and it almost made up for the trepidation that had gripped him.

"What?" Belisarius stared at the Censor. "What did you say?"

"Would you rather free the Roman lady or punish your slave? It's a simple matter of choosing one or the other."

"Are you offering me a bargain?" Belisarius said in disbelief. "I come for justice and you barter with me?"

Athanatadies put his fingertips together. "General, the Emperor is determined to be rid of the Roman influence in this city. He is not inclined to look indulgently on crimes when a Roman is implicated. He is also determined to punish erring slaves. A man who is in your position will not do well by asking too much of Justinian; he regards you with suspicion already and it would not take much for him to decide you are actively his enemy. If that happens, then neither your slave nor the Roman woman will get what they deserve." He paused, giving Belisarius time to consider.

"You will do one, but not the other?" Belisarius asked harshly.

"I can see no way to do both," Athanatadies said.

"What you mean is that you will not act in both cases. You refuse to risk your position, and because I am in disfavor you are free to abuse your trust." He studied Athanatadies. "You enjoy this. You are reveling in your authority. It pleases you to be despotic."

"Those words could be fatal, General." Athanatadies sat straighter, one hand clutching the crucifix that hung around his neck.

"But there is no witness to them," Belisarius said gently. "Is there, Captain Vlamos?"

"I heard nothing disrespectful, General," said the Captain of the Guard.

"You will answer for this insolence, Captain," Athanatadies warned.

"Then I will have to reveal the offer you have made. I

don't think it would be appreciated." His face was blank and he spoke in a monotone, but all three men understood.

"Since you insist," Belisarius said evenly, "we will strike your noxious bargain. But I warn you, Athanatadies, that your victory will be Pyrrhic; this is only the first skirmish—you have yet to enter battle."

* * *

Part of a series of clandestine orders from Kimon Athanatadies to the Guard Captain in charge of detained suspects.

In regard to the apostate pope called Tomus, the Censor in the name of the Emperor requires you to strip him bare in the narthex of Hagia Sophia and batter him with workmen's mallets until no bone within him is left unbroken. He is then to be hung from ropes in the narthex where those Christians of catechumen status may see the consequences of the loss of faith.

In regard to the musician Narsissos, his tongue is to be cut out and he is to be branded on the arm and the chest so that all will know he fouled his mouth with libelous and unholy songs. Also, the fingers of his right hand are to be broken so that he may no longer pluck a lyre.

In regard to the traduced slave Simones, he is to be taken to the public courtyard of the Censor's house where he is to be flayed in strips, so that his skin will hang in tatters from him. Let care be taken that he not die too soon, for when he is flayed, he is to be left for the curs to devour.

In regard to Pope Sylvestros, who is demented: let him be immured in one of the cells in the new extension of city walls where his prayers may strengthen the fortifications and where he will be no harm to anyone. Further, let him be visited often to hear what he is saying. If it is treasonous, then his cell must be walled up entirely.

In regard to the Roman sorceress Olivia Clemens, she is to be held for twenty-one days, until the next full moon, at which time she is to be sewn in a sack and taken into the Sea of Marmara. The boat is to leave the east end of the Bucolean Harbor at the end of the first quarter of the night. Because this is a dangerous sorceress, the sailors are to be told in advance that she is not to be listened to or believed.

In regard to the desecrater of tombs, the heretic Pthos, he is to be sewn into the skin of a fresh-killed goat and taken to the highest Guard tower on the city walls at dawn, and left there exposed to the sun for three entire days, at which time his corpse is to be thrown to the swine to eat, said swine then to be used to feed other heretic suspects.

In regard to Szoni, the smuggler of condemned books, he is to be taken to the main portal of the Emperor's Forum where he is to be flogged with parchment lashes until he dies.

• 10 •

At sunset Captain Vlamos came to Olivia's cell for the last time. He stood in the door, not quite certain what to say. "I have to tell them you will be ready," he said unhappily.

"I am not ready at all," Olivia said in a tranquil way. "I do not want to be . . . executed." She wondered what the Censor would think if he knew what a long and agonizing death he had ordered for her. She sighed and glanced toward the small, high window where a little fading light glowed. "Was it a fine day?"

"Very clear," said Captain Vlamos. "The night should be the same."

"Full moon," she sighed. "Will they let me keep my garments and my shoes?"

"If you request it, yes, if they are very simple. You may wear a dalmatica but not a paenula." He shifted to his other foot, disliking his task more with every passing moment.

"Then I do request it. I am not wanton." She went to the low pallet which had served as her bed. "Will Belisarius be notified?"

"He has been already," Captain Vlamos confessed. "I sent him word myself. He requested it—"

"You needn't apologize," Olivia told him with a faint smile. "I'm grateful to you." There was a very slim chance, she thought, that Belisarius would inform Niklos, and if Niklos learned of her fate, he would do everything he could think of to aid her.

455

"It's not enough for gratitude," Captain Vlamos said, not able to look at her. "If it had been up to me, I would not have issued the orders. It was the Censor's doing. He had to prove to Belisarius—"

"I know," Olivia said, cutting him short. "And he certainly has. At least Simones didn't escape; that's something."

"The Emperor would not—" Captain Vlamos began, then broke off. "Belisarius has filed three petitions on your behalf. He has said that all the charges against you are lies and that it is only the self-serving interests of those close to Justinian that have made it possible for this to happen." He looked at Olivia with remorse. "They would not permit me to testify."

Olivia did her best to look unconcerned. "It was good of you to make the offer. There are many others who would not, who did not."

"Do you blame them?" Captain Vlamos asked.

"Not really," Olivia said. There was an unreality to her situation. After so many, many years, she could not make herself comprehend that it was ending. This time it would be the true death, not that other. The five centuries she had survived were over. She shook her head at the idea; it was not possible.

"Great lady?" said Captain Vlamos.

"It's nothing," Olivia responded. "I . . . was remembering. There won't be much more time for memories, will there?"

"If it had been my decision, you would have left this place the day we brought you here." He paused. "I knew Captain Drosos before he went to Alexandria. He told about you, a little, and I thought he was a very lucky man."

Olivia lowered her head. "Thank you, Captain. And when Drosos returned, what then?"

"He was not himself," Captain Vlamos said with difficulty.

"Yes." She turned away, but said, "If you know where he is, tell him what happened, will you? If Belisarius does,

it will be too painful for him. You need not say more than
a few words. You might mention that I would never forget
him." Then she shook her head. "No; don't say that. It
would only trouble him."

"Great lady, I will be back . . . shortly." He was
finding it impossible to speak.

"I will be here, Captain Vlamos." Her hopes were
fading, but she was determined not to let him know it.
She stared at the locked door when he left, as if the power
of her eyes alone could open it. Then she lay back on the
pallet and let her thoughts drift.

When had it been, that time when she was convinced
she would die? Three hundred years ago? Commodus or
Servius called himself Caesar then; Olivia was living in
Ravenna, and there had been a riot. The reason for the
riot escaped her, and she could not bring it to mind. She
had been trying to return from the emporia where she was
expecting goods to be delivered. She was by herself in an
open chariot, and when the crowd began to throw rocks,
she had been more worried for her horses than herself.
And then she saw two men dragged from their chariots
and trampled, reduced to a terrible flattened smear on the
cobbles, and she knew that unless she was very careful
and unusually lucky, she would suffer the same fate. She
had pulled the chariot to the side of the road and cut the
harness. She had ridden her lead horse through the streets
at a gallop, her legs holding tight and her hands holding
both reins and mane in a tangle. She had been cut and
bruised, but she had escaped. If Niklos had not taught her
how to handle horses so well, she would have been lost.

There would be no chariot, no horse for her now. She
was facing water, the one irresistible force. At least, she
thought in ironic consolation, it would be night, and they
would let her keep her shoes, so that she would be able to
swim, at least for a little while. Eventually she would lose
strength, and when the sun rose, it would sap her vitality,
and she would sink, to lie in the depths, paralyzed by the
water.

As she forced her mind to other thoughts, she became

aware of a distant voice singing one of the chants of Saint Ambrose. She listened to the droning melody with half her attention, and then sat up, for the first time realizing what the text of the chant was: *"Lord God lend Your protection to those who venture on the deep waters."* A single spurt of laughter escaped her before she was able to control that impulse, and she chided herself for clinging to forlorn dreams. The chant was repeated, and this time Olivia took heart from it.

"I am . . . not dead." The sound of her words in the little room startled her; she sounded resolute, determined. "All right," she said, "until the crabs nibble my toes, I—"

The distant chant changed to one in praise of the Virgin Mary and began with the words "Magna Mater."

"Very well, Niklos," Olivia said to the dim light of the little window. "I will not succumb yet." She stretched out on the pallet, her apprehension and fear belied by her apparent languor.

By the time Captain Vlamos returned, she had worked out a skeleton of a plan. It was so inauspicious that at another time she might have found it absurd; now she hoped that she would have enough good fortune to attempt it.

"Are you . . . prepared?" Captain Vlamos was more upset this time than he had been earlier.

"I hope so," said Olivia, getting to her feet unsteadily.

Captain Vlamos reached out to her, pity in his heart. He let Olivia lean against him. "You have courage, great lady, but there is no shame in faltering at a time like this."

"You're very kind, Captain," she said, stepping back to adjust the single wide sash she had tied around her waist. The little ornamental dagger she had removed from his belt was concealed as swiftly and as efficiently as she had taken it. "Do you have the sack with you?"

"It is in the rear courtyard." He indicated the two torches in the hall. "You will have a full escort that far; two of my men will walk with us."

"But you are in no danger from me," she said pleasantly. "I do not know my way about this place. If I escaped I would not know where to go, and most likely you would need to find someone who would help me while I was lost." She went ahead of him into the hall. "Tell me one thing if you can, Captain Vlamos."

"If I can," he agreed.

"I left writs of manumission for my slaves—have they been honored?"

"Belisarius has petitions with the magistrates. It is assumed that they will be granted. That way there will be fewer questions asked about . . . this." He signaled the soldiers to fall in, one ahead of and one behind them.

"That pleases me," said Olivia truthfully. No matter what happened to her, she wanted to believe that she had treated her slaves the way a Roman matron ought to. Especially Zejhil, she added to herself, for her loyalty and bravery.

"Is there anything . . . you want me to say? To anyone?" Captain Vlamos could not look at her as he extended this offer.

"Tell Belisarius that I know he has done more than anyone could expect of him, and that I thank him for what he has done. There is no one else in . . . Constantinople I wish to bid farewell." She did not try to keep track of the turns the soldiers took, nor the placement of doors and halls. No matter what happened to her, she would never return to this place.

By the time they reached the rear courtyard, Captain Vlamos was visibly distressed. "You do not have to sew her in until just before you throw her overboard," he told the men who waited for them. "Let her have that at least. She is not a sack of onions."

The naval officer, an old man with a puckered scar where most of his ear should have been, shrugged. "If the orders don't say otherwise, it's all one to me."

"Olivia?" Captain Vlamos said, looking at her with sadness. "There is nothing more I can do."

She made him a reverence. "You have done more than you know, Captain Vlamos; this last is more generous than—"

He turned on his heel and walked away, unable to remain any longer.

The two soldiers who had served as escort exchanged looks that the pale brilliance of moonlight rendered inscrutable. "We might as well get to it," one said to the other.

"She goes in this cart," the naval officer said, indicating a rickety contraption pulled by a weary donkey. "There will be six men on the boat. She'll be over the side before the monks start to sing for the souls of the dead." He indicated a heap of rough cloth in the cart. "There's the sack. Do you put her in or do I?"

The Guards did the work quickly, their hands clumsy but not unkind. "We're sorry, great lady. None of us thought it would come to this."

"We'll say prayers for you," the other promised.

"I will certainly need them," said Olivia as she felt them adjust the drawstring around her neck, tightening it enough to make it uncomfortable for her to struggle or move too quickly.

"When you get to the place where you do it, loosen this and draw it tight over her head," the taller Guard told the naval officer.

The sack fitted tightly and Olivia could not easily move her arms to discover if the little dagger was still in place. She told herself to bide her time, that she would have enough opportunity for that later, when the boat was under way. One thing encouraged her; since her head was left uncovered, it was not likely she would be left in a hold or put under a deck. So long as she was not too closely watched she would be able to get to the dagger before she was dropped into the water. Her only difficulty would be resisting the intense seasickness she invariably felt aboard a boat.

The streets were almost deserted and the donkey cart was incongruously protected by an escort of six well-armed soldiers. As the decrepit cart rattled down to the Bucolean Harbor, Olivia rolled in the back of it, unable to keep her balance or to brace herself against jolts and turns.

Another contingent of soldiers was waiting at the docks, and they unloaded Olivia from the back without speaking. Two of them carried her aboard a dorkon, its angled lanteen sail still furled.

"There she is, boatmaster," said the shorter Guard. "Handle her gently. She's a great Roman lady, this one, and we're sorry she came to this."

The boatmaster hitched up one shoulder. "They warned us she was a sorceress and that she might try to work her wiles on our boat. Some of the men were for having a last go at the lady, but I said that we'd take no chances with the likes of her." He spat copiously and called on several Saints to protect him. "For it is a bad business, having such a creature aboard."

"You won't have me aboard for long, boatmaster," Olivia reminded him, and resigned herself to rough handling.

"Take her aft," the boatmaster ordered. "There's some chickens in crates. We're bound for Rhodes when we've finished this job."

The soldier obeyed promptly and none too gently. When one of them swung Olivia around so that her shoulders struck two of the crates, he only grunted and shifted his grip on her.

Olivia was starting to experience the vertigo that being on water gave her which not even the Roman earth in her shoes could entirely counteract. She struggled in her bonds to face the front of the boat, knowing the hypnotic effect the sea would have on her. She was oddly pleased to see that there were several small fishing boats out, torches in their sterns, wide nets flung across the sea like the mottled pattern of moonlight. At least, she thought, they will have to get beyond the fishermen before they drop me overboard. The notion was comforting in its silliness, and she discovered that she was almost smiling.

She knew that this levity could be dangerous, but for the moment she welcomed it.

The sailors cast off with a minimum of fuss, and the sail opened like a night-blooming lily as the boat moved away from the wharf. The sailors made it evident that they were not going to pay any attention to Olivia, taking care not to get too near her as the boat edged out into the Sea of Marmara.

Silently the dorkon moved away from Konstantinoupolis, going slowly in order to maneuver through the fishing boats. Even the luff of the sail was muted; the bow whispered through the water as if wanting to keep its passage secret. No calls, no signals from the fishermen disturbed the dorkon as she began to pick up speed, leaving the fishing boats bobbing like fireflies over the moon-flecked water.

They were moving at a good pace when the boatmaster resigned the tiller to his next-in-command and brought two men aft with him.

"We might as well do it now," the boatmaster said as he approached Olivia.

She froze, her hand almost on the dagger hidden in her belt. "Now?"

The boatmaster went on as if she had not spoken. "We'll slack off, slow down and make sure she's in the water. No telling what a sorceress like this might do."

"Boatmaster," Olivia said, speaking forcefully. "I wonder if I might make a request?"

He struck her across the face with the back of his hard, thick hand. "You're not to talk. We were warned about that."

Already slightly dizzy from being on the boat, Olivia fought nausea as she tried to steady herself. Then she fell to the deck and her fingers closed on the dagger.

The boat was slowing down, and it began to rock more as she was brought around, wallowing in the rise and fall of the waves.

"Get her up and over," the boatmaster ordered. "Now. Before she can do anything."

"But we're supposed to tie the sack again, over her head," one of the sailors protested.

"If you want to take that kind of chance, you're free to, but I wouldn't open that sack. She might conjure anything out of it, and who knows what would become of us all. I say throw her in now. The Censor won't know or care unless someone tells him." There was a threat in this last, and two of the sailors made signs against the Evil Eye.

Olivia's brief rush of elation was lost before it had begun; she was wrenched to her feet, then hoisted into the air and flung away from the side of the boat to a host of blasphemous oaths. She struck the water, and for a short time was so disoriented that she dared not move. Eventually her head broke water and she caught a glimpse of the dorkon drawing away from her. She tried not to stare after it, knowing that would only serve to sap her fading spirits to no purpose. The dorkon's wake was froth in the moonlight, then drifted and was lost.

With a terrible effort, Olivia worked her knife out of her belt, trying not to thrash with the struggle. Part of the time she was able to breathe air, occasionally she was under the water, and it stung her nose and lungs, adding to the discomfort and confusion that was gradually overwhelming her. She fumbled with the knife and it dropped to the bottom of her sack; it took her far too long to retrieve it, and when she did, her whole body was lethargic, so that any movement at all was a grueling ordeal.

She brought the knife up to the cord around her neck, but could not cut it. Disheartened, she let herself drift for a little time, then resolved to make another attempt. This time she tried to cut the sack itself. One, two, three times she poked at the rough fabric without success. On the fourth jab, which she noticed was weaker than the others had been, the tip of the knife snagged on a heavy slub in the weave, and as she tried to pull it free, a large tear opened like the mouth of an exotic sea creature. Sobbing, choking, Olivia renewed her efforts, and at last she had ripped away all but the small section of the sack that held the cord around her neck like a bizarre wreath.

She was out of the sack, but her body was exhausted; the earth in the soles of her shoes was wet, steadily losing its potency. Only the power of the night gave her any resistance to the insidious somnolence that tempted her. It would be so easy to stop fighting, to yield to the seductive lure of the water, to drift away from all the turmoil and the pain and the strife.

Only the distant motion of the torches on the fishing boats held any fascination to her, and she clung to that with some small, committed core of herself. If they could float, so would she! Her arms ached whenever she moved them, her head was muzzy, her legs might as well have belonged to someone else for all the sense she had of them. Her knife was gone, dropped some time—she did not recall when—while she strove to escape from the sack. She focused her dwindling attention on the fishing boats and hoped that morning would not come too soon.

Dazed, demoralized, she floundered, sometimes keeping the torches in sight, sometimes not. There were fewer of them, she thought. Most of the fishermen must have their catch and were now returning to the land. She tried to paddle toward them, but the effort was too great.

But it did seem to her, she thought when she was not filled with chaos, that a few of the boats were nearer. One of the torches seemed to be growing larger, and she made a last, pathetic effort to swim toward it. She splashed ineffectively, and for a short time she slipped under the surface again.

When she rose and was able to clear her head a bit, she noticed that one of the fishing boats had come quite near, and was moving back and forth over the sea. She watched it, bemused, her body no longer able to move.

She was gazing up into the immensity of the night, caught by the beauty and vastness of the sky, the constellations no longer clear to her, when something brushed her outflung arm.

Olivia let out a hoarse yelp, then whimpered as a darkness loomed between her and the stars.

"For Poseidon, will you give me your hand, Olivia?" Niklos ordered in an undervoice.

Although she was certain that none of this was happening, that she had actually sunk to the depths of the sea and was lost in a pleasant dream, she did her best to humor herself, and with tremendous exertion, was able to wag her hand out of the water.

Niklos grabbed it, muttering a string of obscenities that would have awed the boatmaster. He was desperate with worry, and took little care about how he got her aboard. Dragging first her arm and then her leg, he wrestled her over the side and onto the rough planks. He wrapped four stout ropes around her, securing her to the mast. All the while he watched her, distracted with apprehension.

"Zejhil!" he commanded, keeping his voice low since he was aware how well sound carried over water.

The Tartar woman came from the shallow hold. "You have her?"

"Yes," he said, and the word itself made him giddy. "Bring that rolled mattress. Wrap it around her. And then head for Cyzicus." He rose from his task and went to the high tiller set aft in the boat.

Zejhil obeyed, her impassive features only once revealing the alarm she felt. "She is half-drowned."

"But only half," Niklos pointed out, letting himself laugh for the first time in days. He kept his eye on the shore, but his attention was more on Olivia than the line of darkness at the edge of the bright sea.

Near dawn, Olivia turned her head. "Niklos?"

Though the word was little more than a croaking whisper, Niklos beamed at her.

"Where . . ."

"We're going to Kythera." He glanced down at Zejhil asleep in the bottom of the boat. "You?"

"I'll . . . heal." She leaned back against the mast. "This mattress is soaked."

"So were you," he pointed out, leaving most of his feelings unspoken.

"That hymn—?"

"I gave a donation to three monks; I said it was for a relative feared lost at sea. They accepted the donation." He secured the tiller with cords, then came to her side. "Shall I take the mattress away?"

"Not yet. I still need it." Her voice was faint but each word was steadier, less strained.

"All right." He beamed at her. "Tell me about it later. There's plenty of time."

Her answering smile was weary and her chuckle ended in a cough, but at last she said, "Yes, centuries. Thanks to you."

Niklos put his hand on her stringy, matted hair. "Just returning an old favor." As he got to his feet, he said, "Sunrise soon."

Olivia turned her head to the stern of the boat and saw the first tarnished glow at the rim of the sea. As she watched, it brightened and smoldered, as if distant Constantinople were on fire. She closed her eyes, and when she opened them, she had turned, facing the bow again, and the pallid moonpath spread over the wrinkled sea.

* * *

Text of a letter from Chrysanthos to Belisarius, delivered to Konstantinoupolis three weeks after the General's death.

To the great and admirable Belisarius, greetings from the godforsaken outpost Colonna Romanum where Chrysanthos now commands, by default as much as promotion.

It has been more than three years since I have written,

and almost nine since I have seen you. For the lack of letters, I ask pardon, but there has been so little to tell. Out here, we are cut off half the time, and the rest of the time we are so bored that there is nothing to report except for the number of flies biting the horses. Ever since Totila was killed, and then his heir Teias, we've had few skirmishes even at outposts like this one. Until two months ago.

Drosos was posted to Mons Falconis, which is a three day ride from here. He was second-in-command to Solonios, nephew of the Exarch Narses, and I do not need to tell you how Solonios got his position, do I?

Yes, I say was. Drosos was killed six weeks ago. Mons Falconis got cut off and Solonios would not order an attack or send anyone for reinforcements, for fear of what his illustrious uncle would say. Drosos took it upon himself to remedy that, and with Fabios, Leonidas' son, rode around the enemy lines. Fabios arrived here, wounded and half-baked with fever and we did what we could for Solonios and his men.

Drosos wasn't so lucky. He was thrown when his horse was lanced, and the barbarians caught him. They staked him out, still bleeding, and then rode to the charge over him. There wasn't enough left to give him proper burial. If he hadn't disobeyed Solonios, none of the men would have survived, and so he had what he told me last year he no longer deserved: an honorable death.

I am sorry to have to send you this news, especially since it is my understanding that in your battles with the Huns last year you were badly wounded yourself. The rumor is—and I hope it is not true—that you have been blinded. It is bad enough to have lost Drosos; to know you cannot fight again would be too much for this old soldier to bear. Let me hear from you much sooner than you have heard from me, with news that you are thriving now that you have saved Konstantinoupolis and are once again in some favor with Justinian.

Is it true that Kimon Athanatadies was found guilty of heresy and hanged on a butcher's hook across from Hagia Sophia? I could not believe it when the story reached here. I hope that it is so, and that he suffered long and hard for all he had done. If it isn't so, I might well be the one hanging on a hook when I am posted back to Konstantinoupolis at the end of next year, but I doubt if it would bother me as much now as it would have when I left there nine years ago.

I hope that the next time I write to you, it is with good news, and the invitation to dine with me upon my return. It is an honor I look forward to with joy and gratitude. Until then, my respect and my affection is with you; it is heartening to know you have been vindicated at last.

Though I am remiss at letters, I am still very much your friend

Chrysanthos
Captain (still)

Epilogue

Text of a letter to Olivia from Sanct' Germain.

To my long-treasured Olivia, Sanct' Germain sends greetings from Naissus, and thanks her for sending news of her travels.

So you are going to Alexandria now that Justinian is finally dead and his nephew Justin rules in Constantinople. I hope you have not decided to do this out of devotion to Drosos' memory. You tell me that you want to find out what is left of the Library and to try to salvage any of the texts that might have escaped the fires. That, I probably need not remind you, is dangerous work; high risk for a dubious reward.

You told me once that Drosos called you a monster and that you did not know how to convince him you are not. Olivia, he was right. We are monsters, Olivia, never forget that. But we need not be monsters simply because we are.

Some time soon, I, too, hope you can return to Roma. I know how hard it is to be drawn by your native earth. Why else would I be in a place like Naissus? In less than a month I will be back in my native mountains, and they will restore me in ways I need not explain to you.

I am pleased to know that Niklos Aulirios is still with you. His sense can stand you both in good stead, for often you have more courage than sense, which is one of the many reasons that I loved you while Nero wore the purple and love you now, and will love you when both of us are nothing more than dust.

Take joy in living, Olivia, else the burden is too great for even you to endure, and loss of you would grieve me more than any other loss I have sustained in all my years.

In this, the Lord's Year 566, you have my love, as you have had it for the last half millennium

Sanct' Germain
(his seal, the eclipse)